THE BATTLE FOR TOMORROW

THE BATTLE FOR TOMORROW

FREDERICK BELL

ILON THE HUNTER SERIES
BOOK 1

Manufactured in the United States of America
ISBN: 978-0-9823079-2-2
Cover Design: Molly Bond
Cover Illustration: Eric Williams/The July Group

9 8 7 6 5 4 3 2 1

First Edition

Library of Congress Cataloging-in-Publication Data

Bell. Frederick
The Battle for Tomorrow /
by Frederick Bell.
p. cm.

ISBN: 978-0-9823079-2-2 (pbk.)
1. Literature—Fantasy and Science Fiction
2. Fantasy and Science Fiction—Fiction
3. Adventure—Fantasy and Science Fiction
1. Title

2001012345

Alternative Views Publishing
Web site: http://www.alternativeviewspublishing.com

For my wife

EARTH RELATIVE COORDINATES
planet: Egris
distance: 15,000 light years
people: Egris
location: Olahn territory
time: Present

Chapter 1

The tree-top prairies stretched all the way to the horizon, a dark line made darker with approaching daylight. In the early light of dawn only the brightest stars remained visible in the sky. The second moon, now sinking beneath the forest, reflected on a spot where the water had collected in a stagnant pool; something stirred near the water's edge and caused it to ripple.

Just before sunrise some of the first animals were awakening. The gray shapes that dotted the field now could be made out more clearly. Moving sluggishly forward one of the herd made a rumbling snort, and the others of its kind soon began to stir—gigantic eight-legged creatures with solid bodies, massive heads, and thick outstretched tails. Tree eaters. Snapping its jaw shut the great beast started to advance. Most in the herd resisted, yet once they saw it lumbering away they too assembled behind the leader and plodded off toward the lightening sky.

Ahead everything appeared to be the same, endless and unchanged. There were no large hills or deep valleys, no visible landmarks that might indicate their traveling direction, though the goud seemed to know exactly where they were going. Even as the day progressed the blazing sun did not deter them from their trek. At dusk they halted for the night, tearing out huge clumps of green vegetation with their beaked jaws and chewing contentedly. Where one of them was browsing a tree branch suddenly cracked and buckled beneath the animal's great weight.

To the untrained eye it was easy to think of this place as an undulating endless plain, growing atop of what might just as easily have been mistaken for solid ground. Yet beneath the living floor, under this intricate latticework of thickly woven branches and green leaves, far, far below, was in fact another world altogether.

At dawn the next morning the goud were awakened by an animal screaming from out of the depths of the forest below. The sun was above the horizon and they were ready to depart. The invisible route they were on took them eastward. After three more days of traveling, from sunrise to sunset, they finally reached their destination. Some of the early arrivals had been congregating here for days. From all across the prairies the goud came. Now tens of thousands were grouping on the field, grazing placidly while the latecomers plodded in to join this burgeoning crowd. As one herd passed by another several of these beasts lifted their heads and bellowed hoarsely.

This was the way it was, every year. When spring came to the forests of the far north countless herds began the migration south, traveling almost to the very edge of their world, where the tall trees ended and the grass-filled plains began. As in the past this was where they came, driven here by an instinctual force to return home to their birth place. After climbing up the tree trunks and chewing through the dense overgrowth they completed the end of their long journey by mating and laying their eggs in the branches.

And then they died.

Their dying began the cycle anew. Soon after their deaths the eggs hatched, and the voracious youngsters, devouring vast amounts of leaves, grew until they were as big as the adults. They ate everything in their path, sometimes eating right down to the bare tree trunks. These ravenous creatures might have devoured the whole forest were they not possessed by the same fierce instinct to climb back down and join their kind below.

It was almost dusk and the goud were still milling about on the field. A trumpeted roar soon broke the spell. The second full moon's light was spilling onto the herd just as the first animals gaped open their huge, beaked jaws and plunged head-on into the floor, wriggling out of sight. One after the other each goud tore through the overlapping branches and vanished into the choking mass of green growth. Now they began the long climb down into almost permanent darkness.

But the worst part of their journey was just beginning. Being on the ground exposed them to a whole new set of dangers. Unlike their tree-top home, there were meat-eaters down here, and undoubtedly some of them were stalking nearby. Luckily, many of the big game carnivores seldom penetrated this deeply into the woods. Even so, and despite the great distance that separated them—some did.

To be sure, there were other animals that were swifter, better armored, but the goud's sheer physical size made them difficult to kill. Nevertheless they had hungry enemies, meat-eaters who were not afraid to risk death for a mouthful of their tasty flesh. So as the goud continued their downward descent it was possible that some of these bloodthirsty creatures were waiting below.

Now in the ink-black darkness the goud began climbing off the tree trunks and spreading out. The main body eventually splintered into smaller groups that were soon following their own path south. Further back, behind one of the trees, something moved. This unknown creature suddenly made a bestial roar and the goud steered immediately back for the trees. However, its sound soon died away and so the herd slowly reassembled on the well-trampled trail, though were ready to leave it again at any time.

But just as soon as the first stalker departed now another one was watching them. In absolute silence a near invisible form crouched in the bole of the tree while the big animals rumbled past. Its huge ears twitched with every footfall. Even up this close it remained perfectly motionless, watching and waiting for the moment to strike. One of the passing goud inadvertently swung its tail around, forcing the creature to jump aside. It did not make a sound when it landed. Not that its silence mattered, for once the Egris found the goud death would certainly follow.

Of all the creatures in the wild world this one was the most devastating predator of all. An incredibly fierce and fast predatory pack killer, who with its deadly rows of spiked teeth and retractable claws could tear apart its prey with bloody efficiency. Using its powerful hind legs for jumping it could chase down even the swiftest of prey. Standing erect on its haunches, at over ten feet tall this was no puny animal that could be frightened off by something as big as a goud. Continuing to watch from its concealed position, now the Egris swung its tail in the opposite direction and leapt away, only a puff of dust showing where it once stood.

The hunter, an adult male, soared through the air with a powerful thrust of his muscular legs. Each jump propelled him skyward in a graceful arc that carried him far from where he landed. His mighty tail slapped the dusty floor as the ground exploded beneath him. Without taking a step he sailed straight back into the air, leaving a trail of swirling debris in his wake. Something was moving up ahead, dark shapes angling toward him, and so he came down just as two more Egris landed in front of him.

One of the two, a female, snorted through her nostrils as she smelled the scent of food on the returning hunter's hide. "I smell goud," Dhorsal growled hungrily, licking her wet chops. "So you found us food at last. Tell us where?"

Gangahar excused her impertinence, for she was indeed hungry and wished only for information that would take her directly to a fresh meal. "Traveling south," he replied. "Through those trees to the trail marker, then straight ahead. Straight to the goud."

"I'll get the others," Magamengon said without delay. Quickly he jumped away, and very soon nine more hunters came leaping in to join them.

"Goud." Takilisk smacked his lips together when he learned of their target. "My teeth will be the first to taste its sweet flesh," he boasted.

"Enough talking," Yaryar ordered. "Talk when your belly is full of meat. Now is the time to hunt."

They left immediately. Since Gangahar knew the way he was the first to depart, with the others of his trod flanking him on both sides. All of them were jumping simultaneously together, leaping high past the trunks of the great trees, heading straight toward their prey.

*****

A low, distant growling noise echoed out of the forest. The fleeing goud reached a spot where the tree trunks were spaced more widely apart, and undoubtedly this was where their attackers would strike next. Instead the karafins retreated, staying well back from the herd, though remained close enough to attack again. Earlier, three of them had boldly surprised the herd. Although slow, a lone goud was not easily killed, and these marauders, perhaps more hungry than stupid, had wrongly chosen to pick this animal for their next meal. Instead the big goud proved itself the superior fighter, and though bloodied by the battle, easily fended off its adversaries. As for the karafins, only two remained. The third, now mortally wounded, slumped to the floor and breathed its last breath.

It did not take very long for the stench of death to reach the scavengers. Very soon a roving band of ethusentaks crowded around the fresh corpse, eager for a mouthful of its still warm flesh. One of the animals, a long string of meat dangling from its open mouth, looked around in sudden fear as it felt the ground shake beneath its feet. A second ethusentak tilted its head and squealed nervously. There was no mistake about what was coming. Immediately it emitted a shrill shriek of alarm and the pack instantly divided and fled back among the trees.

Something dark soared through the air above and there was a sudden gust of wind that followed. The ground shook heavily and then was followed by silence. Further up ahead the thudding sounded again, each time growing more and more distant.

The first goud to hear them coming were at the end of the line and immediately started galloping past their slower companions, retreating back up the trees. So for those who were only now starting to react—it was too late. From high above the first hunter came hurtling down, his powerful tail thudding onto the dusty floor. Saliva dripped off his teeth as he steered straight toward his chosen prey. Using his huge, slashing attack jaws, Magamengon bit deep into the goud's unprotected flank and tore out a bloody chunk of flesh.

Yelping, the injured animal reared on its attacker, though by the time it closed in with its beaked jaws the same spot where the hunter had stood was now empty. Another hunter came plummeting down, then another, each taking their turn before leaping away with bloody hunks of flesh. Although the goud fought back viciously, desperately, wherever it turned there were razor sharp teeth and stinging claws to send it stumbling back. Unable to withstand this relentless attack any longer it charged uselessly forward, then backwards, again and again, finding nothing in its jaws but clouds of its own dust. In this grim, sightless blackness, though, the Egris were leaping all around it, clicking their teeth in wild excitement. The goud was beginning to falter and screeched loudly as it crashed to the ground, writhing in agony. As Dhorsal delivered the killing blow the great beast screamed fitfully and then died.

A loud animal roar of satisfaction reverberated off the rooftop as the hunters gathered around the carcass to eat. Smelling the sweet smell of flesh they wasted no time, sinking their slavering jaws into the goud's meaty hide. Though adept hunters the Egris were particularly crude eaters, often swallowing bolts of meat whole, for it was their nature to eat as much as possible since their next meal might not be for days. Yet the goud was a gigantic animal, big enough that it could have easily filled the stomachs of three other trods as hungry as this one.

While they were partaking of the goud's tasty meat one of the hunters, a female, suddenly broke off and stood outside their circle. Something appeared to distract her, and after a moment she hissed loudly between her teeth for attention. The other hunters, some with their heads still buried inside of the animal carcass, reluctantly withdrew and responded by hissing in return.

"What is it now?" Yaryar growled ill-temperedly. His was the voice of authority. Naturally it was toward him that all heads were turned. Yaryar, the oldest, and leader of trod Yaryar, impatiently thumped his tail against the ground as he awaited her answer.

Instead Horhon maintained her rigid stance, was looking straight into the black depths of the forest. "Listen. Do you hear that? Something is moving in there."

Yaryar frowned. "I hear nothing. Only the wind. Now be silent and eat."

His quick pronouncement was welcomed by the others. No one really wanted to listen to her; no one could think of any good reason to pay attention. Those who had stopped eating quickly bent back over the goud and snapped up some more. Horhon was well known for raising false alarms. Earlier this same night she claimed to have sighted something flying overhead, had foolishly sent them all running for cover. It had proved to be nothing as well. So this time they ignored her completely.

This bold rejection incensed Horhon. The strength of her emotions forced her to turn her back on them to sulk by herself.

"So full," Dhorsal moaned, crushing back against her tail.

"You look fat," Magamengon complimented her.

"I am the fattest," Karkakass bragged, patting her belly.

All but two had finished up. The goud's fleshy ruins and well gnawed bones looked particularly appetizing to the scavengers that were amassing outside of the hunter's perimeter. Some of the smaller tickridents were boldly scurrying in on all eight legs to be first before the bigger animals got their teeth bloody on them. Yaryar, his face and chest stained dark red, joined his corpulent companions to celebrate the end of an excellent meal.

"The eating was good tonight," he said, using one of his serrated claws to tease out the bits of meat stuck between his teeth. "But I think this is our last day. We head for the plains. Tomorrow." As leader, he was a practical thinker and had no intention of waiting for the forest to empty of goud before they were forced to leave. Though intelligent hunters who could foresee nature's cyclical patterns, their world had its own set of rules that either they obeyed, or perished. The goud would continue south to the great plains, and so this was where they were going too.

Gangahar, still licking the blood from his fingers, crouched on his haunches beside Horhon who was pretending to ignore him. "Do you still hear anything?" he asked her.

Her headshake no was his answer.

"So was it the Iranha?" Gangahar continued, trying to get her to speak.

She grinned a little at that because he thought more of her feelings than his own feelings of doubt. "I think it was," she replied.

Behind them, Yaryar snapped his jaw resoundingly shut. "And what foolish stories will you tell us next, Horhon? That these Iranha things are here in our forest right now, stalking us, preparing to skin us all?"

"They might be, or they might come tomorrow or even the next tomorrow. It does not matter. What matters most is that if tomorrow we go south to the great plains, then they will certainly find us and kill us all. We are safer here."

Yaryar looked at her scornfully. "Stay in the forest? Ridiculous. The plains are filled with game, the hunting is good. Everything we need is there."

"Everything—and the Iranha," Horhon grimly added.

The Iranha! Yaryar swung his tail down and scowled, loathing that name. He still remembered the first time he had heard it spoken aloud. None in the trod might have ever believed these stories had it not been for Horhon. She was an outsider. Only recently, home for her was in the desert country, where the grasslands ended and undulating dunes of sand began. Tragically, though, she had lost her entire trod to the Iranha, and she, the only survivor, the only one who knew firsthand of these new and dangerous killers. But he had also heard the rumors that were spreading among the other trods, stories that seemed to grow more fantastic with each telling. In fact most of what he heard was a lot of wild speculation and hearsay. Nevertheless there was some dark and appalling news which only recently was reaching this part of their world. Apparently entire trods were being found slaughtered, and in grizzly ways that no hunter would dare to have imagined, for what kind of animal would take only their skins and leave the flesh behind for the scavengers to tear at? If the stories were true—if they weren't in fact bald faced lies—then there was another kind of hunter loose on the plains, a hunter more ferocious, more bloodthirsty than even themselves. And these Iranha, it seemed, were hunting for them. But for now trod Yaryar was safe from the Iranha. Safe here, or so he steadfastly and stubbornly believed.

Grinding his teeth, Yaryar finally said, "You can't be sure that the Iranha are here to stay. We have looked very carefully, all of us, searched everywhere and found no sign of them. Only you have seen their flying machines overhead."

"The Iranha inhabit our world. You know that, Yaryar."

"I know of these creatures only because of what you yourself have told me," he hissed. "Sometimes I wish that day trod Yaryar had never found you."

Horhon sniffed. "My wish as well. Since you are so stubborn I doubt that the truth will ever satisfy you, and that will be your undoing. But those who you command might die unnecessarily."

"Don't be so arrogant. If you find fault with my leadership, then vote with your feet, and leave."

In this case Yaryar's popularity made it difficult for her to challenge him for the trod's support. To do that she would have to be careful not to alienate herself any further than she had, so she chose her next words to offset any negative feelings the other hunters might be harboring toward her.

"The old ways no longer work. The Iranha are a new problem, and this requires a new solution. You are an old hunter Yaryar, you know many things, but I think you know nothing about these Iranha."

He scoffed at this. "So far I have seen none of these Iranha. But if as you say, they are really here, then it must be somewhere where they are far from us. So we are safe."

"Are we?" Horhon shook her head no. "So long as we stay we are in danger. And the Iranha will certainly come to the plains. I tell you all, we must leave this territory. Now. I see no other solution."

"Well I do!" Yaryar clacked his jaw shut; it was all he could do to keep himself from losing his temper. "We are proud hunters. We do not turn tail and flee at the first sight of an enemy. You say the Iranha has destroyed other trods. You say they might attack us too. But we will not be hunted down like scared animals. So if they come here then we will fight them, kill them, chase them back to the hole they crawled out of."

Evidently his rousing speech seemed to satisfy the listeners, for they were growling with approval, though Gangahar raked his claws in the dirt and thrashed his tail for all to be silent.

"We are simple hunters. We stalk our prey and kill only to eat, to survive. Not these Iranha. They are unnatural hunters who seem to have no teeth or claws for killing, but instead use strange weapons we do not understand. Now this we must consider before we stay and fight them. Like you I have no wish to leave this territory, and yet perhaps this is something that we should all think about while we still can."

However, Karkakass fervently disagreed. Obviously she was thinking and worrying about her unborn child, its grim and uncertain future. "Our world is a big place. There is enough for everyone, even the Iranha."

"No," Horhon protested. "What the Iranha already have is not enough. It will never be enough for them. They want our world for themselves, and to see us dead, destroyed."

Many, but not all, sided against her. What followed then was a heated exchange of opinions and personal beliefs; two hunters were licking bloody wounds so great had been the argument. In the end it was Yaryar who settled their bickering.

"We go nowhere!" he shouted angrily, expressing himself in the loudest and most commanding way. "If you cannot agree that trod Yaryar remains here, then I want nothing more to do with you!"

Although the discussion was ended for now, by no means was it over for good. Crouching on his huge drumstick legs, Yaryar propelled himself high into the air and jumped away among the trees, quickly gone.

One by one the others followed after him, his trail of dust was their way back. Ahead was the uncertainty of the open field. Yaryar had chosen for them, had ultimately made the final decision to return. But what if the Iranha were waiting? They might be. Nonetheless, the hunters were heading for home.

Chapter 2

The demarcation line between the forest and the field wasn't so clearly defined that one ended and the other started. Rather, there was a gradual progression as the great trees thinned, then opened up in places where some of the stars could be viewed overhead. Eventually, the terrain became interspersed with grass and other small plants before withering under the tree cover's choking darkness. Finally, where the last tree stood out like a sentinel, was a vast grass filled field that seemed to stretch all the way to the end of the world.

The open ground was directly ahead. Above, some of the first stars were breaking through the once impenetrable cover, yet even they were dimming down as the light of dawn pushed through. On the field, tussocks of coarse grass rustled under the brightening sky.

From high overhead a flock of soros flew into sight, darkening the sky with their number. These were long-winged creatures of death. Carrion eaters with rows of curved teeth for tearing apart flesh. Flying low, they beat their thundering wings and went swishing past with a tail breeze blowing strongly behind them. Eventually the deafening sound died down, though the breeze kept up well after the flock departed.

When they were a dark patch on the brightening horizon a distant rumbling sound came out of the woods. Several tarsers, grazing close by, stared head-on toward this new disturbance, their huge ears twitching nervously. Alarmed, these small and agile creatures instantly broke from their torpor and bounded soundlessly into the grassy field. Behind these fleeing beasts, dark shapes were moving out from underneath the trees; something familiar was coming closer and closer.

Magamengon was the first to appear. Yaryar had led for most of their trek home, though Magamengon still enjoyed his youth and soared past him on the open field. The others were keeping up, but with their stomachs full no one seemed to be in a hurry to get there. Yaryar had a humorous saying, that anyone who had to jump faster after a meal, was still hungry. Following closely behind him was Gangahar, surging high up into the air in a long, graceful arc. Horhon was next, followed by the others who were taking great leaps behind her. Karkakass however, was in last place, and trailed further behind with every bound, though she was in the final stages of her pregnancy and so this was a comfortable pace for her.

It had rained earlier during the night and the runoff had collected in deep muddy pools in spots where the hunters splashed. Thick splotches of mud now streaked their hides. Nevertheless they were making good time; the sun was yet to be seen above the field, and they were almost home.

Suddenly, without any warning, Magamengon landed to a stop and this quick moving procession piled up behind him.

"What is it?" Yaryar asked quizzically.

"Something here," he motioned.

The urgency of his words was such that Yaryar came over immediately to see what was the matter. As soon as he reached the spot where Magamengon was standing he looked at the ground and gaped with puzzlement at this new and strange thing.

"What do you make of this?" the less experienced hunter asked him.

But Yaryar was equally perplexed. Shaking his head he answered, "I do not know. It appears to be a track of some kind. Gangahar, you are my best tracker. What do you think?"

Strange. That was his opinion. His huge snout hovered over the ground as he tasted the air that was rapidly moving in and out through his nostrils. If these were made by an animal then he did not know which one. Whatever this was had plowed two equally spaced trenches that had flattened the grass and left a visible trail that could be easily followed. And there was something else too. Imprinted in the sand was a bizarre honeycomb pattern of depressions and ridges. Although Gangahar had never seen a track like this before he could tell that it had been freshly made. Yet if this creature was still around then it was too far distant to spot it from here.

"Since it is here we can say that something made it," was all that he could conclude.

"But what?"

He had little confidence that this mystery would be solved today, but he now remembered something else that seemed to be too much of a coincidence to ignore. "See where it goes into the forest?" He then moved his arm slightly. "We hunted over there, and there. Could this be the same thing you heard last night?"

Horhon's eyes widened. "Then—I did hear something."

"It would seem so," Gangahar concurred.

"You can't be certain," Yaryar said brusquely. Undoubtedly Horhon was planning to use this as her proof so he was more determined than ever for an explanation that didn't involve the Iranha. "Does anyone recognize these?"

Those who crowded around him tried to answer, could not, for exactly what animal had tread here no one could say. Again it was Yaryar who finally broke the deadlock of disagreement.

"Then these are of a kind of animal no one has ever tracked before. Obviously this is a new creature we have not yet encountered."

"And what if this new creature is the Iranha?" Horhon argued. "These tracks go south where we go."

Karkakass, one of Yaryar's most fervent supporters, now was having second thoughts about leaving. "Should we go on? Do you think it is safe?"

Even Gangahar was concerned. "Horhon is right. We must find out why this animal is here. Perhaps we should send out a scouting party. Two or three hunters. No more."

Yaryar started to speak, but instead he made a crude expression that bordered on impatience and stomped off in the direction of the tracks. Only Gangahar followed him. Since he was the only volunteer the rest of the pack moved back under a copse of trees and awaited their return.

The daytime sun rose higher in the sky; still the two hunters had not yet returned. At first no one seemed overly concerned, though as the day progressed a few began to wonder where they might be.

Karkakass especially, was worrying about the missing hunters. Her bulbous blue eyes stared across the empty field. An invisible wind rustled through the grass. Nothing else moved. "Shouldn't we go and search for them?"

"No," Horhon warned her. "If they found the Iranha why then should we give them any more of us to kill?"

Of those who were listening none were eager to leave here. Until they were more inclined to act, Karkakass would have to wait and hope that Yaryar's obstinance hadn't gotten him killed. She slumped back onto her tail.

In the mid-afternoon, when the hot sun was blazing down and an arid wind was whipping up the dust, Karkakass noticed two dark shapes on the field, coming closer

"Here they come!" she screamed.

Sure enough, they spotted the dark shapes lifting off the ground, bounding closer. The returning hunters' skins were dusty and splotched where the saliva had dripped down their gaped open mouths; they were panting in the fierce heat of the day.

"This accursed heat," Gangahar complained. Thick strings of saliva dangled from his long black tongue. "Is there water to drink?"

Karkakass led them over to one of the trees where she had clawed a deep gash in the enormous trunk. Cool clear water trickled down into the natural bowl of the tree. Lowering his head Gangahar lapped up thirsty mouthfuls, gasping, drinking some more. He sighed deeply; it was good to finally be out of the blistering sun.

"What did you see out there?" Horhon was quick to ask him.

"Did you find what made the tracks?" Dhorsal asked almost as quickly. Gangahar started to speak, stopped when he saw Yaryar's stern expression.

"We saw something," Yaryar told them carefully. Then slowly he recounted the day's events, telling them all, "What we saw is not easy to describe, nor easy to tell, but I will speak of it as best I can. We followed the trail. Up ahead everything appeared perfectly normal and there was nothing to see. We just kept going and I thought we would never reach the end. Now we both knew that it was time to come back, but Gangahar went on a little further and so I searched on my own, waiting for his return."

A lump came to Gangahar's throat now that it was his turn to speak. "I suppose I should have returned. I now wish that I did, for my head hurts whenever I try to think about what I saw."

"Was it animal?" Horhon asked fearfully. "Or something else?"

Gangahar thought for a moment about what he would call this new thing, saying, "I am not entirely certain." To him there was no simple way of describing it. He knew that he must and so he went on. "Something very big was stopped up ahead on the trail. First I believed this was an animal of some kind, but after I stalked it from behind to get a closer look I thought it was a very strange thing. The risk was too great to be seen so instead I crept away to watch it from atop the hill."

"Then I found the others," Yaryar told his shocked listeners.

Dhorsal gasped. "There was more than one?"

"A whole herd." Like Gangahar, he too had come across these same things on a different part of the field. "I was very close, close enough to see them clearly. I counted eight. They were moving, making strange noises. Their smell made me cough and close my eyes. Only when they were safely out of sight did we return here to tell you." Yaryar felt a stab of anxiety because he was not the sort of hunter to admit his fears. "I was afraid. We both were."

"That is not all," Gangahar told them uneasily. "They did not walk, but crawled overtop of the ground. Propelled themselves forward, making tracks. A double track that the others followed in, flattening everything beneath them."

"An animal that crawls? On land?" Karkakass tried to picture this in her mind, not seeing how this could be done. "I understand little of what you say. Only the simplest land creatures need no legs to move."

"That is what I saw. But how such big things were able to accomplish this . . ." He shook his head to show his audience that he had no satisfactory answer. ". . . I do not know."

"I have hunted in many places where there are all sorts of strange beasts," Negoragil, a hunter of great experience told his listeners. "But where on this wide world are there animals like this?"

Horhon was so convinced what these were that she found herself shivering in the sweltering heat. "The creatures from the sky that brought the Iranha had no wings for flying. Could these strange things belong to the Iranha too?"

Her question posed serious consideration. For once, even Yaryar had to reluctantly admit that this was at least a possibility. Long before he had ever heard of the Iranha there were stories of unstoppable giant creatures roaming in the deep and distant desert. It could not be a coincidence that these might be the same things that were now crawling to within reach of their forest. Still, he quickly pointed out that the trod was out of immediate danger.

"They were well south of here, even further since we left them. I don't see any danger."

Of those hunters who were originally indifferent to Horhon's ideas, now some of them were beginning to take up her cause. Magamengon snorted disagreement. "Suppose they come back. What if there are more of them the next time?"

What could he say? Did he ever want to see them again? "I am sure they are gone for good."

"You can be sure of nothing," Horhon said coarsely. "If you were, you would certainly give this matter more serious attention. What if they saw you? They could be returning right now."

"I can't believe that," Yaryar growled, his lips peeled back to show the full intensity of his temper. "The Iranha—if they were the Iranha, were traveling away from here, and we were careful to avoid them. They are gone. Now we can safely return to our burrow."

Her eyes widened. "That is your plan, just go home?"

In answer Yaryar pounded his big tail across the broadside of the tree. She was a poisonous creature who saw dark shadows behind everything, and for all the good it did her to spread fear about things that might never happen again. He wanted very much to put a stop to their bickering, and never speak the accursed name of the Iranha ever again.

"Since there is a gulf between us that can never be crossed, I see no reason to speak of this any further. You have your beliefs. I have mine. Our place is here, this is our home. Why should we leave just because these Iranha are nearby? They can come and go whenever they wish. I don't care, so long as they stay away from us."

It was a controversial decision. Even Yaryar's loyal followers seemed dismayed with his lack of resolve. Today's events had enlarged their fears. There was no telling if the Iranha might or might not return. But now the hunters had a new worry. Up until today no one had ever doubted Yaryar's ability to lead. He was a natural leader. And yet his rash actions were of uppermost concern in their minds because only Yaryar himself seemed to know what he was doing. Could they afford to risk their lives on a bad decision? They were not ready to abandon him, not yet, though all were watching him closely to see what he would do next.

"What I have said, I said because this battle of wills must end," he told his listeners. "Tomorrow I leave for the great plains. I want hunters—not cowards who hide in the shadows and let these Iranha things shape your fears. So either you come with me, or turn your tails and leave trod Yaryar forever. Now choose."

Grudgingly, a straight line started forming, growing longer. Yaryar was ready to issue the order to leave when Gangahar came to his side and the two of them walked together to the back of the line. Karkakass was lying on her side; she appeared to be in pain.

"I stay. My baby's time has come so I will dig out a lair and birth it here."

Yaryar nodded. "Understood. Shall one of us remain to aid you?" She stared at him, only him. That was his answer. "Then we will look for you tomorrow."

He broke off and strode away. Karkakass sensed the conflicting emotions. He wanted to stay with her, she knew, but his first duty was the trod, always. Tears welled up in her eyes as she watched his departure. He was the last one to vanish from her sight.

As the field opened up ahead of them they bent their drumstick legs and shot back into the air, taking long, graceful bounds that sent them sailing across the open plain. Out in the sunlight the color of their hides began to change dramatically. Within moments they now blended perfectly into the brown and green landscape, almost invisible. Their chameleon-like ability made them the ideal stalkers—and yet, unknown to the hunters, this natural advantage also doomed them to extinction, for the Iranha skin hunters were well familiar and eager to supply a burgeoning population with these decorative and fashionable Egris hides.

The hunters weren't far now. Their new burrow was purposely close. Several days earlier they had shoveled it out in anticipation of the goud that were preparing to come off the forest canopy. Their natural inclination was to follow the meat animals so they dug in here, waiting for them to come. But because there was no telling where they might find their next meal, Egris preferred the convenience of life underground in hollowed out burrows. With all this sand it was easy to dig another one wherever they happened to be hunting, and it was the most functional way of escaping the day's intense heat.

Their sand burrow had been dug into the windward side of a dune, where thick bushes had taken root and grew all the way up the slope. Parting the dense foliage the first hunter pushed through the opening. Inside the air smelled of decaying vegetation. Thick wet roots brushed their faces; it was impossible to avoid them, for as quickly as they were cut down new ones sprouted back in their place.

The passageway was a long one. Numerous corridors angled away from the main branch, then merged at a central chamber that had been dug out and enlargened to accommodate everyone in the trod. Horhon was waiting there when Gangahar came through the passageway.

"We must talk," she said gravely.

Dhorsal wandered past, then Negoragil and Magamengon shuffled through, and as these last two departed for their sleeping lairs the room was silent again.

Gangahar sighed. For his part he wanted a swift end to this tiresome discussion and brought down both hands in a gesture of weariness. "We will talk tomorrow."

"Now," Horhon said firmly, standing between him and the tunnel.

"Then speak and be done," he gestured irritatedly.

"You know what you saw today."

"It was no animal," he finally admitted now that there were no others around to hear him. "It was the Iranha."

"Then why do you let him take us on this insane trek tomorrow?"

"What can we do?"

"What can we do?" Her voice trailed off and she sank into a depression that lasted for the remainder of their conversation. "Leave. But first the others must see that this is our only option."

"And Yaryar? He will not listen. He does not believe the Iranha are a threat."

"He should." Horhon frowned. "They are closer than ever. Each day will bring them back. How many more times are we to find them before they find us?"

"Then you have a plan?"

In a slow steady voice she said, "You must help me, Gangahar. If we are to do anything at all then Yaryar must be convinced."

"And if he chooses to ignore my advice, what then? He is my friend. I will not stand against him."

"That was never my thought. Only that you use your friendship to help him see what we both know and believe is true. Can you do that?"

He nodded hesitantly. "I will support you if I can."

"Good. This is all I ask." Her teeth-filled mouth opened wide, yawning as she exposed her rows of deadly points. "So tired. I must sleep."

Gangahar was already thinking of sleep. With half-shut eyes he slipped into an adjoining tunnel and dragged his tail out of sight.

It was the following day when Negoragil, the first waking hunter, crawled groggily from his burrow. With half-shut eyes he stumbled out into the tunnel. As he entered the central chamber he saw another hunter's blurred shape sprawled on the floor. Negoragil recognized her. Horhon must have spent the night here, was sleeping even now as he approached and prodded her with his clawed toe.

But she did not move.

When he bent to touch her shoulder, her skin was bone cold. Something wet and sticky brushed across his fingertips. There was confusion and fear on his face when he held up his hand, a hand smeared red with blood. Her blood.

Before he could think clearly, before he could decide what to do next, he was thinking only one grim thought: If Horhon was dead, then what about the other hunters?

Chapter 3

"**W**ake up, wake up!"

Yaryar's eyes were two narrow slits, so heavy was his sleep. He awoke when Negoragil's hoarse shouts penetrated his burrow. "What is the matter?"

"Horhon, dead. Something attacked her . . . so much blood."

Even as he led him to the chamber Yaryar was still reacting to the news. Not until he saw her laying still, saw all the blood, did the grimness of Negoragil's words sink in. Opening his mouth Yaryar screamed in horror, sick with revulsion. He was soon joined by the other hunters who were emerging from their burrows. They too reacted strongly, for even though they were well used to killing and butchering, to see one of their own kind dead was a shocking sight.

No one could think of what to say, they were still too upset to go near her. Only Gangahar went closer. His own grief was evident as he placed his trembling hand on hers. Yaryar glanced over.

"Is she . . . ?"

Tense silence followed, then . . . "No. Unconscious, but still alive!"

She was covered with blood. A lot of it. While he wiped away the worst messes with handfuls of wet grass he suddenly spotted something very peculiar. "Look at this."

As the trod crowded around him to see, Gangahar pointed to what looked like a bite mark on her left shoulder. Looking closer what they saw was a triangular shaped pattern with several small marks that perforated her skin. Obviously something had bitten her, Gangahar concluded, thinking to himself, What beast could have done this awful thing, and why?

"I wonder what animal attacked her," Yaryar queried.

"This." Negoragil pointed to the floor where the evidence was clearly visible.

To be sure there was something there, though Yaryar had trouble identifying it because it was so strangely marked. "And what are these?"

"Tracks," he answered simply.

Yaryar frowned. "I can see that. But what creature made them?"

Shaking his head Negoragil responded, "I don't know. Just tracks. Of what I cannot say, or why they have no scent."

"They must lead somewhere. Find out where they go."

Gangahar was wiping away the last traces of caked blood when Horhon opened her eyes and groaned. "I feel terrible."

"You are lucky. We thought you were dead."

She had no idea what was going on, hurting so much she could barely think. Her only wish at this moment was that the fierce pain would drive her back into unconsciousness.

"Stay down," Gangahar ordered. "Do not try to move, that will only make it hurt more."

Ignoring his plea to remain calm Horhon struggled to a sitting position. Huge drops of perspiration dripped off her face; she was in agony. And when she saw her own blood-splotched skin she started to panic.

"What's happened to me!?"

The answer eluded him. What had happened to her was still a complete mystery. Except for the wound on her shoulder there was no other place on her body which might account for all of this blood. No cuts or torn flesh. No openings or wounds. It was very strange. Looking at her now she seemed for the most part unharmed, so when Gangahar was absolutely sure she was all right he bent over her and pressed her for some answers.

"Last night. Do you remember anything?"

Lying perfectly still, Horhon barely shook her head. "No. Nothing. I remember nothing."

Yaryar squatted beside her. "Are you sure?"

"Of course." She blinked up at him. "What do you mean?"

Ordinarily Yaryar would not have spoken so forcefully, but he was afraid, they all were. "Perhaps I was mistaken to ask you, yet there is a reason for this happening and it must be understood."

As he was talking, Negoragil came bursting through the tunnel, his mouth gaped open from the speed of his arrival. Because Yaryar wanted to hear this important news first, he broke off and bade him to approach.

"Did you follow the trail back to its source?"

"Just as you ordered."

"Well," he said impatiently, "Tell us what you found."

"The tracks begin and end atop the same dune. I searched further on the field just to be certain. It was empty too."

"Then obviously you did not search hard enough." Yaryar spoke sharply. "Take some of the others with you and look again."

Although Negoragil protested he did not disobey. This time four hunters accompanied him outside. When the last one vanished from sight every eye was again on Yaryar. There were great mysteries presented here today; things that could not be understood, and his audience was eager to listen to whatever he had to say.

"You Dhorsal. Your burrow is next to Horhon's. Did you hear anything last night?"

Dhorsal scratched behind her ear, thinking hard. "Perhaps I did. It must have awakened me because I remember hearing a noise. Something was moving in the tunnel."

"A noise? That might be important."

"I heard it too," Horhon suddenly remembered. Trying to recall it now was just a blur, though Dhorsal's words had sharpened her recollection. "And a bright light. It hurt my eyes to look at it." Her jaw slackened. "Strange that I cannot remember anything else."

"Nor I," Gangahar agreed. He gestured sympathetically toward her. "How do you feel? Can you move?"

"I think so." She demonstrated by raising her leg, holding it up for only a moment before letting it thump back onto the floor. She closed her eyes. "Sleep. I need to sleep."

Obviously Gangahar was upset. Everyone could see how Horhon was suffering. And it was no secret who he blamed for this vicious and cowardly attack. "The Iranha. It must be," Gangahar growled.

"Might be." Yaryar, as always, was hesitant to acknowledge their name. "To say this is the work of the Iranha means that everything we know about them is wrong. Since they are supposedly killers of Egris then I doubt they would have been so merciful to Horhon when they could have easily skinned us all."

To Gangahar they were the logical choice, the only possibility. All of the evidence pointed to the Iranha. They were nearby, they had already demonstrated a penchant for killing, so they had every reason for attacking them now. What other creature would have been bold enough to enter their burrow? He stared downward at the tracks. "Something was in here. So if not the Iranha, then what was this thing who attacked her?"

What were the alternatives? None that Yaryar could think of. In disgust he obliterated the tracks with his tail, thinking instead of ways to defend themselves from this new and menacing invader. "Our only option is to leave."

But Gangahar strongly disagreed. "Not with Horhon injured like this. Leave if you must, but I am staying."

"Then we must be on our guard. Always. Whatever came here today can come again just as easily tomorrow."

"Agreed. But how can we fight what we do not understand, worse, what we cannot even see?"

Dhorsal's question struck deep into the heart of their fear. They were all paralyzed with fright. What if this same thing were to happen again and again? Thinking about it now made the hunters realize that any one of them might be next.

"It will not be coming back."

The surety of Horhon's words broke down the wall of silence. Yaryar looked around the circle of hunters, snorted. "How can you possibly know that?"

"I suppose I don't," she confessed. "It is only a feeling, the kind a hunter has when a herd is somewhere nearby."

Scowling, he said, "That is no answer. If a hunter finds the hunting good in one place then he is certain to return."

Horhon was in no mood to argue with him. Her head ached, she was dizzy and sank back down. With his strong arms around her Gangahar helped her through the tunnel. She dropped down into her own burrow with a groan, vaguely aware of the throbbing pain in her abdomen. The pain was only a small part of it though, and while the horrors of yesterday pushed deep into her thoughts she fell dead-asleep.

When Gangahar checked on her the next evening he could see that the wound was healing over nicely. The swelling had gone down and the mark was beginning to gray to an ugly scar. For Horhon, all she did was sleep. Each day was the same as the next, empty and formless. By the time she opened her eyes the fever had broken, the pain was over. The worst was now behind her. Horhon groaned and twisted inside her burrow. How long had she slept? Far too long, because when she awoke she was ravenous. Fresh killed meat was what she needed.

Something was troubling her and she could not think of any reason why. She recalled so little of the recent past that thinking of it now was as if it happened a very long time ago, maybe it had. Horhon struggled to understand, but these were thoughts that could not be understood. Something had physically attacked her. In the days that followed she had come very close to death. Had she not the willpower, the sheer determination to live, then she might have died. Yet it felt like her feelings were not her own because she honestly believed her attacker never really intended to harm her. Her head hurt from thinking. If there was an answer then it was beyond her comprehension. Emerging from her burrow, she forced it from her mind, the memory now forgotten.

The stillness around her suggested that everyone was out hunting. Horhon saw that the other burrows were empty and was annoyed at herself for sleeping when she could have been outside stalking prey with the hunters. Thinking about them now she felt a stab of fear that they had actually abandoned her and went south with Yaryar, although this was a foolish thought. Still, she anxiously awaited their return.

It was not a long wait. Horhon heard a noise echo in the main tunnel, the footsteps coming closer. Soon Karkakass strode into the room. Someone was trailing behind her, a smaller figure, though he bore an amazing resemblance to Yaryar. He was still very clumsy, moving as though each step was his first. She could not have birthed him too long ago, for his smooth hide still had a wet sheen.

Seeing Horhon in the room Karkakass brought up both hands and gasped audibly. "Such a surprise, to see you awake. Gangahar told us tomorrow, maybe tomorrow. And yet here you are now. Say something. How do you feel?"

"Hungry." Horhon noticed the youngster circling in the background. Like all Egris newborns he had come into the world ready to kill. Within minutes of being born he would have been on his haunches and ready to eat. Blood stained his teeth; they must have just returned from a meal. "Was the hunting good?"

Karkakass saw the direction of her gaze and moved to get out of the way. "He killed his first tarser tonight," she said proudly. "All by himself."

Killing a tarser was no great feat, Horhon knew. Just skin and bones. Worthless to hunt, worse to eat. Ordinarily it would have scarcely received any notice at all, though she wanted to be polite to Karkakass, and so she praised her youngster's hunting prowess.

To him her talking was just a noise. Horhon could have been saying anything, though this was mostly for his mother's benefit. Taking him by the shoulder Karkakass led him over to Horhon.

"Greet Antayak, my son. He will grow up to be like his father one day."

Like his mother, Horhon hoped. Two Yaryars in the same trod might prove unbearable! While Karkakass talked, Horhon was deep within herself. She saw all the shadows in her thoughts, things that until now she was not really aware of. So many awful things had happened to her. First the Iranha, now this. Horhon ran a finger over the scar on her shoulder, grimaced. Then the brief spasm of pain was quickly gone.

"How long?"

Karkakass blinked. "How long what? The illness you mean?" She nodded to Horhon's affirmative. "Eight days. You were so ill I thought you were going to die, we all did. Don't you remember anything?"

"Only the pain. I choose to forget the rest. Now, you said you were out hunting. Will the others be returning soon?"

"Not before the morning. Negoragil knew where there were goud to eat. They left early to stalk them. I'll take you if you are strong enough to make the trip."

If they traveled quickly and quietly under the cover of darkness the herd might still be there. Horhon could hardly wait to leave, rushing outside to the fresh air and starry night sky, only to wait impatiently for her two companions to join her. On Karkakass's signal the three of them slapped down their tails and leapt away together, jumping high into the air with swirls of dust blowing off their backsides.

They trekked steadily southwest through the grass-filled fields, staying in the hollows of the sand dunes. Overhead the sky was clear. Stars flickered in the darkness and the second moon was clearing the distant plains. A rocky scarp loomed straight ahead. It was not until they reached the top when Karkakass landed to a halt to speak.

"See here where their trail leads?" Her arm followed a narrow track way that wound downward into the dunes. Smacking her lips, she said enthusiastically, "It will take us over that next hill and beyond to the flatlands. To the goud. If the hunters have already departed then we will find our own goud. Attack one, kill one, eat one."

Horhon approved of this simple plan and was eager to move on. She started forward, only to stop when an image filled her mind.

"Is something the matter?" Karkakass said behind her.

Without answering Horhon quietly stared up at the shimmering star filled sky, then pointed eastward toward a cluster of brighter stars. "Do you see anything?"

"Only the lights." She shrugged. "What should I see?"

After a long, ponderous silence Horhon shook her head and replied, "Nothing. I think these things I see must be my imagination. We go now."

The downward climb was onerous, but once they crested the next hill the landscape began to flatten and a wide-open plain stretched out ahead of them. All those long days of immobility now taxed Horhon's strength; even despite her great hunger she was slipping further behind them.

"The hunters were here," Karkahass informed her when she landed.

Horhon could see where the tall grass was trampled flat and the hunter's clawed tracks ringed the area. This was where they had attacked from. Further up ahead a huge shape lay sprawled across the trail and as it came into view they saw the others of their trod bent over, feeding on the goud's now dead remains.

No one saw them coming, though when Gangahar looked up his cry of happiness made everyone turn around. "Horhon, is that you?"

"Too hungry to speak. First must eat," she blurted. Seeing the goud was almost too much to bear, though the worst part was waiting for the others to get out of her way.

Promptly stepping aside Gangahar pointed at the ripped open carcass. "Just killed. Have some."

Without delay Horhon sank her teeth into the meaty hide, tore off a huge bolt and gulped it down whole. She hadn't been eating for very long when she began to make choking sounds and regurgitated much of what she had already eaten. It was unusual that the goud's delicious flesh would cause her to gag. Yet suddenly it was not so delicious after all. In fact the flavor was so revolting to her that she immediately spat out the remaining lumps of flesh.

Gangahar stared at the wet pile. "What is wrong?"

"What is wrong?" Her eyes widening, the answer seemed perfectly obvious. "This meat tastes awful. How can you stand to eat it?"

After exchanging confused glances with the others, Yaryar swallowed another mouthful of meat and said, "I don't understand. The goud's flesh is tasty and perfectly good to eat."

"I cannot eat it."

"Why not? Tell us."

She shrugged. "I cannot. That is all." Horhon had no explanation for it. None whatsoever. Why had only she among the hunters been unable to digest this repulsive meat?

"I think it must be the sickness you taste," Gangahar decided. "Perhaps you will feel like eating tomorrow."

She felt like eating now; she was ravenous. In silence she went off to sit by herself and brood. There were so many worries; she had no idea how to deal with this new one. More than once she found herself looking back to where they had traveled from. The image of what she had seen earlier was still with her, and she could not shake the feeling that they were all in great danger.

"This hunt is over," Yaryar announced. "Time to return home."

Just then, the word home triggered another powerful image for Horhon, so sharp, so clear, that this might have been as real as the hunters before her. Real enough that she sprang to her feet and shouted urgently.

"Stop at once! Right now. Do not return to the burrow."

"Why?" Yaryar asked indignantly.

"The Iranha! They are waiting for us."

Facing in the direction of their burrow, everyone knew that it was a long ways back. But not even Magamengon who had the sharpest eyes could possibly see it from this far away, so even as the hunters were straining their own eyes to look, Yaryar was instead looking straight at Horhon.

"What nonsense. Don't be so ridiculous," he scoffed. "Are we to believe that you see things that we cannot?"

"Then go back there and die! I don't care."

His jaw snapped shut. "Enough! We leave for home."

"Let Antayak remain here with me," Horhon begged Karkakass. "Please don't let him go back to the burrow. Please don't let him die. You must believe me, you must."

"Bring him!" Yaryar ordered, turning his back on her. "We go." The swirling dust cloud from his tail slap was all that remained as he leapt away, heading for home.

As the others started to follow, Gangahar was wracked with indecision. To stay here with Horhon meant that his loyalty was no longer to trod Yaryar. To leave her meant that he was no better than his trod's namesake and deserved whatever fate befell them.

"You're going to your death," Horhon grimly warned him.

But his mind was made up. "I'll come back for you," he promised.

"I hope so," she said tearfully. "I hope so."

No one stayed with her. No one wanted to; their stomachs were full and they wanted to sleep. Daylight would bring her back home.

At sunrise the forest rose as a thick, black line on the distant reddening horizon. The brightening sky was clear except for a few clouds that went scudding past. Stars were dimming out, only the brightest ones still flickering overhead. From the air any notable landmarks were indistinguishable on this formless grass-filled plain. One wrong turn and a hunter could easily be lost for good. But the track they were on was a well-traveled route. Each hunter was spread wide apart, leaping high.

Yaryar made certain that he led the way home lest the others think he feared the Iranha. Not that he believed there were any Iranha. Being first was only so that he could prove Horhon wrong and finally be rid of her at last—this was what he most desired.

Home was now only three short bounds away, though when Yaryar came down he stopped himself from going any further. "What is this?" he said to Magamengon who landed beside him.

The hunter peered at the animal with the same quizzical look. "A nentenen," he answered.

"I can see that," he snorted irritatedly. "But why does it not flee from us?"

The sight of a nentenen wasn't at all unusual. They were fleet footed herbivores that normally roamed in vast herds on the plain, though were not the meatiest animal so a hunter had to be motivated to want to eat one, especially if there were tastier choices nearby.

"Something keeps it from running," Magamengon deduced. "See that?"

Despite its size and strength the nentenen appeared to be struggling against something that was much, much thinner, thin enough that it should have been easy for the animal to break free. What looked like a flexible vine was lashed around the creature's neck. The other end attached to a strange, stick-like object coming out of the ground. Since they had no word for it the hunters could only theorize about its origin.

"What could have done this?" Dhorsal's teeth clicked together in puzzlement. "And why?"

No one seemed to have the answer. Perhaps it had been grazing and gotten itself tangled up, yet being this close to their burrow the animal's presence seemed almost purposeful. Or was it just a coincidence that it had trapped itself just outside of their burrow's entrance?

Obviously their presence was agitating the creature; it pulled wildly against its tether to escape them. But no one appeared to be overly interested in eating any more, though if the nentenen was going to stay here then it would be a convenient snack in the evening.

"How can something this flimsy hold a nentenen?" Takilisk wondered aloud.

Curious, Dhorsal tried to bite through the odd looking vine and could feel her teeth grinding against it. "Not even a scratch." She then ran her clawed finger perpendicular across the taut line and sawed at it uselessly. "Doesn't cut either."

While they were all too distracted to much notice their surroundings the wind changed direction and Gangahar got a whiff of something foul. Air was rushing in and out of his nostrils as he continued to sniff for the source.

"What is that awful smell?" Magmengon now swung around in the same direction where it was coming from.

Karkakass detected it too, deciding the stink was emanating from over there in the deep grass. Maybe some other animal had died—but where were the scavengers? While she was pondering this, suddenly something lifted itself out of the grass, then another one, and another. She counted five. "What are those things over there?"

While they didn't appear to be particularly dangerous looking no one moved. Magamengon stared. "They stink too bad to be alive." Perhaps to prove to everyone that he wasn't afraid he started towards them but one of the creatures reacted to his threatening presence by raising a stick shaped object. He saw the flash of blue light but it was Karkakass who watched him drop down dead.

"Skin hunters!" she screamed in horror.

"Run!" Yaryar roared. "Run fast and don't stop!" As he turned to flee he knew what he had done: he had doomed them all.

The attack came swiftly. Negoragil was hurtling skyward as something tore through him; he crumpled and fell into the grass. There was a sudden explosion as several hunters were tossed into the air. Karkakass rose shakily off the ground; her skin was spattered with blood. Two bodies were close by. She recognized the face of the nearest. Yaryar lay still, his eyes glazed over. He was dead. When she saw his murderers coming out of the grass she lunged toward them with her armament of teeth, thinking only of their deaths. There was a loud crackling noise, a blue bolt of light that arced right through her body. She dropped and died.

Amid all of the noise and confusion Gangahar and Antayak somehow escaped. They bounded away, not turning back to look, for what they left behind was certain death. It was not long after this that a distant voice cut across the path they were traveling. It was Horhon.

"Come on! Come on!" she shouted. "Hurry up before the Iranha find us too."

They wanted to get as far from them as they possibly could, so they went on without stopping, even as the great forest swallowed them up and they stayed under the protective barrier of the tree cover. When they finally halted they slashed their claws across a tree trunk and let the running water collect in a small pool before lapping up gulp after thirsty gulp. For the rest of the afternoon they kept going, though were watching their backs to be certain they weren't being pursued. By evening the sun was setting; it was a safe time to stop.

"Where will we go now?" Gangahar asked gloomily.

"As far from the Iranha as we can get."

He looked at Antayak who was already missing his dead mother. "Do you think anyone else escaped?"

Horhon shook her head. "All lost, they must be."

Although he accepted this he was nonetheless angry at her for not wanting to return.

Likewise Horhon snapped at him. "Had you listened to me then those who died would still be alive."

"I understand that now," Gangahar growled through his clenched teeth.

"You do not. How could you when you left me to go with the others to where the Iranha were waiting for you just as I predicted."

"That is true," he agreed, "yet how did you know this?"

"It is too difficult to explain."

"Try."

"I can't. I just had to stay away, to protect . . ."

"What? What were you protecting?"

Horhon stared down at her belly. Suddenly it was all very clear to her now. "My child. I am pregnant."

Chapter 4

On their third day, the three hunters traveled south towards the desert, moving farther and farther from the Olahn Territory. To the west the sun set beyond the dunes and the evening shadows lengthened under the low hills. Some animal had left its tracks beside a muddy pool, so they stayed with the trail until the second full moon drifted up high behind them and illuminated their moving shadows on the pale sand.

Out this far on the arid plains water was more important than food, where a hunter would eagerly trade a full stomach for a mouthful of water. Luckily they found a meager watering hole; a small group of tarsers saw them coming and galloped away. Horhon just barely quenched her thirst when she glanced eastward and shrieked with alarm, seeing dark shapes moving through the star-filled sky. Gangahar looked, Antayak too. Something moved up there all right, but were they killer Iranha searching for them? Or something else?

According to Gangahar who recognized them first, they were soros, a large flock of them, wings outstretched, toothed beaks showing. No doubt hunting for death. Horhon could see them now, watching as they hurtled down into the shadows and vanished over the crest of the dune, gone.

The next day was the same. The horizon ahead of them was as unchanged as the one behind. Earlier there had been some hills, but the land soon began to flatten out again. The ubiquitous clumps of grass became sparse and there was more sand, little else. Some time ago—Horhon didn't know exactly when—they had crossed an invisible line that put them in the Un desert. While she had had spent most of her life living on the fringes of the desert, this was all very new to her. Few hunters had ever reconnoitered such a vast, empty territory. Even Gangahar had never traveled this far out before, and so what lay ahead was a complete mystery. But even that was far better than thinking about what they had left behind.

What remained of the blazing day lifted with the first moon. To conserve the water in their bodies, earlier they had dug into the side of a dune to wait out the heat, but now that the night was cooler and a freshening breeze blew across their backs, they traveled forward. As the evening progressed, Antayak fell further and further behind, until Gangahar had to turn back and search for him among the dunes. Horhon was reluctant to slow down, until Gangahar's distant roar cut through her worrying thoughts. Sinking into the sand she swung her tail around and jumped back to find him.

She was no longer running, but plodding, certain that what waited ahead could only be another setback. Her first thought was of Antayak. All this day he had been whimpering for his dead mother. It would not surprise her at all to learn that he had now turned back for home. But there Antayak was, Gangahar as well. Both of them were stopped at the base of a dune. The bleached bones of some long dead animal were sticking out of the sand. When Horhon arrived, she could see that something was stretched out on the ground behind them. Gangahar stepped aside.

"See what Antayak has caught," he said, swelling with pride. It was another tarser, a desert variety, its narrow arched ribs showing through mottled gray skin. A mostly worthless creature though. Few Egris hunted them, for they were bony and not very tasty. Yet the way Gangahar spoke made apparent his resolve to praise the young hunter's kill nonetheless.

Horhon feigned surprise. "You did this Antayak? All by yourself? Wonderful," she exclaimed, making known to him the magnitude of her pleasure.

And Antayak seemed to thoroughly enjoy her gratitude, chirping enthusiastically as he snapped up the animal in his jaws and set it down in front of them.

Sinking his teeth into the animal's haunch, Gangahar tore off a limb, the bones cracking beneath his great jaws as he chewed on the tough flesh. "How much further?" he asked Horhon.

"Tomorrow. One more day."

"That day is already here. You said that we would reach its end today."

"I said maybe today. How can I be expected to tell one day from the next if there is not the hope of tomorrow? Is crossing the desert more important than our survival?"

"It isn't if we die here."

Horhon scowled. "That won't happen."

"Are you sure? Lately you say so many things it is difficult to know which is which. We could have stayed in our forest where the hunting was good, and yet you chose this impossible trek across the desert. Why?"

Lowering her eyes, she was thinking hard, and when she looked up at him again she spoke only the truth. "To you it will make no sense, but I know this is the direction we must take. In my dreams I saw..."

She had not even finished speaking out the words when suddenly Gangahar's blue eyes widened and he threw up both his hands. "You mean we have come out this far—because of a dream? Insane!" he shouted. "Insane!"

"There is a hunter who I search for," Horhon said calmly, letting none of his negativity cloud her thoughts now. "Her name is Megog."

"So is this Megog real, or a part of your imagination too?"

She returned his sarcasm with equal vehemence. "Were the Iranha real enough, or have you so quickly forgotten the bodies of the dead we left behind?"

"It is you who I fear more than the Iranha," he admitted. "Something has happened to you. Now when you say things I wonder if these visions of yours will lead us into more trouble."

Horhon hesitated. "I cannot say where this one will take us. I hear a voice . . . and it is telling me to go."

"There is something else," Gangahar said worriedly. His clawed thumb retracted and brushed across the rough surface of Horhon's hide. "Look at your skin. So strange. I noticed this morning, thought it might go away."

"So did I," she agreed nervously. Despite her ignoring the problem, since this morning it had only worsened. For some reason her skin was losing its ability to match the color of her surroundings. When it was still daylight both Gangahar and Antayak's hides blended perfectly with the sand while hers was more a whitish, grey color that still, even in the pale light of both moons seemed to glow more brightly than before. "I do not understand the reason for it."

"There is a reason for everything so there must be one for this." Enough strange things had already happened to her that he feared what might be coming next. "I hope it is not a permanent condition."

"Will I be less a hunter for the color of my skin?"

"Probably not," he decided. "You must be hungry. Eat some."

"This tarser looks well fed," Horhon said with exaggeration as she closed her teeth around the shank and tore off a piece. She was ravenous and gulped down the bloody meat whole, not caring nor wanting to enjoy its taste. However, even before it settled in her stomach she bent over and retched in the sand. The drool was still dripping from her teeth as she stared down at the fleshy pile, wondering what it could mean.

Gangahar was visibly distressed. "Again? What is wrong with the meat now?"

"I don't know," she swore, more to herself than to him.

"You must try to eat something," he insisted.

Horhon wanted to, yet she doubted her next mouthful was going to stay down any longer than the first. Nevertheless she bit off a small strip of flesh and this time chewed it more slowly. "Tastes so bad," she complained. "I wonder how you can eat something this awful."

"I wonder how you cannot."

"Perhaps I am the one who has changed," she admitted reluctantly. "My fear is that I will be this way from now on."

Enough time had passed for Gangahar to feel more confident about his next words. "Your food stays down," he observed.

"Barely. If I have to eat this slowly then I will starve to death before I ever get my fill."

"Maybe the next animal we stalk will be tastier."

"It is not the animal. Rather, I crave . . . It is a craving for a taste that . . ." The image before her seemed to defy explanation. "I cannot describe it."

"Try," he said simply as he sank back against his tail.

"Something first must be done to the meat."

"What? What must be done?"

"Something." Horhon scratched behind her big ears, thinking, until it finally came to her. "Changed. Yes, that is it. It must be changed." But it was not an easy thing to describe. Somehow she could picture it clearly in her mind and knew how it was done, yet the words were difficult. "Do you remember that day when the sky set fire to the field?"

How could he forget about that? This past summer was an especially dry one. It had not rained at all; the grass was brown and crackled wherever the hunters jumped. One day while hunting they saw the dark storm clouds coming up, heard the rumbling of approaching thunder. They left for home immediately, yet before long the storm overtook them, and as they fled bolts of lightning thundered down. Aided by the fierce wind the flames whipped up higher and higher; the air was smoke-filled and hot. The fire spread so quickly they were trapped on all sides with no way out. Two hunters burned to death—it was terrible! The memory of that day still caused him to wince in pain.

"We were lucky to have escaped it."

"We were—and that is why you must remember what fire can do."

"Fire," Gangahar repeated uneasily. "So this fire will help you to eat? How?"

How indeed, for in its explanation were descriptions that even Horhon herself could not entirely comprehend. "I understand only that it must be used to change the meat."

"And where will you get fire?"

Now she found herself thinking about something she had never done before, and oddly, it seemed so simple, so straightforward, that the answer came to her immediately. "I can make fire."

Gangahar snorted. Few Egris had ever seen fire, and he had no great wish to see it ever again. "What you have described is impossible to make. Since no other hunter possesses the fire's knowledge, how is it that only you, Horhon, can do this thing?"

Obviously he didn't believe her. Yet could she believe it herself—especially when she had never made fire? With all these thoughts in her head it was hard to tell which was real and which was imaginary, but she had to try. "To prove what I say is the truth I will show you. But first a fire must have something to eat. It must have food. That is what we must seek out and find."

"We are in the middle of a desert where nothing grows."

"Not true. Last night we passed such a place. Of course that would mean doubling back. Or instead we might try going forward and maybe we will find another spot. What do you think?"

"I think we should go back—and keep going and don't stop until we reach our forest again."

"Do that and we will certainly die."

"We will all die out here anyway if we go on. So why not risk going back?"

"Leave if you must, it is your decision, but I go only as far back to last night."

Growling unhappily, Gangahar could see no advantage to abandoning her now, and so he decided to stay with her even despite what he feared the outcome would be.

After traveling all night the three hunters dug out a place to sleep and rested until nightfall. With the hot sun gone and only the bright stars to guide them they came upon yesterday's track and followed it to its source. They found a natural spring where the water percolated up from deep underground. Some small trees and bushes ringed its muddy banks; animal tracks ran off in every direction.

"Find us something to eat," Horhon told them both.

Up on the hill, out of water's reach the outermost ring of trees were mostly dead. Using her tail to crack off some of the dead wood she collected the broken pieces then threw them into a pile on the sand. Only a short time passed when Gangahar returned with food. It was still wriggling in his mouth and so he bit down hard then dropped the limp thing at Horhon's feet.

"Another tarser," she frowned. "Is this all you could find?"

"It is fatter than the last one," Gangahar said, irritated. He then watched as she crouched low and started working with her hands. Little of what she did made any sense to him, nor was he especially interested. However Antayak bent over and nudged the carefully arranged bits of wood with his snout.

"Stop that," Horhon scolded. "Can't you see I'm busy?"

"Doing what?" Gangahar asked bluntly. "All I see are sticks—and why do you rub them together that way?" He could have laughed because it was so ridiculous, to watch her supposedly making fire. "Lately, everything you do is a puzzle to me."

It worried her too. So much had happened since waking that first day in her burrow. She was no longer the same Horhon; she was changed. Now she saw things, images that were so haunting, so strange, she was sure that these were the thoughts of someone else. Whatever its source, one day soon she would be forced to reckon her own thoughts or she might lose herself forever.

Had Gangahar not seen it with his own eyes he would have never believed it. At first there was a single speck of light beneath her hands, then a second point began to grow out of the darkness, glowing even more intensely as Horhon leaned forward and blew onto the mound. Then Gangahar noticed a gray wisp of smoke curl up through the center, watching as the first spark burned beneath the twigs. Then flame.

"Fire!" he gasped, scarcely able to contain his astonishment. "You made fire!"

Of course she had. It wasn't much of a start but it was enough. The flames came up steadily as she piled on more wood, until the fire roared and was hot on her face.

Gangahar honestly didn't know what to make of her newfound ability, only knowing that he didn't like it at all. The fire both frightened and excited him, though when he overcame his initial shock and could speak at last his fear was such that he said, "Is it dangerous? Should we be so close?"

"You are afraid of it?"

"Yes," he admitted honestly, and then said, "It is a thing of destruction. I feel we should let it die before it grows and eats more than you give it now."

To her it all seemed so harmless, so ordinary and perfectly natural, as though she had always done it this way. To alleviate his fear she explained the procedure at great length, even demonstrated her skill with the sticks, yet when she finished she could see by his blank expression that the meaning of her words was completely lost on him.

"You just don't understand."

"Do you?"

Stirring the fire with a stick Horhon sat peacefully, watching as the bright sparks swirled up and vanished among the stars. She stretched back on her tail and yawned. Now was the time to eat.

"Antayak, go get me some more wood," she ordered. She held up a branch then pointed toward the dead tree. "More wood. Understand?"

He didn't, so Gangahar volunteered to go instead. "I'll do it." He moved off into the shadows. When he soon returned with an armload of fresh wood, Horhon had already torn off a limb from the carcass and was holding it over of the fire. While the tarser's flesh cooked, hot meat juices dripped down, sizzling onto the bed of red-hot coals. Its foul stench made him cough, and his eyes watered immensely. Up until this point her strange behavior had completely mystified him, but this was clearly the most outrageous thing he had ever seen her do yet.

"What is it that you do to that black thing?"

"It must be thoroughly burned," she replied frankly, and then added, "If I am to eat it."

His eyes bulged. "You are going to eat . . . that?"

"I am."

In horror he watched as she now closed her teeth around it. Grimacing, he asked, "How does it taste?"

"Better," she mumbled, not knowing why but swallowing it anyway.

Even Antayak was perplexed, sniffing the black lump of flesh and making a face that caused both hunters to burst out laughing.

"Burnt flesh." Gangahar shivered, watching with renewed disgust and revulsion as she snapped off another fore limb and gnawed contentedly on its cooked remains. "Looks terrible." He poked at the steaming meat pile with his clawed finger and put the tiniest piece between his teeth. And spat it out immediately. "Tastes even worse. Now I will be the one who throws up."

Half-chewing, half-swallowing, Horhon looked over and said, "I crave it, that is all."

"You say things and do things that make no sense. You are pregnant and it makes no sense. I have thought of this over and over and none of it makes any sense."

"Is it so important that you know the reason why?"

"Why? Why?" Gangahar was indignant. "You are too quick to attack the meaning of my words. I am concerned." He was. It was no coincidence. He knew, just as Horhon did too, that all these strange events were somehow connected.

In the fire's flickering light, Horhon's face had a forbidding expression. "Do not be concerned for me, Gangahar. Be afraid. Be very afraid for our people," she warned, the tone of her voice rising dramatically. "I have seen the Iranha in my dreams and know what they will do to us. Thousands will die. Tens of thousands!"

He was paralyzed with fear, her words of doom closing in around him like a predator's jaws. He stared at her with widened eyes, whispered, "That is knowledge you should not have."

"Or asked for," she replied quietly.

"Tell me, will the Iranha attack us tonight? What about tomorrow? Where are they now?"

"I don't know," she admitted. "Understand that I cannot control what I see, but I feel we are safe so long as we keep moving. I know that if we stay out here in the open we are targets for killing. The Iranha are always hunting."

"How can we go on when there is defeat in the very future that we look toward for hope?" Gangahar said dismally. "You see death for all of us."

"It is wrong to think like that. Yaryar believed the Iranha were no threat to us—and died. Those who believe as he did will die too. We must think instead what we can do to stop this from happening. Now it is to be our task to bring this news to all hunters, to spread the message to everyone we see."

"It is a big world," he said skeptically.

"And there is little time. Our future is coming."

With daylight approaching they had to hurry. Horhon led the way, Antayak and Gangahar following swiftly at her side. As the day progressed the warmth of the sun grew, and when it rose high and was hot on their backs they stopped beside a dune and dug into its bank to sleep until the evening. When they awoke the night was clear; the stars were easy to follow, yet the forest was no closer. They went on, knowing that what lay ahead was exactly what they left behind— just more desert.

Days passed by and still there was no forest in sight; the arid plain was empty and endless. The hunting was sparse, the water even more scarce. Once when they found a dried-up watercourse they followed its length for the entire night and found no outlet. And no water. This was no longer a journey but an expedition into the unknown, one that the hunters now worried would never end.

It was the start of another long night and the first thing Gangahar needed to do was search for water. Two solid days without anything to drink made this expedition particularly important since it was either find water tonight or go back, these were their only choices. He and Antayak set off together just as the sun was setting, but by the time Horhon climbed out of her burrow and brushed off the sand they were long gone.

Strange. This morning she had felt like eating raw flesh again but now her stomach was unsettled and she retched up the remains. While it frustrated her to be this sick she was determined to not let it keep her from getting off this accursed desert. With the other hunters already searching for water she decided to scout on ahead by herself.

At sunrise the next morning Horhon was returning to the same spot where they had spent the day before. Gangahar and Antayak still had not returned. She was not alarmed, only worried that there was no water to be found. The sun was streaking up and in every direction they were not to be seen. They might be back soon. Nevertheless now she was tired of waiting for them and so she dug back into the hill and went to sleep.

Sometime during the day Horhon opened her eyes. She heard the sound of footsteps and guessed the others were now returning. But when she poked her snout through the sand and peered outside she saw the face of a stranger looking in at her.

"Greetings hunter, I am Krugjon. And you," he grinned toothily. "What is your name?"

"I . . . I am Horhon, a hunter for trod Yaryar. Or, was," she lamented, now remembering. Once she pushed through the sand and emerged from her hiding place she was surprised to see two youngsters standing nearby. The youngest, his oversized ears twitching nervously, was probably on his first expedition in the desert.

No one moved. For a tense moment all four were rigidly silent. Horhon looked at them, they at her. Then Krugjon scarcely nodded, a gesture that brought the other two jumping forward without delay. He placed his hand on the shoulder of the nearest.

"This is Ilistruk, my oldest. She is a good hunter but she wastes too much time pursuing her male companions." The color of her hide changed slightly though Ilistruk managed to growl out a greeting without further embarrassment from her father. "And this small one is Yahu. He still has many things to learn."

No older than Antayak, Horhon thought. The memory of him suddenly stirred within her and she wondered where he and Gangahar might be now. "And your burrow mate?" she asked distractedly. "Where is she?"

"Their mother . . ." Krugjon's voice broke off and there was a long silence before he finished. "Dead. She went hunting and never returned. So we did not stay." He pointed up the slope. "We were crossing this dune, saw your tracks."

Although it was fortuitous, their meeting this far out in the desert, Horhon was sure she had met him before, somewhere. "Your face, Krugjon, so familiar. We must have met."

He shook his head no. "I don't think so. But tell me, where do you come from?"

"The Olahn territory."

"Then I must say no for certain. That is a far distance from here. Once I hunted north beyond the desert, but that was a very long time ago. Perhaps you confuse me with someone else."

"Perhaps."

Ilistruk then growled at her father and he listened momentarily before turning his gaze back to Horhon. "She wishes to know if there are other hunters who look like you."

Lifting up her arms Horhon slowly rolled them over and sighed unhappily. Except for a few dark blotches now her skin was completely white. How strange it was to not even know if this was even the end of it. "No," she responded. "I am the only hunter who looks like this."

"Do you travel the desert alone, Horhon? Are you lost?"

"Not alone. We are three, the last, the only survivors." Then she grimly added, "The others were killed."

This was indeed disquieting news that caused Krugjon's mouth to gape wide open. "The rest of your trod dead, wiped out. Everyone?" When told that they were, he moaned, "What happened?"

"The Iranha," she growled, hatred and loathing in every breath and movement of her body.

"What are the Iranha?" he asked naively.

She gaped, her blue eyes bulging in their sockets. "Don't you know?"

"No, tell me."

"The Iranha. Killer Iranha. The ones from the sky, the ones who butchered our hunters."

What Krugjon then heard was so frightening that he was forced to send his children away out of earshot. Of all his deepest fears none now compared with the Iranha. Everything about them was disturbing and unnatural, evil. These were creatures that hunted the hunters—and not for food—but something even more grisly.

"Our skins! They steal our skins!" He was aghast. "Why do they do that?"

Horhon simply shrugged. "They are not of this world."

"Then they must be hunted down, these Iranha. Wiped out."

"Not likely." She was appalled by how little he knew, though moderated her comment so that he would not be offended by the strength of her rebuke. "Obviously we both want the same thing, to see every Iranha dead. However you must know that no one has lived to tell us how this might be accomplished."

"If they behave like any animal then they can be killed like any animal."

"No, they can't be killed that way."

"What other way can there be?" He expected her to elaborate further, yet he saw the firmness of her expression and knew that he would have to speak again. "They are that dangerous?"

She frowned angrily. "Infinitely worse. The Iranha are not hunters like us. They possess knowledge we do not have, kill with weapons we do not understand. We do not even know how to kill them, or if they can be killed."

It was a gloomy assessment. Krugjon looked away from her, wanting to hear no more, yet even as he was turning about she came around to face him.

"My trod died, perhaps yours is now dead. Even your mate. The Iranha might have captured her too."

"Please—not like that!" His shock and bewilderment was such that it took extraordinary effort just for him to continue. "To see my beautiful Mako skinned—no! No, that is a death too horrible to imagine."

Evidently Horhon was not finished yet. As she told him more it was as if the entire future ended on her last word. He was astonished and dismayed, shaken. It seemed that the future she painted was very certain indeed.

"There is another hunter who speaks like you," Krugjon told her after a harsh silence. "Many summers ago she came to our trod and talked of terrible things that were to happen. Some have said that no one knows the future better than her."

"Then she must know of these Iranha because they are our future."

"Megog knows many things," he agreed. "One time she—"

"Megog!" Horhon abruptly cut him off. She instantly knew why that name sounded so familiar to her.

"So you know of her?"

"I dreamed of her. I think she is the one I am searching for."

Krugjon slapped down his tail. "Then you are the luckiest hunter alive! We are on our way to her right now. Come with us, Horhon. Speak to Megog yourself. I believe it is very important."

"Yes," she agreed wholeheartedly. "I believe it is."

Chapter 5

For all their time on the wastelands the search for water was only marginally successful. Gangahar had found some, but only after burrowing down deep in the sand so that he and Antayak had to take turns crawling to the bottom to drink. All this physical labor for a mouthful of water, and now it was too late to leave. By the time the sun reached its zenith in the sky the daytime heat was oppressive; hot air boiled up in shimmering waves off the dunes. Despite this he found himself wanting to return to tell Horhon, though it would be better to dig in for the day and bring her back with him this evening.

Meanwhile, Antayak was preoccupied with chasing another tarser up the side of a dune. It was a scrawny thing, not really worth the bother; still he roared enthusiastically as he snapped it up and clutched his prize as if this was his best effort ever. Very soon, however, his huge ears quivered and he looked down to see a dust cloud lifting off the field, arrowing closer and closer. The small tarser clamped in his jaws twitched spasmodically as it thudded onto the sand. Blinking its eyes open the animal suddenly bolted away to freedom, screeching as it fled.

Gangahar heard the rumbling sound too, bounding up the slope to see what was coming. It had to be Horhon, her white hide shining in the sun. But behind her, brown shapes moved over the brown sand, almost invisible except for the glinting of their teeth. Roaring happily he hurried off the dune to greet them.

"The forest is three more days' journey." Horhon pointed toward the south-east. "We leave for trod Megog. She is the hunter I seek. I am certain of it."

Again Gangahar stared at her, dumbfounded. "Amazing! To hear you speak her name, now I believe this must be true." While it was a tremendous relief to know they were almost free of this wretched place, he had his own good news. "I found water." He peered at the other hunters whose hides looked as dusty and dry as the desert. "Enough for everyone."

Krugjon's cracked, black tongue licked his teeth. "So thirsty."

Since the watering hole could only accommodate one hunter at a time each took their turn going down headfirst. Only the very tip of Horhon's long tail was visible to the others while she slaked her thirst.

"Something else happened," Gangahar told her after she climbed out. "We saw the Iranha."

Fear seized her and she spun about in all directions. "Where?" she gasped. "Are they following you now?"

"No. No, they were far away—and we were not seen. The danger has passed," he assured her. Seeing Krugjon sighing with relief he met his gaze and said, "You must know of these Iranha, too."

He nodded unhappily. "I now wish I had never heard that name."

After Horhon introduced everyone they chatted briefly. Gangahar was delighted to learn that trod Megog was right at the edge of the forest where there were malgots, a gigantic, meaty beast that he had only heard of but never tasted. He was eager to leave. They could have gone on, but the intense heat made daytime travel unbearable, so they decided instead to dig in and wait for dusk.

At sunset Horhon climbed from her sandy lair and brushed herself off. She was alone; the others were still asleep. However, as the first bright stars took hold of the darkening sky Krugjon climbed from his burrow to see her sitting atop the dune.

"What is it that you see up here?" he asked, yawning, his rows of white teeth glinting in the moonlight.

"I watch the sky. Ever since I was a small one like Yahu."

"For what reason?"

"Many reasons. Why does the day become night, the night become day? Why does the sun change its course as the seasons change? Why do the moons rise and set? Do you not ever think of these same things too?"

"Why, no," he responded, surprised. "Will looking at the lights make me think like you?"

"They are more than lights. They are like our sun, only more distant. I call them stars."

"Stars," he repeated. "And do these stars shine on other worlds like ours?"

"See that low one over there, larger, brighter than the others?" Krugjon nodded. "That is a planet. And on it I believe there are living creatures like us."

"You mean a world full of Iranha?" He grimaced to show this was indeed an unpleasant thought. "All this thinking is hurting my head. I think we should wake the others and go on."

Despite the great distance they covered, there seemed to be little change in the landscape. Other than a few clumps of grass the desert still remained desolate and empty. They traveled all night and into the early part of the next morning before the hot sun made them stop. But by nightfall they began to notice some spiny plants—these were the first ones, though as the hunters went on they began to see more and more of them. The second moon was coming up. Straight ahead the jagged, dark line of a distant mountain came into view.

It was close to dawn when they crossed through a mountainous pass to find a grass-filled valley beyond. Herd animals grazed nearby in the foothills, yet moved off quickly when they saw the big flesh-eaters approaching. On the way the hunters surprised a large herd of nentenens drinking alongside the bank of a fast running river. They sent these lumbering, four-legged creatures plunging into the water to be submerged by the swift currents. White waves foamed up around their long necks as they swam for shore.

Krugjon stood on the opposite bank and watched them gather downstream. "What should we do? Keep on, or go hunting?"

Naturally they all wanted to eat but trod Megog was now closer than ever. In any case the sun would soon be up and they might have to stop anyway. They were leaning toward staying but it was Horhon who inadvertently forced the decision.

Gangahar saw her trembling and caught her by the shoulder as she gaped open her jaw and retched. "Sick again?"

"I keep hoping this will be the last time."

"It never seems to stop. Maybe it won't."

"It will." Shaking her head to clear away the fog she then turned to Krugjon and said, "Will you lead us on to trod Megog?"

They started off immediately.

When it was too hot to continue, when the sun was scorching on their hides, they halted for the remainder of the day. Horhon thought she would not be able to sleep and yet it was nightfall before she emerged from out of the shadow of the hill and joined her companions waiting up on top.

Only one moon rose this night, and for the rest of the evening its cool light guided the hunters toward the distant outline of the forest. As they disappeared beneath the towering treetops Horhon felt the days of uncertainty lifting off her shoulders. It was a long journey that everyone was happy to see come to an end.

Within a short time they came to a place where the gnawed bones of some gigantic creature lay strewn across their path. There were fresh tracks leading back into the woods and everyone knew they must be close. As they swung around a tree trunk Horhon spotted a group of hunters jumping up ahead. Her sharp growl brought the pack to a standstill. Now as they approached, one of the hunters, possibly the leader, leapt forward.

"I know you."

"As do I." Krugjon nodded to the scarred hunter whose name was Katakana. Her right arm had been bitten off and there were several prominent scars across her ribcage where some animal had savagely clawed her. "These are my friends," he introduced them.

To the onlookers Horhon was a mystery. When it was learned that both she and Gangahar were from the Olahn territory, another hunter asked them, "Then you must know of Sosot, my daughter, who hunts with trod Kuro?"

"I do." It was Gangahar who answered her. Sosot was well-known to him. He, in fact, had hunted with her for many seasons before leaving the plains. "But she hunts with trod Kuro no more. She has her own trod in the Pok forest."

"Wonderful," the old hunter grinned toothily, then added, "I once hunted with Kuro myself. I knew your mother well, Gangahar. Come to my burrow tonight and we will talk of the past."

He bowed his head respectfully. "I'd like that."

"First they must speak with Megog," Krugjon interrupted.

So while everyone went off together, talking, laughing, trying to see what they could learn, news of the Iranha soon spread throughout the trod. After hearing what happened their voices died so low that the listeners' teeth were clicking together uncontrollably.

They were only beginning to be afraid.

Word soon reached Megog that the strangers were coming. But she was not well at all today and had retired to her burrow to rest. When she was first awakened from her deep sleep and told of these new arrivals she angrily chastised her attendants and ordered them away. But something one of them told her changed her mind.

"A white-skinned hunter? She is here, in our burrow?"

When told that she was, Megog stirred sluggishly; she sent an advance message instructing the trod to prepare for her presence.

After struggling through the tunnel, Megog's aides escorted her into the central chamber where the hushed audience was already waiting. Fresh meat and a skin bag containing water were placed in front of her. She shunned the meat, though did lap up some of the water before ordering everything removed. Megog looked at all of the silent faces, knew that they were watching and worrying.

"I heard there were strangers among us."

"I am no stranger," a familiar voice answered her.

"Then come forward and name yourself."

His toothy smile was sufficiently enough for her to remember his face. "Krugjon." Megog's eyes shifted beyond him. "And what of Mako?"

In the meantime Horhon stood watching from behind a cluster of hunters, hoping to see if Megog could recognize her, though she doubted that the two of them could have possibly shared the same dreams.

"Such tragic news," Megog said sadly after Krugjon was through speaking. "Your burrow mate dead, so terrible. When my daughter left us I wished her a long life. May she have died well." The trod answered this with a resounding growl of consonance. "Of course you and your family are welcome to stay with us as long as you like."

"I thank you." He nodded gratefully then stepped back into the circle.

Gangahar decided it was his turn to speak but Megog rudely cut him off in mid-sentence. "Where is this white hunter? Come out and let me see you."

"I am here."

The instant Horhon appeared the old hunter gasped, so great was her shock. "This strange one who is before me. Remain here. Now leave us," she ordered the others. "I will speak with her alone."

It was an unusual request yet one that the hunters instantly obeyed. When the chamber was once more silent Megog crooked her head. "Come closer."

Horhon could not disobey, for this was a hunter of considerable age and importance, one who commanded those around her just by her mere presence. As Krugjon had said, she was indeed very old. Megog's face was thin and gaunt. Most of her teeth had fallen out, her bones showing through her thin hide. Part of her tail was missing, but she had held up well for most of her long life.

"Yes," Megog hissed slowly, screwing up her eyes to see her. "Yes, it is you. Come closer." Placing her trembling fingers on Horhon's shoulder she pulled her down. "Long ago I dreamed of a white hunter. Are you the hunter who can bring the light of day into darkness? Are you that same one?"

"I am."

"Good." Clapping both hands together she shouted for her attendants. "Go outside. Bring me dead wood. As much as you can carry." Horhon knew exactly what the old hunter wanted her to do, and so now as they piled the sticks before her, Megog waved her hand and said, "This skill that only you possess. Demonstrate it."

It did not take her very long to bring up the fire, and as the white smoke cloud rose and filled up the chamber the curious onlookers gasped in horror and fled away into the tunnels. Only Megog remained in her place.

"Does this thing have a name?" she asked curiously.

"Fire," Horhon told her.

"Fire." She repeated the word twice, poking the flames with her finger tips and drawing them out quickly. "It is very hot, this fire."

"Have you never seen fire before?"

"Once, perhaps, a long time ago." Then she asked, "Does it eat what it is given?"

"Yes," Horhon replied.

Megog leaned forward; she was thinking. "Everything?"

"I guess so."

"An important bit of knowledge to possess, don't you think?"

But Horhon disagreed. "Your hunters already laugh behind my back. Others will too."

"So you should laugh at them. You can do what they cannot." Again she rested her hand on Horhon's shoulder. "Now we must talk of more important matters concerning the future of our people."

Horhon said humbly, "It is a great honor to serve you. But how can I, the lowest among your trod, help one who is highest?"

"Something has happened. Something that will change everything." Megog's gaze moved downward. "You are pregnant," she told her matter-of-factly.

Her expression changed instantly. How could she have known about that? She was not dismayed, only surprised, shocked. "Why yes," she admitted.

"Just as I thought." Megog continued to stare in amazement. "Do you know what this means?"

She didn't, but even while Horhon was trying to fit the pieces together, Megog went on, telling her, "Your world is in the Olahn territory where few of us have ever ventured that far from our home here. The Un desert divides us so we live apart, but we are still the same people. There are many other such places in the world where we Egris are separated, yet we have an enemy common to all."

"The Iranha," Horhon growled through her clenched teeth.

"The Iranha, yes. You seem to think of little else."

"I hate them."

Megog nodded. "And so you should. They are the killers of Egris. I foresaw their kind long ago, knew that they would come here, taking home with them their cargo of death. Our world is not theirs to have, so they learned to hate us long before we hated them. It is our total and complete annihilation that they plan, every Egris dead, or so that is what they want. Thoughts of these despicable creatures fill my dreams, day and night. I have spoken of this to those few who could understand, for it is difficult to carry such a terrible burden all of these years."

"I understand."

"Some of it. And now I will tell you more." She wheezed, then coughed long and deep in her chest, her voice dropping so low that Horhon was just barely able to make out her words. "I am very old. It is a good thing to die old. Before me, Mogul was leader. He too was very old. He has since died. Now I look forward to death, to be with him, and those who have gone before me. But know that there are many hunters who will no longer have that choice. Now wherever there is death these Iranha creatures are certain to be there."

While Horhon listened in silence she was greatly impressed with Megog's immense knowledge, especially her keen awareness of the Iranha. No other hunter had spoken with such vehemence. And it was a great relief to know that someone else shared these same thoughts.

More importantly though, Megog's information provided new insight into her own situation, the things that were yet to happen, and so she was careful to remember every detail.

"How long have you possessed this knowledge of the Iranha?" Horhon asked her.

"Too many years ago to remember. Or perhaps I have always had it. Anyway I have known about them for a very long time."

Horhon was getting ready to speak again. Megog spoke first. "We Egris, the Iranha, all are inextricably linked to one thing, Horhon. Your child."

"My . . ." Her eyes widened. "Are you sure?"

"Of course. Do you doubt what I tell you?"

"If you say so then it must be true, for it is my belief that you can look into the future and see many things."

"This one could not have come to you in a natural way. He is so different."

"Then you have seen him?"

She nodded. "The child who is not a child. The one who is Egris but who is not Egris."

"What do you mean?"

Her interrogative only strengthened Megog's temper. "You have no appreciation or understanding of what I have just told you, do you?"

"Only the tiniest bit," Horhon admitted. "Maybe it is better if I did not know the reason why this has happened to me."

"It is better to know the truth than to be ignorant and die for nothing," she replied testily. "Now pay attention. It is our age alone that separates us. Do not doubt your own abilities. You have already made good use of them, have you not?"

"I have, but only to escape the Iranha."

"And so you are here now. Safe."

Horhon, as usual, was cynical. "The Iranha will come here too. There is no place to hide where we cannot be found."

"Then you had better start thinking of ways to protect this life within you. Because without him, there is no future at all. No hope whatsoever. Growing within you is the very future itself." Megog poked an angry finger into Horhon's abdomen. "Many will die so that this one will live. If need be, are you willing to die for him too, Horhon?"

It was a very serious question, one which she had better quickly answer. "Yes."

"Then you must pay strict attention. Listen very carefully to what I have to tell you. Your listening will make the difference between life and death."

She talked a long time, mostly about ordinary things relating to the trod, though some of it was about Megog's own personal feelings. Occasionally she asked Horhon deliberate questions just to be sure she was listening. But by the end of the evening Megog was rambling. When she finally began to slow and closed her eyes with fatigue, Horhon called her attendants and they came at once and took her away.

As Megog's health quickly deteriorated, the days they now spent together were fewer and fewer. So when Horhon was summoned to her chamber three days later the old hunter's slumped figure was a discouraging sign that there was not much time left.

Today Megog coughed so much that most of what she said made little sense to Horhon. It was not until after another day with her that the words slowly began to sink in. Understanding grew, a word, a sentence at a time, until it was perfectly clear what she was telling her.

"What you ask of me is impossible, insane! I cannot do it."

But Megog paid her little attention. "After my death you will lead the trod. This is the way it must be, the way it was planned."

"No."

"Silence! If you must speak then speak only of your gratitude to what I offer."

"But I refuse. I must."

"Refuse." Megog was incensed. "Idiot! Listen. Understand. You cannot refuse. I have waited a lifetime for you, always knowing that some day you would come here. Now it is happening just as I foresaw."

"But there must be other hunters more worthy than I."

"There is only you. This is your future. Now accept it." Without further argument Megog motioned for her attendants. She was exhausted and needed to rest. "One more thing. The fire. Do you remember what we talked about?"

"Everything. I will not forget. I promise."

"Good. Then I can now embrace death and die in peace. May you be successful in every venture."

Horhon stayed there, was thinking carefully of her response, yet she could think of nothing to say, only watch her leave.

In the early evening a hunter came hurrying from the tunnel. It was one of Megog's attendants. "Come at once," he said urgently to Horhon. "It is Megog. She is dead."

Now the hunters were looking toward her, looking to the future of trod Horhon. All of them.

Chapter 6

The many days that followed Megog's death were unhappy ones for the trod. The hunters were in a somber and restless mood, but it was the burial preparations that penetrated their innermost thoughts. As the final day of grieving ended they were ready to begin at last.

Just before dark the funeral procession marched silently onto the field. It rained during the early part of the day but the sky was starting to clear behind the forest; a cool, wet wind was blowing from that same direction. Once the heavy clouds lifted the first faint stars began to appear in the eastern sky.

While there was still daylight some of the hunters went on ahead to stand beside the pyre of wood where it had been carefully stacked. The pallbearers moved slowly toward it, carrying Megog's prepared corpse high over their shoulders.

For Horhon it was another exhausting day. Her mouth gaped open with fatigue as she fought to stay awake. With so many things to be done it made sleeping impossible. And because it was Megog's fervent wish that she take charge, the funeral arrangements were now her sole responsibility. The old hunter was very precise about her death. She spoke of it in infinite detail before she died. How this and that would be done, how much wood for the fire, who would carry her body, who would sing her death song, on and endlessly on it went. It was an impossible list.

But now Horhon was leader, speaking with Megog's rank and authority, delegating the least important tasks to those who attentively came to her side, obeying her every command as though it had always been her they faithfully served. And Megog not even buried yet.

Since this was a period of mourning no one was permitted to hunt, for it was customary to fast until the dead were buried. Once when Ilistruk returned with her mouth stinking of animal flesh Horhon reprimanded her so harshly that the listeners backed away in fear, not wanting to incur her instant and ready wrath.

The transfer of authority had not been an easy one. Having the leadership and so many new responsibilities thrust upon her made it incredibly difficult for Horhon to remain calm. Consequently there were many angry outbursts. So now when she stopped in front of the procession and raised her hand they halted, their eyes trained on her, their ears straining to hear her every word.

"This is far enough. Gangahar, go into the forest and find me some dry sticks. You know the ones I need. Those of you who carry Megog. Put her on here."

Carefully, they laid Megog's body upon the prepared pile, the branches cracking beneath her stiff weight. The ceremony was to begin at once. Encircling her corpse the hunters looked on in silent thought, thinking of the past. Those who were old enough to remember recalled the days when Mogul was leader, and Megog a hunter just like them. Even fewer could remember back when she hunted with another trod. Now as they stared at her face for the last time, many of the hunters were feeling particularly heavy-hearted.

Amink, an old hunter like Megog, suddenly fell prostrate before her corpse and wailed in anguish. Katakana, too, joined in, and soon there were few faces not wet with tears of unhappiness. Horhon, like everyone else, was caught up in this groundswell of emotion. It took a long time to recover, but when she could think clearly again, when she could talk of Megog and not burst into tears, then she talked as leader.

"This unhappy day has finally come. As a trod we gather together to honor the dead. Megog, our sister, now joins those hunters who have died before us." Scooping up a handful of dirt Horhon gingerly sprinkled it overtop of Megog's body, saying, "We give her back to Agorgagoran from which all life was formed, and to where the dead must all return. Her physical body mingles with the dust of the dead, yet her eternal spirit now lives within us all."

"Should we not properly bury her in the ground?" Katakana interrupted.

"Megog would have preferred it that way," Saskakel agreed with her. "I do."

"Enough!" Horhon roared. "Did I not explain what would be done? Did you not listen?"

Under the burden of her angry words her detractors instantly quieted. In the meantime Saskakel deliberately clubbed his tail in protest. He was angry and could find nothing about this strange ceremony that was satisfactory. Nevertheless Horhon continued.

"Everyone take your places." Slowly, deliberately, the hunters formed a complete circle around Megog's body. Horhon stood in the center. "Bring me the sticks."

From all of the ones Gangahar collected in the forest she selected the two best pieces and was soon vigorously rubbing them between her hands. Few of the hunters had seen this strange thing done so they crept closer to watch, though were ready to flee at any time.

Okinaw scratched his head in puzzlement, was startled when he saw the ring of smoke, the red sparks glowing redder, and screamed aloud as the first flames rose up beneath Horhon's hands.

Katakana's blue eyes were enlargening in the firelight. "I told you," she whispered to Amink beside her.

Until tonight many in the trod had never seen fire. Seeing it now, this close, filled them with awe. Without thinking Amink reached towards the burning pile only to have Horhon slap his hand away.

"Do not touch it! Fire burns," she told him. Holding up a burning twig to show him Amink watched in amazement as it disintegrated before his eyes. Afterward she bid them all to join her at the fire, passing to each hunter a thick branch and giving them explicit instructions. At first they looked bewildered and confused, yet when she demonstrated by lowering her stick into the flames, for some of the watchers it was almost too much to bear.

"Must we do this?" Ilistruk protested, her arm trembling.

"There is nothing to fear," Horhon assured her. "So long as you do not touch the flame."

Still she was shaking so badly that Horhon had to clamp the flaming stick in the young hunter's hands until she was able to hold it herself.

"Gangahar. Here, take this."

Although he wanted to appear unafraid, as he reluctantly took hold of the burning branch his teeth were chattering together.

Even despite Horhon's orders Katakana refused to put her stick into the fire. Likewise Saskakel refused. However, Amink was determined to be an example to the others and lowered his stick into the fire until it caught and blazed brightly against the darkening sky.

One by one the assemblage encircled Megog's body and set their torches into the bed of branches. Most of the wood was still damp but the grass was reasonably dry and caught. Thick gray smoke swirled around them, sent them leaping backwards, coughing and rubbing their eyes. The flames grew in intensity, and so did the heat. A strong gust of wind fanned the fire, brought up the flames higher and higher, completely engulfing Megog's body. Layers of flesh began to peel away, the exposed bones blackened, everything was being consumed.

"This is not right," Saskakel grumbled. "Her bones belong with the dead. We should have buried her." Just then a piece of timber crumbled and a spray of red sparks shot up. "I do not like it."

No one answered except for Horhon. "It was her death wish that I do this for her."

"For what reason?"

"For the same reason that prevents me from telling you now." She smiled coldly at his attacking stance. He was arrogant and deserved to have his self-importance lowered a notch or two. "Since she never told you then it is a secret you are not permitted to hear. So do not ask me this again."

His nostrils flared and he snorted angrily. Her treatment of him was deplorable and he dug the claws of his feet into the ground, raking up clumps of earth to show everyone how much he objected.

Saskakel had always believed that when Megog died he would be her natural choice for leader. It was no secret that he had lifelong aspirations for her position. After all, this was his trod since birth, and he was the popular choice to replace her. Everyone expected Megog to chose him. Now to see this outsider taking over, and doing these unnatural things. She was a troublemaker, he could see that already. Deep down he secretly hoped her hide might fall into the hands of the Iranha.

"Megog was old before I was born," Horhon told her listeners. "Yet she led this trod until the day of her death and was respected by everyone because she proved herself a capable leader. Certainly no one among you ever questioned her ability to make decisions. I now lead. This was never my choice, to be responsible for your lives and the lives of your children. Megog did this well, but I know I will never surpass her leadership. I promise nothing, only that if you wish it then I will try as I can to continue the task of keeping this trod together, and alive. Know that there is a new danger out there. I have seen these Iranha kill, have seen two whole trods wiped out, and nothing could stop them. Somewhere, I am certain this slaughter is happening again. And so we must prepare for the future. Our future together depends on what we decide today, right now. What say you, hunters?"

For many of them, there was never any question as to who should lead, since it was Megog herself who had chosen. Even despite her choice, right or wrong, the decision was ultimately made for the good of the trod. Megog would never have selected Horhon as her successor for any other reason—they knew the old hunter too well.

"Megog's dying wish was that it be this way," Amink said. "I think so too. Like her I believe this trod must change as the world changes. The Iranha are a new problem, and so we must learn what we can to survive. I see no one among us better than Horhon to command. She knows these creatures so I think we must follow her as Megog wanted."

Because Amink was so admired for the veracity of his words no one doubted what he was saying now. In fact the majority of them were convinced that Horhon was their best choice, although she was an inexperienced leader. In time she would improve, but until then they would also be forced to live with her mistakes.

"I approve of Megog's choice as well," Okinaw announced. Others in the group nodded and growled out their approval.

"And you, Saskakel?"

"I honor the decision of my trod only because I must."

Katakana then spoke up. "I believe Horhon will lead us well."

"That is to be seen," he snorted.

With his anger still unspent, Saskakel couldn't look at her without having to taste the bitter bile in his mouth. Megog was dead. She had made her choice and so for him there was nothing, although he fervently believed that her protégé would ultimately disgrace herself and those who she commanded—if he waited long enough. In the meantime he might have to leave. There were other trods out there. He could reach one of them before morning. But if Horhon wanted to be rid of him, she might be doing that now. Obviously his own status in the trod threatened her position. She would have to be on her guard, watching him, so perhaps he would stay just a while longer.

Even though the fire was almost out Horhon ordered more wood stacked on top. Flames roared up high and the dry branches crackled. A plenary moon, the first, drifted above the field; it was all very peaceful. Later, when the second moon appeared, Amink climbed to his feet and began to chant Megog's memory. His was a plaintive, melodious cry that brought the others to tears. When he finished each hunter rose and took their turn, until the last one dropped down and was through. For the remainder of the night they kept a silent vigil while the fire burned lower. By the time Horhon threw on the last of the wood it was a simmering red bed of coals. Gangahar crouched beside her.

"How long?"

"How long what? The fire you mean?"

"Yes."

"Until everything that was Megog has burned. Then her remains must be collected and stored away for the future."

He had absolutely no idea why, nor did he wish to know. He simply wanted this to be over so he could stalk some game and eat. She must have known what he was thinking because she immediately changed the subject to food.

"You must be hungry. Antayak and Yahu could stand to sharpen their hunting skills—and what better hunter than you to teach them. Why don't you take them hunting."

"I mean no disrespect to Megog," he said guiltily.

"I know that."

"Aren't you coming with us?"

"Until I am finished here—no. Now go."

Everyone else left for the hunt; Horhon stood alone on the field. Once the last of the embers glowed no more she dug her hands into the warm ashes and scooped them into a thick branch she had specially hollowed out for this purpose. Whatever was left she covered it over with sand, then started back for the burrow just as the sun was coming up behind her.

With all of Megog's wishes now satisfied, except for the very last one, she could sleep.

Chapter 7

Sambalor heard the airship groan. Now she detected a subtle change in the air pressure and it felt to her like they were descending. "They're bringing us down."

Blilo Yim, one of her two male companions, got up from where he was sitting. There was a small portal that he waddled over to look through.

"Well?" Sambalor asked him impatiently. "What do you see out there?"

"Lots of sand." He said, fear-filled and visibly shaking. "They've brought us out to the desert."

Scowling, she said, "This is what happens when I put my trust in males. At the first threat of physical harm you shriek like chebollas in a fire, tell your jailors everything."

"At least we are willing to die for our beliefs," Taluine said indignantly beside her.

"And what good are beliefs if your environmental cause dies with you?"

All three of them bumped hard in their seats as the airship settled on the ground.

"We're here!" Blilo Yim panicked.

"But still alive. Remember, if we stick together we can find our way back."

"More male foolishness." Obviously Sambalor didn't share their misplaced optimism. "We will be eaten well before we ever walk off these dunes, before we ever—"

"Shut-up!" Taluine snapped at her. "Can't you see we're frightened enough already? Instead focus your intelligence—that is, if you have any—on how we might escape this place alive."

"You are dreaming if you think Midlothian wants us to escape. Putting us out here alive is just an illusion that will evaporate as quickly as a mirage on the sand. We are already dead."

While they were heatedly arguing, their compartment suddenly filled with hot, dry air as the door hissed and slid open. Outside a dozen heavily armed soldiers encircled the perimeter while Lophine Lorim, their hahlok commander, stood at the doorway looking in.

"Welcome to paradise," she greeted them. Her grotesque smile increased. "I trust everyone had a comfortable flight and is looking forward to getting outside to enjoy this wonderful place."

Even Sambalor had to admire Midlothian's ingenuity. She had found an effective way of making her problems disappear without having to deal with the mess since the evidence usually wound up in some predator's stomach. "I'm surprised your abdominous leader is depriving herself of her entertainment," she said coarsely.

"Unfortunately she was busy with another important matter that required her attention, yet she deeply regrets not being here to see you off."

"No doubt she is killing someone more important than us."

"She prefers to involve herself in the decision making, and leaving the fun part for those of us who enjoy seeing her enemies suffer."

"How fortunate that she was able to find another shallow-brained sadist like herself to do her dirty work," Taluine glowered. "I wish her a short life and hope her fat corpse rots before I set eyes on her again."

Lophine Lorim's laughter shook her corpulent bulk. "Her wish for you, too. Now, please." She eagerly waved the wedge of her hand. "Do come out."

Sambalor volunteered to be first, stepping past Lophine Lorim with a killing glare in her beady, black eyes. Physically attacking her might get her killed, yet the opportunity to close her wedges around this idiot commander's scrawny neck seemed so much more appealing than being ripped apart and eaten.

"Why Blilo Yim, my dear, you look positively frightened to death. Don't you want to come outside and play with your little animal friends?"

He had backed himself into the furthest corner where he was determined to stay. "No."

"Leave him alone." Taluine stepped between them.

"This is your cause, isn't it? Protecting the indigenous wildlife from Epiphilinian aggression."

"There is no moral justification for exploitation," he argued.

"Well then, come out of there and let these wild beasts decide if this morality of yours will improve or degrade your tastiness."

Stepping into the sunlight, Taluine raised a blocking arm to protect his eyes from the blinding glare. To be this far out of his city felt like he really was on another world. Strange, because back on his own world, the massive environmental destruction was more hostile to him than this wild world ever could be. And still, he was going to die. Behind him, he could hear his companion squealing as Lophine Lorim hauled him from the passenger compartment and tossed him face first onto the sand.

"You should thank me for bringing you out here to see this. Is it not beautiful? Look at these dunes. In pristine condition, untouched by us Epiphilinians."

"Like all things Epiphilinian, I expect it will be destroyed in no time to put something of lesser value on it. Profit before life. Destruction before preservation."

Her head-shake was slow and deliberate. "Such a shame to waste two young and pretty males on these bestial animals when you could be entertaining my troops instead of filling your feeble minds with the same sort of environmental nonsense that you were preaching back in city Anaxerxes."

Taluine remained obstinate. "I'd rather die in the jaws of some beast than have to lie on my back for even one of your dregs."

"Very well." She waved her arm to signal that it was time for them to depart. "My preference would be to watch and see what happens to you, but I have to return to my city. You do know where your city is, don't you?" Looking around to see if any of her dregs were listening, she acted as if she was giving up an important secret that might help them. "Tell no one that I gave you this. It's that way," she pointed. There was a dark line visible on the horizon. "Through that forest. And straight on to city Anaxerxes."

"Straight to our deaths," Sambalor said grimly.

"That's not a very positive attitude," Lophine Lorim chided her. "Why, a big, strong female like yourself shouldn't have anything to be afraid of. And with these two males to assist you it will be an easy walk from here." But the real sting was in her final words. "Have a safe trip home."

The dust cloud swirled up around them as the aircraft started to ascend. Blilo Yim watched as it departed and shrank to a faint dot that already seemed to be an infinite distance away from them. He was trying to be realistic about their chances of survival. "We are going to die, aren't we?"

Now Sambalor was sounding like the optimist. "In the military I took survival training, and believe me, there are much worse situations to be in. If we can reach the forest then those giant trees will protect us so long as we can keep ourselves clear of the stalking animals."

However, Taluine was more pessimistic. "The engineers constructed impenetrable walls around our cities for good reason. This is not Epiphiline where we eliminated all of the predators. There are no cute and cuddly animals here, just the ones that want to eat us."

Sambalor nodded because this was the reality they were living in. "Then I hope we make it."

"As you said already, we won't."

"I'm scared, Taluine," Blilo Yim shivered.

He put his arm protectively around his friend. "I am too. Pray to Ashimmah for protection, but I fear she has never met a segathar before."

"So what now, stand and wait to be eaten?"

"We walk. Even if it is to our deaths we are doing something instead of nothing."

"Do you suppose Midlothian will discover that it was Poxiciti who told us that she was profiting from the skin traders?"

"Perhaps he is the one who she is killing at this very moment," Sambalor said.

"Then I hope not, because he is our only hope for this world now."

"No," Taluine disagreed. "Even he is not enough." He stared in the direction of the forest where they were heading. "To save it, there has to be something else."

"Or someone else."

"Then let us hope he is coming soon."

Chapter 8

Just how long Gangahar had been asleep he was not entirely sure. His eyelids were drooping back down and he thought he might close his eyes and sleep some more, until the next shrill shriek penetrated his burrow. This disturbance roused him and he hurried through the tunnel to find Katakana waiting outside of Horhon's burrow.

"She dreams again," Katakana told him.

Another anguished shriek caused him to look past her. "I worry."

"You should not."

"But these nightmares of hers seem to worsen by the day."

"When a pregnant female's time is near she can dream the dreams of the unborn," she explained. "And since Horhon has said that her baby is coming soon this is what must be happening to her."

"It is much too soon," he told her. "Less than half the time that it normally takes. This one is not even a full season yet."

"Perhaps she was pregnant for longer and just didn't tell you."

"She had no burrow mate," Gangahar insisted. If she had then it would have been him, or so he hoped. "Horhon told me herself. She swore that however it happened it was not one of our hunters."

Katakana's smile suggested otherwise. "Something happened."

"I know what it was." Unknown to her there was some additional information that only he had knowledge of. "Something attacked her."

Her big, blue eyes widened. "What attacked her?"

Even despite what he told her, she was unconvinced that this had anything at all to do with Horhon's pregnancy. "Gangahar, in this world of ours, goud produce goud, efedaifents produce efedaifants, and Egris produce only Egris. How could such a thing have produced her child? It had to have been a hunter."

"This thing was no Egris hunter. I saw its tracks."

"Then what?"

Before he was able to answer, Horhon cried out in her sleep again. This time Katakana couldn't prevent him from getting past her; he peered down into Horhon's burrow. She was still asleep-awake, her rigid body writhing in agony.

"It is unwise to wake one who dreams," Katakana cautioned him.

Perhaps he should have heeded her warning because when he touched Horhon on the neck she grasped him tightly about the arms and shook him until his hoarse shouts penetrated her waking nightmare. On her face was a look of terror.

"Such a terrible dream," she gasped. "So many awful things that I wonder if I am awake now. Am I?"

"Better for me that you are." Unclasping her frozen fingers from his arms he said, "Was it the same dream again?"

She nodded. "It felt so real, maybe it was." Then she quickly added, "My head, these thoughts. I can't make them go away." She looked at him tearfully. "Make them go away, Gangahar."

He couldn't. Eager as he was to please her there was little he could do.

"Is she all right in there?" another voice said from behind him.

"Katakana, is that you?"

Her snout poked through the opening. "I warned him not to wake you, but he is stubborn and wouldn't listen to me. I heard you shouting. Are you well?"

"I think so. It was a bad dream."

"This was my first thought, that you were dreaming awake again. Then I return to my burrow to sleep."

"Sleep well," Horhon told her.

"Tell me what it was you saw," Gangahar asked inquisitively.

"I do not think I should tell you. It will frighten. Perhaps what I feel you will not even understand."

"Then I will listen as I only can," he said, then made motions of respectful silence.

It had not gone unnoticed, his fawning, his attentiveness. She believed that he genuinely cared for her, and they were close friends now so she would tell him whatever he wanted to know.

"I was . . . someone else. Something else. In another body." Holding out her hands in front of her she wiggled her clawed fingers. "My hands, so different they were from these. The others of my kind, their faces unlike any animal I have ever seen."

"Can you describe them?"

"Two-legged animals, walking upright like us, but running on their feet, not jumping. No tails, no claws or sharp teeth. Instead they use sharpened sticks for weapons. They have fur on their bodies but they wrap themselves in animal skins to stay warm."

"These are very strange creatures," he agreed, "and I can see why they frighten you."

"They are not what frightens me. The reason we are running, is to escape."

"From what?"

"Other creatures." She stared at him, her face full of gloom. "The ones who are attacking us."

As she described the attack she was possessed by a hatred of such intensity that she blindly smashed her fist into the sandy wall. But even while she was trying to comprehend it she found herself becoming more and more upset. She could scarcely breathe, she was that angry.

Panting, Horhon cried out, "I know this anger is difficult to control. I also know I cannot speak about these other creatures I see without feeling hatred towards them. I must, but I know not why I feel this so strongly."

It seemed there was no end in sight to her despair. Although Gangahar remained calm in the face of her pent-up anger, he realized he would never find the answer if he let her continue like this. So instead he decided to go with his gut feelings and speak what he believed.

"Perhaps this is not your dream." His eyes shifted downward. "Perhaps it is his."

Her hoarse bellow of surprise was such that Gangahar drew himself backwards, expecting her sharpest rebuke yet.

"No. Stay. I do not mean to shout," she apologized. "None of what I feel is intended for you. Rather it is because I think you must be right. These are his thoughts, his anger, that fills my mind."

"Do you think they are real?" he asked.

Her eyes were closed in deep concentration before she opened them and spoke again. "It feels real. I see their faces, I know their names. They are all dead. And their killers seem to be a lot like the Iranha. "

Perhaps her interpretation was a bad one, and these bellicose creatures she described were in fact the same ones who were attacking them. "If they are living here somewhere then these others you speak of are the Iranha, too."

"No," she disagreed. "I sense they are very far away, somewhere that is not Egris. Do you remember in the past when I told you about the hunters who will die?"

"Unhappily—yes. You said that the Iranha will destroy many trods, that the fight will be long and hard."

"I did. But now I must tell you that this has happened somewhere else. And the ones they killed are gone forever, gone forever . . ."

"What are you saying?" Gangahar sank back and was filled with despair. "This is what you see for us as well?"

"What has happened to them is in the past, and what will happen to us is in the future, so this does not mean that we cannot change it. We can."

Of course he was thinking purely out of his own fears. He may have to hear more, so he calmed himself down and tried to think. "If these things are not the Iranha, then what are they?"

"I hear a voice inside my head that speaks their name, over and over." Her entire body began to tremble. "I hate it. Hate them."

"Them?"

"Uta. This is what I hear. This is what I hate."

Gangahar's face creased in puzzlement. Was that even a word? He attempted to make the same sound too. It was barely pronounceable. Nevertheless he tried several more times and when he finally came close to saying it correctly Horhon nodded.

"That is it. Uta."

A sharp spasm caused her to grimace.

"Your child?"

"Yes. Even now he moves with hatred as I speak his enemy's name."

He understood, maybe a little too well. "Just how different will this child of yours be from us?"

"So different that it terrifies me to think how he will survive in this world of ours."

"Then it worries me too," Gangahar said. "He is coming soon?"

"Very soon." She was clear about her wish for him. "I hope he is ready."

Chapter 9

"**N**o, no, no! That is not how you stalk game," Ilistruk said to her brother, highly irritated, watching as the herd of nentenens bolted away into the field. Antayak was no better a stalker. In fact the two of them together were doubly worse, and even while she was angry she felt an uncontrollable urge to laugh at them. "Now watch me. Here, like this," she demonstrated, bending low into the grass and creeping forward on her stomach.

Yahu chirped enthusiastically, trying to do just as she did, though he was still clumsy and stepped on Ilistruk's tail. Her resounding roar of rage echoed across the field.

"Stupid! Stupid! You will never be a hunter!"

His face wrinkled. "Already I know a lot."

"You know nothing. I don't know which one of you is worse."

Antayak wasn't even paying attention. Instead he was staring out into the grass, concentrating on something. Even despite his inattentiveness Ilistruk no longer cared. It was hopeless, just hopeless, they would never learn. What she really wanted was to be with the adult hunters, stalking the big game. A big meaty goud, or efaifedent, that would be tasty too.

"Where are you going now?" Ilistruk called after her brother. "Come back here!" Her eye caught the end of his long tail sliding into the tall grass. Whatever animal he was after, his only hope of catching it would be that it was deaf and incredibly stupid to not hear him coming. Even Antayak went in after it, running as if he was the one being chased. "Unbelievable," she grumbled. So long as these two neophytes accompanied her she would never catch anything alive.

Suddenly her big ears twitched and she turned in the same direction where only moments earlier her two overzealous students had disappeared. Something squealed loudly.

Her thick tail snapping, Ilistruk instantly sprang into the air, hitting the ground twice before coming back down in the grass. It was just as she expected. Both Yahu and Antayak were bent over something on the ground. They both straightened up when they saw her stamping forward. Now the two of them were grinning proudly, though it was Yahu's blood-stained teeth that showed who had struck death.

"What is that you have killed?"

"Tarser," he clicked happily. "I catch tarser."

"That is no tarser." Indeed, it was a very ugly thing. Ilistruk could see the gaping wound where he had torn it open, the bright yellow blood still seeping out. She leaned over its dead mass and sniffed. How strange. It had another layer of skin beneath. Slimy, mottled gray and black skin, smelling of something long dead. What was this thing?

At first she believed the dead animal was a tharank, large dirt eating creatures that lived mostly underground, but this grim looking mass had arms and legs so it could not be. And what was this laying beside it? She retracted her claws and touched the shiny object. It made a hollow sound as her finger thunked against it. Here was a mystery needing to be solved, though she was certain that her brainless companions were readying to consume the evidence.

"You are not to eat this. Is that understood?"

Although Yahu was shaking his head yes she knew it would be devoured the instant she left his sight. Undoubtedly it would be a pile of well gnawed bones upon her return. She considered this, and arrived at what she thought was the best solution.

"You must go tell father what has happened. You must bring him back here. Can you do that?"

"I tell him I kill tarser," he grinned again. "Yahu is good hunter."

"Yes," she agreed, careful to show her appreciation lest he think about staying. "Here, give him this."

He grasped the shiny object in his hand then leapt away. Antayak was close behind him. To be rid of them both was what she had most wanted. And yet now for the first time today, she hoped they would be coming back.

Chapter 10

This night had been a restless one for Gangahar. He thought about hunting; he was hungry and sensed the taste of meat as he licked his wet teeth clean. Yet he could not leave Horhon alone so he propped himself up against his tail and waited for morning to come.

By night's end the hunters were beginning to return from the forest. Gangahar's solid, unmoving frame was the first thing they saw as the group came bounding in.

"How was the eating?" he asked them.

"You were not out hunting?" Katakana knew exactly where he had spent his night.

"I do not know what to do," he said with concern. "She refuses to eat, nor will she leave her burrow. Katakana, you have children. Is it always this way?"

She grinned and told him, "Always," and then added, "You worry like a father, Gangahar."

The others burst out laughing at his shocked expression, but he did not find this to be amusing at all and shaped his body to show his true feelings.

"I will tend to her now," Katakana said. "You must be hungry. Go and eat."

He was ravenous. Even so, her disarming words did not penetrate his thoughts until she twice repeated her simple order. Eat. That is what he would do.

Later, when he returned from the woods, his mouth bloodied, his appetite now sated, Krugjon greeted him outside their burrow as he approached. "It is starting to happen. Horhon's baby is coming."

It took only a moment for the full import of his words to sink in. But Krugjon must have anticipated his reaction and seized him by the arm even before he started for the burrow. "Katakana said you would be more a bother than a help. The females are expert. Let them attend to her. They will know what to do."

"So what can we do?" Gangahar asked him pointedly. What could he do? He wished he could be there now, at her side, as he always was.

Krugjon was looking away—and that was his answer. "There is something important you must see. Here." He handed over a strange object that Gangahar could see his own reflection in. He examined it thoroughly before his gaze returned to the hunter.

"Where did you find this?"

"Yahu brought it to me just now. I understood little of what he said, although I believe it was Ilistruk who sent him."

Again he peered at the object. But what he saw was clearly beyond his comprehension. "Doesn't scratch. And see, it cannot be dented either. You say this came from Ilistruk?"

"There is only one way to know for certain. We will go find her together."

Just as he finished speaking the sound of Horhon's birthing screams echoed out of the tunnel, the last one dying to dreaded silence. Gangahar looked alarmed.

"Perhaps I should stay."

Only once before had Krugjon ever watched a birth. It was nothing like he imagined at all. Through the haze of time he remembered his new daughter, the good feelings he felt then, but the excruciating pain it had caused his burrow mate was not something he wanted to burden Gangahar with, so he wisely did not speak of it now.

"She is fine. When we are tracking for Ilistruk you will soon forget."

He sincerely hoped so.

The two of them turned tails and bounded for the field, soon crossing the invisible line where the great forest ended and the grasslands began. Here they were leaping high, traveling further and further, until the tall trees became a flat line on the vast open horizon.

As Krugjon expected, Ilistruk was waiting for them, her big ears and head sticking out over the grass. She was happy to see them, though the next moment the elation of this meeting quickly turned to a more immediate concern.

"You must see this thing for I do not know what it could be." Ilistruk led them over to the body. In that short time she had turned her back something was now crawling over the stinking corpse. "Get away from that!" she roared, snapping with her jaws at several tickridents who were scrambling away with shreds of flesh dangling from their mouths.

Krugjon gazed upon the dead creature with obvious disgust. "Smells like it's been dead for a long time."

"As I said, Yahu killed it only this morning."

With some trepidation he fingered the fleshy corpse. "What is this oozing from its body?"

"It stained Yahu's teeth where he bit the thing. I believe it is blood."

"What sort of creature has yellow blood? Do you recognize this ugly thing?" Krugjon queried Gangahar.

He could only shake his head no, though when his clawed foot rolled the creature over he almost fell off his feet, so great was his shock.

"Iranha!" he hissed in hatred. Remembering the destruction of trod Yaryar filled him with a fierce rage. His emotions were in turmoil, seeing this Iranha now here, this destroyer that he so fervently wanted to kill. With his bone crushing teeth and claws he tore it to pieces, hurling the dismembered corpse as far from him as he could, even bending to pick up the pieces and fling them away, out of his sight.

While it satisfied Krugjon to see it decently destroyed, there was something else on his mind. "For what reason did it trek out this far, alone?"

"It escapes me. And yet it is here so I can only wonder why."

"Even more importantly, you said the Iranha could not be killed."

"I said that only because I have never seen them be killed." His eyes opened wider with this new and interesting revelation. "They can be killed."

"Then there will be many more deaths to come," Krugjon promised.

Gangahar's nostrils were close to the ground, sniffing. "See how closely spaced apart these foot prints are? This thing could not have moved very quickly. Should we follow its tracks to see where it came from? There might be more of them."

As much as he wanted to, Krugjon felt less certain that they were going to find any Iranha in the desert once he spotted the black cloud building on the horizon. "Not today. A wind storm is coming," he said. "We better get off this sand before it hits."

The hunters simply called it Chuduk, the windy season, when the heat of the desert whipped up the sand and sent roiling storms that could block out the sky for days. It had started early this year and they were lucky to have reached the forest in time. The sky behind them was already clouded over and their hides were dusty and dirty. The wind was howling above the tree-tops when Katakana saw the three hunters bound into sight. She amplified her distress with movements that brought them jumping forward.

"Inside! Quickly!" She waved her one arm frantically in the air and wailed, "The baby . . . It is . . ."

Dead, Gangahar thought in horror as he rushed forward and seized her by the arm. "Is Horhon's baby all right?" he demanded.

"You must come and see for yourself."

There was no happiness in her voice, only a grimness, a darkness that he thought for sure was death. Together they hurried inside. As they proceeded in tense silence Gangahar heard a scream that caused him to ask her, "What is that awful noise?"

Shuddering, Katakana answered hoarsely, "The baby."

As they came into the central chamber where Horhon had birthed him, the three who were following behind Katakana now finally got to see what was making all this noise. From the shocked look on their faces it was all too clear that this was not the savior they were all expecting.

"What is this thing?" Krugjon finally dared to ask.

Lying on the floor was something totally alien to him, that even the dead Iranha he had seen outside now seemed only moderately revolting in comparison. Since its body was still covered in a wet sheen from the delivery he knew this was not something they had dragged in to eat.

"My son," Horhon growled at him for his rudeness. "As you can see, a male."

"Yes," he shivered, "but what kind?"

"The one who is Egris but who is not Egris," she answered. Those had been Megog's very own words to her.

Gangahar recognized something familiar about him. "Like the ones in your dream."

"The same. The ones who are no more, so he is one of us."

While he appeared to have some of the fundamental body parts—legs, arms, a head and torso—everything about him was physically different from them. About the same size as an Egris newborn he was missing a tail, and maybe this was what made him appear smaller, but there was much more wrong with him. Little hands and fingers that were clawless, a mouth that was full of tiny, flat teeth—if these were even teeth. Gangahar guessed this was his mouth because that was where all of his noise was coming from. Even his ears were no more than a hole on each side of his head. It would be better if he didn't say what he was thinking: he had the face that any mother would have wanted to eat.

"This small one is to lead us against the Iranha?" He opened and closed his mouth, thinking. "How?"

"In the fullness of time he will deliver us from our hated enemy, destroy them all, as it was already foreseen."

"Why does he not stand up?"

"He is just born," she explained wearily. "Maybe it is too soon."

An Egris child stood up almost from the moment it dropped out of its mother's womb. And within a very short time it was jumping, and killing as efficiently as an adult. This one just lay there, flopping around as if life was abandoning him—perhaps it should.

"So much pain this small one caused you," Katakana remarked. "You should return to your burrow to rest."

"I stay." Horhon had no intention of leaving him here alone with them. He was rolling around on the floor, moaning fitfully, yet she felt sure this would soon end.

"Such tiny legs," Okinaw noticed. "How will he ever jump?"

"I do not think his kind can jump."

"Then . . . can he hunt?"

"All meat-eaters hunt."

It was his diet that most interested Gangahar. "Meat that he must kill for?"

This incessant questioning was draining her. "Yes," she answered testily. "But only when it has been burnt over the fire."

With each new thing she said his understanding grew. His forehead creased as he thought what next to ask her, though the frowning-faced hunter, Saskakel, spoke first.

"Can his noises be stopped?" he complained.

"No!"

Her listeners scattered into the tunnels as she roared. Horhon was greatly annoyed and happy to be rid of them all at last. Undoubtedly the hunters were just as happy to be gone too. Over time his presence was something that they had better start getting used to, for even as the seasons changed nothing else did.

Only Gangahar and Katakana remained but they were afraid to speak out of fear that she might bellow at them again. However, Katakana was the first one to notice that something had changed, and wandered over to look at him.

"Look, his eyes have opened."

All three hunters bent over to stare at him, pushing their big snouts to within inches of his face. He seemed to have some awareness of their presence. When Gangahar moved backwards he turned his head to see where he was going.

"He sees you," Horhon said.

As soon as she spoke his head turned back and he was looking directly up at her. Now he raised one arm to touch her on the face, and slowly dragged his fingers along the curve of her mouth, feeling the sharp points of her teeth.

"Do you think he understands what we are saying?"

"It is too early to know. Other Egris speak their first words after a full season, so he will learn." While she sounded hopeful there were other things about him that she now expressed her private fears to them. "Whether he speaks or not, I worry that our ways will be difficult for him, that he will be among us, yet feel that he is not one of us."

"He is so different," Katakana agreed. "If the Iranha attack us, he will be an easy target for them."

"For now the Iranha are the least of his worries. Until he gets bigger than this we will have to protect him from the other animals who might find him an appetizing meal."

Still Gangahar seemed worried. Their natural inclination was to follow the meat animals so he would have to be able to keep up with them or die. "What if he does not get up, and this is all he can do?"

"He will."

As soon as she said the words he started struggling to sit up. In a moment he was sitting upright on his own, looking around in the dimness of the chamber. Their own eyes were accustomed to the perpetual darkness of their burrow, and the forest under which they were living, so she paid close attention to him to see if he possessed this ability too.

After a while he rolled over and lifted himself up so that he was on his knees. Sensing that he was trying to stand up, Horhon shifted her tail and stretched it out in front of him. He must have known what it was for because he grasped hold of it and now climbed to his feet. As he stood shakily, his legs wobbling beneath him, he let go of her tail only to fall back down, though this did not prevent him from trying again. As soon as he was back on his feet he took his first step, then another one.

"He is walking," Horhon said excitedly. "He can walk."

Gangahar sounded relieved. "Then this is a good sign because the next thing he will have to do is hunt for food." This may have been wishful thinking on his part, but he was hoping for the best nonetheless.

While he wasn't exactly running circles around them he was moving over his own two feet. Several times he stumbled down yet he picked himself right back up and kept going. What he needed to do was strengthen his legs so each of them took turns walking him around the chamber. Katakana had just finished her turn and was now debating what to call him.

"He needs to have a name," she said. "Have you considered one?"

"Not yet," Horhon replied. "First I shall have to give this some thought."

"Something important," Gangahar added.

Katakana then said, "If he is our salvation then let him be called as one who delivers us from the teeth of our enemy."

"I have a name."

"He speaks!" Gangahar gasped.

All three hunters' mouths fell open; they stared at him gape-jawed, with their big blue eyes bulging.

Horhon could scarcely believe it. "You can understand our words?" At his headshake she asked him, "Then what do you call yourself?"

"Ilon," he answered in a clear, strong voice that everyone heard. "My name is Ilon."

Chapter 11

For Ilon it was like waking from a long, dreamless sleep. There was no awareness of time. Instead there was only the slow, bit by bit realization that he was alive.

I am alive, he thought. *In some other place.*

In another body? Even as he pinched at his warm, fleshy skin, he had doubts whenever he thought about it. No. This felt too much like his old body. Yet he remembered the pain of coming into this world, lying under a creature that had just given birth to him. Then if he was a newborn why was he so big? He had not the delicate, tiny limbs, or the helplessness of a baby, but the thick, muscled arms and calves of an adult who could stand on his own feet. Even all his teeth were here in his mouth. And yet he had no hair, not any his body, nor on his head, so maybe he was something else now.

Half-consciously he remembered pieces of his past, yet he recalled only enough of it to know that his existence here made no possible sense. Therefore his knowledge of the past held the key to his present. Had he been alive once before, another person? Indeed, these were important questions to ask himself. Yet even more importantly, where was he now, and, *what was he?*

What he remembered came to him day by slow day, filtering into his consciousness. Ilon recalled a distant memory. While at first it left no more than a vague impression, it seemed so old that it might well have been a dream, or something that someone might have told him. Yet he saw himself as he once was, or it could have just as easily been someone else. He was a man, a hunter. Very old, he remembered that much. And he also remembered a cave, although unclear to him at first, but this too coalesced into a single, clear thought. He had survived all those years just to be there. *Yes, that must be it,* he told himself. *I returned to that place, the home of my people. To die.*

Only for the very first time since he could remember did he finally accept that these memories were really his. That person had been him. He was *Taal,* he knew that, knew it as clearly as though the familiar word had been spoken in his ear. The very cave where he had come back to die, was where he had been born. His people, his family, his harden, living the life of the hunt and following the old ways. The images flooded back. *Lende,* his mate, and *Aisahl,* like a mother to him. And yet he knew—but he could not say how he knew, returning to that cave as an old one to die—that all the others were dead. All dead.

Because of the *Uta*.

More a feeling than a memory, the word washed over him like fire in a howling rage. *Uta. Enemy. Death.* And then he knew, with sad insight, that he had died alone because he was the very last of his harden—and what was more, perhaps the very last of the Taal who walked the world.

If I died, then is this death? Ilon asked himself.

Perhaps it was because now strange and terrifying creatures hovered over him, black mouths gaped open, rows of pointed teeth shining. They were like something out of a nightmare. Their teeth, their claws, designed for efficient killing. These were superior killers who far exceeded even the most ferocious meat stalkers that he recalled from his memories. But they were hunters too, like him, yet beyond that he shared little else in common with them. However, they did speak, using a snarled, growling language that Ilon was certain could not be the language he remembered. So how did he know their words? How could he speak and not even recall where he had learned them? For him this was another mystery.

Egris. This word he knew to be the people these creatures called themselves. The one who had birthed him had said he was Egris too, like her. So then he had two identities, was of two different peoples. But how could that be? Ilon knew he was physically different from them, in every conceivable way. Egris or *Taal*—which was he? For these endless days and nights he struggled with the insanity of it.

On another night a second vision of his past life appeared. The memory of it was painful, disturbing, and so he tried to push it away, but he could not forget the light, the light that hurt. Looking into it, he had felt its thoughts, yet understood nothing of what it was, or wanted. It was not a good thing to remember, but it was an important thing, something that made his existence seem very important now. And important to these Egris creatures. They were protecting him, he knew, watching him constantly, every waking and sleeping moment.

So far, all of his young life had been spent here inside the sand burrow. The fire beside him was a constant companion. His trod was all he knew. Ilon had no encounter with anyone else other than these same hunters who bent before him each day. He wasn't permitted to go outside, so other than the occasional glimpse of daylight through the tunnel Ilon saw little of the outside world. Although from what he heard and understood he managed to piece together a picture that was disquieting. The world was not as he remembered it. Indeed it was a very different, even frightening world, and he could only imagine what it must be like for hunters as these, with their mouths full of sharp spikes, and knife-like claws for tearing flesh. What other unimaginable creatures of death might be lurking out there? Suddenly Ilon was glad that he knew very little of this strange and hostile world.

One early morning he was awakened by something in the tunnel. Since his mother left with the pack to go hunting he guessed that she was now returning to feed him. It was natural to assume that, for he had little else to think about but food. Yet when he woke from his dreams thoughts of hunting filled his head. He had not forgotten what it was like to be a hunter. The memory of it moved through him as though it was something he experienced right now. The spear was in his hand, the herd of fallow deer grazing in the deep grass before his rigid and silent form. Of course that was when he still lived among his own people, lived and hunted like them, with crude sharpened sticks. What must it be like to hunt as these Egris hunted?

With his eyes half closed he was suddenly alerted to something crawling right outside his burrow, only to now realize that this was no hunter. Deprived of even a simple stone implement to protect himself with, Ilon could only squirm in his hole like some helpless animal waiting to be killed and eaten.

"Help!" he screamed. "Help me!"

Something large was climbing inside; he knew that it was something dangerous. Though his eyes were well accustomed to the darkness he saw little of the black thing—long stick-like appendages, a vague outline, that was all. A damp sucker pressed against his cheek, another touched his foot. Ilon shivered. To die this soon made his short life seem all the more pointless.

Suddenly he heard the scraping of toenails in the corridor, running footsteps coming closer. Gaping jaws reached inside and closed around the creature, its hard shell cracking easily under a hunter's powerful dentition. The feral beast emitted a shrill shriek before dying to silence.

Gangahar stood at the opening, Katakana behind him. "That was too close."

"What is it?" she queried him.

"A despicable creature of disgust. Look."

He dropped its dead mass at her feet and spat out the remains from his mouth. Katakana shook with revulsion. A tree turlin. A blood sucking parasite, it had only one goal: to firmly attach itself and suck the life from its host. Had Gangahar not killed it immediately,

Ilon surely would have been lost, for one as small as he would have been quickly drained.

"Ilon, are you safe in there?"

His frightened face appeared in the burrow's opening. "Is it dead?"

As if to prove to him that it was, Gangahar's clawed finger speared through it as he held it up to show him. "At least you were not its last meal."

To finally see it caused Ilon to shiver. What other horrors were hiding out there that he might not have the luxury of calling the hunters for help?

Ordinarily turlins were ambush stalkers, preferring to hide in the trees and fling themselves onto unsuspecting prey. How it had slipped into their burrow unnoticed was a moot point. Under Gangahar's direction they soon discovered that it had in fact crawled through an adjoining tunnel, one thought to have been sealed up. After a thorough search of the entire sand burrow they determined there was no further danger.

Ilon was waiting for them in the central chamber where he had built up a fire, perhaps in the belief that this would keep away the predators, though as he was finding out in this strange and hostile world, he really was a baby, or at least he was as helpless as one.

"It will not happen again," Gangahar promised.

"Until you grow larger, here is where you must stay," Katakana agreed.

"From what I remember of my other life, this is as large as I will grow."

"Then I hope you are wrong because you will fit very nicely into a bigger animal's stomach."

Gangahar asked him curiously, "Were the animals not dangerous where you hunted?"

"Some were very dangerous," he admitted. "And what animals do you fear?"

"None except the Iranha."

"You have said little about these creatures."

"I promise you will hear more," Katakana replied uneasily. But before he could ask her she changed the subject back to tonight's incident. "Since only Gangahar and I possess this knowledge of the tree turlin no one else need ever know—especially your mother."

"I won't tell her," he agreed, otherwise she might never let him out of the burrow.

At dawn the hunters returned, jaws bloodied, stomach's full; everyone was happy to be home. When questioned by Horhon of the evening's events there was much yawning and complaints of boredom. Fortunately for Gangahar she believed his small lie, though he felt a stab of guilt when she asked about Ilon. Yet he knew the mere mention of trouble would generate unnecessary anger, endless enquiries and precautions that he had already taken great pains to correct. And so it was never spoken of.

Ilon lost track of the days. Boredom seemed to be his only distraction; this sitting around and doing nothing was taking a toll on him. His requests to leave the confines of the burrow grew louder. It became a tug of war between him and his mother. He wanted to go out, while Horhon wanted him to stay put. She realized that eventually one of them was going to have to give in to the other.

"The time has come for you to go outside," she said one afternoon. "I have told you of the forest and plains and all the animals that fill it. For any hunter these are things that must be seen."

"Are we going hunting?" he asked excitedly.

"For goud."

She was easily double his height, and the goud she had described to him were much bigger than her. They sounded even larger than the mammoths he remembered hunting on the plains, but he suspected even the biggest mammoth wouldn't have a chance of escaping one of these hunters.

"I have thought about how best you might travel with us, so that you can be safe, and I do not have to worry about where you are. This is for you," she grinned with satisfaction. Between her thumbs was a mottled green skin that she held out to him. "I made it myself." And Horhon was immensely proud of it too, for she had carefully scraped off the wet meat and stretched the thin remains onto a frame to dry in the hot sun. This particular one was still warm.

To Ilon it looked like a pouch with carrying straps, having openings for his legs and arms. But mostly what she showed him revealed little of its true purpose. At least, not until she lifted him up and fitted him in. With the straps now tied securely around her neck and waist it looked as much as something the Taal women might have used to carry their babies about—perhaps this was where she had gotten the idea.

When it happened the first time Ilon thought he was flying. He watched the ground fall away beneath him, then return with the same force that had propelled him off. The other hunters beside him were leaping high, jumping together in long graceful bounds, legs pumping, tails snapping rhythmically behind them. They continued at the same pace for a while, yet it was not until the pack halted and the dust cloud settled that he had his first real glimpse of the world.

What he saw was unlike the world as he remembered it, unlike anything he had ever seen. Huge scaled trunks plunged skyward together, so tall that they seemed to vanish into the blackness. Were those branches above him? Dark creatures were flying underneath that he was sure were not birds. Now he was beginning to regret ever leaving the burrow. What was this forbidding place? Krugjon called it the Pok forest. A forest? Then these huge things were trees? It seemed impossible to believe that a tree could grow so tall. And what of the distant plains? Sparsely planted grass and brush. Beyond that, sand, dunes of sand, hills of sand, a field of sand. Just an empty endless desert. This might have been the plains someone else remembered, but not him. Even the sun seemed brighter. And it was hot, far, far too hot.

Something was moving into the forest, creatures of immense size, stiff tails dragging behind them, huge beaked jaws, tearing mouth-sized bites out of the tree trunks and chewing contentedly. From their great size and the color of their skin he guessed they were goud, a giant herd of them.

The dissimilitude of this place frightened him. He wanted to go back inside, to close his eyes on what could only be a bad dream. If this ever was once his own world then it was no more, a world lost and gone forever. What remained was too different, too menacing. Obviously he did not belong here, he could see that now, and he wished to be dead again.

He should have been dead.

Why was he here, still the same creature living among a world of monsters? If there was a reason or a purpose for his existence then why did he have no knowledge of it now? His head hurt from trying to think of a logical explanation, yet there were many more questions and too few answers.

It was near dusk when the sun appeared through thinning cloud before it set. The first stars were brightening in the eastern sky; a plenary moon was lifting over the field. Yet there was something different about this night sky too—particularly that moon, larger, brighter than he recalled. But when he saw the second moon rising Ilon knew then that he was far, far from his home.

Back in their burrow his mother had talked of a world that was immensely bigger than this vast forest and plain. What he had once thought was the whole universe was in fact only a tiny speck in a vast sea of other lights. Now he knew those flickering points for what they were in the sky. Seeing those two moons was confirmation for him that he was somewhere else, so out there among those same stars must be his own world. What would it be like now? Ilon wondered. With the Taal gone and the Uta crawling all over it, he had a very bad feeling about its future.

"There are more goud coming in off the plain," Amink had just come back to tell them. "Plenty enough to fill your stomachs. Are you ready hunters?"

All were in complete agreement; now was the time to hunt.

"Hold on tight," Horhon warned Ilon as she pumped her legs and leapt away with the others, straight towards the herd.

The size of these creatures was unbelievable. Had Ilon seen one of these back in his other life he would have been the one to have run away. Not these hunters. They were fearless and ferocious. No need to cull the weakest, slowest animal, just pick whatever one suited them and attack. Within moments a giant goud was lying on its side, being efficaciously ripped apart. The Egris were rudimentary eaters. It turned Ilon's stomach to watch them devour the animal, yet this was their world, and they were the masters of it.

"We will search for some wood and build a fire to cook your meat," Horhon said.

Other than himself, she was the only Egris who knew about fire. This puzzled him because she also knew things about him that only he could know, as if somehow her mind was connected to his and they were seeing and remembering the exact same things. This was a very strange second life he was living.

The sky was darkening as the second moon set, but by the time the pack reached the forest there was a blur of gray light growing above the horizon. Gangahar and Krugjon were waiting for them at the burrow. Yet when Horhon counted for the three who had left that evening, only two returned.

"What happened to Ilistruk?" she asked them.

In a slow trembling voice, Krugjon said, "My daughter is lost. Dead."

There were shocked gasps, even young Yahu understood some of it and trembled hearing the name of his sister. What Krugjon had said was death, but death how everyone was wondering.

"We were after nentenens," he continued. "We killed a big one near the river gorge and were feeding well on its meat when—"

"You left her body there for the scavengers to eat?" Katakana interrupted amid everyone's cries of protest. "We should go and retrieve it at once."

"No!" Gangahar shouted so strongly that she would have fallen backwards had her tail not supported her shifting weight. "Return, and we die the same death."

No need for Horhon to raise her hand for silence. With those few words everyone was subdued, so she merely motioned for Krugjon to continue.

"As I said, we were feeding when we heard a noise coming out of the forest, so we went closer to investigate. What we found were the Iranha." With his mouth gaping open, he told them all, "They are pulling down the trees! There is an ugly scar where they now cut through the forest. At first I did not know what to think, for they do many strange things, but as I watched them I began to understand. They are building something to cross the river. And that will bring them and their world even closer to ours!"

He tried to continue, could not, for he could no longer repress the true emotions that possessed him, so Gangahar now spoke in his place. "Ilistruk's only mistake was that she hid behind the wrong tree. There was a terrible noise, a lot of bright light and smoke, a deep crater where the tree once was, and Ilistruk dead. We returned at once to tell you of this."

"Dead for nothing," Horhon growled bitterly. "If the Iranha are tearing down our forest to build this thing then we must leave at once before they get any closer."

Everyone agreed. Except Ilon.

"No. Fleeing will only give them more of what they are taking away from us. What we must do is find a way to stop them, for their presence here can only mean there will soon be Iranha everywhere."

"But we have no real weapons to use against them," Gangahar argued, lest anyone was thinking about staying.

"You have your teeth and claws."

"And what good are these against their death sticks? They point them, and we die."

"Did Yahu not kill one of these things on the plain?" Since Krugjon had told everyone Ilon knew he couldn't disagree. "If a youngster can kill an Iranha, so can you."

Although each hunter had an opinion no one seemed able to provide the solution. While they despaired of an answer, Ilon walked over to the fire and removed one of the burning branches, waving it in the air to bring him the attention he wanted.

"Perhaps this is the weapon that we seek."

"Fire?" Saskakel said doubtfully. "What is that against creatures like the Iranha?"

"Are these trees they bring down not made of the same wood—wood that will burn?"

When the full extent of his words sank in Horhon quickly said, "Why then this thing that they build to cross the river will burn just as these sticks, be consumed—and destroyed! Yes!" she roared aloud. "You are right. A weapon." And she knew how to make fire. Closing her fingers around the burning stick she held it aloft. "Wait until dark, then we strike. Burn it into the river and let the wreckage be floated away."

The plan was quickly made and everybody agreed that it was the right thing to do, for now their very survival depended on fighting back. All shared the same desire for revenge, all wanting to see the Iranha's creation destroyed. The pleasure of attacking the Iranha, instead of running away, thrilled them.

As Ilon watched them go to their burrows to sleep he knew that they too were fighting to destroy an enemy that could not be beaten. Taal and Egris, two cultures, two peoples, and he, here to bring these two worlds together at last. Suddenly the future and his place in it were now very clear.

Chapter 12

"**S**omething terrible has happened."

Nalanusat was the only passenger to emerge from the open hatchway. Even as he waddled off the landing platform and onto the deserted field he rehearsed the same unhappy words over and over out loud to himself.

"Something terrible has happened."

Not since first arriving by air transport had he seen anyone else on the runway. Nor were there any posted guards in front of the main terminal. A vehicle was supposed to have been sent to escort him back to the city, but there was no sign of that either. With news this important he could not wait here any longer, and so he started off by himself, moving forward with slug-like speed.

It was near dawn when he arrived at the walls of city Soligcetis; the sun was an undulating yellow swell just above the dunes. When he reached the main gates armed guards were waiting to stop him.

"Let me pass," Nalanusat puffed, though gesturing more than talking. Finally, after he pushed several more breaths of air though the pores of his skin, he was able to make clear what he wanted and said, "I have come all the way from Betelgesel bearing an important message that only Poxiciti can hear. He must be awakened from his sleep at once."

As the huge metal gates swung slowly open he pushed his bulk inside and hurried on; a guard was calling out directions behind him as he plodded away. Dim yellow lights guided his way down a deserted street, past the city's administration building, finally ending at the dormitory. More warders were stationed outside of the building.

After repeating the same urgent message the guards pressed Nalanusat to answer more of their questions before deciding to let him through. The door briefly hummed then hissed open to a dark corridor beyond. One of the Epiphilinian soldiers, a heavily armed female with a dreg's rank on her blue neck band, escorted him the rest of the way inside.

"Let him through," she barked at a second locked door. Eventually she led him to an elevator, then up to a expansive waiting room from which Poxiciti was summoned.

While Nalanusat waited he took out his bottle of tesano and applied a fresh coat of makeup. The nozzle hissed as the bright green paint coated his face, a color that was said to attract even the most unresponsive females. After checking himself in the window he then focused his thoughts back to Betelgesel and wondered how he would bring this dark event into the light of day.

"Tell me what it is you want and be gone."

Turning quickly around, Nalanusat saw the scientist approaching, his many attendants trailing behind him. He walked with a noticeable limp, had also a scarred face and a black eye socket from a recent laboratory explosion which had disfigured him. Now he was an important member of the Vulana, the ruling party comprised mostly of scientists and environmentalists.

Once regarded by many as a subversive, male-dominated organization, they had gained considerable power and popularity during the agharl plague back home on planet Epiphiline. Poxiciti himself had successfully organized several protest campaigns against the ruling government, whose environmental policies many believed were responsible for the disaster that claimed millions of lives. His importance had given him the red band which he now wore around his neck. So when Nalanusat addressed him directly he spoke respectfully in his presence, as he could see that Poxiciti was indeed a powerful figure.

"Are you Poxiciti, one who is imminently known and revered for his great works of science and learning?"

"Of course I am," he said clearly in the presence of everyone, indicating his rank by words alone. There was a trace of condescension in his voice. "And you?"

"Nalanusat." Since it was customary to avoid eye contact when speaking to one of higher status he lowered his head then spoke formally, indicating to him the importance of his own position. "I am the administrative assistant to Midlothian, who is head of city Anaxerxes and all those who she commands."

Poxiciti's body trembled when he heard that name. She was notably one of the Vulana's staunchest opponents. They had clashed several times in the past, although now she was currently embroiled in a corruption scandal involving fraud, kickbacks and political payoffs. If this low male worked for her then he was a traitor, to be hated and despised.

"I find her incredibly stupid and wonder how one of such low intelligence could have possibly attained so high a position. Those whom she employs are idiots and incompetents." He spoke directly to Nalanusat to ensure he clearly understood this fact. "And clean that disgusting mess off your face. I find it revolting to stand in the presence of one who uses such conveniences merely for garnering female attention. Males have brains too. We are equal to females. Seeing you this way diminishes the status all we males fought for."

Humiliated in front of everyone, Nalanusat withdrew a facial cloth and quickly wiped himself clean. Poxiciti nodded approvingly.

"Much better. Now—what is this urgent news that bloated imbecile orders you to wake me before daylight?"

With the evening's events still fresh in his mind, Nalanusat fought to control his emotions. "Bad. Worse than bad. Terrible. Horrible!"

"Stop!" Poxiciti sharply commanded. When he spoke that strongly the dense pores covering his skin hissed loudly as he sucked in the air. "There is no intelligence behind your words. Find it, and explain yourself immediately."

"I will." Nalanusat apologized as one who obeyed his superiors. Though it was extremely difficult, he went on, saying, "Something terrible has happened."

"What? What has happened? Tell me quickly you fool."

"I have just come from Betelgesel."

"From where?" Poxiciti was already angry and spoke in the rudest possible way. "Speak at once and make no more riddles lest I have my guards beat the words from you."

"Forgiveness is asked, and the explanation is forthcoming. It is a bridge we are constructing across the Betelgesel river."

"Understanding at last. Then I can assume there is a problem that warrants my special attention?"

Indeed there was. Under the threat of his movements alone Nalanusat conveyed every sense of disaster. From his garment pocket he withdrew a crumpled slip of wet selp paper and unfurled it on top of the table. The light-activated nanoparticles embedded in the paper quickly formed a detailed map. Using the wedge of his hand he touched the specific area so that it now re-formed a magnified image that he pointed out the recognizable landmarks. Poxiciti quickly deduced the bridge's exact location.

"I know this bridge," he confirmed.

"The last link between city Anaxerxes and city Tykrerek, a bridge of countless delays and accidents. What has taken the entire season to construct has in a single night been utterly destroyed."

"Destroyed? How?"

"By fire. While we speak it is spreading to the forest beyond and burns out of control." Through his tiny yellow eyes he made a pleading expression. "What can be done to lessen this terrible disaster?"

"Unfortunately—nothing. A burnt forest is an incalculable loss. Since it was an accident of stupidity then there is little I can do. Your bridge is destroyed. Build another one."

"It was no accident."

Those who were present in the room, some assistants, a few environmentalists, Poxiciti included, looked at Nalanusat in absolute silence, no doubt hoping that he would further elaborate on this new and distressing news.

Nalanusat tapped the selp paper, leaving a trace of slimy residue where his wet wedge touched. "There are two other bridges on this same road. Were," he said, correcting himself. "All three were deliberately burned last night."

"All set by the same offender?" Poxiciti gasped audibly. "Then you had better quickly apprehend those responsible before they do this again." From Nalanusat's grim expression and raised hand signing for continuance, Poxiciti guessed that worse was to follow this already shocking news.

"Eleven guards were found brutally murdered, five more are still missing, presumed dead. The sight of them is like nothing I ever want to look upon again. Flesh ripped apart by claws, bones smashed with teeth. Even while we were discovering the bodies flying carrion things were devouring their remains."

As he went on, Poxiciti found the grisly details of the guards' dismembered corpses revolting and interrupted. "It seems to me that you should return immediately to city Anaxerxes for help. Even if only to assure the populace that their killers will be quickly caught and punished for this horrendous crime."

"I don't think so. That is, what we are looking for is not of Epiphiline, but is in fact a wild animal, a deliberate and cunning destroyer, yet one who also is a bestial slaughterer that we must find and eliminate completely."

"An animal who plots murder in the night and burns our bridges too? Ridiculous," Poxiciti said testily, reacting with vehemence and disbelief. "What you have described is a creature possessed of intelligence and planning. There is nothing like that on this new world but we Epiphilinians. However, a more satisfactory explanation might be that a group of armed terrorists committed this atrocity. We know of two such organizations that are already operating here on the planet, killing and destroying to advance their religious cause."

Nodding, but not agreeing, Nalanusat reaffirmed his city's official position by saying, "The guards were first killed, then the bridges set afire. Animal tracks were discovered beside the bodies in all three locations. An animal that killed but did not eat. One witness reported seeing black creatures as I described earlier, fleeing the bridge while it burned behind them. One other survivor repeated very much the same story. If it is these creatures that are attacking us then there is no telling when they might strike again. What do you think?"

"I think you are wasting my time," Poxiciti said abruptly. "I am a scientist, not a fortune teller. If there are clues to be found then I may ascertain the only possible answer from the evidence. Not from mere speculation or wild reports."

Nalanusat arched his body to show this was exactly what he wanted to hear. "That is good. So if you, an important figure of science, searched these same sites, why then I believe your findings would prove to everyone that it was these monsters who did this."

"I?. . . I?" Poxiciti at last began to understand the point of this suppliant's visit. "Then your fat master wishes me to visit these places?"

"She thought that you might give this single matter your fullest attention."

"For that ugly thing?" he hissed. "Why should I want to help her?"

"Only because it magnifies your great intelligence and diminishes her own status as a problem solver."

"True," he said without any hint of modesty. "What else?"

"I assure you that is all." Then he carefully added, "Someone as powerful as Midlothian would not request aid unless it was of vital importance. You should not refuse her."

"And if I do?"

Nalanusat heard this, and the strong emphasis was in his ready response. "She has many important friends. With such a tenuous grasp on power, Poxiciti, why risk having any more enemies?"

There was a sudden flurry of movement as those in the room hurried to get out of the way. Poxiciti was trembling with rage. Had Nalanusat spoken that way to a female he would have died on the spot. Nevertheless Poxiciti had to fight to keep his emotions under control.

"You talk big, yet I can see that you are one of small intelligence and thinking, and merit only dismissal. But tell me before I have you sent from my sight, why does she so steadfastly believe that a feral animal is the culprit?"

"Stupidity does not permit me to answer this," Nalanusat admitted angrily, feeling the harsh emphasis of his own words and knowing that he should now lower himself before Poxiciti had him forcibly ejected. "Only you would dare to prove her wrong."

He would.

The building soon filled with the hum of activity. Messengers waddled in and out of sight, assistants gathered supplies, technicians packed equipment and instruments while important instructions were being issued for the journey. Poxiciti then led his retinue outside to the waiting transport which took them promptly to the sky port. After the shuttle was loaded they boarded and took their seats while the engines started to whine. A cloud of dust and debris came off the field as the shuttle arced skyward toward the rising sun.

From the air, Poxiciti could see that most of the roadway below was completed, for it cut a wide swath through the forest and terminated at what must have been city Tykrerek, just barely visible on the distant horizon. In between were the burnt remains of the bridges; an ashen cloud of smoke rose visibly above each one. However they were heading first to Betelgesel, since that was reportedly the initial source of the attack.

Upon arrival the first thing Poxiciti did was interview the witnesses. From the start there were some discrepancies with their testimony, but after further questioning he determined that most of what they recounted seemed to corroborate the basic story. After that he inspected the destroyed bridge for any clues that might reveal the true nature of the attack, though could see there was little left to study. The charred bones of wood floated downstream; massive broken beams rested half submerged in the running water.

Curious onlookers crowded nearby; talk of what Poxiciti was doing here was starting to spread. There was no time to waste. His investigation would have to be completed before these witless workers ground the remaining evidence underfoot. And so he worked on through the morning yet was no closer to finding what he wanted. By midday, when the hot sun was directly overhead, he was looking about and realized that the wild animals he had so quickly discounted were perhaps now the most plausible explanation. In several places rimming the shore were their telltale footprints, now baked rock-hard in the mud.

"Look at these." Poxiciti traced out a clean track in front of his assistants. "Seven toes, marked by claws. A two-legged creature, with a long length of tail. See where it has dragged it through the mud? This is a very big animal," he remarked, noting the depth and size of the prints. "Has anyone bothered to follow these tracks to see where they might lead?" He scowled when he saw all the silent faces. "Were it not for my curiosity then all of this would forever be a mystery. See that they are followed to their end," he ordered.

As they were making their way past the rows of makeshift tents one of the construction workers appeared in a doorway and called them over. Inside Poxiciti saw several neatly spaced mounds, each covered with a dark sheet.

"And these are the bodies?"

A slow headshake answered his interrogative. "We picked up what we could find. Are you sure you want to see this?"

He nodded for her to proceed. The worker gingerly peeled off the covering so that he could examine the remains for himself. It made a tearing sound where the dried blood and flesh had adhered. Obviously the sight of it must have been disconcerting for him because he was speechless for a long time. And when he did speak his voice sounded cold and detached.

"The victim has extensive tissue and organ damage, multiple lacerations about the head and chest . . ." He touched the cold skin and took a deep breath of air. "Death occurred sometime last night, I'd say nearer to dusk. Interesting. The bite wounds are undoubtedly that of a wild animal. See these lateral incisions here and here, where the mandible bit cleanly through the backside and severed her spine. She died instantly." The worker replaced the sheet and the moment of discomfort was over. "Whatever did this is obviously some sort of carnivore, although I didn't see any clear evidence of consumption."

"As I explained to you earlier," Nalanusat reminded him. "Now tell me what kind of animal kills only for the sake of killing."

"Only we Epiphilinians," Poxiciti answered with harsh sarcasm.

"We kill only to bring about peace and order," Nalanusat responded angrily. Until now he had kept quiet strictly for the sake of the investigation, though this surge of anger he felt loosened his mouth. "You pacifists are all alike. Naturally you enjoy the benefits of our society without having to bear any of the cost."

"Your lack of intelligence is appalling. But for you I suppose it was far easier to rise to your position on your back than use what little brains you have to solve our people's problems."

Just as the two of them were squaring off for another round of fighting, one of Poxiciti's assistants, a young, hotheaded environmentalist named Inelefar, waddled into the tent, his arms swinging wildly to show the importance of the news he was bearing.

"In the forest. I found something."

He led the party, though armed soldiers scouted the perimeter as they went forward. As they followed the trail deeper into the forest what they saw was indeed very peculiar, for these same tracks were now spaced much farther apart, as though this animal was able to leap great distances.

"Now I know these creatures," Poxiciti announced. "That is, I know of some ruthless profiteers who risk death to hunt them. It is a very dangerous beast I have only heard of but never seen, though one which is eagerly sought out by our detestable poachers and sold back home on Epiphiline." Then he added with disgust, "Criminals who harvest life for profit—a monstrous crime! But they fetch a good price, these animal hides, for apparently they have certain luminescent properties that enable them to change color to match the background."

"Segathars. Their hides are very popular. And expensive," Inelefar agreed. "In city Tykrerek I hear there are cargo cruisers being loaded every day with segathar skins."

"Of course in my city we have strict hunting regulations against that sort of thing." Nalanusat felt compelled to say something affirming because it was known that both cities had close dealings. "Midlothian would never permit it unless—"

"Unless she could profit from it," Poxiciti broke in. He halted on the path. "I believe your words mask the darker truth—and that is, what she and her brain-deads really want is for me to sanction this wholesale slaughter, all in the name of public safety when it is really the money she is thinking about. Now tell me what I wish to know. Is she not already hunting these segathars to death?"

Although Nalanusat never intended to disclose this information, he had never tried to conceal it either. In fact it was common knowledge back in the city. Bounty hunters were seen every day at the market place with their load of skins. For a dangerous service that Midlothian happily rewarded, they emptied the forest of a menacing and troublesome pest.

"Since you prefer to put it that way—yes," Nalanusat confessed. "She has granted special permission to cull this particular beast because it is a nuisance animal, better dead, for not only is it a marauder who depletes the forest of other, more valuable animals, but now it has proven itself to be a life-threatening danger to our own people."

"How convenient," Poxiciti said with as much sarcasm as he could muster. "A nuisance, and yet one who's hide fetches an exorbitant price on the market. It seems as though Midlothian has found an effective solution to her problem while still making a handsome profit. And of course, with my approval she can now increase her efforts to kill even more. Had I her low cunning then I too might stupidly believe I was above the law. When news of this reaches the Vulana—and I promise it will—she will certainly be punished for her wickedness and disobedience."

It was no mere threat. Poxiciti could do that, report any offender of the strict environmental laws. His duty as the Vulana's ecological enforcement officer was very clear. Any activity that might pollute or degrade even the tiniest part of the planet first had to have his approval. It was a very long process of environmental impact assessments and public hearings—the backlog was enormous. And any polluters or breakers of the law were to be dealt with severely.

But the Vulana also had many opponents. For countless generations, the low males had little influence on matters of government legislature. The female power brokers, greedy, and politically corrupt, had brought Epiphiline to the brink of economic and environmental ruin. Now its oceans were polluted cesspools, its atmosphere nearly unbreathable, one global catastrophe following after another. Yet for the first time ever, voter dissatisfaction had swept the males into power, had given them the opportunity to fulfill their promises of a cleaner and better world. But so far they were failing, the damage was already done, their planet dying. Now this new world was their only hope, but because of their own stringent laws they were being criticized by the same environmentalists who now demanded a more cautious settlement. However the females, eager to regain power, wanted to see their own world quickly abandoned for this new one. Poxiciti felt the mounting pressure, but for as long as the Vulana ruled he would keep on fighting them to ensure a bright future for everyone.

Finally they reached the spot Inelefar had spoken of. When he pointed down at the pile and kicked over some of the charred black wood, Poxiciti was as stupefied by its presence as everyone else.

"A fire pit, still warm. I don't understand. Tell me, did you look carefully for any sign of disturbance, anything that might show us some other force was at work here?"

"Of course. I counted at least a dozen tracks, and they were all made by the segathars."

"Fascinating, yet highly improbable. Wild animals cannot make fire. Nor do they have the mental capacity to launch a well planned attack."

"Apparently," Nalanusat said, terror in his voice, "this one does."

No doubt news about what they had found would be carried back to city Anaxerxes, would spread to the other cities as well and begin a groundswell of panic. Soldiers were dead, bridges were burnt down. That would not be easily forgotten. It was going to be a formidable task just to keep the people under control. Midlothian, the brute that she was, would order her armed forces to scour the forests and exterminate every last segathar—and what could Poxiciti do to stop her? If he interfered then his party risked losing the support of the people. Had none of this ever happened then perhaps both segathar and Epiphilinian could have lived apart, in peace. But not now.

Poxiciti stood staring at where the segathar's footprints and the fire pit came together. While he refused to see the connection, there was something at work here that had put these animals in Midlothian's gun sight. What exactly was he going to tell the Vulana?

Chapter 13

Midlothian was Tomauk of the greatest city on this new world, and her rule was sure and absolute. Of those who knew her—if they could be believed—she was the driving force behind the Vulana's decision to bring the whole of Epiphiline here. Even if untrue many still saw her as their salvation from the monstrous waste-land that once was home. To be sure, she had many supporters in her city, yet those on whom her shadow fell would tell a different story, one that if they should live to tell would surely describe her as this planet's primary polluter and destroyer. And so for those who dared oppose her the punishment she dealt them was as swift and severe as her judgment. Death.

Malquilimbe, battered and bloody, fell to her knees as the aircraft trembled beneath her. Only the strong arms of the dreg towering above her kept her from toppling over. The aircraft rattled and shook tenuously. Hot air from outside gusted in as the bay doors now hissed open.

Standing at the edge of the platform, Midlothian gazed out across the undulating grassy plain. Long necked creatures, too many to be counted, moved gracefully through the grass with just their heads visible. Other creatures circled in the sky overhead, shrilling noisily at this mass of metal hovering in their midst.

"This new world is too beautiful to imagine, wouldn't you agree, Malquilimbe? You must come over to the door and take a look." A short silence followed. Midlothian's own heavy sigh was of disappointment for her prisoner's reluctance to move. "Bring her to the door," she ordered.

"No, please, great Tomauk. I beg you to reconsider."

"Reconsider?" A cold humor was in her voice as she spoke. "Is this not what you and your followers were trying to protect? Well then, go out and join these creatures you fight to preserve. And before they strip the flesh from your bones and consume you, tell them I will have no dissension spread in my city."

Malquilimbe felt herself being pushed forward, ever closer to the edge, realizing that what was about to happen, would happen if she did not speak out. "My life is in your hands, mighty Tomauk. To one who is highest in the city I humbly ask for your absolution."

Standing erect, with all the power that was hers to command, Midlothian touched her yellow neck ring. "There is a decision to be made here. It is still not too late for you to make up my mind. Just name the names of your companions and I promise you shall go free."

"So hard," she answered. "Understand, these are my . . . my friends." She struggled inwardly, caught in emotional turmoil.

"I can see you are an honorable creature. Loyalty to one's friends is a difficult bond to break. I understand. You see, I have friends too. So now I must think about this. How can I still have what I want, and you, without having to betray your friends? Let me think." She was in her thoughts. What she was thinking no one knew for certain, though Malquilimbe's tension increased when Midlothian was ready with her answer.

"I believe I have the solution—and I offer this only to please you." Opening the wedge of her hand she spoke firmly. "Two names. Give me only two names and you will live. Are these two worth your one life?"

Slowly, imperceptibly at first, Malquilimbe shook her head. "No."

"Good, good. So—the first name?"

"Lohastahana," she trembled.

"A criminal of small importance. And the other one?" Her response came even more slowly than the first, though when Midlothian heard the name she smiled and her plans of death were made. "Well done. You did the right thing, telling me. As I promised, you are now free to go." She waved her arm in the direction of the open doors.

Malquilimbe appeared confused. "Go? Now?"

"Yes. Throw her overboard," she commanded the dreg.

As soon as it was done Midlothian peered over the edge to see her deep in the grass, shrieking to be brought back aboard. "Walk quickly, Malquilimbe. It is a long way back to my city. And if you happen to see Sambalor out here somewhere, do say hello to her for me."

Her rude roar of laughter diminished as the doors slid shut and the aircraft nosed skyward. This was the start of a good day, and it was only going to get better.

Chapter 14

To the other creatures of the forest, Ilon must have looked very tasty. More than once Horhon had to leap over him and close her jaws on some hungry predator that had strayed too close, her white teeth now red where she had bitten through the last animal that had tried to taste him. She had the solution, yet he was determined to be free of his carrier, and so she reluctantly permitted him to walk about freely even though another karafin was preparing to have him for its next meal.

Clearly Ilon had forgotten what it was like to be alive again. That was another time, another place that could have been days, or a thousand lifetimes ago. He had no idea, only that he remembered it, yet whatever he once was he was not the same person now. Perhaps he looked the same, but he was changed forever and could never go back. Nor did he want to. In his memories he was still Taal. This seemed as natural to him as breathing, yet as each slow day passed he sensed that he was changing into something else, and that old life was slipping away from him.

"What is this darkness I see on your head?" Horhon noticed.

With his hand he brushed the top of his head and felt the nascent beginnings of bristly growth scraping under his fingers. "Hair," he told her. "It has started growing."

From the look she gave him this was an unfamiliar word that required explanation. However, very soon she moved with understanding. "In my dreams I remember seeing this hair. So you will have hair on your head like them."

Not only his head, but all over his body. Because he was looking, Ilon could see where hair was growing out on his arms and chest. It was one more oddity, something that should not have concerned him, but it was another reminder of how different this life was from the past one when he started his life as a small baby and had waited years to grow into the body that he had now.

At sunrise the next day his mother took him outside, traveling onto the sunny field before going deep into the dark depths of the forest. Everywhere he travelled felt like a new adventure of discovery. Today he watched a herd of goud scale a tree. Ilon could not help but marvel at their ability for climbing. Though immense creatures of size they were excellent tree climbers, using their eight limbs and divergent outer fingers to reach the uppermost part of the forest. There was much to be learned here. Indeed, this forest and everything that it held was still very much a mystery to him.

And then there were these Egris, intelligent creatures like himself who knew of life and death, who dreamed like him, felt emotions like him, but were nothing like him at all. They were brutal killers, savage, raw meat eaters. The way they devoured their food was too much to bear watching. Ordinarily, it might have been easy to mistrust them, for there were rows of sharp teeth behind their smiles. And yet to hear their true feelings made him feel ashamed for ever thinking them animals. For them life was as it had been for generations—unchanged. Yet now the Iranha's sudden and unwelcomed presence here changed everything.

Once, Ilon had seen an Iranha corpse. Horhon carried it all the way from the river just to show him one. They were sebaceous things, creatures of disgust. Like oversized slugs, he thought, for their smooth gray and black hide was slimy to touch. The two legs were short and stumpy, without any toes. The arms were longer, but again there were no fingers, only two spatulate stumps. Faces that were chinless, jawless, hardly a mouth at all, just a thick slit with rows and rows of tiny teeth. It was hard to believe how something that ugly could be so dangerous, yet he realized they possessed a kind of cunning that easily made them the most deadly creatures alive.

Outside the forest was darkening. Ilon's day long exploration ended the moment he climbed into his burrow. He was soon fast asleep. However, for the many creatures of night, sunset signaled the beginning of the hunt. This was also true of the Egris hunters, who by nature were nocturnal feeders. At dusk they too were moving up through the tunnels, hungry, and ready to kill.

Katakana was on the field when she saw smoke near the dying horizon. Yet this was not the smoke from a campfire, for with each new day she watched it drift above the trees and knew that it was a little closer than before. Seeing it now she could not help but feel some bitterness about what they accomplished. From the very beginning it had been a bad idea. Yes, the bridges were destroyed, the Iranha stopped dead at the river. Unfortunately what they risked and won was nothing more than a reprieve. After that the Iranha redoubled their efforts, also posted more armed guards and laid deadly traps. Now each day began and ended with killing. Expeditionary forces were sweeping deeper and deeper into the forest, striking death at the very heart of their existence. More trods were being wiped out than ever before. Perhaps the hunters had unwittingly plunged themselves into an unwinnable war. If they had even once considered the hard-heartedness of their enemy before attacking them, then none of this might be happening now. Even so, the last bridge was now completed; road construction was going on as though it had never stopped. No one ever talked about attacking them again.

There was a new moon tonight. Some of the first bright stars were starting to appear in the sky overhead. In the background an animal screamed in distress; dark forms moved off the field toward it. Lifting her head, Katakana sniffed the thick, hot air, then glanced down at the ripped-open corpse and licked her red teeth clean.

"Are your stomachs full?"

"This one was not very meaty," Saskakel complained. He spat out the animal's gristly remains to show her he was through. "It is still early. We should keep hunting."

"And you, Gangahar?"

"I think I have tasted better meat on the scrawniest tarser." He freed a bloody lump of flesh caught between his teeth and threw it to the ground. Katakana took his actions for agreement.

"Then let us move on."

Soon afterwards the hunters spotted a large herd of crested mullatods wallowing in the shallow part of the river. The nearest of them saw the attackers coming and splashed to get out of the water. In an attempt to cut them off Gangahar ran across their front while the other two circled and closed in from behind.

With his teeth dug deep into the animal's hide Gangahar inexplicably broke off the attack and let it gallop away with the herd. It was very strange behavior. "Flee now!"

Behind them, Katakana and Saskakel saw the reason for his departure and took off after him in swift pursuit. Nor did they stop when they reached the forest, for just as they cleared the first trees monstrous machines were landing on the field behind them.

"Jump faster!" Katakana screamed in terror.

All Ilon remembered was a pair of hands suddenly closing around him before he was spirited outside and tied to his mother's waist. He had no idea what was happening, though as the trod fled away he saw the bright lights cutting through the darkness, heard the sound of heavy machines approaching.

"Go after them!" Midlothian shouted.

She had ordered the advance. Now she wanted to kill them all, would have gladly done it herself had her personal escort not slowed and let the armored troop carriers pass. Soldiers in full battle gear emptied from the vehicles and quickly formed a skirmish line that spread out between the surrounding trees; their heavy lag guns blazing blue in the darkness.

Watching the proceedings from atop her private transport, Midlothian screamed out orders to those who ran past. She was an accomplished military leader, and head of an important city. Yet those who served under her knew her as one who ruled by fear and brutality. She enjoyed her work too much, enjoyed the hunting and killing—it was a very satisfying thing to be doing. Now as one of her hahlok commanders emerged from the forest she climbed down from the vehicle and bid her to come over.

"I wish to hear of your progress. How many dead?"

"There is a problem," was all she said before Midlothian cut her off.

"I don't want to hear about your problems commander, only your successes." She crossed her thick arms. "Well, report what you found."

The trembling hahlok commander made motions of servitude and obedience. "The animal lair is presently surrounded by our troops. The chodox gas we used is highly toxic and kills instantly, yet after we searched inside we found no segathars. It is empty."

"They escaped? Every last one?" She was furious. "How could they have known our soldiers were coming? Could some of them have alerted the others?"

"I doubt that dumb animals could be so pragmatic as to anticipate our attacking forces and give warning."

"Nonetheless, something has chased them off. There are fresh tracks that lead into the forest."

"Shall we pursue them now?" The commander was quaking in fear of Midlothian's clenched fists.

"You have a mandate, and that of course is to rid the surrounding area of these filthy things. I want them all exterminated. Search the forest. Find them, and kill them. See to it at once."

As the terrified commander turned and hurried away, Poxiciti said from behind, "If they are feral as you say, then why are so many getting away from you?"

Midlothian snorted through her swelled nostrils. "I wasn't aware you were keeping a record. Are you still convinced that they possess more than bestial intelligence?"

Poxiciti frowned angrily. "I can be sure of nothing," he replied. "They are unpredictable, as wild animals usually are, but if they kill our soldiers and do not eat them, then surely it is more out of hatred than hunger. Would a mindless animal destroy valuable equipment while ignoring potential food?"

"What nonsense," Midlothian fumed. "You have thoroughly examined the ones I sent you, have you not?"

"I have."

"And?"

"And they are only corpses. The dead can make no plans against the living. If I am to make any sort of scientific analysis based on proving intelligence, then I need a living specimen to study."

"So we will capture one for you," she assured him, summoning a nearby dreg and issuing orders so that his wishes would be immediately fulfilled. When she turned back to Poxiciti she gleefully added, "Any knowledge you provide us will also aid in their destruction."

However, Poxiciti shared little of her zeal. "You wish to destroy life and that is wrong. For so few who are guilty you are undeservedly punishing an entire species."

"Undoubtedly true, but they destroy everything that is Epiphilinian. My city Anaxerxes is strong, and it grows stronger each day. I wish it to remain that way."

"And it is my responsibility to see that this particular species of animal is preserved."

"Preserved!" Midlothian jumped quickly to anger. "They are a pestilence needing to be wiped out!"

"Enough of the creatures have already been destroyed. The Vulana permitted you this only because a few have proven their bestial nature. Yet I doubt they will permit this slaughtering to continue only for furthering your ill-gotten wealth."

"Your precious government is on the verge of collapsing," she angrily retorted. "I hear news from Epiphiline of food riots in the Jhordlax district, widespread looting and killing. No one will want to preserve a killer animal here when everything they have there is falling apart."

Now it was Poxiciti who was incensed. He pointed accusingly at her. "The ecological crisis was precipitated by the very same powers who now work to undermine our government. You female hard-liners want to see an end to our conservation policies. And that would bring the garbage pile you created back on Epiphiline—here."

With equal vehemence Midlothian replied, "Females are the natural rulers. That is the way it has always been. We make the important decisions affecting our present situation, instead of you males who think too much of the future. I seek only to do what is best for our people—and that is to ensure our continued survival at any cost." With her raised hand she terminated all further discussion before curtly dismissing herself from his presence.

What a tremendous relief to be separated from her at last! The pain in his head was only now beginning to ebb. But deep inside him his thoughts were in turmoil. How did I ever allow myself to be talked into this insane scheme of hers?

Midlothian and her rich cronies had been illegally poaching the segathars all along. Not that this was a secret. Unfortunately after the recent attacks the public was happy to see these animals hunted down, even if only to fill Midlothian's warehouses with expensive segathar hides. He could not allow that to go on, but to stop her right now might make him and his government very unpopular. What he really needed was some condemning evidence, something that would put her away for good. He knew what he must do.

Later, while Poxiciti was exploring some of the subterranean tunnels, one of the low ranking dregs shuffled through the passageway and made motions of urgent attention.

"There is something they want you to see."

A hahlok commander was waiting for him at the end of the corridor. She directed Poxiciti into what appeared to be some sort of large chamber. Midlothian was conferring with some of her aides, waiting for him to approach.

"What do you make of this?" She pointed to a black spot on the floor; Poxiciti bent and looked closer.

"Fire," he said with apparent surprise, seeing the burnt bits of scarred wood piled inside a ring of stones.

"Of course it is. But can you think of any logical reason for its presence here?"

"None."

"Then guess."

"Very well. We have been in many of these same animal lairs but have never seen any evidence of fire. Now we have indisputable proof that creatures other than ourselves are responsible for its making. We also know that this one lair might also be the source."

"Of what?"

"Perhaps those who built this fire are the same ones who burnt down our bridges." He had dared to make the obvious connection, but there was even more mystery here. "Down here, look at this."

Brushing off the thin layer of sand he handed the object over to Midlothian. To her it appeared to be just another well-gnawed bone, the floor was littered with them. But at Poxiciti's urging she held it close to her face and sniffed.

"Burnt flesh. Disgusting." Repulsed by the sight of it she hurled it back to the floor and wiped her hands clean. "I thought they ate their meat raw?"

"So did I." He was just as mystified by the sight of burnt black meat. "For whatever the reason it is here, obviously these creatures have brains. They can make fire. This changes everything."

"Then if we are dealing with a thinking animal after all, it is a beast who plots our destruction, who kills and destroys what we have so resolutely created. Every last one of them must be hunted down before this insidious plan is achieved."

Poxiciti ardently disagreed. "No. I doubt their primitive fires will ever prevail against our superior armed forces. And since it is we who are the invader I fail to see how killing more will stop them from attacking us. Enough of them have died. No more. Today the poaching and slaughtering ends. By my authority I declare all segathars a protected species. That means if I find anyone trading their hides in your city, Midlothian, then it will be you I hold responsible. Now order your troops back to the city."

"I will not be ordered!" Midlothian could no longer suppress the tide of strong feelings that was surging within her. Reaching for her gun she stopped herself just short of using it. "Be assured that others will hear about what we found here today. And they will not be pleased to know that you dedicate our resources to the segathars' preservation when now it is obvious they are thinking of our destruction. Protected or not, I choose to do what is best for all Epiphilinians. The hunt will continue as planned."

"You forget which of us is the superior." He was unmoved by the coldness of his own response, for what he had to do next was clear in his mind and must be done. "From this moment on your reign of greed is ended." With his hand he summoned one of her own hahlok commanders. "You. See that she is returned to the city and imprisoned for her crimes. For her treachery and irresponsibility I strip her of her powers of office. She no longer has the authority to command. She who was highest now is lower than the lowest among us. Now get her out of my sight."

When the commander hesitated, even turned to the other officers to seek needed advice, Poxiciti screamed, "Do as I order!"

Though she struggled with the invisible burden of his command, she finally issued orders to her company of dregs who reluctantly took Midlothian into custody.

Back in city Anaxerxes news soon spread of the prisoner's arrival. People gathered along the streets to watch the procession pass. For Midlothian this was the most humiliating experience of her long career, to be paraded in disgrace through the streets of her own city. Though stripped of her power, shackled and flanked by armed guards, she walked proudly, lest anyone in the crowd forget that she was still in control of this city.

Actually nothing had really changed. To Midlothian her incarceration was merely a temporary setback. All Poxiciti had done was stop her for now. Even despite his best efforts to punish her, what he had in fact done was seal his fate. When news of the arrest reached her business associates they would see him dead. Midlothian herself was already thinking of possible ways to kill him. Not today or tomorrow, but some time very, very soon.

Chapter 15

Nalanusat was just returning to the city when word came of Pulima Cos's imminent arrival from their home world. Even as her shuttle was landing he was hastily assembling a welcoming party of important city officials and dignitaries.

As the dust cloud dissipated, armed troops in yellow and green uniforms paraded across the tarmac, saluting to attention while Nalanusat walked between the straight lines. Oneteesel, a powerful merchant trader from city Tykrerek, accompanied him to the platform.

There was a hissing sound as the shuttle's metal gangplank slid onto the platform. Soon a dark figure appeared in the doorway. Fat, dressed in a flowing purple gown, Pulima Cos proceeded down the ramp in stately silence. Behind her was her train of attendants, her advisors and personal aides, a line so long that it seemed to take forever to empty the craft.

"Welcome to our city," Nalanusat said formally. "How was your journey?"

"Very boring," Pulima Cos yawned through her open cavity. "I miss the comforts of Epiphiline already." Without saying another word she then rudely brushed past him and stopped in front of Oneteesel, who was introduced by one of her attendants as the planet's richest investor.

Oneteesel, her head lowered, spoke clearly in the presence of the delegation. "Pulima Cos is known among our city as one who appreciates beautiful things."

"I find little about this planet that is beautiful."

A special wet chair had been prepared for her. Cool water now bubbled up through the chair's pores. She was seating herself when Oneteesel began to speak admirably of the richness of this new world, the countless varieties of plants and animals which they harvested for sale in the market places of Epiphilinian cities. On this last topic Oneteesel was expert, though Pulima Cos interrupted her when she mentioned the segathars.

"Beautiful—those hideous things? I have seen stuffed specimens back on Epiphiline. I prefer them that way."

Oneteesel nodded agreement. "Yes, of course, but an ugly thing made beautiful. I have many skin hunters in my employment, professionals who are committed to providing the finest animal skins money can buy." She motioned her aides forward. They held up several fashionable segathar skin robes before passing them over to Oneteesel who selected the most expensive. "Try this on. It is of a most excellent manufacture. Feel the texture. Quality like this is not easily available to the public. Is it to your liking?"

"It is."

After trying on a few, Oneteesel asked her, "So which one do you prefer?"

"All of them," she answered.

Oneteesel nodded. "I trust that you will remember my name whenever you might require my services."

"And what service is that?"

"Why to aid you and your Tomauk in the destruction of these despicable creatures." Her eyes shifted towards Nalanusat.

Pulima Cos frowned at the sight of him. "I see only a low male standing in her place," she answered disdainfully, leaving no doubt whatsoever to who her harsh words were intended. Facing Oneteesel, she continued the conversation, leaving Nalanusat clearly aware that trouble was coming.

"Your offer of help is an admirable gesture. Then you must also know of our problems with these accursed things?"

"Yes, certainly," she agreed. "And so I offer my people's knowledge and expertise, anything you need that might lead your troops in their total elimination."

"Does this apparent generosity have a price?"

She closed the two wedges of her hand. "A very small price. Only that you allow my skinners exclusive access to your killing sites."

"Done. My aide will see to the contract details immediately." Now with her attention suddenly back on Nalanusat she said, "Am I to be impressed that Midlothian should send you as her representative instead of herself? Is this task so beneath her that she sends an underling to greet me?"

"I am Nalanusat," he said with supplication as he stepped before her and bowed reverentially. "As one who serves Anaxerxes, I extend greetings and welcome you to my city."

Before the air hissed from his hide, Pulima Cos backhanded him hard across the face. "Has she given you charge of her city? No? You shake your empty head no, and yet you dare to greet me as one who commands. I see that you wear her emblem of authority. Disgusting." Seizing him tightly by the throat she tore off the yellow neck band that signified his rank as Tomauk and flung it into the crowd. "I heard rumors that she rots in her own jail, imprisoned by you males on charges of corruption and ecological genocide. Is this true?"

The shock of what had just happened was still sinking in; Nalanusat was utterly speechless. Before he could recover, Pulima Cos, perceiving his cowardly stance as a sign of male weakness, railed her immense anger against him.

"Patience is a male trait. So answer me quickly!"

Quailing before her closed fists he cried out, "It is true."

"Release her. Have her brought to me at once. And send for that traitor, Poxiciti."

In the afternoon Poxiciti answered the summons to appear before Pulima Cos. As he entered the building his personal body guards were surrounded and disarmed. He himself was taken forcibly upstairs under heavy guard. Until he entered Midlothian's private suite of offices he had no idea what was happening. But seeing her ugly bulk seated next to Pulima Cos instantly filled him with dread.

"Your despicable government is gone," were Pulima Cos's first words to him. "The military now controls Epiphiline. And I alone control the military."

"What of the others?" he managed to croak out before his own shocked gasps cut him off.

"Executed. As punishment for their crimes against Epiphiline. You should be dead too. Yet I graciously spare your life so that you may better serve me."

"You—never! Better that I be dead with the others than serve one who rules only to further her own self-interests."

"That may be your wish, mine too, yet I still have need of your ability to placate these rebellious and stupid environmentalists."

Poxiciti was belligerent. "The power that you grasp at will be yours for only as long the people permit it. Once they hear the same promises and see the garbage pile up at their feet, they will pull you down. The truth will ultimately prevail over your powers of deception."

"You ignorant fool. The only true power in the universe is the power of fear. With it I have the power to rule, the power to crush my opponents. The same power to expel you from your position of importance. You would die quickly in the forest. I can do that. I will do that," she threatened, "if you do not obey my every command. This I promise you, for I have no recourse but to end this environmental nonsense that preserves a planet yet destroys a people. Fortunately for you there are still many believers of your ridiculous teachings, people who would preach to others of sedition and dissension. They need to be weeded out—and silenced. You will do this task for me."

He accepted this new responsibility with great reluctance and loathing. Already he was feeling the turmoil churning within him, the conflicting orders. No doubt Pulima Cos had already given the order for a full planetary settlement. And with none of the environmental restrictions in place it was going to be an ecological disaster. His home world was dead. They might be forgiven for this mistake only once, but twice, not twice, they would never live to see it again.

And maybe it was already too late.

Chapter 16

Ever since Pulima Cos declared the new world officially ready for colonization, the floodgates swung open and thousands began to pour in. The shuttles transporting these new immigrants were booked solid. Often, a hefty bribe guaranteed passage, since there was now an interminably long waiting list. As more and more citizens decided to leave planet Epiphiline, much of the activity there was slowing to a dead stop.

And yet here the growth rate was incredible. Industrial output was tripling every day, cities were expanding, people were working. These were the boom times. Indeed, even Pulima Cos and her despised government was riding an incredible wave of popularity. The people no longer cared about environmental issues and soon forgot the problems of the past. In fact the whole environmental movement lost many of its supporters, and those activists who were still brave enough to speak out were arrested and thrown into jail. As was often the case, public executions provided cheap entertainment for the masses.

Even Poxiciti, once considered to be one of the founding members, was branded a traitor by the same environmental organization he was now helping to destroy. Although he vehemently disputed his close relationship with Pulima Cos, after two attempts on his life he knew that his future was bleak. Whatever was left of the movement was driven underground, and those who now worked in Poxiciti's place would eventually see him dead.

In the meantime his research continued at city Soligcetis, in the same laboratory where he and his assistant, Inelefar, were now forced to labor exclusively for Pulima Cos's own personal interests.

"Has the segathar eaten anything at all?" Poxiciti asked pointedly. The door slid closed behind him as he entered the laboratory and halted in front of the animal pen.

Inelefar shook his head no. "This is the ninth day now. The animal appears to be weakening. The last two died of slow starvation. I fear this one is dying too."

Pressing his face close to the metlaglass Poxiciti peered inside. The big segathar was sitting on its haunches, its tail coiled around, looking back at him with the same apparent fascination. "Amazing that it can survive for this long without food or water. Look at it. Such a magnificent animal. To see it die, here, purely for the advancement of . . . of knowledge," he said distastefully, ". . . is a tragic waste."

"Knowledge—not to create, but to destroy. That is our duty now," Inelefar coldly reminded him. "To study all aspects of the segathar's physiology and report anything that will aid Pulima Cos's forces in their extermination." He did not sound pleased either, for he was merely repeating Midlothian's exact orders. "I hate her too, but we have no choice. If we refuse her then undoubtedly we will be this segathar's next meal."

"She can dig into my brain, yet she will never alter my beliefs." Poxiciti was momentarily startled when the segathar lunged forward, jaws agape as it smashed uselessly against the impenetrable wall separating them. "You want to kill me, don't you?" Sighing, he turned his back to the creature and said, "You would not be the first one to try."

Advancing to his work station he picked up a thick pile of memory sheets and began sorting through them one at a time. "So, what has that fat tyrant sent us today?"

"A new problem. City Tykrerek reports that the blottan they planted on the fields is now poisoning its citizens."

"Those idiots!" he shouted. "Of course it is poisonous. City Tykrerek was built where a particular species of grass produces a highly toxic residue in the soil. To plant anything there without first neutralizing the contaminated soil would poison anyone who ate what was grown there. First have them remove all of the blottan and burn it immediately. Then tell them to treat the soil with a concentrated solution of ataxapag before they replant the new seed. Such stupidity. I wonder how we ever manage to survive here."

All that day Poxiciti found himself having to deal with the same set of problems—their old world struggling to come to grips with this new world. Almost every single day there were reports of someone being poisoned, or worse, attacked by a wild animal that had strayed too close to the city. The security force's response to these attacks was automatic. The offending animal was immediately tracked down, captured, then destroyed. A growing list of animals was already in danger of being wiped out forever.

In the evening, after their work was completed, both scientists retired to their separate sleeping quarters. Later, after everyone was asleep Inelefar crept back downstairs to a small waiting room where he knew all of the listening devices had been removed. When he secured the door Poxiciti rose from his chair.

"Tell me, what news of the movement?"

"Borobos sends word that one of her contacts in city Tsilix has incriminating videos of the military. Apparently they were spotted dumping toxic waste into the river."

"Excellent. Have more money transferred to her account."

"This is an insane scheme, Poxiciti. If Pulima Cos were to discover our involvement in this affair, she would have us both killed in an instant."

"Has all of this clean air softened your brain? She intends to kill us anyway. But before that happens I will gladly risk my life to expose the people to what she and her corrupt government are doing behind their backs. You know what is happening out there. And every day we do her dirty work we bring ourselves that much closer to her, to those like her who destroy purely for profit. Because of them our home world is now dead. And when this next world is dead too—what then? No amount of money will ever undo the damage or bring back the destroyed lives. We might die trying to stop her, yet we are the only ones who can stop her."

"You are right, of course," Inelefar conceded. "Certainly I will help you in any way I can." He would. After all, what other choice did he have?

"Good." Poxiciti went to the door to show that this meeting was now over. "I must go to city Anaxerxes. Tomorrow. You will accompany me." As he was about to leave he abruptly spun around. "One other detail. The segathar. Have it returned to the forest, and released."

Inelefar's shocked expression was such that Poxiciti decided some clarification was necessary. "I do not wish to cause its suffering any longer, nor will I allow its hide to fall into the hands of our jailer. We shall say it died."

"Midlothian will demand an autopsy."

"Just do it," he ordered, and then exited from the room.

The next morning he was up at dawn, working diligently in his laboratory on some new project which he allowed no one to see. Inelefar eventually caught up with him at the sky port, and just as soon as they boarded they promptly departed for city Anaxerxes.

Although a vehicle was sent to take them directly to Pulima Cos, as soon as they were within the city limits Poxiciti ordered the driver to stop at a location he pointed out on the map.

"I wanted you to see this first," he told Inelefar as their vehicle was pulling away. Naturally the driver would immediately report their whereabouts, so before they were apprehended he grabbed hold of Inelefar's arm and hurried him across the street.

Up ahead a group of rough looking females were milling out in front of an abandoned building. One of them said something crude as the two males walked past, then turned and started to follow.

"We're asking for trouble if we stay here," Inelefar whispered as he glanced nervously over his shoulder. All three females were keeping pace behind them.

"Just a little further." Poxiciti checked the map again, then angled left onto one of the side streets.

"You!" A harsh voice penetrated Poxiciti's thoughts, and he turned to see an overbearing female stomping forward. "Not you," she said coarsely. "The pretty one. Come here," she ordered.

Before she realized what was happening Poxiciti pulled a gulun gun from his robe—and now he fired it into the air as he charged forward screaming as loud as he could. As he anticipated, the three frightened females made a hasty departure.

"This accursed city is full of ruffians and hooligans."

Inelefar's tiny yellow eyes enlargened. "You . . . you brought a gun, a killing weapon? You Poxiciti?"

"What, this thing?" To Inelefar's shock he pointed the weapon directly at him and fired. "Just a noise maker," he laughed at his assistant's horrified expression. "See? A harmless toy. Now be quiet and stay on your guard."

Were this not city Anaxerxes, Inelefar might have guessed he was back home on Epiphiline. The street was filthy, strewn with garbage and derelict equipment. Many of the older buildings were now empty, though he could hear some kind of heavy machinery emanating from the one across the street.

"Where are we?"

"Terrasote sector." Lifting his arms skyward Poxiciti slowly spun around in a circle. "So what do you think of our fine city now? Is this not the pinnacle of all our achievements here?"

Obviously his sarcasm was intended to launch them both into some sort of philosophical debate that Inelefar had no wish to participate in. It could not come at a worse time. They were two defenseless males, alone, in a dangerous part of the city. And undoubtedly Pulima Cos was searching for them right now. Of all the places to go, why had they come here? Could all this stress and mental turmoil be making him crazy? Inelefar thought for sure he was when Poxiciti walked over to one of the sewer grates and pried it open with his hands.

"Over here. This is something to be seen."

Reluctantly, Inelefar squatted overtop the black hole, grimacing as the sewer's acrid stench bit into his pores. "Poxiciti," he said urgently. "We have to leave. Now."

"Is anyone still watching us?" he asked distractedly.

"No."

"Good. Hold onto this." He handed over a gnarob, a highly sensitive instrument used for detecting the presence of various toxic chemicals. "I recalibrated it this morning."

"For what?"

He declined to answer, though Inelefar's curiosity was piqued when Poxiciti attached a line and began lowering it into the hole. While they waited for the device to take an accurate reading Inelefar checked over his shoulder again. To his immense relief no one else was in the area; still, he couldn't be sure they were out of danger. In any case when he looked back, Poxiciti was hauling the gnarob back up.

"Ah-hah! Just as I suspected. These readings indicate the usual concoction of deadly chemicals and poisons which city Anaxerxes's citizens are illegally disposing of. And something else." He noted this one particular discrepancy and immediately pointed it out to Inelefar.

"Helixarum? This figure can't be right. According to this data, there's a significant amount of helixarum accumulating down there."

"Correct." Poxiciti regarded him grimly. "They're pouring it straight into the city's sewers."

Inelefar was aghast. "Who would do such a stupid thing?"

"I suspect poachers. There are several operating in the vicinity. And since helixarum is extremely corrosive, why they're probably using it to dispose of their animal carcasses. That would explain the elevated levels of carbon in the reading."

"It's insane! To use helixarum for something like that. Why at this concentration, if it combusted, it could . . ." Inelefar caught himself slipping backwards, so great was his shock. "It could wreak the entire infrastructure, knock down whole city blocks, kill thousands! We have to report this at once."

"And what do you expect the authorities will do? Hunt down these polluters, arrest all of them, jail every last one? No," Poxiciti said firmly. "Instead, the lives we save will be our own."

"Then—you're asking me to say nothing, do nothing?"

"I am."

"But . . . thousands of people."

"Only thousands. It is a small price to pay if we are to prevent the deaths of millions. After all, it is the people who are precipitating this crisis. Their lust for fashionable animal hides has attracted these same exploiters and criminals who now pollute our cities strictly for profit. So long as there is money to be made this sort of thing will continue to happen."

He was appalled by Poxiciti's cold-blooded reasoning, though Inelefar had to admit to himself that a devastating explosion might be just what they needed to get the people back on their side.

"Here, help me put this back on." Together they slid the grill over the opening. Poxiciti rose and brushed the dust from his robe. "We better get going."

After a brief walk they again encountered another group of females, though managed to get past them after Inelefar promised to come back with some of his friends. Fortunately, their driver spotted them crossing the street and promptly delivered them to the city's main headquarters located behind the protective walls of the old city. An armed escort met them at the door and took them upstairs to Pulima Cos's private suite of offices.

Her specially equipped wet room misted out just the perfect amount of humidity and water vapor. Invisible droplets of water condensed on their bodies and dribbled off. The cool wetness was luxuriating. Ordinarily, Poxiciti might have enjoyed this frivolous convenience, yet seeing Pulima Cos's fat frame wreathed in heavy moisture was too ugly a sight to behold and robbed him of this one pleasure.

"You were to come straight here as I ordered. So what were you doing in Terrasote sector?" she demanded.

"Why out enjoying the sights of your beautiful city," Poxiciti answered with only the slightest trace of sarcasm in his voice.

"Very amusing," Pulima Cos said dryly. She frowned. Seeing him again, this soon, was almost more than she could bear. His annoying presence brought back the anger she had felt during their last encounter—and now made her wish he was dead. He should have been dead, she wanted this very much, though regrettably he was much more valuable to her alive. Yet hopefully, this might soon change.

"Did you bring the information as I asked?"

"Of course," Poxiciti answered. "Here it is."

As she swung around to face him she spotted his new companion and all thoughts of work were instantly forgotten. "And who is this pretty one?"

"He is Inelefar," Poxiciti said formally, stepping aside so that he might better introduce the two of them. "My assistant."

"Assistant? So you are a scientist, Inelefar?"

Reluctantly, he nodded.

"Wonderful. And so lovely too." She rose from behind her desk and squeezed his hand. Inelefar nervously avoided her eyes though could feel them burning into his wet flesh. "You must join me for dinner tonight, Inelefar."

A personal invitation from Pulima Cos was impossible to refuse. Not that they would be eating food. Her sexual appetite was well known among the ruling circles. Though he had nodded yes, he was already thinking of possible ways to cancel their engagement.

However, Pulima Cos wanted him right now; it was difficult to think of anything else. But once she was again seated behind her desk, looking at Poxiciti's ugly face, the discussion quickly returned to the present problem.

"Your work. Is it progressing?"

"Slowly," he admitted. "Understand that this is a new world and everything in it is a mystery needing to be solved."

"Then you and your lazy companions need to work harder. Were you not given a live segathar to study?"

"It died."

"Then get another one. I want answers, not excuses." In anger she thumped the top of her desk. "Have I not made available to you every scientific convenience, provided you with some of the planet's best scientists?"

"You have."

"Well then, what have you discovered?"

"As of yet, nothing conclusive. The segathars I examined showed an intense fear of fire, nor were they able to demonstrate any skill whatsoever that might be interpreted as intellectually motivated."

"Then you are wasting my time. I know those creatures are out there. I want them found. And destroyed. My ability to protect the public depends on knowing if these animals can make fire. You have three more days to unlock this mystery."

"Or what?"

Her silence was his answer, and so he and Inelefar departed for home under this new threat of death. Even so, it was not worth thinking about. Whatever she decided to do to them she would do. Poxiciti limped slowly; he did not let her bother him.

"She frightens me," Inelefar whispered beside him.

"Do not fear her. She is more afraid of us than we of her. Remember, for all her powers she is nothing but a fat blowhard."

Inelefar snorted. His mentor's sense of humor was atrocious, yet he appreciated these brief moments of levity if only to remind himself that he was still alive.

Poxiciti looked to the end of the corridor and saw that the guards were still out of earshot. "The killing of the segathars will not be ended. Therefore we must work against her to ensure that these animals are protected. I propose a non-profit organization of concerned citizens, funded by private donations to ensure that these and other endangered animals are saved from permanent extinction. I want you to go to city Tsilix and begin this task immediately."

"And what shall I call this new enterprise?" he asked him.

"Exactly that. Segathar Scientific Enterprises."

A vehicle was waiting outside, and as soon as they climbed in, Poxiciti ordered the driver to take them at once to the sky port. Still he was thinking of Pulima Cos, though he was happy to see her accursed city vanish in the dust cloud behind him. He cared nothing at all for this city, for already it was a dirty, polluted place, growing wildly out of control. That had never been his wish, to see the surrounding forest burnt down, the wetlands drained dry. Sadly, he knew that some day all this would be indistinguishable from the overcrowded, filthy cities they had abandoned on Epiphiline. Some day very soon.

Then an odd thing happened. Unknown to his two passengers, the driver turned at a crossroad and headed south away from the sky port. Only when Poxiciti realized they were going in the opposite direction did he order the driver to pull over. He pressed a switch on the com panel. Now as the privacy shield slid open so strong was Poxiciti's reaction to the driver's face that he fell back into his seat.

"You!"

"What do you want?" Inelefar hissed in hatred.

"Only your attention," Nalanusat said quietly. "There are no listening devices. We can talk."

"We cannot. Now drive," Poxiciti commanded.

"First, you must promise to listen."

"I promise you nothing. You are one of Midlothian's paid informants."

"No more. It was in her jail where I learned to hate her. But it was also there where I met others who made me see that the females are our oppressor. We males have no voice, no power to change anything. Unless we act against them now I fear this new world will become like the one we left."

"And what proof do you have of this amazing conversion?" Poxiciti asked him skeptically.

"Only this." He rolled up his garment sleeve and showed them the red tattoo burnt deep into his flesh. And though it was only a small and simple design both of the lookers instantly recognized it as a symbol of rebellion.

"I cannot imagine it. You, a terrorist."

Even Inelefar managed to snort out a laugh. "What would Midlothian think of you now?"

There was a long ponderous silence, Poxiciti was thinking very seriously of how he would now respond. Finally, he lifted his eyes and spoke. "So tell me what it is you want, Nalanusat."

"I know you have a fifth column operating in several cities. Your spies are collecting information to use against this government. So are we. Why should our two groups work apart when we are both working against a common enemy?"

"Then . . ."

"We want to join you."

"No. Never!" Inelefar shouted. "Besides, what do you and your converts know about our cause?"

"Absolutely nothing," he said unabashedly. "We only want the same as you—to see the power shared equally, male and female together."

Even while Inelefar fully expected his mentor to refuse and say no, Poxiciti found himself unable to turn down Nalanusat's offer. "Before I give you my answer I want to know more about this movement, your members, your political connections, and your covert activities."

"Done," Nalanusat agreed happily.

When they arrived at the sky port Poxiciti produced a wet slip of selp paper which he handed over to Nalanusat. "Here. Her name is Borobos. She will examine your organization and decide how it might be integrated to better serve us. For now, until things change, we will have no further contact."

"Understood. The next time we meet I hope this world will be a different place."

"I hope so," Poxiciti told him. "I sincerely hope so."

Chapter 17

"**K**rugjon is very sick. I fear he will not survive."

Horhon was so still that to the watchers she did not appear to be breathing at all. "And Ilon?"

"He is the lucky one." Katakana sighed. "His sickness is not as bad as the others. Of course he is still not able to leave his burrow, but I believe he is recovering."

Then the news was not entirely bad. Still Horhon could not allow Ilon's present condition to draw her away from an even more pressing matter. Two had died yesterday, and soon maybe another would join them. With tremendous effort she forced aside all thoughts of him and concentrated on her greatest worry.

"This sickness you speak of. Has anyone else succumbed to it yet?"

Of all the grim faced hunters only Katakana seemed marginally relieved. "I believe not. Only the four who returned together, only they complained of sickness—and that has not happened to any of us. Not yet. I have questioned everyone here, and since one more day has passed without any sign of it spreading to us, why then I suppose we are safe."

"Then what could have caused it?"

Again it was Katakana who responded, though she was no authority and was the first one to admit that this matter was outside the realm of her understanding. "We see its result, yet we know none of the reasons. I only know that the death of two, and the possibility of even more death, brings great fear to our trod. Who can think clearly when so many terrible things are happening at once?"

"You should not worry," Gangahar told the frightened listeners.

"I do worry," Horhon interjected, digging her sharp toenails deep into the ground to show him how resolutely she felt. "Something out there is killing our hunters, and while we wait here the answer eludes us. Now tell me Katakana, do you have the answer?"

"Perhaps. They left together, they returned together. So therefore whatever found them is not here, but out there."

"Where did they go hunting?"

"I believe it was west of here." Antayak straightened his stance because every hunter was now looking at him. "Before everyone sickened, Ilon told me they tracked a herd of nentenens to the river where they killed one."

"Then that is where we will look first."

The journey was largely an uneventful one, though Horhon ordered everyone to be on their guard, for there was no telling what kind of danger they might find up ahead. Gangahar was looking about the field when he spotted a nentenen lying on its side in the grass.

It was dead.

As they circled the carcass Katakana noticed a repellent stink. She moved in closer and pointed out something very peculiar. "Look. This one has no wounds. It just died."

Horhon bent toward the gigantic corpse and sniffed. "It has been dead for a while. More than a day." Glancing skyward she noticed a flock of soros circling overhead. "Strange, they should have picked its bones clean by now."

"Over here," Gangahar shouted from across the field. "I found another one."

This time it was a crested mullatod, its spotted hide torn open where some animal had fed on it; several soros lay sprawled on the ground nearby. Horhon looked up as Antayak came speeding in.

"There are more bodies at the river. Others are spread out on the field. They too are dead," he informed them.

Gangahar grimly agreed. "So many animals dead. What could have killed them all?"

"Something. We must look closer." Horhon was determined to resolve their ignorance surrounding this mystery. Seeing all these bodies made her want to find the answer all that much sooner because this awful thing might happen again. However the answer eluded her. She was greatly troubled by this fact, that what should have been easy to understand was not, and though the sun was now up high this whole affair was still a complete mystery.

"Whatever happened here is still happening. Look." Katakana pointed to a soro that was flopping about in the grass, writhing in agony. She drew her claws and killed it quickly. "Two of our own hunters dead, others dead here. I fear there will be more death coming."

"Then our lives depend on us finding the cause of it that much sooner. Now find me the answer," Horhon told everyone urgently. "It must be here, somewhere."

An animal track led straight down to the beach. There was a narrow strip of coarse sand running to the water's edge, though the river itself was filled with larger stones that the breaking waves splashed over.

And something else was caught there.

Wading out into the white foaming water Horhon pushed the animal's dead bulk over. A tarser. It had probably died somewhere upriver and the current carried it down here and washed it up onto the rocks. But what had killed it? She looked across the water and spotted another one beached further down. There were probably more bodies. She would never find out standing around here. Climbing back onto shore she shook herself dry and leapt away.

Gangahar was the first one to notice Horhon was missing. After a brief search he picked up her scent and tracked her to the river. There the trail ended. She must have crossed over because her tracks were nowhere in sight. Perhaps he should return to tell the others. The sun was hot on his face and he licked his dry teeth as he approached the water. As he was about to drink, something landed with a splash behind him. He felt a pair of strong hands tug on his tail and pull him forcefully backwards.

"What is the matter with you?" he snapped. "Let go of me!" Again he tried to wrench himself free yet Horhon still held fast to his tail.

"The water . . ." Her mouth gaped open, she was breathing that hard. "Don't drink it!"

Though Gangahar was still angry his face had a puzzled expression. "Why not?"

"Because I found something. But first we must go back and tell the others."

He was piqued for her not telling him now. Whatever it was she was going to show him had to wait until they returned to the others. Curiously, she also ordered them to not drink from the river. After a short while they came to a place where a small stream emptied into the larger river. Oddly, the thick shrubs and grass that grew along its banks were brown and shriveled up.

"Do you see this?" Horhon pointed.

He did. The water flowing out of here was thick and black and it smelled incredibly bad. Gangahar had to stand away and take a deep breath of air.

"Smells terrible," he choked. "What is it?"

Instead of responding, she leapt away at a fast pace. Further upstream Gangahar finally caught up with her. That was when he noticed the odd-shaped rocks piled up on the bank behind her, yet after a closer inspection he realized that these in fact were not rocks at all, but something else. Several of them were broken open, their smelly contents drained dry, though many of the others were still leaking directly into the stream. Gangahar had a bad feeling when he saw that this was the spot from which the foul stench emanated.

"What is this strange place? And what is that spilling into the water?"

Finally Horhon spat with fury. "Poison!"

"So you believe this is what killed our hunters, also killed all those animals?" He took her grim silence for agreement. For a moment he glanced back at the heap of drums. Undoubtedly she was thinking the same thought. "I can think of only one place from where this might have come."

"There is death in everything these Iranha do," Horhon said bitterly. "It is not enough that they trap and kill us. Now they poison us with their garbage."

"At least we know. No more of us shall die."

"I fear there are other places like this one, and we shall see more deaths in the future."

"So what now?"

"We return to tell the others. Come on," she said. "I want to get out of this place immediately and never come back again."

Chapter 18

These past four days had been the longest in Ilon's short life. Katakana told him he could have died, yet he never actually considered the possibility since most of that period was just a painful blur. While the illness was still with him, he was improving. Yesterday he was able to stand up. Today he could walk, though not very far, yet each time he went a little further he knew that he was getting stronger.

On the sixth day he managed to climb outside and hobble onto the field, though by the time he sat down in the grass he was so exhausted one of the hunters had to carry him home. After three more days he was close to normal. The only reminder of the past now was his interminable headache, but this too was starting to ebb.

Unfortunately Krugjon's recovery came at a much slower pace, yet he was beginning to show some signs of improvement. His fever had broken and he was able to speak again. However his vision had not improved at all, and after waiting and hoping it would change, everyone in the trod knew this disability was a permanent one. He was blind and would never see again.

At first Krugjon refused to believe it. He swore it was just a temporary condition that would soon correct itself. Although this never happened he persevered, going outside every day to hunt. It had been days since he had eaten, but he was more stubborn than he was hungry. When Horhon insisted that he eat some of her food he hurled it to the ground and screamed that he would sooner die than eat something that he was unable to catch himself. It was insane for him to go on like this. Everyone in the trod could see he was wasting away, yet he was a hunter and could choose whatever he wanted. Any sort of discussion with him always ended in argument. He never listened, until the day he ran head-on into a tree and broke his arm. The pain was awful and the broken bones never set correctly. That was when he finally gave up trying. Now all he ever talked about was his death.

Out on the field the sky was beginning to cloud over and distant thunder was the first sign that rain was coming. Some of the hunters were already asleep inside their burrows before a heavy squall sent the others jumping in off the field. Katakana was the last. In her mouth was a bloody hunk of meat which she deposited on the floor and nudged it gingerly forward with her toe.

"This is for you. Just killed."

Krugjon sniffed, then grudgingly accepted her offering only because he had no other choice. Making the slightest nod of gratitude he leaned forward and closed his jaws around the food, swallowing the meat whole.

Taking his eating as a sign of acceptance, Katakana mistakenly said, "You should come hunting with me tonight. I know a place where you can easily kill—"

"No!" His snarled response caused her to draw back; she would not ask him again. "I am useless to everyone, including myself. What good is a hunter if the only thing he can see is the darkness? It would be better if I were dead. I should have died with the other two," he said bitterly. "Then I would not be such a burden to everyone."

"The only burden is the invisible weight you put upon yourself. You are turning to skin and bones and will never get your strength back if all you ever do is sit around here. Instead you must adapt. You must find other ways to hunt."

"I cannot do it!" Close to tears, his teeth clenched, so great were his emotions. "I am not a hunter anymore, will never be one again."

Katakana turned away whenever he spoke like that. "I am going to sleep. This is now the time to think about tonight."

As expected, when she rose later in the evening Krugjon remained in his burrow, though she never bothered to ask him because she knew the decision was made. Sure enough, when Horhon tried to rouse him she was sent away after he told her to leave him alone.

"He will surely die of unhappiness," Horhon said to Katakana as she passed her in the tunnel.

"What can be done? He is a proud hunter who will never accept our help."

"The Iranha are the real cause of it. This would never have happened had he not drank their poison. To see him this way now makes me hate them more than ever."

"You must stop thinking so much of these Iranha," Katakana scolded her.

"You are right. I should just stop. I should never think of them again. And while all those around me are falling into their hands I should be thinking of anything but that."

"That is not what I meant," she scowled.

"Do you understand what is happening? I know you must, but I feel as if I am the only one to keep them from being forgotten."

"All your thinking and talking about them is starting to rot your brain, Horhon. To hate them as much as you do—and what has all of this accomplished? Are we any better off now?"

"If it is results you want then let us seek them out tonight."

"You mean strike at them again, risk our lives. For what? To be chased away, even worse—killed. No, I choose to stay here."

"And wait for them to come here to you?" Her anger was so great Horhon clenched her fists and shook them. "How can I make you understand that while we wait, while we do nothing, more hunters are being killed. Undoubtedly our turn is coming, unless . . ."

Katakana rolled her eyes, knew exactly what was to be said next. "Unless we listen to Ilon? He is too strange."

"Maybe to you," Horhon retorted with genuine pride in her voice. "Yet I see great things for him in the future."

"I see him just as he is now. The same," she added in the hopes of strengthening her argument. "It is hard to believe one like that can ever hope to accomplish so impossible a task, when we, strong hunters all, cannot face our enemy without dying."

"They are not invincible. Even they can be killed. So like us they too must be vulnerable, must possess a weakness that can be exploited. Ilon knows of things that we cannot. If there is any way to wipe out the Iranha for good, he will find it."

"Then he will search only to find what others have already found. Death." Her next thought she spoke with a level of honesty that few other hunters would have admitted. "I think I would rather run away from them than decorate the floors of their city."

What she said was not a good thing to say, though it was the truth and even Horhon herself was forced to acknowledge that she too, preferred this option. However, the situation and the circumstance were such that their only possible choices were to fight back, or face extinction. Horhon would have to convince her to fight, somehow.

"The time has come for us to leave."

"But why?" Katakana protested. "The hunting is good here—and the Iranha are almost certainly everywhere else."

"Is that all you want, to stay here and eat?" Appalled by Katakana's hard-heartedness, Horhon's sneered coldly. "Other trods are being destroyed. Can't you understand that to survive, to have lasting peace, we must fight."

"Then let the other trods come to us instead. I have no great wish to join your mission in death."

"We have no choice. Wherever we go the Iranha will find us just as they did in the past. Found us, attacked us, and chased us. Twice we escaped. Only the next time we might not be so lucky."

"I stay with you, Horhon, only because you are a proven leader. More than once you have guided our trod to safety. But Ilon . . . follow him . . ." Her deep voice trailed off to a low, steady hum. "I do not think so."

"Like it or not, one day you will. We all will."

"You can't be so sure."

"I can be. Was his birth not a sign to us all that someone or something knows of our plight? Why else do you suppose he is here among us when it is obvious he belongs on another world?"

Not all of her predictions were absolute, Katakana knew. In fact more often than not Horhon was wrong, or at least had given them information that any of the hunters could have figured out for themselves. All these seasons of waiting, hoping to see this bright future come about, only to see it worsen, discouraged her. But Ilon himself was proving to be the biggest disappointment of all. Saskakel was right. He was no Egris, nor was he any sort of decent hunter either. Yet Horhon was listening to him while ignoring the advice of her best hunters. Deep down Katakana secretly wondered how much longer she could bear listening to Horhon tell her about the future.

Not even once more, she was sure.

Chapter 19

"**W**hat is that you are making?" At the end of her question Horhon leaned forward and waited expectantly.

"A spear," Ilon replied.

Some of the others who were watching from nearby, saw what was going on and came over to get a closer look.

"What exactly is that?" Gangahar asked inquisitively.

He tried to explain, yet little of what he described made sense to his listeners. These were only vague impressions, old memories dredged up from his previous life, or it may well have been someone else's past. However he did recall an image of fur clad hunters, though his own interpretation elicited snorts of laughter from the audience. Finally he gave up and said simply, "A thing of death."

"Really? Let me see it."

One by one they passed the sharpened stick around, until it reached Saskakel, who as usual saw only what he wanted to see and pronounced it worthless. "Better thrown onto your fire to burn. Then at least it would be good for something."

Ilon would hear no more of his disaffection and took back the spear with a swing of his arm. "Just as you kill with your teeth and claws, I kill with this."

"You kill?" The shock of hearing him speak about killing for the first time set Saskakel stumbling backwards. He expressed astonishment, disbelief. "You plan to kill—with that—your death spear?" His jaw was clenched so tight that it was all he could do to keep himself from bursting out laughing.

Insulted by Saskakel's blunt remark, Ilon plunged the sharp tip of his spear deep into the ground. "Is that so hard to believe, that I can kill?"

"It is," Katakana admitted reluctantly.

As he stared around at the silent faces he knew they were all thinking the same thought. These hunters took his day to day presence here very much for granted. In fact many in the trod were still as yet undecided about his status, though most actually considered him just a helpless thing that needed their protection. He stomped his foot to show the strength of his feelings. No more! All that changed now. The future would be very different from the past. Yet he had no illusions about the future either.

"When I come back with blood on this, you will see that I can kill," he told them all.

The next morning Antayak's eyes were almost closed when Ilon poked his head through the opening of his burrow where he just had curled up to go to sleep.

"I'm going hunting."

"Not this morning." Antayak yawned. "So tired. We'll hunt after the sun falls."

The others were fast asleep in their burrows so Ilon slipped outside on his own, his spear at his side.

It was an excellent day for hunting. Already he had walked a good distance onto the field, never even once stopping to rest, and all the while his body dripping with sweat. Shielding his eyes from the sun he surveyed the shimmering territory ahead of him. Some sparsely planted grass ringed the sand dunes. Further to the west, where the hills flattened out, he could just make out the pointed, snow-capped teeth of a mountain range beyond. Snow. Ilon touched his forehead and wiped away the film of grime and sweat. He had forgotten what it was like to be cold, for he had lived all his life here, close to the desert. But being within sight of the mountains reminded him of his other life, when winter reached down into the valleys and hills, bringing with it fierce winter winds and blowing snow. It was a lifetime ago, yet he could almost smell the frigid wind right now, feel its icy blast shocking through him. Maybe he would go to those mountains and see, some day.

An animal trail crossed in front of him. The track was made by a creature he did not recognize, yet he could see where its claws dug into the sand. Ilon raised his spear. With much practice his aim was improving and he could now throw his spear and seldom miss its target. Yet he and his tiny spear were no match against a big meat eater, and so he steered clear of its spoor and headed north instead. Only later did he come upon the freshly butchered remains of a nentenen. An experienced stalker had killed it and would undoubtedly soon return. And these were the same tracks he had seen before. Ilon hurried away.

Something was just ahead of him. Climbing warily up the steep side of the dune he peered over then lifted his spear with satisfaction. Three tarsers were grazing below in the grass. Taking aim he drew back his arm and fired. His spear arrowed straight and struck one of the creatures in the midriff. It dropped and writhed in a spasm of agony before it died. He ran forward as the others escaped. They were well out of sight before he reached its body.

As soon as Ilon wrenched his spear free, he sighed. This tarser's vile meat would sustain him. How he wished for a deer instead, or better yet, a big mammoth. He knew it was pointless to think about these things. That world was gone. He was here now, so this was where he would hunt.

The tarser was heavier than he first thought. As he reached the next dune he tugged on the animal's dead weight and struggled uphill, knowing he still had a long ways to go. Perhaps he should not have come out this far. With no wood to burn, he decided just to butcher the animal here, carrying only what he needed to eat. Severing the hindquarters, he heard running footsteps behind him, turning just in time to see a karafin lunging straight toward him; its teeth-filled mouth was gaped wide.

Without hesitation, Ilon reached for his spear, plunging it deep into his attacker's chest, though not before the animal raked its claws across his shoulder and arm. Red blood gushed from the open wound. Falling backwards from the force of the blow he grimaced as he struggled back to his feet. The big meat-eater was nearly double his size and could easily outmaneuver him. It stood poised on its haunches, ready to strike again.

Now the two of them stood unwavering, each waiting for the other to attack. Finally, Ilon took the first slow step backwards, waited, and then stepped again. With no spear, he had no wish to die fighting over a worthless lump of meat.

The air was dry and hot under a thickening gray sky that had only the appearance of the sun behind it. A strong wind gusted from the northwest, sending with it darker storm clouds that obfuscated the sun completely. Soon fierce winds whipped up the sand around him, obscuring everything, yet he struggled on through this blinding haze, hoping to find his way home.

By the time the storm was over he realized that he had wandered out even further into the desert. While he brushed himself off he felt the throbbing pain in his shoulder and saw that it was still bleeding.

That was when he noticed something very peculiar.

Surrounding him on all sides were several huge bumps in the sand where the windstorm had covered over. There was something very large buried under here; he could tell they were not a natural part of the landscape. Any hope that this might be a dune vanished when he climbed up the side and brushed away the sand. Whatever this thing was, its shiny green surface was rock hard and could not be scratched. What exactly had he stumbled upon here? And what was this? As he brushed away more sand he saw what appeared to be ice. Smooth, clear, but not cold, and he could see right through into its belly. He decided this was very strange and interesting, so he jumped down and started looking around to see what else he could find.

There were more pieces to this puzzle. Directly ahead of him appeared to be a walled structure with a black hole that he could see straight into. A cave? Ilon thought curiously. If it was, then it was a very strange looking cave. The shifted sand had buried most of the doorway and spilled down onto a floor of some kind. Lying flat on his stomach, he crawled closer and peered inside. The room had a very large interior that extended for as far back as he could see. Up on the cavern's ceiling shone rows of bright lights that he was sure could not be fire. Where he was looking there were odd shapes, stacks of things that could not have been put here by this desert. Rather, it appeared to be a purposeful construction. With this understanding came the grim awareness that only one creature could have possibly built this place.

Iranha.

Ilon cursed his bad luck. In his stupidity he had inadvertently walked right into the middle of the Iranha. Luckily, their cave appeared to be deserted, yet he wished no other surprises like the karafin's unexpected attack earlier, so with the utmost caution he climbed onto his feet and started backing away. One step. Two.

Suddenly he stopped dead in his tracks, his eyes frozen towards the horizon. Straight ahead, something was coming this way. In a panic he quickly retreated, running, stumbling over top of the sand. Once he crested the dune he threw himself down. Though he was out in the open, he was reasonably well hidden and lifted his face just enough to be able to get a good look at what was approaching.

A four-passenger road vehicle rolled up quietly towards the compound, passing the big earth movers and heavy construction equipment before its six wheels squealed to a dead stop. There was a hissing sound as the passenger compartment unlocked and slid open. Two Iranha exited from either side of the vehicle.

"I hate the desert," Nalanusat complained, dabbing his dry skin with a moist phillum bar. His female companion, an ex-combat soldier named Qantoquil, surveyed the surrounding territory with a trained warrior's keen eye.

"That sand storm has made quite a mess of things, buried all of their construction equipment."

"Unfortunately, not enough to slow them down."

He was right. Despite all this sand, she could tell that once the workers returned, things would return to normal before this same day ended. "Their work here is progressing quickly."

"Then we shall have to put a stop to it." Nalanusat walked behind their vehicle and pulled the latch. Inside were several small canisters which he now unfastened and quickly deposited on the ground.

"Be careful with those," Qantoquil warned him. "If not properly handled, gnarox can be highly unstable."

"I know what I'm doing," he replied testily, only because females always questioned male competence.

She looked up to see the sun breaking through the thinning cloud. "The storm is over. That means we don't have much time."

"Enough to complete our task here. Take these and start over there." In his haste to hand them over he clumsily let go of one, and watched, horrified, as it fell freely to the ground. Qantoquil reached downward and quickly retrieved the device.

"You idiot! We're not trying to kill anyone—especially ourselves. Now put those down immediately before the workers return to find us in pieces."

"Here," Nalanusat huffed. "Do it yourself."

Once Qantoquil was on her way some of the anger left her face. She had spent too many years in city Tykrerek's armed forces to know what this sort of explosive could do. As a trained explosives expert she had seen the results of her own work, innocent people blown to bits, if only to further a corrupt government's baseless claim of terrorism. The truth was, they were murdering their own citizens to stoke the public's outrage against the environmentalists. She no longer wanted any part in sanctioned killing. Not that she cared about these environmentalists; there were many more pressing matters than picking up garbage. Poxiciti and his wild-eyed followers were merely a popular diversion who filled their listeners' empty heads with promises of change. He was a publicity seeker, a fast talker who ultimately would ruin himself with the same excesses that had corrupted this present government. Then the fickle public who once supported him would refocus their attentions on the next messiah. Nevertheless for now she would continue working for them—their money was as good as anyone's. What did she care of their pitiless environmental anthem? To see Pulima Cos and her evil regime destroyed was always her first and strongest desire.

The charge was magnetized and adhered to the machine's metallic shell. Closing the wedge of her hand on the arming mechanism there was a high pitched whine now emanating from the canister. After placing another five charges she returned to their vehicle to pick up some more. Nalanusat was working on the opposite side.

"How goes it?" he shouted over to her.

"Almost finished. Three more."

"Did you place charges in the storage facility?"

"Enough to collapse the roof. All that sand piled on top will do the rest."

"What about those machines over there?" he pointed.

"Impossible. There are not enough charges to destroy them all."

"This is our one chance to strike at them. The next time we return to this place it will be a city, filled with polluters and destroyers who will sully the landscape like an animal that defecates its waste. So think about this before we leave. We can prevent that from happening."

"A delay, that is all. This city will be here despite what we do. And do not include me in your environmental fanaticism. I don't care about your cause. What matters most to me is that we get out of here in one piece."

Nalanusat turned to the smaller pieces of equipment with his gulun gun. He fired one burst; blue flames and smoke erupted from the center of a smashed digger. This was one less machine that he knew would hinder the builders. In the meantime their environmental movement was regaining popularity. Resettlement from their home world to here was bringing not only more people, but the same problems that everyone back on Epiphiline was in such a hurry to get away from. Nalanusat remembered the stinking, choking air, the daily pollution alerts. All that could easily come back, and would, if cities like this one continued to be built. His attention returned to the present when he realized that Qantoquil was standing next to him.

"Done. Now let us go."

Ilon had been running for a long time. The forest was closer but still a long ways off. Once he looked back, only to see thick black clouds rising in the same direction he had come from. He knew that if he slowed for even a moment he would collapse from exhaustion, so heavy were his legs. Eventually, even despite his great stamina he tumbled over and fell face first into the hot stinging sand. His teeth were clenched together as he moaned in agony, unable to move.

With much effort he hauled himself up, just to flop back down, clumps of sand sticking to his sweaty face. He felt too miserable, too exhausted to get up.

A cackling sound opened his eyes and he was startled to see three soros maneuvering around him; six others were circling overhead. Each of them, exceeding the length of his arm, was testing his responsiveness by coming ever closer. A handful of sand was all he needed to send these ugly, buzzard-like things skyward.

Back on his feet Ilon forced himself to keep walking. Something rustled in the grass and he was keenly aware of a dark shape crawling in and out of his sight, keeping pace with him. His only weapon was a sharp stone that he used for skinning; hardly enough to scare off whatever was stalking him now.

Leaping across the field two Egris hunters swung straight towards him. Horhon was first to come down in the grass beside him while Antayak overshot his mark and landed a short distance away. There was a horrible screeching noise, and the next time Antayak lifted his head red blood splotched his face and teeth.

"So once again I find you on these plains. Alone," Horhon said angrily. It was not a question, but a fact he couldn't deny. "Were you not supposed to take Antayak with you? That was our agreement." She was furious. He had disobeyed her, even lied, or at least he had attempted to deceive her. This would not happen again. Folding her arms across her chest she said, "All sorts of dangerous animals are stalking out here. See, Antayak has just killed one now." She bent forward and noticed his gashed arm. "What attacked you?"

"A karafin. I stabbed it with my spear, ran."

"As you should have. What is your puny spear against a big stalker like that? For what reason did you foolishly risk your life to be out here?"

At first Ilon didn't want to tell her, he even considered lying to her, though she would easily see through this bald-faced deception. Then he thought of the Iranha. Talking about them would make her forget everything else.

"I was hunting," he admitted, then quickly told her, "But that is only a small part of what happened. A wind storm sent me wandering in the wrong direction. I was lost. When the storm finally ended I knew at once this place was not where I wanted to be." Ilon pointed to the horizon, the black clouds were still clearly visible. "I should have left immediately, walked away, but once I knew what I had stumbled onto it was too late."

"What happened?" Horhon now had to ask him. "What did you see?"

"The Iranha."

At once her eyes looked towards the horizon. Perhaps it was a good thing he had seen the Iranha first. If they were that close then the whole trod had better leave the area before the Iranha saw them.

"How many?"

"Only two," he answered.

"Where there are two, there will soon be more. Were you seen?"

Ilon was sure he couldn't have been, otherwise he would be dead. His slow head-shake indicated a negative, though what strength he had left to support himself now departed, and his legs collapsed underneath him.

Picking him up in her arms Horhon quickly carried him home where he lay recovering for the remainder of the day in the cool comfort of his burrow. At nightfall he stirred awake and walked out of the tunnel into the central chamber where he found the hunters anxiously waiting, maybe for him.

"Are you well tonight?" Horhon asked concernedly.

"Better," he acknowledged. On the floor was a slab of raw, bloody meat someone had brought in for him that he now hacked off a piece and held it to the fire. Fat juices dripped off the meat and sizzled on the hot coals.

Gangahar stirred behind him. "Tell us what you saw today."

He had expected this, that everyone would be curious to know what happened to him out there and maybe to decide for themselves if they were in danger of being killed. As Ilon recounted his wild adventure in front of everyone, gradually, he could see from the look on their faces that this story of his sounded like an elaborate prevarication that no one wanted to believe.

"It did happen," he protested. "Exactly as I said."

If anyone had any doubt about his veracity it was Saskakel. "These Iranha things destroyed their machines?" He turned to the others. "Or perhaps what he saw was his own imagination. Not only is this creature no hunter, he is a liar too."

Angrily, he hurled his meat at Saskakel, catching him off guard by striking him square on his snout. "I am Egris!"

The big hunter opened his great jaws and roared. "You are not one of us!"

This time Saskakel had gone too far. Ilon could feel the pressure in his chest building, barely able to keep himself under control. Had he been holding his spear, he might well have driven it into him, he was that close to killing.

No doubt Ilon's very presence here among them was an ambiguity in the natural order of things. He was as much out of place in this world as were the Iranha. He should not have been here. Rightly so, at the very least he should have been hunting on the endless grasslands, or wintering in the mountain caves of his ancestors. How had he come to be here? This was an important question to ask himself, yet even more importantly, what power had resurrected him from the dead—and why?

But the answer to that was right before him. He was to be the nexus, the link between two disparate peoples. For him his future was already charted, the path he was on so clear, so straight, that he knew the ending just as surely as the beginning. Although Ilon's life was just short of three seasons, still a baby, somewhere else he had lived an entire lifetime. And so when he spoke next, he spoke the words of a man and hunter.

"You have puzzled over my existence, have argued that I cannot possibly be Egris, and yet trapped inside of me is the mind and heart of a hunter who thinks and believes just the same as you."

Even with Horhon's icy stare bearing down on her, Katakana spoke her innermost thoughts aloud. "How is it that you, small one, are Egris, when you appear to belong on another world?"

Of course she was absolutely right.

"The fate of our two worlds is inextricably joined together," Ilon simply and grimly explained. "Mine is dead, yours is dying. And without me, yours too shall come to the same end."

Most would have gaped at his audacity—a few did, yet it was of paramount importance he make his thoughts perfectly clear on this matter. He knew there were contrary opinions to his own, yet he spoke with such assurance that even his detractors kept silent.

"Have none of you ever wondered why I am among you? You should. Is it coincidence that I am here just as the Iranha are here? Once I lived and saw the world in a very different way. But this does not mean that the problems of the past are any different than the problems of today. Here the Iranha are everywhere. There we were oppressed by this same kind of enemy. They were ruthless killers who could not be talked to or bargained with. So we fled and died in the miserable cold of our mountains." Talking about the Uta opened up old wounds. And though he did not wish to remember any more he was determined to finish.

"You hate the Iranha." Holding up two fingers he said, "I doubly hate them. Hate them once because they are exactly like my old enemy, a different kind of killer, yet the same destroyer. And hate them twice because I see your future just as I once saw my own. If I speak so strongly of the past then it is to impress upon your brains just this one thing: we must fight the Iranha. Or die." In his first lifetime a cruel history of circumstances had driven the Taal to their doom. That did not have to be the same eventual fate awaiting these Egris.

"Fight them? With what?" Katakana broke in over the strong objections of the other listeners. "We attacked them once before and have been running away ever since. If you know these Iranha as you say then how do we stop them? Can we stop them?"

"No. We cannot. Not alone. What is a single trod against a city of uncountable killers? To be successful we must band together, unite our forces and drive these creatures away forever."

Her eyes widened with disbelief. "You wish to attack them head on. A quick slaughter ending in a quick death. The end of us all! Insane!"

"Only if we are united together by our desire to destroy the Iranha can we ever hope to be victorious. There are other trods out there. They too must know about the Iranha, must hate them with the same intensity, and wish them dead. So they must be recruited for this great task."

"And this is your plan for us?" Saskakel roared with anger as he smashed his tail against the floor. "To unite our trods just to be wiped out that much sooner!" He leaned over Ilon, his mouth agape, his deadly rows of teeth glinting in the firelight. "Better for all of us if today you had been eaten! May that day come soon." He spun about and left. Norgolash, his burrow mate, started getting up to go after him.

"Leave him," Horhon ordered. "We could all stand a little less hot air."

The evening passed by quickly and very soon it was dawn. Behind him, Ilon's deleterious companions were still huddled together. But rather than discuss anything of relevant importance they preferred instead to complain, mostly because it gave them something to talk about, though after last night's melee they avoided the thorny issue of the Iranha altogether and lowered their voices whenever he was nearby.

Ilon was tired of listening; he knew what they were saying about him. Still, he was unhappy because he had forced them all to think about their eventual fate together. Regrettably he realized little of what he said had influenced them. Like him the Egris lived their lives from one day to the next, hunting and eating. However, where they differed was their outlook on the future. What really mattered most to them was today, only today, for that was as far into the future as any of these wild hunters ever bothered to think about. Maybe he was just wasting his time, yet he had to convince them, force them to see his way, somehow.

"Time to sleep," Horhon said as she uncoiled her tail and stretched.

As she was walking past Gangahar the tip of her tail brushed up against his leg. Understood. After she was gone he rose from his place and disappeared into the tunnel behind her. Katakana grinned toothily, as did Norgolash. However Ilon was unsure about what had just transpired, although he was sure that if he asked no one would tell him.

By early dawn the next day Antayak returned to the burrow to tell everyone how he had spotted the Iranha on the field. Something was going on, so during the night while the Iranha were gone, the hunters slipped out of the forest to see what they were doing. To those who saw these big machines for the first time it was a very disturbing thing to look upon because now the Iranha were really here. Ilon was not at all surprised to see them, for this was exactly what he had warned everyone about.

Over the next several days more of these machines appeared. As each day progressed the hunters could see that something was taking shape on the field. Apparently the Iranha were erecting some sort of barrier. To Horhon what they were doing was appallingly clear.

"They are building a city. A place where their kind congregates and lives."

"Not here!" Katakana screamed. She had heard that there were Iranha cities in the north, but now they were coming here. "What will we do? Leave again?"

"I think we must."

Leaving was the best thing to do. After all, staying here meant certain death, for their close proximity to this new city made them a sure target. And though the thought of leaving their hunting grounds was an unhappy one, fortunately Saskakel was the only real dissenter.

"I am staying."

Horhon was dumbfounded. "How can you think about staying when the Iranha are this close?"

"If we leave them alone, stay away from their cities, then why should they continue hunting us?"

"Why should they stop?"

"I'm not afraid of them," he growled. "Are you?"

"Your over-confidence will get you killed," she answered, irritated. "Again I ask you—will you come with us?"

He was looking in Ilon's direction. "No."

It was his own personal decision to remain. Even as one who commanded, for all her powers of persuasion Horhon could not prevent him from staying. In the trod everyone was equal. Members cooperated jointly together for each others mutual survival. Disputes were normally settled by consensus. Though she herself was leader and issued orders, Saskakel could do whatever he wished. So that was the end of it.

"Then—be well hunter."

They departed at once. Gangahar took the lead, and soon he and the others disappeared into the black depths of the forest. Just before Horhon joined them she glanced back one last time to see Saskakel standing alone. Raising her hand she waved goodbye.

He would not be alive for long.

Chapter 20

Trod Horhon had trekked for many days through the deep woods before coming out of permanent darkness into blue sky and sunshine. It was a welcome change to be jumping on the grassy fields again.

Happy to finally reach the end of their journey, Horhon ordered her hunters to scout this new territory. Later Norgolash reported seeing nentenens crossing the river. And when Gangahar returned to tell them of a giant herd of goud everyone was convinced that this was indeed a good place to be. But the best news of all came with Katakana, who now jumped in from the field and spoke as the dust settled around her.

"Game is plentiful. Meat animals are to be found everywhere. All that we need is here. Except Iranha. Perhaps we shall never see them again."

This too was Horhon's desire, though what Katakana had said was not even close to reality. "Never is a very long time, and I fear we shall see these Iranha much sooner than that."

Nevertheless, now was not the time to be thinking of them. Other details needed her close attention. And first among them to be done was to dig out their new burrow.

"Dig here." Horhon scratched her clawed foot across the ground. Norgolash was only too eager to start digging. Thick clouds of dust swirled upward out of this deepening hole, and very soon only the tip of her tail was visible.

By early next morning their task was completed and everyone admired their new sand burrow. Scraping the dirt from his claws, Antayak came through the tunnel into the central chamber. A small fire burned in its center, which by now seemed so ever-present that most in the trod walked past it without even noticing.

It was daylight and those who had labored all night now retired to their burrows to sleep. Even with so much to do Horhon felt herself being unconsciously pulled to her own burrow. The others were already curled up inside fast asleep, though she noticed that Ilon's hollowed out hole was empty.

"And where do you sneak off to so early this morning?" He had left a strong scent that was easy to track. Her big eyes narrowed when she noticed his spear. "Hunting? Do not even think about it."

"I do as I wish," Ilon said, the firmness of his words telling her that this would be his decision alone. "I am a hunter, not a baby."

"There must be another way," she told him firmly, implying that he was the one who would have to change. Horhon knew she was being overprotective but it was for his own good. "There are too many dangers, too many opportunities for something to go wrong. You must promise me not to hunt alone again."

Although he did try to argue she was resolute in her determination to make him do this for her. And so when he went out hunting the next day Gangahar was close behind him. Ilon did not like this new arrangement at all. How was he ever going to kill anything on his own with Gangahar's hulking presence scaring off the animals that saw him coming? In his other life he had gotten used to fending for himself. However he could not rationalize his beliefs completely because he was no longer there—but here. If he did something stupid and died then all this would be for nothing, so he grudgingly accepted his hunting companion, but only for now.

"Time to go back," Gangahar said.

"It is still early," Ilon complained. "I want to keep hunting."

But he disagreed, saying, "You have speared your first tarser already. Is one not enough?"

"It is no good for eating." He spat on the carcass to show him how strongly he felt about having to taste its foul flesh. "I want to find a nentenen and kill it myself."

"Only a nentenen? Why not a big goud instead, great hunter?"

"Yes, why not?"

Gangahar knew very clearly what Ilon was thinking, and so he must quickly deflate his overblown ego lest he start believing this fantasy of his and get himself killed. "You misunderstand the meaning of my words. You will never get close to the goud with your pointy little stick. One tail swipe and you would be flattened, or perhaps fall under its feet to be trampled. Either way you would die just as quickly. So why foolishly risk your life to kill something that can easily kill you?"

"I have told you that I must hunt."

"I know that you must—but you are going to get yourself killed." His ears twitched slightly as he stared in Ilon's direction. "Come over here," he said, his voice low. "There is something hiding in the grass close behind you." As soon as Ilon was out of the way Gangahar leapt forward and roared violently. The dark shape of a karafin suddenly appeared upright in the grass. As expected his menacing presence sent it hurtling away into the field.

What he had just done made Ilon feel all the more bitter. Walking over to where Gangahar was now standing he threw down his spear. "You are right. I am no hunter. Not on this world."

"I do not understand. The danger is gone."

"Yes, but if not for you I would have been its next meal."

"They are noisy things. I heard it coming before I ever saw it in the grass. You should not worry because my ears are bigger than yours."

"I don't. I only want to hunt the bigger animals like you do."

"Those are for big hunters. You are a small hunter, Ilon."

He sighed in unhappy agreement. "Then for me it is this tarser, and there will always be plenty to kill because no one else will eat them. Now we go home, before I change my mind."

The day was bright, the sun hot, the sand sparkling through the shimmering waves of heat. Something appeared out of a dark hole and skittered across the dune. There was a high pitched scream, and whatever it had been chasing after, it now loped away with this same creature writhing in its closed mouth. In this crushing heat there was little else to be seen moving upon the field, except now as two solitary figures appeared at the crest of the hill, plodding slowly, steadily forward.

"Look, they are coming now," Katakana said.

His arms caked in sand, his face dripping with sweat, Ilon glanced up occasionally as he hauled the tarser closer and closer to home. Only when he was off the field, when he crossed into the shadow of the first trees and the scorching sun was gone, did he recognize the hunter Katakana and his mother looming closer.

Seeing him with yet another tarser was not very encouraging, though Horhon was able to conceal her real feelings and tried her best to praise him nonetheless. "Your tarser looks very meaty," she remarked as she bent over and sniffed the hot carcass.

"Have some," he told them both, doubting their teeth would ever touch it..

Horhon looked away from Katakana who was shaking her head no. "We go hunting tonight." For better tasting meat, yet she dare not speak this thought aloud.

Frowning, Ilon tried to think of something good to say, could not, so instead he dropped the animal's dead bulk in front of them, groaning as he rubbed his bruised shoulders where the leather thongs had bitten into his flesh.

"Gangahar could have carried this dead weight for you," Horhon told him.

"Next you will have him do all of the hunting for me as well," he told her scornfully. He was unrepentant and would not be deprived of the one last thing he was capable of doing himself.

Horhon was very close to losing her temper. He was getting more and more rebellious all of the time. Antayak and Yahu were now his only companions, as he often criticized the others and referred to them as his baby-sitters. Even if she had put a stop to his going outside by himself, whenever she tried to regiment his other activities he disobeyed her orders and undoubtedly he would do the same in the future. What could she do? There had to be a solution.

"We must talk," she said firmly, indicating the space in front of her. "But first you must promise me that you will not get angry at what I have to tell you."

"I promise nothing." He stabbed the point of his spear into the ground and squatted down beside it.

Without thinking she bent over him and bellowed, the forcefulness of her breath blowing the hair off his shoulders. She did not care for his kind of backtalk. However, after her anger abated she realized he was not a child and could say whatever he wished. That would still take some getting used to.

"There is a baby coming soon," she quietly told him.

Somehow Ilon wasn't too surprised with this news, although he now felt a little jealous because very soon there would be another sibling to compete with for her attention. "A new brother or sister. This is good," he smiled thinly.

"Then you are not upset with me?"

"Maybe a little," he admitted. "Then I am no longer your baby?" All along this was his hope, that she would let go of him and start letting him make his own decisions.

"You are a hunter. But that does not mean I approve of you going off by yourself," she repeated. "Whether you agree or disagree I am still your mother, and that is a bond that can never be broken."

Her decision was made and he had no choice. Ilon rose to his feet, trembling with pent-up frustration. He would not be restrained by her fears, but before he was able to express these feelings Katakana came in between them.

"Wait. I see two problems—and the solution to both is simple. Ilon wishes to be free to hunt. Krugjon is blind and needs a guide. If one cannot hunt and the other cannot see, then why cannot one help the other?"

"Why of course," Horhon said, suddenly excited. This was exactly the solution she had been seeking. Ilon, however, was still warming up to the idea and needed convincing. "You are his eyes, he is your teeth. Think about what the two of you might accomplish together."

He scowled. It sounded like another way of controlling him, and yet despite his suspicions he slowly shook his head yes. "I will do as you ask. I will go to Krugjon and explain exactly what you told me."

"No," Katakana said. "He has his pride. Instead tell him you desire his help. He will like that."

Ilon wondered if it was the other way around. In any case, with Krugjon as his weapon he could now hunt the larger, faster animals, and still have no one but himself to decide when and where he would go. It might just work.

Later, while he was hacking up his tarser to eat, Yahu and Antayak came over to see what he was doing. Of course when he offered them some they shook their heads and politely declined. As soon as the smell of the roasting flesh reached their nostrils the two of them escaped outside, happy to be away from the stinking meat.

"What have you caught today?" Krugjon, the last to wake, appeared from out of the tunnel and stopped just short of the fire. He sniffed the polluted air, then made a face. "Smells terrible. It must be another one of your tarsers."

Ilon's laughter was automatic. If Krugjon had anything still left inside of him it was his brutal sense of humor. "Will you eat some?"

"Of your burnt meat? No," he gasped, holding up his one good arm in front of him. "But some raw meat. Is there any left?"

"Plenty."

For an Egris the size of Krugjon this was no more than a snack. Sniffing the tarser's remains he bit into it with his great teeth and swallowed it whole.

"Tastes worse than it smells," he complained.

"There are tastier animals out there," Ilon agreed. "You should try to catch one."

Then Krugjon fell silent and remained at bay. At times Ilon felt like him, desperately alone, and so deep inside himself that no words could describe his real feelings. Krugjon was alive, yet he was not living.

"Can this dark cloud of yours ever be lifted, for each passing day I watch you and wonder if there is any hope still inside you?"

"None," Krugjon assured him. "None at all. But do not despair for me. I am lost in this accursed darkness, a prisoner by my own choice, for had I the courage to bring about my death this pitiful existence need not be."

"You have the courage to live, that is what I firmly believe, for I know of no other with your strength of will."

"Don't say that. It is because I am too afraid to die, and were this fear of mine not so great I know I would happily embrace death."

"So you are blind, but does this mean you cannot see the world in other ways?"

"I see it only as a dark place, and my fervent wish is to see the end of it soon."

"Then unhappiness is your joy. You know that I am right because you stay here when you could be out hunting with the others."

Now the same bitter unhappiness was back in his voice. "No one would hunt with a cripple."

"I would." They were alone. He saw the moment was right and explained what he wanted.

It sounded very complicated, what Ilon was suggesting. And there were certain parts of his explanation which Krugjon outright rejected, though the more he listened the more he believed it could be done.

"I will help you," Krugjon said when Ilon was through. Ilon excused himself from Krugjon's presence and disappeared into the tunnel. When he returned he was holding out his riding harness.

"Here, let me help you put this on."

At first it was a very clumsy operation. Krugjon immediately became entangled and broke one of the straps.

"This is not going to work," Ilon decided. Being on the front was fine when his mother could see where she was going. "I need to be on your back so I can be your eyes."

Later, after making some changes to the harness they set out for the open field.

"Right! Go right!" Ilon screamed, pulling tight on the reins to bring him back on course. But Krugjon was going left when instead he should have veered right. Fortunately they barely missed the tree, and Ilon sincerely hoped they would never come that close again.

Nevertheless their early attempts at navigation proved unsuccessful, mostly because Krugjon was unaccustomed to taking orders. Twice he sent Ilon sailing through the air. The first time Ilon was lucky because the soft sand broke his fall, but the second time he landed hard on solid ground and they did not go out again for three days. After that incident Krugjon promised to listen to him and was his willing student.

Their training continued for many more days. Originally they both started out together as raw and undisciplined. They made many mistakes too, but they were slowly improving. Each day they rehearsed the same exercises, turning, stopping and starting, practicing until it was perfect. After the field they tried the forest and managed to negotiate all of the trees without a single accident. For Ilon it was a tremendous feeling of accomplishment. No longer was he just an unwilling acolyte riding on the back of his companion. Now he was part of an organized team, an active participant who planned and aided in hunting. Theirs had become a kind of symbiotic relationship, each of them depending on the other. Krugjon was in his thoughts as Ilon was in his.

Daylight soon became dusk and this was now the time to hunt. Climbing up onto Krugjon's back Ilon strapped himself in. The trod was to accompany them on their first hunt, for this is what they most desired.

"Are you ready hunters?"

Despite himself, Ilon was more excited than usual. Krugjon was a little nervous too, and had to pay close attention to Ilon's shouted commands once they were underway.

The pack traveled north together, out onto the open plains with only the stars showing in the dark sky. After a while they swung west and headed back into the forest. It was there they discovered the fresh tracks and stopped to get their bearings.

"Goud," Gangahar said, licking his chops. "I count seven, going that way."

Just as soon as they started they heard the distant sound of running footsteps; something was coming closer, and closer. Dark forms soon emerged from the darkness.

"There they are!" Ilon shouted. He tugged on the leather reins and steered Krugjon in their direction. "Go!"

They had to hurry because once the herd made it to the trees they would never catch them. As they closed in on the fleeing animals the hunters split apart into three groups and thus began the attack.

Although Katakana was in the lead, Ilon and Krugjon were closing the gap behind her. Ahead of them the herd was beginning to scatter.

"Go faster!" Ilon shouted. Steering Krugjon closer they were now jumping alongside one of the goud. "Ready . . . Ready . . . Now!" he cried out.

With a final thrust of his mighty tail Krugjon propelled himself high up onto the goud's broad back. Sinking his teeth into its hide he felt the hot blood gushing into his mouth. He bit deeper into the wound, wanting to taste more.

Moments later the rest of the pack converged on the goud, closing in on both sides so that it had no chance to get away. The animal came crashing down into the grass as it died.

"Meat, meat, meat," Krugjon said happily after he leaned over the animal's dead mass and tore away a bolt of flesh.

Nearby, Ilon watched and waited. These Egris take their hunting skills very much for granted, he thought jealously. Their teeth and claws were the only weapons they had, yet they were natural killing machines who seldom ever worried about going hungry. But to him hunting was much more than killing and eating, for the dead goud symbolized his ability to kill as they killed. He was one of them now. As for Krugjon, being here with his trod, this day, this moment, was the single greatest feeling he had ever felt in his entire life.

He was a hunter again.

Chapter 21

It had been a long summer and no one noticed it was over. But much further north, beyond the desert to the end of the great forest, in a remote region of their world that no Egris had ever seen, snow was falling. Here it never changed; the day after seemed no different than the day before. Sometimes it was difficult to tell one season from the other, yet seeing tens of thousands of goud rumbling off the plains and into the forest to ascend to their tree top world, was a sure sign that spring was coming.

The first thing Ilon did after killing the crested mullatod was to go back and search for his spear. He cursed himself. It was a bad throw. The fleeing animal had dislodged his spear before he and Krugjon were able to chase it down and finish it off. Not that his spear hadn't gone missing before, yet this time he was less certain about where it might have fallen.

After pleading with Krugjon to stay until he had made a thorough search of the area, at daybreak his crotchety companion talked of giving up and returning to the burrow to sleep. But Ilon refused to abandon his search.

"It is lost," Krugjon said confidently.

"No," he answered, pulling on the reins so that his reluctant companion would keep going forward.

"Why do you search for something that can be easily found? Are there not plenty of other sticks you can pick off the ground?"

Ilon did not want to speak about its importance because he feared Krugjon might laugh at his foolish beliefs. Yet he steadfastly believed that losing his spear was a loss infinitely worse than any kind of death. When a hunter died their spear was the most important thing that be buried with them. If he died without his spear he would not be welcomed into the spirit world; he would be rejected and lost forever. Egris beliefs were more mundane. They simply died, and whatever life-force they possessed became part of their world. A living world to which their souls mingled and joined. Agorgagoran, they called it. The return. The reunion of all things in the life force.

Antayak and Norgolash came in at dawn, both of their faces red with the blood of a fresh kill. Those who had gone out to hunt were now returning for the day, and all activity soon quieted as everyone went to sleep. This was life, simple yet satisfying, for if anyone had ever complained of it then no hunter could remember their name.

By early dusk Ilon was outside, sitting pensively by himself. Actually he had slept little during the day. Not having found his spear deeply disturbed him. That, and the meat-eater who had managed to crawl to within an arm's length of him before Krugjon killed it from behind. Too many times he had been close to death, and he now was frightfully aware that this fragile life of his could end at any time.

Krugjon was a heavy sleeper and would not be awake for some time yet, so he built up a small fire and fanned it until the wood crackled and burned. Yahu soon appeared, followed by Norgolash, then Katakana, who left the others to come over and join him at the fire.

"You have eaten already?"

"No," he acknowledged. "I still wait for Krugjon."

"You will wait a long time," she muttered to herself. Obviously there was something on her mind, so she stated her thoughts without any formality or delay. "I wish to talk to you of a matter important to the both of us. For the moment I will say only that this is more important than hunting."

There were things being planned, and whatever was forming in her mind Ilon suspected it would not be good for him. "What is it that you want?"

"Not what, but who. I speak of Krugjon."

Perhaps it was just a coincidence because he saw his friend coming out of the tunnel right now.

"Greetings, Katakana." Even without his eyes Krugjon knew she was in his presence, unseen, yet visible to him, and he now shifted his weight so he was facing towards her and away from Ilon.

"I was thinking about chasing after nentenens tonight," Ilon told him.

Instead the hunter answered with silence.

What is going on? he wondered. Katakana was here, Krugjon was here. Yet it felt like he was not here at all. Even in the silence Ilon could hear their thoughts telling him to leave. He rose to his feet, determined to break apart whatever was between them. "We should go hunting."

"Not tonight." Oddly it was Katakana who answered for him. When she touched Krugjon's face the harshness was gone from her voice. "I wish a child, Krugjon. And I choose you as my burrow mate. Do you accept this responsibility and promise to stay with me until our baby has fully grown?"

"I do." They went off together.

Had Ilon not stopped them outside of Katakana's burrow he would have never retrieved his riding harness. Nevertheless she gave him a look that he was sure meant death and he should certainly not return again.

"I'm going hunting," Ilon huffed as he passed his mother in the tunnel.

"So where is Krugjon?"

He scowled. "With Katakana."

Obviously she was aware of this arrangement. "Do not be jealous of them. He is a hunter. She is a hunter. It is their wish to be together. There will be other nights to go hunting."

"Krugjon can stay here forever if he wishes it. I go."

"Name the hunter who goes with you."

"Not to worry," he assured her. "Antayak joins me this night. We hunt for nentenens."

While she approved of his plan outright she had one additional request. "Take Sanbat with you."

"Sanbat?" He shielded his face so that she wouldn't see his unhappy expression, yet still she heard it in his voice

Horhon crossed her arms. "And what is wrong with your sister?"

"Wrong?" Though at first he pretended ignorance she saw through this ploy easily enough and now waited expectantly for his real answer. Frantically he searched out his thoughts for the one right word which she might accept and relinquish him of his charge, although none were forthcoming.

While Ilon was thinking, dark memories of his younger sibling flooded in. Sanbat was still very much a youngster, having yet to speak her first few words of intelligence. Although Egris newborns had never been a cause for concern in the trod before, Sanbat's sudden presence opened their eyes to a new and unforeseen problem. Just born she was a creature of pure instinct, who attacked and ate anything that moved. Unfortunately for Ilon, she welcomed her new brother with open mouth. He grimaced when he recalled the hunters who had wrestled with her, who had pried her jaws open and pulled him free. And he had her teeth marks across his back and chest to prove it! However he objected to having her along because she was a clumsy and undisciplined hunter. Yet despite all of his excuses, in the end Ilon had no recourse but to obey the wishes of his mother.

"There is nothing wrong with her," he answered sullenly.

"Good. Then you will take her hunting with you."

"Yes." Ilon sighed. The excitement of trying out his newly made spear diminished since he expected their quarry would flee from her noicy presence.

After his riding harness was lashed to Antayak, Ilon mounted him and clung on tightly as they made off for the open country; Sanbat was leaping along beside them. They made good time. Behind them the red sun was setting beneath a nigrescent sky as the first stars appeared and the forest dimmed to a dark line. As their journey lengthened, Sanbat was trailing farther and farther behind. When she was lost behind a dune Antayak slowed to a walking pace.

"We should stop and wait for her to catch up," he said.

Ilon shook his head. "No. Do that and we could be chasing after her all night. As long as we lead she will keep following us."

"If you say so." Slapping down his tail Antayak took off into the air; the swirling dust cloud was all that remained.

Under the two moons' light they halted upon seeing a well-marked trail in the grass. Eagerly, they followed the scent west, only to find it eventually dead-ended on the muddy banks of a river. Sanbat was still well out of sight, but Ilon was angry that she was slowing them down and let some of this show through when Antayak spoke to him.

"Should we not go back to find her?"

"I'm staying right here," he said firmly. "I know her. She has more stomach than brains. She's probably eating."

"She could be lost."

His mood shifted a little when Antayak said this. But it was still not enough to cause him to change his mind. "Will you hunt, or waste the rest of our time looking for her? Decide now."

"I want to hunt."

"This is what I want too." Yet there was unhappiness in his decision. In a way he felt responsible for her and this was ever present in his mind so now he must choose. "We go back." He sighed deeply. "We go back."

Sure enough, within a short while Antayak picked up her scent and was quickly on her trail.

Where could she be going? Ilon wondered. They had already passed the point where they expected to see her. Still Sanbat was nowhere in sight. Nor could she have returned to the burrow because she was heading in the opposite direction. As they crested the hill Ilon saw that he was staring down into a shallow valley. Beyond was some thin cloud covering the horizon, wide enough where he could see it reflecting the lights of some nearby Iranha city. With both hands pulling back on the reins he dug in his heels as Antayak came to sudden halt.

"What is the matter?" As soon as Ilon pointed east did Antayak shake his head. "I see the problem. Her tracks lead down that hill, straight to the Iranha. Should we follow?"

"I think we must."

Their search ended very quickly in the valley, for it was here that they found her, bent over, tearing the flesh off of some creature she had chased down and killed.

Ilon was still too angry to think about eating, seeing the bright lights of the city and wanting to be as far away from here as possible. The moment Sanbat lifted her head to see him coming over he slapped her soundly across the snout.

"Well that was really stupid to run away," he scolded her. Again his hand was raised but he lowered it down when she started to whimper. "Do you know where we are? Do you know the Iranha are close by? Of course you don't. Because your brains are made of dead meat."

"Iranha," Sanbat growled, speaking that name more out of recognition than understanding.

"That is correct. Look over there." Ilon pointed to the glowing lights. "Iranha. City of death. Do you see it now?" He shook his head no just as Sanbat did.

"She doesn't understand you," Antayak said.

"You are right," he sighed. "I might as well be speaking to a rock."

"Make no sound!" Antayak whispered severely. Suddenly he threw himself down flat on the ground and lay completely motionless. Ilon crouched beside him while he sniffed the air and looked head on into the forest.

"What is it?"

There was a long space of time before Antayak answered. "I don't know. A strange noise." He lifted his clawed finger ever so slightly. "Over there."

In absolute silence they crawled through the undergrowth, moving out of the woods as they made their way across an open field under the cover of darkness.

Antayak was the first to see it, hissing a warning through his clenched teeth. "Iranha!" Sanbat started to growl but Ilon slapped her into mute silence.

What they were approaching was a compound of some kind, a large four-walled building with an adjacent fenced in enclosure, perhaps a holding pen. When Ilon crawled closer he saw that this was indeed its purpose. There was a large animal lying on its side in the corner.

It was an Egris hunter.

"What should we do?" Antayak whispered beside him. "Return to the burrow and tell the others?"

"And what will they be able to do that we cannot? This one is a prisoner and must be freed."

"It is too dangerous. The Iranha are here."

While they debated, it was Sanbat who made the critical decision. "Stop! Come back here!"

Ilon dropped back down, wild-eyed with panic. No time to think rationally. "Stay under cover and do not move from here," he ordered Antayak.

Except for Sanbat and the imprisoned hunter the surrounding yard appeared to be completely deserted. Ilon cautiously climbed to his feet and ran toward them.

All this commotion brought the hunter to her feet. Of course she was very much surprised to see Sanbat staring in at her, but then alarmed to see this other creature, whatever it was, come running over.

"Go back to Antayak." Ilon pointed to the bushes then spoke to his sister with great intensity. "Go now!"

When she disappeared back into the undergrowth the hunter crooked her head and stared at Ilon through the thick bars of her cell. "What are you, creature?"

"A hunter like you. I am Ilon of trod Horhon."

Her mouth gaped open. "You—You are Egris? How is that possible?"

"Silence. I will ask the questions," he said forcefully. "Tell me quickly, what is this place?"

"A slaughtering ground. A killing place where hunters are taken to be butchered and skinned. We were attacked three days ago, some killed, the rest of us brought here."

"There are others?"

"Were. I am the last, soon to die."

"Then these Iranha are here?" He tested the fence with both hands.

"They do their killing inside. You should get away from here, Ilon, before they find you and kill you too."

"Not before I set you free. My friends are hiding over there. I promise I'll be back soon."

He bent down into the grass and crawled back to his hiding place, finding Antayak just where he had left him. Sanbat growled but quieted the instant he raised his hand. "This is what we must do," Ilon explained, and then quickly shaped his thoughts into a plan.

Once they were in position he picked up the rock and threw it as hard as he could, watching with great satisfaction as it thudded loudly against the door of the building. On his fourth attempt a lone Iranha appeared in the doorway, then pushed the door wider as it stepped outside.

In a single bound Antayak hurtled out of the darkness, mouth gaping wide, claws extended, eager to rip it apart. Scrambling to his feet Ilon ran over to him as he tossed the creature's limp corpse into the bushes.

"Come on."

Inside was a lighted corridor which they followed to the end, through a second doorway, then into a large room filled with noisy machinery and huge vats full of foul smelling yellow liquid. There they parted. On his whispered orders Sanbat and Antayak slipped silently down the aisles.

Then suddenly Ilon heard shrieks of terror, instantly followed by screams of death. A sharp movement caught his eye and he braced as an Iranha lumbered straight toward him. Clutching his spear, he fired at his running target, but not before the despicable creature got off a shot that was too close. Ilon screamed and dropped to the floor as the wall behind him exploded in a flash of light and color. He rose and brushed off the debris, seeing the smoking ruin, now an immense hole where the solid wall had once been. As he approached the dying creature it squirmed and made horrible noises that made his head hurt. Withdrawing his spear, he struck again, happy to see the end of it. Now there was one less Iranha in the world.

After a thorough search of the whole complex Antayak returned with Sanbat and said, "All dead. None escaped us."

"Good. Go back outside and bring me wood," he ordered. "We must destroy this place completely so that it can never be used for killing again."

While Ilon awaited their return he found the sealed doorway leading outside to the animal pen. Frustrated, he swore and kicked at it, but the door wouldn't budge. In his desperation to free the trapped hunter, his mind returned to the burnt hole where the Iranha had shot its fire-stick. After retrieving the weapon he first studied it closely to see how it might work. He had a picture of it in his mind as he turned the barrel towards his face and peered at it with intense curiosity.

The blast shattered the ceiling above him.

Calming himself, this time he pointed the weapon and took aim. One burst from his gun was all he needed to bring the door down. "You are free hunter. Now come outside the walls of your prison and taste the sweetness of freedom."

She moved her body with pleasure and gratitude. "My name is Kykiris. I am grateful to be spared so terrible a fate, happy as well to see my captors deservedly dead. Are they all dead?"

"These ones—but not all. We will never be rid of them all until this is so."

"That would be my greatest wish. If only to live until that day, to die seeing their end."

"My wish too," Ilon said. He then told her of his hopes for the future.

Antayak soon returned with an armload of thick branches. Sanbat, close behind him, squealed happily as she handed over her one stick to Ilon.

"What is it that you are doing?" Kykiris asked him, now seeing that he was rubbing two sticks violently together.

"Making fire," Ilon puffed.

"What is fire?" She did not have to wait long. Within moments there was smoke, then . . . "Fire!" Kykiris screamed, watching with astonishment as the wood pile caught and flamed up high.

"Get more wood," Ilon urgently commanded. "Hurry!"

Soon the entire building was engulfed in flames and the hunters fled outside to escape. From a safe distance they watched with pleasure as the building collapsed under a great explosion of smoke and flames.

"A happy day this has happened," Kykiris said. "I marvel at your abilities, friend Ilon, and remember as I go what you have told me."

"Then you will speak of our future together with the other trods?"

"You have my word. I promise. For this task I pledge my life."

They parted friends. As Ilon watched her go he knew that he had his first real convert. And what was the beginning of a new friendship, he hoped, was also the beginning of the end of the Iranha.

Chapter 22

"**D**estroyed!"

Pulima Cos, her body quaking with rage, beat her fists on the shiny wet metal of her desk. So great was her anger that the messenger instantly recoiled in fear as she picked up her wet chair and hurled it as hard as she could at the wall. She could hardly speak, could barely move the air through her pores. When she reached the cowering messenger and seized him by his wattles of skin, only one important question needed to be asked.

"How?"

"By fire," he blurted out, recounting the exact message given him so that he would get every word right. "An explosion of great magnitude that leveled the entire building, destroying it utterly and completely."

A financial disaster, Pulima Cos thought, her body slumping under the weight of this devastating news. When news of this event reached the other cities many important and influential people were going to be very displeased with her. Some might even demand a return of their investment. Now she could only worry and wait for the inevitable fallout that was sure to come.

"Tell me what happened," she ordered him, her next words even more demanding. "Explain every detail. I want to know everything."

"I—I do not know," the messenger replied haltingly, wanting to please her with information but having nothing to tell her.

"Then were there any witnesses, any survivors at all?"

"Again, I do not know."

"You know nothing, stupid one!" Pulima Cos gestured annoyance. What she needed was accurate, first-hand information. Perhaps if she told him just how close he was to death then that might improve his memory. As she waddled across the floor there was an undulating swell of fat underneath her purple gown. "Who knows? Who sent you? Who is in charge of the investigation?"

At last the messenger moved with comprehension, eager to speak his answer and be gone from her sight. "Why Poxiciti himself is looking into this matter."

Pulima Cos writhed at the very mention of his name. "He is there right now? You saw him?" When the messenger indicated he had, she fought to compose herself. "Why that ugly thing? Why him? What does he think he will find out there?"

The messenger started to respond, only to be cut off by his own gasp when he realized that she was merely thinking her thoughts out loud. Fortunately she was too deep within herself to hear anything else but her own worries. He shrank back and awaited her next order.

To Pulima Cos this could not have been worse news. If Poxiciti was on the case he would undoubtedly learn the truth and ruin everything. Better for her if she had never let him live. From that first day she seized power she should have killed him. In the shortest time he had become her greatest enemy, and every day he lived was another day to regret his existence.

Not killing him when she had the chance was a critical mistake that might still yet bring her government down. One of her own now deservedly dead hahlok commanders had given him classified documents showing that city Tykrerek's main generating station had failed several safety inspections and yet somehow continued to operate despite supposedly strict government regulations. Further investigation showed that several well-connected company officials managed to avoid a public inquiry by paying off the inspectors. In addition, their superior was given explicit orders to bury the reports in return for an undisclosed cash settlement. It was so scandalous an affair that Pulima Cos and her administration were still reeling from the exposure. New charges were still being laid, and there were fresh allegations that several of her top aides also received expensive gifts and interest free loans.

Luckily for Poxiciti the people were still on his side. Pulima Cos tried to have him arrested, though his imprisonment sparked a revolt that very nearly toppled her government. Now her powers over him were limited, yet not so diminished that she still couldn't reach out and crush him. She wanted that very much. His outspoken tirades on animal rights and environmental lies were turning many of her own supporters against her. What a pleasure it would be to see him dead. Already she was busy plotting his happy and much anticipated demise.

After dismissing the messenger Pulima Cos sent for her attendant who promptly contacted Poxiciti. In the late afternoon he strutted into her office, his one good eye on her as he seated himself in a comfortable wet chair.

"You summoned me here? Why?"

She was not used to being questioned, yet she responded politely only because he was incredibly egotistical and might not tell her everything if she wasn't at least gracious. "To question you of a disturbance early this morning in the Noxada sector."

"Out of whose big mouth did you hear that?"

Snorting derisively she said, "Surely you, Poxiciti, must know that everything you do bears my closest scrutiny. Now—what can you report of this event?"

"Not much. Had I been allowed to conduct my investigation uninterrupted then I might have more to tell you," he huffed, indicating that his ordered presence was a great nuisance to his work. Despite this he managed to give a brief description of the event, then added discreetly, "The damage was rather extensive. There was little left on-site to salvage. However we did manage to retrieve something of significance from the rubble."

"What?"

"An important piece of evidence, without which we could not have completed the puzzle." Seeing her confused motions Poxiciti further clarified this point by telling her, "A surveillance camera was pulled intact from the ruins. I believe that when its contents are examined we will discover the nature of the building's demolition—and even more importantly—the identities of those responsible for the felonious activities going on inside."

Pulima Cos squirmed uncomfortably. "I don't understand."

"The building was an illegal facility being used to harvest segathars for skins. Also employing uncertified skinners and opportunists. Poachers!" Poxiciti said with all the vehemence he could muster.

"Monsters who should be punished," she quickly agreed and then carefully asked him, "Were any of these criminals apprehended and taken into custody?"

"Unfortunately, no. But happily they had the deaths they deserved. The bodies we discovered were burnt beyond recognition. All were incinerated by the blast."

"And the cause of the explosion?"

"Chemical. That kind of damage is indicative of orghalax, a popular yet highly combustible cleaning solvent."

"Then it was an accident of immense stupidity," Pulima Cos quickly concluded, hoping to deflect any further discussion and bring about a swift resolution. "Some wicked poachers are dead, and their facility rightfully destroyed. No doubt an immense victory for you and your followers. Now this whole sordid affair can be turned over to the district prosecutors, and I, happy to hear the end of it."

"I think not." Poxiciti then spoke with a firmness and resolve that made clear his intent. "This neat solution that you so readily and speedily advocate clearly smacks of a cover-up. No sooner had I given you this evidence would it have disappeared—and probably those of any knowledge along with it."

How he hated and despised her. Just seeing her made him want to kill her. He had unhappy memories of the past. As part of her austerity measures she had purged her new administration of males, replacing them with female conspirators and profiteers, anyone who supported the ecological rape of the planet. Political opponents were arbitrarily arrested and thrown into jail, or worse, disappeared. Environmentalists were kidnapped, then only to be found tortured and murdered. It was a very bad time.

But the dark days were behind them and the light of the future was shining up ahead. Activists were now rallying against her, the opposition was speaking out again. Pulima Cos's impervious armor was beginning to rust.

"There is working within your government an organization of complicity and corruption, one I believe that starts at the bottom and climbs to the very top."

But she repudiated his charge totally and absolutely. "Ridiculous. How can you make so absurd an allegation?"

Producing a piece of selp paper he proceeded to unfold it in front of her. "To operate this large a facility so close to the city requires the protection and financial backing of some powerful people. Traders, merchants, city officials. I wonder if Midlothian herself might know of its existence."

Pulima Cos could no longer sit still. She rose from her chair and paced the floor nervously. When Poxiciti handed her the paper she first looked it over with trepidation then strongly rejected it by crumpling it up and saying, "This proves nothing."

"Hardly that. According to those figures your own Tomauk is demanding a hefty salary for supplying soldiers to an undisclosed station outside of her city. Yet apparently this damning bit of information was retrieved from within the destroyed walls of the building."

"So now I see your insidious plan. That is to tear down my government with your fabricated evidence and untruths."

Poxiciti laughed hysterically. "Your ability to deceive is as inflated as your brains. You might address yourself to the real truth, and that is, while you conduct these nefarious activities and shady dealings, I come closer each day. The animals you slaughter are gone but your slime remains, a trail that if I follow will inevitably lead me straight to you."

"Get out!" Pulima Cos roared. "Get out of here!"

He had struck too close this time, and she believed that he could strike even closer. He would learn the darkest truth of which she shared the greatest part. Favors would have to be bought. And it would be very costly, Pulima Cos knew, though she was desperate to eradicate every shred of evidence which might condemn her. When Poxiciti was far removed from her sight she summoned her closest aides. What she needed was a diversion.

Chapter 23

His visit to city Anaxerxes was brief but decisive. Poxiciti knew the risks of such an encounter, but to see her corpulent bulk shaking with fear was pleasure among pleasures. Certainly he had wounded her. Now as he returned to his own city he looked forward to any new revelations that might deliver the final killing blow.

Under a dark, heavy sky, Poxiciti exited the shuttle and forged on through the blowing wind toward the main terminal. He made a wide track in the accumulating sand. Guards escorted him inside where he shook himself off and waited for the next transport to arrive.

Outside the storm was worsening, the wind hurling the sand against the windows with unrelenting fury. During this onslaught a bolt of lightning crackled across the sky, and the room suddenly blackened. Inside there was a lot of confusion, everyone was shouting, but none louder than Poxiciti who spoke with authority while those around him scrambled to do his bidding. Despite their best efforts those who labored under his direction were unable to restore the power, and so he sat down in the darkness and brooded. It was a frustrating end to his day and he was greatly displeased with this time-consuming delay.

Finally a passenger vehicle pulled up alongside the building and signaled. Poxiciti barely had time to open the door when Inelefar leaned over the driver's seat and shouted into his auditory hole.

"Came as soon as I could," he gasped breathlessly. "So much has happened since this morning." He seized Poxiciti's arm. He could scarcely contain his excitement. "We have to get back to the city." Poxiciti eagerly climbed aboard and awaited his stunning news.

"Then you have found incriminating evidence against Pulima Cos and her band of cut-throats?"

"Not exactly," Inelefar hummed as he pressed on the accelerator and sped off toward the city. "Something even more important."

He stared at him incredulously. "More important than seeing our arch-enemy and her army of polluters and profiteers eradicated? More important than overthrowing her corrupt and evil empire? I doubt that. Explanation of facts. What exactly did you find?"

"A discovery of incredible significance," Inelefar hinted without the slightest betrayal of information. "Evidence of a kind that will not be believed."

Now Poxiciti was more than puzzled. What could he mean? Inelefar was a good assistant but proved himself a worthless communicator. To pry information from him required the strictest attention, the greatest of patience. Poxiciti sincerely doubted that he would learn anything until they reached the city.

A small crowd was waiting for them inside the auditorium, an expansive room decorated with ornate marble columns and gold and onyx inlaid floors. Plush wet chairs lined the three main aisles, arranged in a semi-circle so that each occupant had a clear sight of the enormous view screen. As Poxiciti entered the room the onlookers immediately quieted down.

"So what is this momentous news that I still know nothing about?" he said after seating himself in a front row chair. An echo of silence was his only answer. Then a voice that he recognized rose behind him.

"A matter so vital to our future that I instructed Inelefar to tell no one, lest word of this reach the wrong people." Borobos, a solid and strong female, rose from her chair and thudded to the front of the room. A bio-genetic engineer, now a staunch environmentalist, she wore her scars like an emblem of pain, attesting to her years of torture and imprisonment in one of Midlothian's many jails. Indeed she was a creature of stature and political sway, having contacts that some said reached into Pulima Cos's closest circle.

"Tried to contact you in the city," Borobos apologized. "The storm was intense. . ."

"Understood." Poxiciti quickly dismissed it; he was more impatient for answers.

"The video we extracted today. Your conclusions proved correct," Borobos continued. "They were operating an illegal processing and distribution center. Had it not been destroyed it might well have soon emptied the forest of segathars."

This was especially good news to her listeners. Naturally everyone was pleased to hear of its end, delighted that every block and beam had been pulled down, although unhappily, Borobos reminded them that just as quickly as that one had been destroyed, another one would soon replace it.

Looking around the room Poxiciti saw all of the angry faces. Borobos elicited more hot emotion than rational thinking and that was not the way to see behind their problems. "Did you find any condemning evidence?"

"Some," she answered. "Solid and indisputable proof linking three of the dead to Oneteesel, a key trader from city Tykrerek."

"Small game, waste of time. What about Pulima Cos herself?"

"As of yet, nothing substantive."

Now he was more angry than impatient. "Why all of this mystery? Why is it that we climb hills when the mountain is still before us?"

"Because of this." Borobos ordered the lights dimmed. Moments later the view screen illuminated and on it appeared an image of what had to be the destroyed facility's interior. There was little of significance to see. Empty corridors, noisy equipment, people working. Very boring, Poxiciti thought.

That was until Borobos touched him on the shoulder and whispered, "Now watch carefully. You saw the destruction. Now you will see the destroyers."

He did as he was told, seeing a guard suddenly appear and angle into the main corridor. She went outside. Now the events quickly unfolded. Poxiciti was unprepared for what he saw next. He straightened up the moment he saw what came inside. It was astonishing, unbelievable! He sat riveted in his chair and stared in stunned silence.

"What is that thing?" someone gasped out behind him. Everyone was speechless. The big pack killers they knew of, but the one leading them was something entirely different. A small, repulsive thing, barely half the size of the segathars, its waist bound with skins, its head covered with fur.

Up until that moment Poxiciti had been rigid with concentration, but the magnitude of what he was seeing suddenly struck home and he leapt out of his chair and shouted, "Why their actions suggest a simple plan! Create a diversion, draw the guard outside. Then attack! Is it possible there is some intelligence within their bestial brains after all?"

"I believe so," Borobos replied. "These segathars appear to be thinking ahead. The strange one who leads them. See how it opens its hole and emits the same noises? It points and one goes that way. Points again and the other one goes that way. Could that be communication?"

"Very possible," he agreed.

The next scenes were grizzly ones, and few in the audience could look on while the segathars closed in and finished off the workers in brutal but efficient fashion. Even more dramatic was the small creature's method of attack. It made no use of teeth or claws, but instead rendered death by throwing what looked remarkably like a spear—in fact it was.

Again Poxiciti rose to his feet, utterly astonished. "My eyes see it. My ears hear it. And yet my brain rejects it. Borobos, are these images real?"

"What you are seeing is no illusion," she calmly assured him. "It is very real."

"This is inconceivable," he protested. "A feral animal cannot know the workings of a spear, much less determine its killing purpose."

"Evidently it is not feral, nor is it an animal of bestial nature. It has a thinking brain. And it has a spear, so train your mind to accept this as fact because you will be the better for it—especially if you should happen to cross its path."

"There is more to be seen here," Borobos advised him.

"Still more? Then I certainly hope there are no more heart stopping surprises. I do not think the shock of what I have seen so far has worn off yet." He settled back into his wet chair as the projection continued.

Again they watched the proceedings in rapt attention, saying little, thinking less. They had no idea at all what the creatures were communicating to each other. However it was soon obvious that the purpose of their planned attack was to liberate another segathar from one of the animal pens. Until this night no one had ever witnessed such a thing. And then they saw the image of the gun in the creature's hand, blasting the door open. Most of the spectators, including Poxiciti, wanted to believe that what they were seeing was simply being misinterpreted. However, when two of the segathars returned with wood and piled it onto the floor all his doubts immediately crumbled away.

"Is that...?"

"Fire," Inelefar said. "Crudely done, but yes, fire."

"Incredible. The rubbing together of two sticks to create friction, heat, then combustion. Our own ancestors might have done it that same way." As Poxiciti watched the flames spread higher he then moved in sudden remembrance of events long past. "I know this creature. Remember Betelgesel? That was so long ago only the memory of it now comes to mind. Once I stood in its animal lair, saw its spoor, poked its fire. Only then it was a mystery. Now it has made itself known to us. A creature who plots death and kills with its brain. And uses our guns. This is a strange world and there must be yet even stranger things out there, as evidenced by what we have seen here today."

"Surely this threat you speak of is a limited one," Tosostenos, once Midlothian's military strategist, said. "Even if proven to be intelligent are we now to quake in fear of it just because it brandishes a gulun gun? I carry one too, and I'm certainly no threat to the empire."

"Stupidity abounds in this room. Think," Poxiciti told them all. "If it can communicate with the segathars, and it knows how to make fire, then . . ."

"Then the segathars must also know how to make fire."

"Precisely. So now if we follow this reasoning to its logical end then we can also assume that if it knows how to use a gulun gun . . ."

Borobos lifted both hands to her face so shocking was this revelation. "Could such a thing be possible?"

"To accept what we are theorizing we must first abandon all presumptions. These segathars have proved to be far more clever than even we could have imagined. Obviously their motives are guided by planning and mutual co-operation. Even more importantly they know we are their enemy since it was our installation which they destroyed. And because they were successful I can only assume there will be more of these kinds of raids in the near future."

"This will only bring death to them that much sooner," Nalanusat said gravely. "If Pulima Cos learns of this creature's existence—and she will—then I see a swift end not only to it, but to the segathars as well."

"You are right," Borobos agreed. "She will stamp them out completely, burn down the forests, ruin the entire planet if only to conceal this one terrible truth. And that is we are stealing their world away from them. We are all hypocrites to our own beliefs. Our most fundamental law is to preserve life, and yet our very presence here brings sure death to the creatures we wish to save."

"Even worse," Inelefar said. "Everything we've worked for and believed in will ultimately be used to aide Pulima Cos in their extinction."

"So what are we to do?" Nalanusat asked despairingly. "Hide the truth and the creatures die for profit. Reveal it and they die for Epiphilinian colonialism."

"The survival of this species is our first and greatest concern." Poxiciti closed his one eye for a moment, thinking of a way to frame this so unpalatable solution. "Some of you may not appreciate this because it means the end of all hope of staying here. We have been polluting for so long we forget our mistakes only to discover we are repeating them now. This is not our world to save, so we must return to Epiphiline if we are to find true salvation."

Those in the audience broke into an heated debate. Borobos lifted her hand and made a firm gesture for silence. "Poxiciti has spoken very clearly of what we all must do. We must find indictable evidence against Pulima Cos. Even she cannot escape her own laws. We are very close, but not close enough that she cannot wriggle free and close her fists on us. Remember that a wounded animal fights more viciously than a hungry one."

"That we must do," Nalanusat said. "Pursue her, catch her, and convict her. We have no other choice."

Speaking like a true scientist, Poxiciti said, "What we have all witnessed here today is a discovery of immeasurable scientific importance. We must not forget that either. Somewhere in the uncharted wild forest is a thinking creature like us. And whoever finds it will be the first to make contact with an intelligent life-form other than ourselves."

Apparently for the moment their curiosity outweighed their conviction. And as they discussed the situation none realized that Pulima Cos had been all but forgotten. Poxiciti, deep in his own thoughts, stood in the corner by himself.

He was already thinking of ways to capture it.

Chapter 24

"What is it that you see up there?" Krugjon asked.

Ilon lay motionless on his back. Beside him the fire sputtered out then burst back to life as a globule of animal fat dripped down. When the black smoke lifted, the bright stars soon reappeared and the night was still again. "When you could see, did you ever look up at the sky and wonder how many other worlds are out there?"

"No. Never," he confessed. "I have heard others talk of such things. Thinking as you do I can imagine that there must be an uncountable number, and yet I wonder how many of them are free, living in peace."

Sitting up, Ilon sliced off a bolt of blackened meat, pushed it into his mouth and lay back down. "If you want to be free, Krugjon, then you must conquer whatever is keeping you a prisoner."

He dredged up memories of the past that for Krugjon were bitter reminders of his life still yet to come. "My mate died. My child died. I am blind. All this because of these accursed Iranha. You say that if we fight them then we become free. I think there is nothing you would not risk to bring this about. How many of us must die to prove this sky bright future you speak of belongs to the Iranha instead? I see no victory for us. My only wish before dying is to taste their blood."

Undoubtedly no argument would sway his decision; he was so sure that his death was imminent. What Ilon needed was something that would permanently change his gloomy outlook. This trek they were on might just do that, bring about the change he desired. Of course his attempt might fail—he knew that could happen too—although this time he was convinced that these Egris were finally ready to fight.

"We must learn from our mistakes," Ilon told him. "If we look to the problems of the past, then why can we not change what happens in the future?"

Krugjon frowned angrily. "What happened yesterday or what will happen tomorrow is unimportant. Only today matters, this moment. That is my personal belief."

Shaking his head Ilon answered, "You are wrong. Your kind of thinking is why the Iranha are winning. They live in the present yet are planning their future every day. Without a plan we are working apart. How can we hope to succeed when so many of us are fighting against ourselves? Instead we must be organized. First we must work together in order to make this victory happen."

"Your eyes see into tomorrow and I am sure you know the future already. But none of this helps to change what is happening now. Convince me that fighting them to the death is better than holding onto our lives. If you can, then this hunter shall be the first to join you."

The sky was beginning to cloud over and a windstorm was coming. Climbing up onto Krugjon's back Ilon secured himself then pulled tight on the reins. Krugjon automatically obeyed, jumping toward the forest directly ahead. This part required the greatest concentration, for the slightest deviation from the path could send them both hurtling into a tree. Yet they were a skilled team, working together to do what neither of them could accomplish separately. And despite their personal differences each was the other's closest companion, for they were constantly together, traveling and hunting. Except for when he was with Katakana, they were never apart. Each could almost tell what the other was thinking, so close now was this bond of trust.

"Veer right. Now!" Ilon shouted as he steered him past the approaching tree trunk.

There was another tree straight ahead and Krugjon traveled as easily around it just as if he was seeing it himself. They loped a while at a fast pace, until Ilon sensed his mount was tiring and so he decided it was time to take a brief rest. When he lifted his face he sniffed the moist air and knew there was water nearby.

Krugjon smelled it too, and when they reached the river's edge he wasted no time, plunging himself into the cold clear water with Ilon still strapped on his back.

Thrashing about in the river, Ilon fought to keep himself afloat, although his head sank beneath the foam and he coughed up a mouthful of water the next time he resurfaced. Krugjon was a natural swimmer and moved through the water with ease, climbing up onto the bank while he waited as his drenched companion struggled to reach the shore.

Ilon spoke sharply. "Why did you do that?"

"You were starting to stink," he grinned mischievously. "A good washing will do you some good."

Still dripping wet Ilon crouched on the ground beside him. "It will be daylight soon."

"How much longer?"

"Today. By early this morning I hope to be there."

"With Kykiris?"

"Yes. I think I must have told you of her."

"If you did then I do not remember. I once knew a hunter named Kykiris who hunted with trod Argugun."

"That is her. She is the hunter I freed from the Iranha. Only she survived. Those who were part of trod Argugun were lost to the Iranha."

Many things were on Ilon's mind, particularly this hunter. Although her message came to him only two days ago it had probably originated at the beginning of Summer, since the normal means of communication between trods depended on which hunter happened to be traveling in this direction.

"Time to leave. Are you ready?"

At his affirmative, Ilon kicked sand over the fire to be certain it was extinguished, then climbed up onto Krugjon's broad back and assumed his riding position, signaling he was ready to depart.

"I hope we will find her soon," Krugjon said.

"Just beyond that field over there, you will see."

Chapter 25

"**I** grow tired of waiting," Midlothian complained. "Look, the sun is coming up. How much longer?"

"Very soon," the hunting guide assured her. Her hands were trembling slightly for she knew that the Tomauk was becoming impatient with her. "Try to be patient."

"Patience does not reassure me. I paid you good money for this expedition, and up until now you have failed to deliver even a single segathar. All this waiting becomes unbearable. We are wasting the whole night out here."

"Very boring," Oneteesel, her hunting companion, agreed. "You promised us there would be plenty of game to hunt. So where are these creatures?"

Dullacima nervously pressed the button once more and there was a loud, rumbling noise on the field. In the deep grass their decoy lifted its head and bellowed as another electric jolt pulsed through its body.

"Try it again," Midlothian ordered. Slowly, she scanned the horizon from end to end in the hope of seeing just one of her quarry. "I don't see anything."

"Use your thermal visor only," Dullacima suggested to her, "As I explained to you earlier, these segathars are almost impossible to spot visually."

Scowling, Midlothian did as she was instructed and pulled the visor over her face, looking for any recognizable heat signatures. Despite seeing a few blotches moving upon the field there was nothing of any significance. After a while she lost her patience and the first thing she did was strike the vehicle's metallic shielding with her clenched fist.

"Nothing!"

She was not only less than pleased, her facial expression was such that Dullacima fully expected her next words to force a deadly confrontation.

"I demand a full return of my money."

"But Tomauk," she pleaded. "Surely you cannot expect me to guarantee our agreement. I help only to guide you to where game might be found. After all, how can I control the minds of feral animals?"

"You make excuses, Dullacima. Perhaps we shall use you instead for target practice."

"No, please, I beg you, high one." Her cold humor was greatly unappreciated, and Dullacima looked at her nervously, her whole body shivering with apprehension.

"Unless you can produce something worth killing very soon then our agreement shall be terminated. And I expect you to pay me back with interest for this miserable waste of my time."

"As you wish," she grumbled. She pressed the button uselessly, again and again, with every attempt hoping to see something moving out on the horizon. Just as Dullacima was giving the order to depart one of her spotters suddenly called out, "Wait! I see them now!"

This was exactly what Dullacima wanted to hear, rushing over to where her spotter was stationed. After pulling down her visor she eagerly scanned the horizon. "I see them too!" she shouted excitedly, waving at Midlothian and Oneteesel to come over and join her.

"What kind are they?" Oneteesel queried her as she strained to look across the field.

"Segathars. Precisely what you wanted. Be very quiet now," Dullacima instructed them both. "Your weapons. Are they ready?"

After checking her gun, Midlothian nodded. Oneteesel latched the arming trigger and the big gun hummed to life. "Ready."

Now they waited and watched from their hiding spot as the segathars moved in closer and closer. These were big animals and were easily clearing the tall grass with every bound. Dullacima swallowed nervously and hoped her two customers were good shots.

As expected, when the decoy bellowed the pack animals came jumping forward. Midlothian had her gun trained on the lead, the wedge of her hand ready on the trigger. She had waited this long to kill one. She couldn't wait that much longer.

"They are a sight to behold," Dullacima said eagerly. "Just as I promised. So. What of our bargain?"

"You can keep my money. And do not even think to ask me for more. Now get out of my way," Midlothian commanded, shoving her roughly aside.

They were just coming into range when Oneteesel lowered her gun. "What is wrong with them? Why have they stopped?" she whispered to Midlothian beside her.

"Quiet," she answered, for she was now keenly aware that the animals were looking over in this direction.

"Above you!" Dullacima screamed out a warning.

Both hunters twisted around just in time to see the segathar's tail disappear over the other side of their vehicle.

"Where did that one come from?" Oneteesel shouted hoarsely.

Midlothian could not have cared less, since she fully expected the pack to disperse at any moment and ruin her chances of killing one. "Shoot them!" she screamed.

Almost immediately the segathars scattered in every direction. With practiced motions both hunters took aim and fired. The first creature went down. After several more shots a second one crashed into the grass.

"Wonderful! Good sport animals," Midlothian crackled, discharging another round into the fleeing pack.

Naturally her hunting companion was enjoying herself immensely. Waving over to Dullacima she told her, "We want to kill more. Go after them."

On her order the camouflaged vehicle suddenly lurched from its hiding place. While they followed in quick pursuit they continued firing their guns, felling another before the main body split apart and angled away.

One particular animal caught Midlothian's eye. "Leave the rest. That is the one I want."

"If it reaches the forest we will never catch it."

Her icy stare was enough to shake Dullacima into immediate action. "Go faster!" she shouted to the driver.

Taking aim Midlothian fired off another round, missing the first three times before the forth shot hit its mark. "Got it!" she roared with satisfaction.

The segathar lay still on the ground. While the hunting party climbed down one of Dullacima's crew members ran over to where it lay, kicking at its backside just to be certain it was dead. Soon after that the hunting party came over to stand beside it.

"Good shot," Oneteesel complimented her.

"Of course. I am expert," Midlothian boasted. "Here you can see a perfect example of my superior sharpshooting skills."

She looked over her prize with enormous satisfaction. "Perfect skin. No blemishes or marks. See how well its hide blends into this grass?" Indeed, a segathar hide of good quality was very expensive, and so Midlothian was eager to see it lying on her floor.

Two of Dullacima's skinners were preparing to slice open the carcass when Oneteesel happened to be walking past. She was startled and almost fell over backwards when she saw the animal's arm twitch. "Get away!" she screamed. "Move!"

The big segathar suddenly reared up on its haunches and closed its jaws around the first crewmember, shaking her as she screamed hysterically. It took several shots at close range to finally bring it down for good.

"Is it dead?" Oneteesel gasped out breathlessly.

"This time it must be," Midlothian answered, firing another blast into it just to be absolutely certain. She stopped beside the first of the two crumpled figures. "This one is dead. And the other one?"

"She is badly bitten," Dullacima answered gloomily. "I do not think she will survive."

"How unfortunate. Leave them both here so that we can return to city Tykrerek. The last thing I want is someone asking questions."

"What of the segathar?"

"Bring its head."

"And the rest of it?"

She stared at the black scorch marks that riddled its body. "Its hide is worthless now."

Obeying, Dullacima signaled to one of her skinners. Oneteesel, her gun still slung across her back, went over to stand beside Midlothian.

"What good fun," she said. "We must do this again."

Chapter 26

"**H**ow many are dead?" Ilon asked gravely.

"Once we were twelve. Now," Gattagat trembled. "Now we are only six."

"Half is still better than nothing. You are lucky to be alive."

"Only because of you. Your warning saved us from certain death, I am sure of that."

The nentenen that the Iranha had tied up to draw them in was an effective ploy, so it could have been much worse had he and Krugjon not reached them in time. "My wish was to have saved you all. It should never have happened. No matter. It is done and cannot be undone. Is Kykiris among your dead?"

"She left early in the summer for trod Sandisand. None have seen her since."

"Then we will never know," Ilon sighed.

"You seek her?"

"I do. Word came to me that there was something of great importance she wished to share. Yet I fear this trek of mine has been for nothing."

A hunter named Amissaiked stirred when she heard this. "Kykiris told us of a strange hunter who might be coming. Are you that one?"

"How many other hunters do you know who look like me?"

"You are the first," she said unabashedly. "And no doubt the last. Come with us, Ilon. There is something you must see."

They traveled a short distance before crossing into the dark shadow of the woods. There, under a tall tree whose uppermost branches reached almost to the clouds, Amissaiked, with the others helping her, dug into the hard ground. Blind as he was, even Krugjon participated, his one good arm throwing the broken lumps that the others now pushed up towards him.

Gattagat called out enthusiastically, "I found it."

Digging her claws aggressively into the same spot, Amissaiked felt them scratch the hard surface beneath. "Good. I worried that it was lost." She looked over at Ilon whose eyes were widening with interest. "Buried in the spring," she explained. "Kykiris said it might be important."

Whatever they were uncovering it was something very large, and as Ilon watched and waited he felt more and more certain that the dark shape forming below him was of an unnatural creation. The Iranha were still on his mind, and very soon he knew why.

"Come down here and see this," Amissaiked ordered.

Obeying her, Ilon jumped into the pit to stand beside her as she was brushing away the last covering of dirt. The top portion appeared to separate as Amissaiked lifted her arms higher, still higher, until it landed with a wobbling noise against the opposite wall. As Ilon now peered inside the realization of what he was seeing struck him like a bolt of lightening.

"Iranha weapons!" he gasped. Reaching into the box he grabbed hold of one and pulled it out. Much bigger than his own gun, more like the ones he had seen the Iranha use on the hunters. And he knew just how to use it on them.

"A weapon you say." Gattagat hesitated, and then slowly ran his thumb along the edge of the barrel, the feel of it causing him to wonder aloud at this new and frightening revelation.

"Yes. A thing of great killing power and destruction. The very thing they use to kill us we shall use to kill them. Where did these come from?"

"We watched one day. The creatures brought them here, left them."

No other reason; that was simply it. None of their thoughts would answer why this had happened, only that it had happened and he now possessed the means to bring this war back to the Iranha. Of course his success or failure depended entirely everyone's participation.

"Stay here in your forest and there will always be something to eat, but do not forget the Iranha are hunting here too. Join me in our fight against them. Until all Egris are united together we shall keep dying. There should be a hundred dead Iranha for every one of us they kill. We know where they live, and it is there in their city where they must be destroyed. We watch and learn and soon we will know everything about them. Then we must strike. Tomorrow is coming. So decide now."

There was silence, and he could see they were thinking. With six already dead it would be easy to choose, for revenge was still hot in their minds. Yet Ilon hoped cold reasoning would prevail, that they would seize this opportunity to rid themselves of the Iranha forever. Finally he heard a murmur of voices and saw Amissaiked looking over.

"We shall do it," she told him. "We shall go with you. Whatever must be done I will not leave your side until I see them and their kind dead."

Ilon believed her. For as long as he could remember he had hoped to hear those words. Kykiris was the first, now these ones, and soon others like them would follow. They would be his missionaries, to spread the word and proselytize the others, and eventually bring these new converts to him. There was still much to be done, so very much, and yet, somehow, he sensed that this was the turning point.

"Take this," he said, passing her the big gun. He reached down into the container and gave each of his new recruits the same. "These are your weapons. And this is how you will use them."

Chapter 27

"It must be captured alive," Borobos firmly instructed. She pressed a button and the view screen on the wall blackened. "And unharmed."

"That ugly thing? You wish it alive?" There was astonishment, even disbelief as the bounty hunter rose from her seat and looked to Borobos for clarification.

"Yes. Absolutely no killing. Is that clearly understood?"

"That will be difficult," she responded, fingering her side-arm. "And very expensive. 14,000 konats. I regret having to ask for so much, but understand my price guarantees a safe pickup and delivery."

Borobos's tiny eyes trembled with rage. This crude hunter was as much a liar as she was a deceitful negotiator. "Is there no end to your greed? What kind of treachery is this? We had a bargain."

"Capturing it alive wasn't part of our agreement."

"Nor was tripling your price. It's outrageous!" she exploded. "I won't pay it!"

"That's too bad. Other people might gladly pay for your animal-thing. But I'll mention it to Oneteesel. Perhaps she might know of someone else who can better handle this so secretive and delicate task for you." She turned about and headed for the doorway.

"Filthy, despicable creature," Borobos hissed under her breath. "Wait!"

There was an expression of immense satisfaction that radiated from every line on the bounty hunter's face. "Then you have my money, all of it?" When she saw Borobos nod she strode back down the aisle and held out her hand to seal their agreement. "Good. You were wise to settle this with me. Others might have taken less, and undoubtedly would have botched the job. Perhaps they might have even talked to the wrong people." Her voice was low, unctuous. "I understand your dilemma. Why an important scientific discovery like this could provoke a lot of controversy, maybe even panic. Some people might be happier to see it destroyed. But you can count on me. Anything to advance the cause of science."

"Naturally. For a hefty price."

"For a fair price," she corrected her.

Borobos quickly signed her authorization to the contract and handed it back over. "And does this buy your complete silence as well?"

"Of course."

"Then I wish to hear nothing further of this matter, nor do I want to see you again unless it is with this creature I specified." She then moved her body to show her thorough disgust of the proceedings. "You are a well paid exploiter and profiteer, part of Oneteesel and her loathsome band of cut-throats, and I cannot bear your presence here any longer. Now get out of my sight."

"As you wish," she grumbled, turning about and stomping out of the room.

Poxiciti and Nalanusat soon appeared in the doorway, eager to hear all about what had just transpired. Both had been absent from the bargaining process mostly because their presence might have over-inflated the bounty hunter's normally exorbitant fee. So when Borobos reported the actual cost Poxiciti very nearly toppled over.

"That much?" he gasped, his skin hissing with the sudden rush of air.

"Do you not realize how much this creature has already cost us?" she said coarsely. "How many of our own attempts to capture it have failed? I thought it was clear that we employ a professional hunter. Under your orders I made inquiries, paid informants so that all this be done in secret. Now, is this still what you want?"

"Unhappily—yes. Thinking of it that way the creature is more important than the money."

"I don't like it at all," Nalanusat broke in. "She might run straight to Pulima Cos."

Poxiciti was thinking and worrying about this too. "Can we risk it?"

"I'm afraid we have to now." Her next words were brutally cold. "That is, unless you want her killed."

He pretended not to hear what she said. Even so he writhed at the very thought of it, for sanctioned killing was a distasteful matter of which he wanted no part.

"Do you think she can be trusted?"

"No," Borobos replied truthfully. "But she is incredibly greedy. I believe that she would snare Pulima Cos herself if the price was right."

For a brief instant Poxiciti found himself thinking about it. Her death he wanted very much. "That is my greatest desire, of which I would have the greatest pleasure. To wipe my feet on her wretched hide every morning."

"It can be done. Easily done. I can bring you her head. Simply order it and—"

"No!" He swiftly and sharply rebuked her. "Killing her will only bring another like her to power. Instead I need you and your female infiltrators to bring me condemning evidence, to pull down her entire government and grind her and her sleazy cohorts into the dust. Now is the time to act. We have to close in on her before these witnesses disappear entirely."

"Then our next logical course of action is to prosecute her business associates, those who we know are guilty of environmental crimes."

"Midlothian would be a good target," Nalanusat said.

"Particularly her," Poxiciti agreed. "Do you know something?"

Apparently he did, for his enthusiasm was so great that both his listeners felt a surge of excitement as he talked. "Normally all waste producing businesses have to be registered with the city. The environmental fee is exorbitant, and then there are the clean air taxes. To bypass all that, all anyone has to do is set up their operation outside of the city's jurisdiction. However it is known that many of these people are operating within the city limits. But rather than drive them out of business, Midlothian is extorting a hefty operators fee, and uses her military muscle to keep the dissenters in line."

"And do you have proof of this?"

"Plenty. If we agree to protect their identities three of these polluters will press charges against her."

"Well done, Nalanusat. Well done. Out of fear for her worthless life she might implicate her other accomplices too, maybe even Pulima Cos. Have her arrested and jailed with the others."

However, in the days that followed, the legal campaign they mounted became an insurmountable wall of stone. In spite of the evidence against her it was an accusation which Midlothian vehemently denied, even after several of her key staffers testified to the contrary. When confronted with charges of blackmail she protested mightily about receiving a large sum of money in exchange for dropping the investigation against a known polluter. Likewise, Falix Loax, a high powered political organizer for Pulima Cos, was also under investigation for awarding lucrative government contracts to some of her biggest financial contributors. She, of course, refuted the charges absolutely, citing her years of dedicated service to the Epiphilinian people as proof. In fact, whenever suspects were fingered for prosecution, the investigators who were sent in—disappeared. Others were harassed or physically assaulted. In one case, Oneteesel was named in connection with an influence peddling scam. She flatly denied any wrongdoing, calling the prosecutor a vicious liar and fabricator of untruths.

Just when it appeared that there was no hope of ever convicting her, insiders reported a rift had developed between Pulima Cos and Godderam Gorta, a wealthy investor who apparently balked at Pulima Cos's demand for restitution after some of her investments went sour. Evidently there was a brief power struggle, and Godderam Gorta soon mysteriously disappeared. Though her body was never found, everyone suspected murder. And after her office was found torn apart, no one doubted the rumors. Important documents were missing, as were large amounts of money. Investigators charged that a high level cover up was going on, but still no one was able to produce any hard evidence.

That was until the arrest of a scandalous character named Loggernod. He was wanted in connection with a sex-for-information scheme, and numerous other sex related charges including bribery and prostitution. But even more importantly he was once a close companion of Godderam Gorta's and was with her on the day she disappeared. In the interests of saving his own skin, Loggernod was eager to co-operate, so what he told the prosecution was incredible, amazing. In return for dropping all of the charges against him, he agreed to turn over evidence, implicating none other than Pulima Cos herself as Godderam Gorta's murderer.

When these new allegations surfaced, Poxiciti and his political supporters quickly sprang into action. Had he not ordered Loggernod's immediate transfer to a more secure facility, then

Loggernod would have certainly joined his dead companion, since a squadron of Pulima Cos's soldiers soon showed up demanding that he be turned over to them.

Now under a constant threat of death, Loggernod had no choice but to tell them everything he knew. Although the information came from a dubious source the prosecution was convinced of the legitimacy of his story. His eye-witness testimony was sure to sink any chance Pulima Cos had to remain in power. To prevent Pulima Cos from learning of his whereabouts, each night he was moved to a new location, sometimes to another city. In the meantime, Pulima Cos had been summoned to appear in court to face charges of murder. And now, on the eve of her trial, Poxiciti went to sleep convinced that her reign of tyranny was finally over.

That night, while everyone was asleep, a distant shout pulled Poxiciti awake. Soon there were more shouts, joined by screams, then the sound of running footsteps. Someone thumped on his door.

"Wake up! Wake up!"

Alarmed, Poxiciti crawled out of bed and waddled over to the door. A dark figure burst through the doorway, stumbled and collided in the darkness of the room. Falanandor, one of his attendants, seized Poxiciti by the arms and shook him.

"Fire!" he screamed. "Our building burns!"

As they made their way downstairs a dense black mass of smoke roiled up in the stairwell. It was impossible to see anything. Choking, eyes streaming with tears, they climbed downward, step by slow step, finding the sealed door at the bottom. But when Falanandor pushed it open there was a sudden rush of air, followed by the roar of flames. He died on fire.

Panic-stricken, screaming, Poxiciti turned away from his assistant's smoking bulk and hurried back up the stairs. After he made it to the next level everything was burning behind him, burning on both sides, so he stumbled the only way that he could.

"This way!" someone shouted through the pall of choking smoke. He reached the end of the corridor and saw a guard holding the door open. "Come on! Hurry!"

By the time they were safely outside smoke and flames were shooting high out of the windows. The speed at which the flames were spreading was unbelievable. The screams of those who were still trapped inside was a grim reminder to the few who were lucky to have escaped. It was too late to do anything. So the building burned.

Poxiciti was confused and speechless, shocked. What had just happened was still sinking in. He had escaped, only later to pick through the smoking, charred remains to find those of his friends who were not so fortunate. He lived. They died. And his building was destroyed. Those were the grim facts. However, during the course of his investigation his suspicions, in the end, became depressingly and inescapably clear.

"There is a killer within our organization, a low and shameless conniver, a filthy collaborator, one who is the eyes and ears of Pulima Cos herself."

Shocked gasps circulated the table, followed by shouts of disbelief. Poxiciti slowly circled the table, letting none escape his close scrutiny. Everyone was uncomfortable, especially Tosostenos, who now found herself staring into his one beady yellow eye. Perhaps to distract herself from this examination she blindly smashed her fists against the table.

"I want to kill her!"

Females were often noted for their brutal physicality and excessive displays of force, but even these inefficacious males felt the same as she. Nalanusat too, felt revulsion and rage. He began to beat his fists on the table and scream out obscenities of a like that would have given even the most ardent female observer a yellow face. Everyone seemed too preoccupied to think, though it was Inelefar who saw through all of the emotional nonsense and raised the important issue at hand.

"Poxiciti is right as always," Inelefar said over the noisy hum of agreement. "If that repulsive thing can reach us here, why then there is nowhere we can be free of her. Instead we must cut off her information before any further disaster strikes us."

While everyone was thinking about how exactly this might be accomplished, Borobos entered the room and was taking a seat when Poxiciti rose to face her.

"What news?"

"It is very bad," she answered immediately, lest anyone think otherwise. "Loggernod is missing. His three guards were found dead. I can only assume that—"

"Get out!" Poxiciti screamed, tearing violently at his clothing. "All of you. Get out of here now!"

One by one they filed out of the room. As the door slid closed he was alone at last. Poxiciti slumped back into his chair. It was her most devastating attack yet. In a single night Pulima Cos had effectively wiped out his entire case against her. And whoever provided the information was undoubtedly still operating under her authority. Deep down he had no idea who this despicable infiltrator was. Nor could his closest advisors help him now. He trusted no one. All that morning he wracked his brain, his thoughts were spinning uselessly in circles, and still he was no closer to the answer.

Finally, at last, he knew what he must do.

Chapter 28

Malanorbe, Pulima Cos's appointed executive secretary, watched the great doors swing open and Poxiciti approach. Opening her appointment book she scanned the wet pages, then looked up and spoke with an impenetrable hardness.

"Have you an appointment?"

"No."

"Then you'll have to come back at another time." She terminated his dismissal with a rough swing of her arm. "Now leave."

"Out of my way, you imbecilic, stupid thing!"

He pushed past her, bursting into the office with armed guards trailing after him, stopping suddenly as strong hands reached out to pull him back. He was amused and disgusted, watching as Pulima Cos pushed a naked male off her ugly bulk and hurriedly dressed.

"What do you want?" she hissed.

"Only to speak with you about your spy." With a wave of her hand Pulima Cos sent everyone else outside. Now it was just the two of them. "You are far more enterprising than even I could have imagined."

"You flatter me, Poxiciti."

"Despise you, hate you—yes. But flatter you—never!" It required the greatest concentration and effort just to restrain himself. To be this close to her sparked feelings that were difficult to control, though with forceful concentration he did manage to reach the point of his visit.

"Your fire last night was immensely successful. Had I your crude thinking I might have anticipated it beforehand."

"I understand the entire building burned down. People killed. Terrible," she said with mock sympathy.

"And Loggernod, too?"

"Yes, yes," she sighed. "So unfortunate, but he was far more bothersome than he was useful."

"So you had him murdered."

"He admitted his guilt to killing Gotteram Gorta and was summarily executed for his crimes." Pulima Cos looked at him with contempt. "That is what you were going to do to me!"

"And no doubt any knowledge he had died with him."

"Apparently so. Important knowledge that went directly from his brains to his mouth." Her tiny eyes glazed over and her expression grew rigid. "Now tell me what it is you want."

"Why the same as you. To see an end to the killing. Peace."

"Peace?" She looked at him as though it was an unheard-of word. "Why?"

"You fight me, I fight you. Where will this lead us, Pulima Cos? How many must die?"

"As many are needed to win," she said, coldness and finality in her every word. "To see your death, your accursed followers crushed underfoot and destroyed completely and totally. Nothing would please me more."

Shaking his head Poxiciti looked at her. "Then I see no possible solution."

"Nor I. While you are still alive there will be no peace between us, only the bond of hatred." Reveling in the strength of her command she admitted the truth without the slightest subterfuge. "Know that it was I who ordered your building burned down. Just as I did that I can easily do it again. I can reach out wherever you are, bring about your death whenever I wish. So now you see that I am the one who controls your very life."

"I see only a bloated bag of hot air," Poxiciti said harshly. "If you were not so fat I think you would float away. Very well." He forced aside all pretenses of civility. "If we fight, then we fight to the death. Die in the defeat I hand you."

"My fervent wish for you also. Now go," Pulima Cos ordered.

In silence he turned and walked from her office, pushed open the main doors, then hurried down the corridor, head lowered, arms swinging faster and faster, using his good leg to get away. Outside he almost stumbled when the ground suddenly shook beneath his feet. Behind him there was a deafening explosion, shattering glass, a cloud of thick black smoke. And as Poxiciti glanced up at the burning building he was thinking and hoping for only one thing.

That Pulima Cos was dead.

Chapter 29

"**H**ide me."

There was terror in Poxiciti's voice; his whole body trembled, shaking with fear. Yet even as he desperately pleaded for help he knew that he was taking an incredible risk by coming back here. Instead of fleeing as he should have, he had returned to city Sologcetis; worse still, to his own compound. Now as Borobos held open the door she had to decide, and quickly, what she was to do.

"Come in. Hurry." She glanced outside then secured the door. After escorting him upstairs to her private chamber she faced him and spoke aloud her fears.

"You should not have come back here. Soldiers are everywhere. They are looking for you right now." She went over to the window and anxiously watched a troop carrier rumble past. "How did get into the city undetected, past all the guards?"

"No time to explain. Been on the run since yesterday," he gasped hoarsely. "First bring me something to drink, then we will talk." He drank thirstily, draining the water jug of its contents and almost half of the second one before he slumped into a wet chair and spoke in a low, fear-filled voice.

"I need a safe place to hide."

"Impossible! You cannot stay here," Borobos insisted. "Midlothian and her troops will almost certainly be back to search for you. They were here twice already. Some of our people were taken away for questioning. I might be next."

His own selfish fears blinded him to the truth, but now that Borobos had spoken, Poxiciti began to realize more and more what he had done. He had single-mindedly and selfishly acted for himself, and even worse, he had inadvertently turned the whole world against the entire ecological organization which he represented. How better to destroy a movement than by tearing down its leader? He himself delivered the killing blow. Now it was over for him, maybe the end of everything, and everyone. Sadly, he was just now beginning to realize these facts.

While he was thinking Borobos became so distressed that she tore at her garment and exploded into anger. "Do you know what you've done, Poxiciti, do you?"

"Yes. Killed Pulima Cos."

"More than that. Worse. You murdered her. You, a renowned and respected peacemaker, a pacifist! Whatever possessed you to do such a crazy thing?"

"I am not sorry that I did it, only that I should have done it sooner. Had I not killed her, I believe that our own deaths were imminent."

Borobos snorted derisively. "They are now. Her death will end in our deaths. Not only ours but the thousands who follow us. Midlothian will seek revenge. She will rail the people against us, if only to guarantee her own place of power."

"That must not happen again," he warned, his voice so grave that his immediate fears were forgotten for the moment. "You must act for the others, take charge. As long as the people see that you are still against the polluters and destroyers of this world then Midlothian will have no power over you." Passionate as he was, it did not take very long for the grim reality of his present situation to sink back in. "However, my own fate is sealed. I am doomed to live out my existence in hiding, as a criminal, fleeing from one place to the next, always on the run."

"Why did you do it, when I could have had her killed for you? You had only to order it."

"Perhaps what I did was rash and ill-conceived," Poxiciti admitted. "Anyway, I am not exactly sure why, but the important thing is that we are rid of her at last."

But Borobos's own words reflected a nagging doubt. "Are we? Is she dead?"

"She must be."

"You can't know that for sure."

"If she survived then I would sooner be dead for having foolishly risked all and gained nothing."

However he did acknowledge that there was at least the possibility of her surviving, though he was now thinking more of his own escape. The sound of running footsteps forced him to look outside.

"The soldiers might be out there now," he said fearfully. "They will hunt me until they find me, and kill me. I do not wish to die yet. There is still important work to be done."

"Then we need help." She headed toward the door. "I will have to tell some of the others."

"No!" Poxiciti sharply commanded, stepping between her and the doorway. His hands were trembling so badly that he clasped them tightly together. "Do that and her spy will betray us all." Looking into her eyes he tried to speak as calmly and honestly as he could. "After all these years together you are the only one I can trust Borobos. If I am to stay alive then you must tell no one of my whereabouts."

Borobos sighed heavily. "Only if you leave city Soligcetis right now and promise to never return."

He nodded reluctantly. "Agreed."

"Then wait here."

On her return she escorted him outside to a waiting vehicle. After Borobos covered over the false bottom she drove the transport onto the main road and headed directly for the city gates. A few minutes later she saw the roadblock dead ahead.

"Get down and stay quiet!" she whispered fiercely.

One of the guards approached and waved Borobos to a stop. Her silver neck band indicated that she was a city Tykrerek soldier, obviously providing some sort of cooperative assistance to Midlothian's armed forces. The chances were good that she wouldn't recognize her. When the soldier spoke her voice was harsh and demanding.

"Your destination?"

Borobos tensed as a second soldier opened the back door and climbed inside. "City Sorgasoragus. Picking up an important shipment of cyrillus filters for our water treatment processors. Here are the papers."

She examined them briefly before handing them back over, then looked toward the rear of the vehicle. "Find anything?"

"Nothing," the voice returned. "It's empty."

"All right, move on through."

Borobos had little trouble at the city gates. The guard merely glanced inside, then waved her past. Within minutes she was driving across the open plains, heading south, and the city, growing ever more distant, was now just a bare patch of light on the dying horizon.

After returning to the city the next morning everything appeared normal. Guards met Borobos at the gates, questioned her briefly, then let her pass. But at the next stop a contingent of soldiers surrounded her and brutally pulled her out of the transport. They shoved her toward a waiting vehicle, from where she was then quickly taken to the air field and loaded onto a cruiser bound for city Anaxerxes.

The first familiar face she saw was that of the ugly and brutish Midlothian herself, who was seated behind her desk, glaring up at her. When the guards removed Borobos's shackles Midlothian dismissed them, then assumed a standing position directly in front of her.

"Where is he?"

"Who?" Borobos was deliberately evasive, though Midlothian easily saw through this feeble deception and struck her on the face as hard as she could.

"Does that help refresh your memory?" she snarled, again lifting her clenched hand and holding it over her. "Last night. You were seen leaving the city. Why?"

The sureness of her questioning filled Borobos with dread. Even so, Midlothian could exact whatever amount of physical pain she wanted. Borobos would never talk.

"To get away from your foul stench," she quipped.

With equal hardness Midlothian delivered a second cruel blow, then retracted her fist when she saw Borobos's stony, unrelenting expression. "We won't get anything out of her this way."

"Then maybe she will discuss it with me."

There was something horribly familiar about that voice, a voice that made her whole body shiver, her skin crawl. As Borobos swung around she was shocked to see the unmistakable fat face of Pulima Cos. "You!"

She snorted humorously in recognition. "You look surprised, Borobos, maybe disappointed. Are you?"

"I am," she hissed. "To see you still alive is no pleasure. I wished you dead, as did Poxiciti."

"That venomous thing tried to kill me. He would have succeeded too had I not gone to speak with my aide. Unfortunately he perished."

"Where? On your bed?" Borobos said sarcastically.

Pulima Cos pushed her face close to hers, shouted angrily. "You know where he is! Tell me!"

Borobos struggled under the threat of her command. Eventually she would be forced to speak, to reveal all of her secrets. She knew that the truth was inevitable and inescapable. She also knew the longer she delayed the better Poxiciti's chances were for escaping.

"I don't know."

"Liar!" Midlothian's fist thudded resoundingly off the back of her head. Strong hands seized her tightly by the arms and shook her. "Now tell us where he is or you will die in his place."

"I haven't seen him since yesterday. Really!" It was a small lie, a pebble of lies among a mountain of untruths.

"Really?" Pulima Cos's voice dripped sarcasm. She returned to the desk and picked up a piece of selp paper, then glanced at it briefly. "All the way to city Sorgasoragus to pick up a shipment of cyrillus filters." She crumpled the paper into a ball and threw it disgustingly at Borobos. "That were delivered five days ago! Your lies increase in magnitude and audacity! We found the secret compartment you used to conceal him. Very clever. Since no other city reported your presence I suspect you've hidden him somewhere in the desert. I assure you that we will find him and punish him for his despicable crimes."

Just the mere thought of his public execution filled Pulima Cos with so much pleasure that only when Borobos spoke for the second time did it cut through her thoughts and provoke her to listen.

"And what is to become of me?" Borobos asked haltingly. Her own involvement in this whole sordid affair was so obvious that it left little doubt of her punishment. It was easier to admit her guilt than deny it, though at the present moment she held fast to her innocence, however tenuous it might be.

"Abetting a dangerous fugitive is a serious crime. I could have you thrown into jail." Borobos shivered when Midlothian touched her scarred arm. "You remember my jail."

She pulled her arm roughly away. "Only too well."

Pulima Cos smiled grotesquely. "Why do waste your abilities helping those brainless weaklings? I could use someone like you. Someone to command her own city, to share in the riches of her people. It could prove to be a very profitable venture. You'd like that, wouldn't you?"

"And how do I repay such generosity?" Borobos asked pointedly, though the meaning of her offer was appallingly clear.

"Why simply show me where Poxiciti is. His capture is inevitable. So why not profit from it?"

"Only if to see you dead first."

The harshness quickly returned to her voice. "I can see now that you are as stupid as the others. Too bad. Perhaps you should have died and spared me the misery of your detestable presence."

Pulima Cos angrily wheeled about and seated herself behind the desk. Having Borobos killed without a trial would undoubtedly be impolitic. She was far too popular. People might question it. Nevertheless she had a plan that would ultimately rid herself of this loathsome band of troublemakers once and for all. Picking up a handful of documents she sorted through the pile and plunked each one down in front of Borobos.

". . . lag guns, sequasel fire grenades, butamin air mines. Quite a stockpile of military hardware, wouldn't you say, Borobos?" The features of her fat face showed a gloating expression. "In fact my troops recovered these very same weapons at a secret location in city Tsilix. The warehouse where they were stored was leased to Segathar Scientific Enterprises."

Hearing that name sent a shock wave of fear through her whole body. As Borobos started to rise, Midlothian pushed her back down into the chair.

"Does that name sound familiar to you? It should." Pulima Cos then produced a document and pointed to Poxiciti's own signature at the bottom. "See? Obviously he and his followers were planning to overthrow this government. My attempted murder is proof of that. Do you deny it?"

"Of . . . of course," she sputtered. "Its . . . insane! Lies and fabricated evidence. No one will believe it!"

"If the lie is big enough then everyone will believe it." She checked the time. "The weapons are being shipped right now. And when they reach my city tomorrow I will expose your entire movement as a fraud. Your seditious and rebellious environmental terrorists will be rounded up and executed—the end of everyone!"

As her final words closed in on Borobos, she thought desperately, Is this the end, is it? Poxiciti on the run, our organization in disarray, people dying. Who can help us?

Chapter 30

The sky was beginning to darken. Even darker clouds, under lit by the sun, glowed blood red. Earlier a heavy downpour passed through the distant hills, the streaming water running far out into the flatlands beyond, forming broad fan-tailed deltas in the shallow pools. At the base of one dune a big goud had died there just recently, though it was already half-buried in the accumulating sand and silt. Several long-legged creatures were snapping up its remains when a distant sound broke their feeding frenzy. One of the creatures looked up and hissed warning. Soon it was joined by the others who made off into the shadows, outstretched tails riding behind them as they fled swiftly away.

Something else was moving upon the field, coming closer and closer. There was a brief flurry of activity as even smaller creatures scurried to get out of the way. The low steady thud of footfalls could now be heard; before very long a swirling dust cloud was visible.

Out of the evening darkness the first Egris came into view, leaping, jumping, striding forward. One by one they passed the dead bulk of the goud, and within moments the last hunter dropped down behind the hill and vanished from sight.

In the evening, after the sun vanished completely, the pack halted at the top of a dune and peered down into the shallow valley below. At the first sight of the road, Kykiris motioned for attention by thumping her thick tail on the sand. She then pointed toward a bright patch of light near the roadway.

"That is where they pass each day. I do not know why, for everything about them is strange, but the Iranha machines always stop there."

"That high ridge," Ilon noticed. "You can see the road more distantly from up there. Gangahar, Katakana, go and watch for the Iranha. Signal if you see them coming."

He issued orders easily and they obeyed him because this bold venture was his idea. This was to be their first combined effort. Trod Horhon, trod Targasesk, and trod Sandisand, all united together under a mutual bond of hatred toward the Iranha. Now every hunter was watching him, waiting expectantly for his next command.

"Targasesk, take your hunters to the other side of the road and wait. When we are sure their building is empty then I will send someone to tell you. The rest of us will go forward quickly and quietly. Spread out. Watch for the Iranha. If any are down there try to kill them as silently as possible. But be certain to kill everyone."

What they had to do was simple and clear. One by one they slipped down the hill, then across the road, invisible shapes moving in absolute silence. Horhon was the first one to reach the building, her sharp claws extended, her mouth open, white teeth showing. Ready to kill. She was soon joined by the others who were moving out of the shadows and into the bright lights of the building.

"Did you see anything?" Ilon queried.

"Nothing." Horhon indicated the door. "It is deserted."

He nodded acceptance, then looked toward the empty road. "Then we wait."

By nature the hunters were eager to kill; most preferred to do it sooner than later. And so as the night wore on the hunters became more and more impatient.

"How much longer?" Katakana complained.

Deep down Gangahar wished she would take this task a little more seriously, although he too was starting to believe that the Iranha might not come this night. "Ilon says we must wait."

"Ilon says," she huffed. "Do we now do everything he tells us?"

"I suppose we do," he smiled, subtly implying that she did not have to enjoy his orders, she merely had to obey them.

She turned her back and growled. Nothing Ilon did would ever convince her that his way was the only way. With so many hunters now dead how could they expend more lives on these suicide attacks? Despite what she was thinking, at that very moment something moved dead ahead. White lights blazed in the darkness, flashed, then blinked out behind a low hill. Too bright to be stars. She immediately recognized them for what they were.

"They're coming!" Both she and Gangahar raced back to tell the others.

In haste Ilon issued just the minimum of instructions before everyone quickly dispersed back into the shadows and waited to strike. The only sound now was that of the approaching vehicles.

As the lead driver swung around the curve she saw the lights of the fuel depot straight ahead. Since leaving city Tsilix this morning the convoy had been on the road all day without stopping. Now with her fuel gauge indicating close to empty, she slowed and angled the transport toward the deserted station.

Drivers queued up in front of the automated fueling bay while each waited their turn for the equipment to move them into position. There was a hissing noise from some of the vehicles as the cab doors swung open and their occupants climbed down. They met at the building's main entrance and talked briefly; one by one they went inside to use the facilities.

No one came back outside.

After waiting what seemed an inordinate amount of time two more drivers climbed down, then walked on impatiently toward the building's main doors. Just as the nearest one pulled the door open she screeched in pain as the spear point pierced her body. Pulling his blood-dripping spear free Ilon took aim at the second and thrust it deep into the stunned creature. She too crumpled and died.

Something came out of the shadows, too black to be clearly seen, moving swiftly toward the transports.

Horrified, one of drivers struggled desperately for her firearm, only to die in the jaws of death that reached in and pulled her screaming from the cab. The Egris so outnumbered the Iranha that in the end few hunters had wet their teeth, though some did bite into the already ripped open corpses just to taste their blood.

"We have done it!" Amissaiked shouted victoriously. "Defeated the Iranha. Killed them all."

However Ilon did not share her happy enthusiasm, for he knew that they had not killed enough to make any bit of difference. "Do not be so eager to celebrate victory yet. We have killed some Iranha. But not all."

"Then it is a good beginning," she replied. "Wait here and more will come."

"Wait here and death will come. We must destroy this place and leave."

"What of their machines?" Targasesk asked. "Destroy them too?"

"Everything," Ilon acknowledged. "But first search them. There might be something inside we can use."

After going through the cargo holds he pried open one of the sealed crates. "Iranha weapons!" he shouted, seizing the gun between his hands and lifting it up to show them. "More than we can carry."

"These ones over here are much bigger," Amissaiked reported.

Indeed, of all the guns Ilon had handled this was the largest. He examined it briefly, then ordered everyone to step back while he sighted carefully at the empty building. His attempts to discharge the weapon failed and he was ready to throw it down when Gattagat came forward to help. The two of them were eager to make it work so they collaborated together, soliciting the watchers for any bits of useful information.

"It is an interesting problem," Gattagat admitted. "Those who made it I am sure never intended that we Egris know its secrets."

"That will be their undoing." Ilon twisted the barrel and pulled; his smile increased as the big gun hummed to life. "Let them feel what it is like to be running away from this."

The air crackled, followed then by a brilliant bolt of light that arced toward the nearest wall. It blazed brightly, making a thunderous sound as it struck; the air had a burnt ozone smell. All looked up to see the smoking ruin where the building had once been.

Sandisand touched the weapon with his trembling finger, a look of terror etched on his face. "They can do that?"

"We can do that," Ilon said confidently. "With their own weapons we will crush them, turn their cities into dust. This is my promise to you. We will not stop until every Iranha has been driven from our world, until their machines are set afire and burned." With both hands he raised the lag gun high over his head.

"There is a storm coming. And soon it will sweep them all away!"

Chapter 31

They never discovered what had been the real cause of it. The bodies were so badly burnt the only real evidence of their fate was the tremendous explosion which had ripped apart the entire station and scattered the debris over a wide area. The investigators who were sent in to deal with the wreckage acknowledged that a powerful force had leveled the building. And since the transports were carrying explosives it was easy to make the connection, so no one bothered to search any further.

Had they looked closer they might have found the spoor of the segathars laid down in the sand. From their location and number they might have even deduced the station was attacked. Someone suggested the possibility of a terrorist attack, since one of the blast points showed evidence of gunfire. Luckily the senior investigating officer chose to ignore her underling's theory because it countermanded her own tidy solution. A horrific and tragic accident. That would be her final report to Midlothian.

For the time being, Borobos had temporarily won her freedom. Yet she knew as she walked along the streets of the city that the shadows were following her, watching her every move. Pulima Cos had given herself sweeping new powers to arrest people and disperse crowds. Furthermore, many of Borobos's aides and associates were rounded up and thrown into jail on trumped-up charges of insurgency and inciting riots. Although she was now under constant watch it was of paramount urgency that she contact Poxiciti. But she dared not, for Pulima Cos was ready to close her wedges on them the instant she went to him.

One afternoon Pulima Cos summoned Borobos into her presence. Undoubtedly she wanted to question her about Poxiciti's whereabouts again, so today's meeting would be no different than yesterday's. As Borobos expected, when she arrived Pulima Cos was seated at her usual spot. Midlothian, now her constant companion, hulked close beside her. Seeing her gesture, Borobos stepped forward hesitantly into her ominous presence.

"Another installation was attacked last night." Those were Pulima Cos's only words. Instead she held up an object of interest which Borobos took in her hand and examined closely.

"The damage is indicative of a pulse weapon, most likely a lag gun," Borobos told her as she handed the burnt metal fragment back over.

"You know something about this, don't you?" Even while she was shaking her head no Pulima Cos went on uninterrupted. "I strongly suspect that these armed terrorists are fighting under your leadership and direction."

Borobos simply rolled her eyes. "I know nothing of it. Nor would I be so cowardly to order the deaths of innocent people."

"Poxiciti would. If he is the one who is behind this killing and destroying—and I believe he is—then you are part of his scheme to subvert my law and order."

For Borobos this was nothing new to hear. Only one thing really mattered to Pulima Cos, and that of course was Poxiciti's capture. Nothing else. Despite her accusations Borobos genuinely doubted his involvement with killing. His attempt to kill her was a perfectly natural response. Had Borobos been holding a gun right now she surely would have finished the job herself.

"You attempt to blame him for what I believe is of your own doing. It is no coincidence that as these nightly attacks increase, so do your charges against him."

"That I would attack and burn my own city just to see him charged, convicted, and killed, is a possibility too wonderful to consider. No, he will not escape that easily. Poxiciti cannot hide from me forever."

Obeying her orders Midlothian pulled out her sidearm and pointed it directly at Borobos's head.

"If she speaks anything other than the truth, even the tiniest lie— then kill her instantly. Is this understood?"

Midlothian happily acknowledged her command, then trained her weapon on Borobos's cowering form and awaited her killing orders. Pulima Cos stepped forward, her pendant flesh wriggling beneath the folds of her scarlet gown.

"Every day I question you, and every day you lie. I believe that you will keep on lying. But today will be different. Today you will tell me exactly what I wish to know. The truth. So I will ask you one thing and you will answer me only one thing. And that is, where you have hidden Poxiciti. Then I will seek him out and destroy him for good. I will know if you lie. Because if you lie I will order Midlothian to kill you. She will shoot, and you will die. Tell me, is this what you want?"

Borobos had little choice. She saw Midlothian's killing stance, the pointed gun close to her face, the motion of her ready wedges on the trigger. It was a very real threat, one that Pulima Cos promised to fulfill.

"No."

"Good. Very good. A simple answer, yet you have spoken truthfully and now live because of it, even if only to save your miserable hide." She stepped out of Midlothian's gun sight. "Now. Where is he?"

What could she do? With so many other lives at stake was Poxiciti that important? Borobos moved her mouth, not wanting to speak, but knowing that death was her only alternative. Her eyes swung across Pulima Cos for an instant.

"He is . . . in . . . in Buloxus prefecture," she gasped out. "At an agricultural facility near the Betelgesel River." Midlothian lowered her gun and the threat of death was over for the moment.

"But by now he will be gone."

"Where?"

"I don't know." When Borobos again saw the gun coming up she covered her face and screamed, "I swear it! He will try to contact me. He knows your spies surround me every day. That is all I know."

Summoning one of her aides, Pulima Cos unrolled a map and forced Borobos to point out his exact location. "Dispatch my soldiers to this place at once. Arrest everyone." After her aide turned and left the room she glared at Borobos. "I had better find evidence of his presence there, or I promise that you will be returned here and killed."

A curt dismissal followed her menacing words. For Borobos it could not have come any sooner. She rushed outside to a waiting vehicle which took her to the sky port. The further city Anaxerxes shrank behind her the better she felt. Dealing with Pulima Cos the way Poxiciti must have, she too was wishing for her death. Far better to be leaving, because as soon as that fat wind bag discovered she had deceived her, it would be the end of her freedom. Worse, Borobos told her a lie. Now she had only to wait, and death would inevitably seek her out.

Upon reaching the sky port she hurried inside the terminal and waited impatiently for the transport back to city Sologcetis. She was incredibly tired, her body finally slumping from exhaustion as she lay against the bench and closed her eyes.

Suddenly there was a loud explosion outside, followed by a lot of smoke, then flames. People started screaming, running to get out of the way. Borobos was on her feet, moving toward the door when someone grabbed her from behind and pulled her back.

"Get back inside! We're under attack!"

The soldier, her weapon drawn, disappeared through the doorway just as another explosion crumpled the wall and knocked Borobos tumbling to the floor. Bleeding, frozen with fear, she watched in horror as a second transport erupted into a ball of fire. Smoke and flames were shooting out of the wreckage; dead bodies were strewn across the tarmac.

Just as Borobos was struggling to her feet an intense heat wave gusted in through the broken windows, then a choking pall of black smoke. Fire! The building was on fire. She stumbled outside, coughing, gasping for air, in all the confusion not knowing where to run. Hearing the sound of a discharging lag gun, she saw the blue pulse of light as it hit a building nearby. The ground shook from the force of the explosion, followed then by a shock wave that spread outward from the epicenter. Those who were running away were knocked down, presumably killed. Borobos looked about in horror. With so many dead the only alternative now was to run for her life. Just as she was about to go, a second, even more powerful explosion, struck from behind and threw her into the air.

The next thing Borobos remembered was waking up on the ground. She was in terrible agony. Her leg was throbbing, the pain of it causing her to groan whenever she tried to move. For several moments she drifted in and out of consciousness, waking only to feel the fierce pain in her leg push her back under. Blinking her eyes open she was scarcely aware of a growling sound. Something dark swam into her vision. Tall, black hide, its sharp toe-nails clicking on the pavement as it approached. What she saw was a waking nightmare, a hallucination. Had she not been depositing weapons at sites where the segathars were known to congregate, then she might have never surmised the horrible possibility. Laying absolutely still Borobos watched the big segathar turnabout, lag gun in hand. The monstrous creature was so close that it could have easily leaned over and bitten into her. To make even the slightest movement now she would be killed. With practiced motions the segathar hoisted its lag gun and fired off three quick bursts before slinking back into the shadows.

Later, when Borobos awoke, someone was leaning over her as she was being wheeled toward an awaiting emergency shuttle. "You're lucky to be alive. Did you see anything?"

Before she lost consciousness she glanced up and said firmly, "No. Nothing."

Chapter 32

The day was hot, the sun shining fiercely down. A dry dusty wind was blowing in from the north, bringing with it a shimmering wave of heat that was visible all the way to the horizon. The sun was well above the field when Ilon walked out of the shadow of the forest. His mother stood alongside him, her blue eyes nictitating in the bright sunlight. Shielding his own eyes he gazed out across the empty plain, into this translucent sea of hot air. Something metallic glinted near the surface.

"The Iranha city. Do you see it?"

Horhon's jaw clacked loudly shut. "I smell it."

What she stated was undeniably true. There was an unnatural brown haze floating visibly over the plain, a choking, stinking length that extended well beyond the city boundaries, reaching them out here. Some of the forest's mightiest trees were beginning to show signs of deterioration; other plants were drying up and blowing away to dust. A new kind of death was coming from the sky, poisoning their very existence.

While Ilon was busy thinking, Horhon saw the intensity of his movements and spoke calmly. "We were successful last night," she reminded him. "Many Iranha were killed, many machines were destroyed."

"Hardly enough. Not enough to make even a dent. We need more Iranha weapons."

"Weapons we have. Hunters we don't have. We are only a small force fighting against a numberless horde. To even return from such an encounter still alive is a victory for us—it must be."

True, there were victories, they were striking back, but Ilon was finding the slow pace frustrating. What he really wanted was a single swift attack, to wipe them out utterly and totally. Perhaps that was never going to happen, yet he saw the future and in it was a world without cities, without Iranha. Nevertheless he wasn't encouraged by their snail-pace progress and wished for the future to be here now.

"Then we must find more hunters," he said simply and firmly. "Scour the forest and plain, bring them here."

Horhon frowned. It was an impractical idea. How would they feed such an army? Egris were voracious eaters, and since there were already several trods feeding here it would not be long before the forest was depleted of game.

"There are too many of us now. Surely the hunters you want cannot all stay here."

"Turn some of them away? That will be hard to do."

"Hard, yes, but even harder is keeping such a large number together, and fed. You know the problems."

"I do," he sighed.

Sweat was pouring off his face when Horhon indicated that it was time to return. Ilon walked all of the way home in thinking silence. He was disillusioned by what he had accomplished so far. But mostly he worried because he knew the Iranha were still winning, which made it very difficult for him to convince these hunters to keep on fighting. Circumstances had made him the leader of this movement, yet how much longer would he be able to keep them all together?

Sleep was the only opportunity he had to not worry about the problems, though when he awoke at dusk his first thought was of the impending battle. So far, their guerrilla tactics had worked surprisingly well. Rather than a direct confrontation they conducted the raids at night under the cover of darkness, going in undetected, destroying their target, then slipping away. Outwardly all of the trods were in complete agreement and no one disputed the satisfactory results.

However, Ilon himself was his own greatest critic. Yes, they were killing Iranha, but ultimately how would this stop the Iranha from killing them? The hunters wanted to see that happen today, now. This was his biggest problem, making them understand that their present and their future were very much a part of the same reality. They, like him, shared the same vision, though their interpretation differed from his own. To them the future was fixed and unchangeable. Therefore it could not be planned out or initiated, since what would happen would happen. Not so, Ilon believed, for it was what they did now, in the present, that would bring about a better future for everyone. So for as long as he remained their leader this battle would continue.

Just after dark Ilon climbed to the surface. He built a small fire and sat down to wait. As he expected, the hunters came up one by one to sit beside him, and when this large group was assembled he rose to his feet.

"Horhon, Alpeak, Targasesk, Sandisand." In all there were thirteen names, all leaders whom he addressed with respect and courtesy. "And brave hunters," he said to his audience. "You are all here. This is what we must do tonight," he told them, laying out the plan in detail.

It was a strange and disturbing concept, there were even some gasps from those in the audience, but because of his past successes everyone listened on, eager to hear more.

"Sandisand. Your trod comprises the smallest fighting force, yet you have the greatest part."

The hunter puffed out her chest for all eyes were upon her. "My hunters are yours, so may your thoughts be ours. Let your words guide us all to victory. What must we do?"

"We must take the war to their city. The Iranha are the city, the city is the Iranha. To destroy it is to destroy them. You have been to the Iranha city?"

"Close enough."

"You will have to go even closer. Inside. Beyond the great wall. I have told you of their buildings, and it is there where you will strike them, in the heart of where they live." Ilon showed him three fingers. "Three is an important number. Three buildings, three fires. Three. One fire is good, but it would be too easy for them to put out. Two is even better though these Iranha are clever and might think this is the end. Three is the best of all because they will fear that more destruction is coming. More fires, more deaths. In fear they will send all of their hunters to aid the others. Then we strike!"

Some of the hunters were so eager to get started that an argument broke out over who would be the first among them to kill Iranha. Ilon enjoyed this banter but soon lifted his hand and the onlookers quieted.

"The risk will be great, so I must ask you again, Sandisand. Are you and your hunters strong enough to do this?"

"This, and more."

"It is enough that you do this one thing. Your success is our success. To fail we all fail."

"Three buildings, three fires. We will not fail."

"That is my hope."

He outlined their objective in detail. With the Iranha too busy fighting the fires the bulk of his Egris army would hit the city reservoir. Although they knew only a little about their enemy, water was the one substance the Iranha needed. So therefore they would cut off their water supply. Deep down he hoped this might render them the killing blow, though he realized it was just one among countless targets. A speck of sand on a beach. Too many had suffered to abandon the fight now, so he pushed through his feelings of unhappiness and looked upon the coming campaign with a great deal of anticipation.

"When do we attack?" Targasesk asked him.

"Soon. Very soon. When the second moon drops below the horizon," he told his audience before excusing himself from the circle of hunters. "Arm yourselves and be ready when I return."

"Norgolash. Go with him," Horhon ordered.

Taking only his spear Ilon set out for the field. When he found a comfortable spot he lay down in the grass and gazed up at the brightening stars. He knew that his own world was up there, somewhere, one of those dim points. The past was not completely forgotten. He had submerged his feelings so deep that only now when he looked up at the night sky did he remember the world as it once was. He had spent an entire lifetime hiding from the Uta, a life lived in fear, never knowing when they might attack. Running and hiding had only brought about the Taal's speedy deaths. What about these Egris? Were they doing the right thing, attacking these Iranha?

"Get on your feet," Norgolash warned him.

"What is it?" he responded, now trying to see where he was looking.

"Something over there. A strange sound. I heard it twice."

She appeared concerned, and Ilon took her warning seriously because Norgolash was not the sort of hunter who ruffled at every insignificant thing. If something was over there then Ilon better be on his guard.

"Stay here, I will drive it away."

As she crawled stealthily out of view Ilon suddenly heard a scream and stood up, hoping to see what had made it. "Norgolash," he called out. "Is that you?" He smiled at his own irrational fear, walking forward through the grass where the hunter had crawled. It would be alright, he told himself, his hand unconsciously tightening on his spear.

To his horror what he saw approaching was not Norgolash. He had to get away, but he was too late. There was a bright flash of light, followed by the sound of a discharging weapon. Ilon crashed helplessly to the ground, too stunned to move, too terrified to scream. Laying face down in the grass he was unable to see his attacker, though he could feel its slimy hands on him.

Tossing him over its shoulder, the creature carried him off into the darkness, away from the world he knew, toward a place of unimaginable terror.

Chapter 33

"**S**o this is the creature." Pulima Cos looked in through the bars of the cage. "It is incredibly ugly. And it smells terrible too. You should have had this filthy animal properly cleaned before bringing it into my sight."

"Apologies, high one." Harsabar acknowledged her complaints by lowering her head in deference. "That was my wish too, but your contacts desired for you see it without further delay."

"Very well. But if it must be now, then let me see it quickly and be gone."

As she removed her segathar skin cloak the creature suddenly sprang forward to the front of the cage and snarled at her. Again Pulima Cos's attention was fixed on the repellent animal-thing, and those in the room clearly saw her expression of disgust when it opened its tiny mouth and barred its flat white teeth.

"Is this all it can do? Just growl?" She bent forward, even closer. "It doesn't look very dangerous. Has it been injured?"

"No. Only stunned," the bounty hunter assured her. She then handed over a sharp-tipped pole. "It was carrying this when I captured it."

Pulima Cos examined it closely and pronounced it a crude instrument that no doubt had originated from this creature's bestial mind. "And what of the gulun gun it was supposed to have been carrying?"

"There was no gun," she assured her. "Perhaps there never was. A sharp stick is one matter, but certainly it could not have grasped the knowledge of Epiphilinian weaponry."

"Why not give it your gun, Harsabar, and we shall see."

Those surrounding her broke into wild laughter yet Harsabar thought little of her humor, nevertheless she was quick to follow the others. "A good joke, high one. Yes, perhaps I shall do just that. But we will all be waiting a long time and I know you are in a hurry."

"Yes, yes," she scowled. Her estimation of this hunter's worth was decreasing. "Before I leave here I want a closer look at what I am buying."

"Be careful not to get too close," she warned. "It is small, but still quite possibly deadly."

"Really?" Pulima Cos was unconvinced. Reaching in through the bars she roughly prodded the creature with her closed wedges, laughing as it howled with pain. "It will make an excellent addition to our city zoo. I want Igna Lox to examine it first. See that it is sent to her immediately."

"Wait." Harsabar stepped in front of the cage. Her voice was low but firm. "There is still the matter of payment."

"You will be well compensated for your efforts." She directed one of her aides forward, who in turn passed over a translucent slip of selp paper. Harsabar read the amount.

"Others have offered to pay more."

When Pulima Cos heard her final price she snorted, "That much? You are far too greedy, and stupid if you think I would pay 20,000 konats for such a scrawny thing. I will give you half that, no more."

Touching her sidearm, Harsabar looked at her shrewdly and said with equal malice, "Not nearly enough."

Pulima Cos regarded her effrontery with deadly anger, and responded in a voice so cold that those in her service quailed and turned away as every bone in her rigid body cracked.

"You dare to demand more! You are nothing but an insignificant trapper, a cheap peddler of animal flesh. Here is my final offer. Nothing. Because you are so greedy and unscrupulous you get nothing. For you there is only the remembrance of your failure. What you once had is now mine. I take possession of your prize, and you return to your city empty-handed. That is your reward."

"I promise others will soon know what you have done here," Harsabar angrily blurted out. She swallowed only as an afterthought, just barely aware that she had unwittingly doomed herself.

Certainly Pulima Cos could not let this insolent creature's challenge go unpunished. She permitted no one in her presence even the illusion of defiance. Spinning around she glanced briefly at Midlothian, then away. Her unspoken order was clearly understood, but the accompanying words were strictly for Harsabar's grim benefit.

"Kill her."

Before the bounty hunter could reach for her gun there was a loud crack as Midlothian's weapon discharged. What was left of her was little more than a smoking pile of burnt flesh and broken bones. Midlothian looked immensely pleased as she hovered over the mutilated remains and poked it with her foot.

Pulima Cos nodded her approval. Just another garrulous mouth permanently silenced. Brushing the singed pieces of cooked meat off her gown she ordered her aides to attend her. "And clean up this disgusting mess." She then turned and strode away, planning her next victory.

*****

Ordering the fat scientist into her presence, Pulima Cos leaned forward and rubbed the wet surface of her desk with her oily palms.

"Have you studied the creature I sent you?"

"Extensively."

"Well," she went on impatiently, "what have you determined? Is it some new species of segathar which now infests our forests?"

Igna Lox's gross mass writhed at the sheer stupidity of her question, though she dared only to answer as this stone-brained politician had directed her. "Absolutely not. I found no evidence whatsoever to substantiate even the remotest biological similarity. From what I have observed I believe it is feral, though it appears to be capable of some sort of crude communication. Dissection might tell us more about the creature's thinking processes."

"For now I want a living creature—not a dead one. Where did you put it?"

"In with the segathars, just as you ordered."

"Good. Then we will go there presently."

It had been another day of storming, though it stopped by the time they went outside. The sun was briefly out, piercing the gray, canyon-like walls of the city before vanishing behind a bank of dark clouds. An escort drove them to the zoological complex on the city's outskirts. Pulima Cos talked most of the way there. Inga Lox nodded only whenever she thought her stupid master had reached some important part of the conversation. When they pulled in front of the complex it was squalling again so Pulima Cos took this opportunity to soak herself in the cool rain before going on inside.

Boa Loam, the smarmy, greasy-faced curator, greeted them at the door. Inside she indicated a large map which showed the locations of the various exhibits, explaining how most of their collections were rare animals brought all the way from Epiphiline, the vast majority of which were quite possibly the only ones in existence. She led the way, talking incessantly, pointing out some of the displays which neither Pulima Cos nor Igna Lox showed any interest in. When they reached the animal pen where the segathars were housed she ingratiated herself in their presence until Pulima Cos tired of her speaking and rudely dismissed her.

"Thought she would never shut-up," Igna Lox said.

To Pulima Cos this part of her trip had been an inordinate waste of time, and Boa Loam she was happy to be rid of. Ordering her thoughts she pressed her face to the metlaglass window and searched the grounds within.

"Where is it?"

Ordinarily the segathars blended so well with the terrain that they were difficult to spot. After careful inspection, Igna Lox slowly circled the perimeter, then went down to the next level where a special underground enclosure had been constructed to enable the crowds to watch the segathars sleep. He pointed out the creature-of-interest lying among the curled-up bodies. "It is here with the other three. Sleeping. Do you see it now?"

Fighting back her revulsion she moved closer and stared for a long empty space of time. "Why do they not rip it apart and eat it? How do you explain its presence among them?"

"I can't. I have puzzled over this relationship for a considerable while, yet I am still firmly convinced that it cannot be a segathar. As on Epiphiline the laws of inheritance must be the same here. Within a species there is an extraordinary range of individual variation, but when similar animals breed they must produce similar offspring. That is, segathars produce only segathars. Therefore the probability of producing such a creature from this kind of union is zero. If that does not convince you then there are some other remarkable differences that clearly distinguish it from these animals. For instance, its diet. It could be an omnivore."

"Then, it does eat meat?"

"Examination of its gut had led me to believe that it does. However, high traces of carbon indicate that the meat was burnt prior to its consumption."

"Burnt? The creature eats burnt meat?"

"It would appear so."

"How revolting." Pulima Cos made an accompanying facial gesture to show her disgust.

"We've also done a complete analysis of the creature's biology," Igna Lox continued, "using biochemical, metabolic—every conceivable medical test. The body of evidence, the indisputable facts, is in here." She tapped the thick wet binder before handing it over.

Pulima Cos studied the first few pages closely before slamming the binder shut. There was a lot of technical jargon and indecipherable equations, little of which she understood. Her one eye was on Igna Lox who she was sure was thinking her the fool.

"Explain this nonsense at once."

"Very well," Igna Lox huffed. "I seriously believe the creature did not originate on this planet."

She was flabbergasted, stunned and stupefied. Rarely had someone been able to render her speechless. Had it been anyone else she might have had them stripped of their rank and driven from her sight. Nevertheless, when she was able to speak again her voice was cold and menacing.

"You should feel shame for bringing me this deplorable information. Am I to believe that such idiocy flows from the mind of a scientist? Evidently all of that food you eat has added more to your bulk than your brains."

Igna Lox was insulted by her rough manner. Nor was she used to having her theories so ridiculed by a rank amateur, though forced herself to be calm in the face of her growing anger. "I assure you that my hypothesis is strictly in accordance with the facts."

"Demonstrate, speak, explain!" she demanded.

"First you must promise to listen. It is abundantly clear that this is information you do not wish to believe. Can you do that?"

"I can," she answered testily. "Go on, but be careful not to drift into the boundaries of stupidity again."

"There are quite possibly more than eight million different kinds of animals living on this planet. Each species arose by a slow modification of earlier forms, tracing their existence back in time to a common origin. That is to say, all roads lead back to a single ancestor who is the progenitor of all life forms. So because of this phylogenetic kinship the morphology of every living creature shows a varying degree of similarity. Their nucleated cells clearly share a common unity in composition, structure, reproduction, and . . ." Igna Lox stopped herself when she saw the blank look on Pulima Cos's face. "Do you understand any of what I am telling you?"

"No."

She stepped back and fought to control herself. The emptiness of her mind appalled her. Pulima Cos, who, unlike herself, was impulsive and reactionary. The majesty of her thoughts, the beauty of her knowledge, certainly could not be appreciated by a crude and uncivilized thinker as this.

"I will try to explain it again."

"I find you extremely boring," Pulima Cos rudely interrupted. "Do you have a point to make? If so it escapes me."

She scowled and was full of contempt. "You take issue with things that you know nothing about. So listen closely and I will elucidate. This particular creature is unique in all the vastness of the world because its genetic makeup differs markedly from any other existing life form. To put it simply, it is utterly impossible for it, or any of its kind, to have existed here."

But Pulima Cos continued to remain skeptical. "I can't believe that." She expressed her reservations further with her next two questions. "Then where did it come from? And what is it doing here?"

"Regrettably, the answers elude me."

"Then you have a mystery. Every problem must have a solution. Find it."

This new task did not please her in the slightest, and she unconsciously wriggled her pendant flesh in hatred of this domineering and overbearing administrator. If Pulima Cos had any idea what she was asking! She could command her to search the length and width of the world, yet as Igna Lox parted company and went on her way, she knew that tomorrow and the next tomorrow would bring her no closer to the answers than today.

Chapter 34

Ilon's original plan to get himself and his hunters into the Iranha city had only been partially successful. His presence here was proof of that. Yet he had little choice and accepted his fate as one who was already dead. No hunter had ever returned from the Iranha alive, he knew. Only dead. Had he ever thought it possible that he could escape then he would be thinking it now. Instead he was thinking of his death, and hoped it would be soon.

For a long period he sat motionless in his cage, seeing only the strange buildings outside the windows of the moving vehicle. It was daylight, yet there was darkness in his thoughts as he wondered of his hunters. Had the Iranha gone back to exterminate them completely? Were they all dead? He could only wonder and be afraid for them.

When the vehicle drove out onto the open plains his worries were forgotten for the moment and he was overcome by a longing so strong that he clenched the solid bars with his hands and shook them until the cage rattled. But this feeling was not to last. He was soon loaded into one of their flying machines and the next thing he knew he was in another Iranha city.

As they wheeled him down the corridor some of the Iranha stopped to look at him. Lumpy, gray-black mottled skin, and unbelievably ugly. A few pressed their faces against the bars and looked in. Two of the ugly creatures were wearing an Egris skin on their backs. How Ilon wished he had his spear. To run it through their hides was indeed a very satisfying thought.

There were four Iranha waiting for him in a large room. From what he could tell they all looked alike. All were strangely garbed in green gowns, their hands and faces covered with the same bright material. In the center of the room was a circular table with restraining straps. Overhead a bank of lights glared down from the ceiling. Ilon sniffed the air. It smelled like blood and death and he was genuinely afraid. Backing himself into the corner of his cage he howled in terror as one of them reached in and stuck him with a sharp instrument. He suddenly felt very tired; he wanted to sleep. Now barely able to keep his eyes open he felt the cold metal of the table beneath his back, saw the bright lights directly overhead, and blinked his eyes shut. They did not open again.

When Ilon awoke the next day he was sore and bruised from where they had poked and prodded him. He had no idea what they had done but parts of his body were covered with a sticky material which adhered to his skin. Ripping off his bandages he saw where they had cut through and bled him. He touched the red weal of puckered flesh and grimaced in pain. After he slept some more he was fully awake when a single Iranha entered the room.

It was carrying a tray between its stumpy hands as it stomped forward and screeched at him. Crouching in the corner of his cage he snarled back, though he knew that it was he who was the prisoner. When it left the room he reached forward through the bars and thirstily drank down the bowl of water. In another bowl was something that looked edible which he picked up and sank his teeth into. He was too hungry to care. Pushing the gobbet of food into his mouth he chewed on it while he began to think. Whoever had captured him seemed to want him alive, and he wondered what his life could possibly mean to these Iranha. Thinking about it made his head hurt, so he stretched back and closed his eyes. He would probably never know.

Only later, when Ilon slowly regained consciousness did he realize that he had been moved again. He felt too groggy to sit up; the back of his head was throbbing. Something creaked behind him. He felt wet nostrils touch his leg, a snort of hot air, then a wet tongue.

"Stop that!" he sharply commanded.

An Egris female was wide-eyed with amazement, shocked, incredulous, and gaped at the other two males beside her who also wore the same stunned expression. When they fully recovered one of the males expressed disbelief, but it was the female who bent forward and peered quizzically at him.

"Speak creature. Say something to us."

Ilon sat up and looked about his new surroundings. A circular enclosure with a high domed roof. The grounds crudely resembled prairie terrain. Sandy hills, clumps of grass, a few small bushes, yet a prison nonetheless. "Like what?" he asked, focusing his attention on how he might escape from here.

All three clicked with excitement; their heads bobbed rhythmically together. "Amazing! A creature who speaks just like us. Do you understand every word?"

Ilon snorted. "Of course. I speak better than you."

"There are more mysteries in this world than can be imagined," she remarked. "Are there others like you?"

"I am one of you."

"One of us?" She appeared puzzled. "I thought you were a meal. You are lucky. We had already eaten our fill before they put you in here, and so we were saving you for the next time one of us got hungry."

"Then I am happy to not have been devoured by my own people."

"Then you are Egris?"

It was too difficult to explain, nor was there time to elaborate because he wanted to know everything that he could since the Iranha still might yet take him away. Suffice for the moment he very simply said, "I am Ilon of trod Horhon. And you, hunter?"

"Nagris of trod Nagris."

The two males behind her were introduced as Krunod and Sekak. They briefly conversed and exchanged information. Ilon told them about the other trods and his efforts to unite them together. In return Nagris told him how her own trod had been ambushed, captured, and killed. It was a sad story which he had heard many times in the past. But now that he had answered their questions it was his turn to ask some of his own.

"Are there others?"

"There were. One died, the other two are gone now." Nagris lowered her head. "Dead I suppose."

"Do you think they might have escaped, Ilon?" It was Sekak who spoke. He was the youngest among them, and the most excitable. With a single word Ilon very quickly severed his optimism.

"No." Then he added with grim finality, "They are dead. Just like us." All sadly agreed. "Tell me, Nagris, what is this strange place?"

"Something between life and death," she glumly told him. "We are fed, but we are not free. See there?" She was pointing to the wall. When he approached he could see that it was constructed of a transparent material. Outside there was a lighted corridor all around the perimeter.

Frustrated, Ilon kicked uselessly against the hard surface with his foot, reflecting only the pain that was evident by his expression. "Then we are trapped here, living in the shadow of the Iranha. Why?"

"The Iranha come each day to watch us."

"They watch you? I don't understand."

"Neither do I. Some watch for a very long time, then they go away. That is all they do."

Shaking his head, Ilon said, "Keep you alive, feed you, watch you. I can fathom none of this."

Unfortunately Nagris was unable to provide any better explanation. The only certainty was that he was trapped in here just as they were. Ilon felt completely helpless. There was nothing he could do, nothing at all. As the day wore on he saw more and more faces behind the wall.

Now they were looking in. At him.

Chapter 35

City Tsilix was the ideal place to meet.

Still a frontier city, it was far enough removed from the influences of distant city Anaxerxes that there were ample opportunities for its citizenry to engage in all sorts of illegal activities—many of which the local politicians actively participated in. With transports full of new Epiphilinian immigrants arriving daily the city was growing at a spectacular pace. Still others were coming in from the outlying areas, eager to make a profit on these new arrivals.

Consequently there was a large criminal element thriving within the city. All sorts of nefarious characters were commonly seen on the back streets peddling their wares. Anything could be bought or had. For instance, those who had a taste for military weapons had their choice from among several of the planet's top arms merchants. Mercenaries and terrorist organizations wishing to stock up on the latest and most sophisticated weaponry could find it all right here. These various assorted thugs and exploiters were all part of a complex web of crime. In fact, a substantial part of the city's trade and commerce was illegal, though the local authorities tended to look the other way since it was known that well connected politicos were controlling the operations. Therefore bribery and corruption were rampant among city officials. As public representatives, they were used to demanding added inducements whenever it concerned a discretionary matter, or a speedier and more favorable zoning permit. Everybody was on somebody's payroll. This colonial profiteering and capitalism all meshed nicely together with its increasingly cosmopolitan population, making city Tsilix a good place to be in the world.

Borobos disapproved of this city. As they edged along through the busy traffic she pointed out sights that not only were displeasing to the eye, but an ominous sign of what was coming for the planet. "Rampant urbanization, untreated industrial waste, stinking rancid air, heaps of garbage. As on Epiphiline it is all here again. A waste. A terrible waste. Stop here."

The passenger vehicle creaked roughly as it came to a halt at the street corner. As Borobos waved her arm a cloaked figure suddenly appeared from one of the buildings and climbed quickly inside.

"Were you followed?"

Inelefar glanced out the driver's window as he angled the vehicle back into traffic. "Of course not."

"You are quite certain that no one knows of your whereabouts?"

"Absolutely," Borobos calmly assured him.

Poxiciti then lowered his hood and leaned back in the seat to catch his breath. "Good."

"What is our destination?" Inelefar asked him.

"Just drive for now." He indicated the direction with the swing of his hand. "Anywhere." After he was fully satisfied that no one was following he directed Inelefar to turn at the next road and head south.

"You look well," Poxiciti told Borobos formally, though his next words did show some genuine concern. "I heard there was an . . . accident."

"I am none the worse for it, although now I limp just like you." Pulling up her garment slightly she ran her wedge along a long length of scar where the doctors had reconstructed her smashed leg. "See? It heals nicely."

Inelefar showed little interest. When Borobos was sure he wasn't looking she reached over and touched Poxiciti's hand. He in turn grasped hers firmly and was secretly filled with desire for her. They stared at each other in silence and held hands until Inelefar's shouted query for directions broke the spell. Poxiciti pulled his hand quickly away and the moment was over, although when he spoke his voice was gentler.

"The pleasure of seeing old friends increases with the time apart, your companionship sorely missed, yet I feel that for us to be together the risk is too great. Perhaps you should not have come."

Borobos enjoyed his attention but dismissed his worries and spoke instead with an intensity that made him remember the point of her visit. "I had to come. The turn of events made it imperative to contact you. Important news has reached me. It seems that Pulima Cos has our creature in her possession."

The mentioning of her name was as if a floodgate had been loosed open within him, tearing through the reinforced barriers and flooding his mind with feelings of revulsion and animosity. Borobos sat patiently while he shouted out obscenities.

"You know how much I hate her. I would try to kill her again if I could," he admitted breathlessly.

"So would I."

Thinking of the captured creature brought to mind the real reason for his anger: his helplessness to stop her. "Is their nothing that grotesque thing does not already possess?"

"You."

This plain and simple truth lessened his anger and he felt ashamed for the way he was acting in her presence. Still he needed to grapple with the abominable truth: Pulima Cos still held onto the reins of power. She, his hated and despised enemy, still alive. And he, living his life under a constant threat of death every day. How he wanted to sink Pulima Cos and her ilk to the very bottom of the ocean, to see her crushed under the weight of her own evil doings.

"Then we must hurry up with this meeting, for she will soon learn of our whereabouts."

"To know that her spy would have to be at the very top of our organization. And if she does know, well then this traitor will undoubtedly be exposed."

"Her shadow is everywhere in this city." Unlike Borobos, he did not believe this one spy was her only source of information, and so he was eager to see a speedy end to this meeting. "Has the creature been harmed?"

"Apparently not. At least for now it has been imprisoned at city Anaxerxes zoo, though I cannot determine with any certainty its eventual fate."

"I can. For what reason does she still keep it alive?"

Her response to Poxiciti's interrogative hinted of more things to come. "There is something about the creature you should know. Something extremely important." Reaching down between her legs she opened a sealed case and handed over a mholic memory binder. "Here. Read this."

His reaction to seeing it was instantaneous. "The creature's medical file?" As he began flipping through the pages his curiosity soon turned to astonishment for the information that was contained within it. "How did you ever get your wedges on this?"

"Pulima Cos is not the only one with her spies," Borobos chuckled, proud of her small victory, and those in her service who had appropriated this vital piece of intelligence.

The holographically imaged binder was displaying the data above each sheet that he turned over. After Poxiciti reviewed the pertinent facts he forcefully slammed the binder closed and fought to control his emotions. "Unbelievable! Knowing that Igna Lox has more fat than she has brains, still I must concur with her findings. Did she uncover anything else of importance?"

Borobos tapped one of the pages in the binder that she was now holding and another image appeared. "When they examined the contents of its stomach they discovered burnt animal flesh. See here?" She pointed to a three dimensional chart that was showing the chemical composition of the material, then flipped over to the next page. "Organic compounds found in the smoke particulate matter are undeniably the result of meat charbroiling. The segathars are raw meat eaters. This animal eats cooked meat. Therefore it must have fire."

"So now we understand the how and the why. Fascinating. Do you suppose there are other creatures like this one in the world?"

"Possibly, although I am mystified by its existence. According to the data it is not an indigenous life form."

"And yet it is here. So where did it come from?"

"That is important to know, yet there is something I have not told you, and it is of far greater importance." Borobos's voice was hushed when she leaned forward to tell him, "Enough that we must try to think of a way to wrest it from Pulima Cos and her city." She made a gesture that signified the conversation was becoming much too sensitive and needed to be discussed in private.

"Pull over here," Poxiciti ordered, directing Inelefar toward a row of warehouses. He stationed the vehicle in front of the first building and waited for their return.

Up until now Borobos had disclosed this information to absolutely no one, and now as she finally divulged her secret to Poxiciti it felt like a great weight was lifting off her shoulders. "Just as you deduced. The segathars have guns. Even better—lag guns—and they know how to use them."

"No!" he gasped, horrified, though once this incredible news had sunken in he forced himself to cold reason as any good scientist would. Since Borobos had stated it as a fact, then it was an indisputable fact to her, so he did not doubt the integrity of the information, only the telling. "Are you absolutely certain? Even our own soldiers must be thoroughly trained on their proper use. And yet you suggest that wild beasts from the forest can somehow understand the complex workings of a weapon such as a lag gun."

"I suggest nothing. I am telling you. You yourself once theorized it was possible. That has happened. These segathars are learning, organizing, finding new ways to fight back. Unhappily I am forced to believe it is this creature who is teaching them this violence."

"Again, just as I predicted. Our presence here soon became their reason to survive. But the gulun gun was the first hard evidence that an armed incursion was possible. Now segathars with lag guns. Where do you suppose they got them?"

Her stance was as solid as her expression. "From me."

"You?" There was confusion, even surprise. "Explain. You gave the segathars weapons?"

An ambiguous question which could have been taken two ways. His befuddlement was such that Borobos hastened to explain. "Like you, I reasoned that if this one creature can master our gun, the others could learn, so I scattered weapons throughout the forest, places where I knew the segathars hunted. Apparently Pulima Cos discovered our weapons cache, was going to expose us all as—"

"You were stockpiling weapons!" Poxiciti was aghast. "For terrorist activities!"

"It was necessary!" she shouted back with equal force. "You submissive male pacifists are going to get us all killed. If a fist strikes, how can words alone make the beating stop?" She clenched her own fist and held it before him. "This will make it stop."

"Perhaps it is I who was wrong," Poxiciti apologized, lowering his voice because he was through with arguing. "Ordinarily you know I would never condone such violence, but now I see that these are desperate times and we must do what we must do. So then, the segathars have our weapons."

"Evidently so. The shipment was presumed destroyed while in transit, yet I searched further and found evidence to the contrary. I am convinced that it is these same segathars who are hitting targets near the city." Borobos described her experience at the sky port.

"Incredible," Poxiciti said after she was finished. "Almost unbelievable. I heard reports of terrorist gangs. Now armed segathars. You were right to risk coming here with this information. Does anyone else know about this?"

"No one but you."

"Good. See it remains that way." As he thought about it he realized that something else needed to be done. "I want you to give the segathars more weapons."

"More?" She started to protest. "They have more than enough now. With that kind of firepower they can level a whole city."

"Precisely. And with any luck, city Anaxerxes will be their first target."

"But they kill indiscriminately. Innocent people have already died. We risk a wholesale slaughter."

"Every one here is guilty—including us. Had we stayed on Epiphiline then none of this killing would be necessary now. I am convinced our presence here is leading us to another global catastrophe. Our only choice is to go back to Epiphiline and fix what we did wrong."

"Go back? It will not be easy to change the people's opinion, especially with Pulima Cos still in power."

"Only she stands in the way. So long as she reigns we will never succeed. Therefore, if we cannot convince the people to leave, then perhaps these segathars can. As for their teacher, it must freed at all cost. With Pulima Cos increasing her efforts to see them disposed of, it may be their only hope for survival."

"And ours."

"Now we must focus our attention to this one concern. Can it be done?"

Once Borobos understood the problem finding the solution was just a matter of mental application. "I think so. It is dangerous, maybe foolhardy, but I will do it."

Hearing this he realized just how much he was asking of her, the risk was enormous, and yet with so much at stake he depended on her success. "What exactly are you planning to do, Borobos?"

"You said it must be done. It will be done. Now you must not be afraid." Before she could speak her plan she heard the thud of running feet, then the creak of the door. Inelefar suddenly appeared in the doorway.

"Someone is coming!"

Her only concern was for Poxiciti. "Go! Quickly, quickly, you have to get away from here."

She rushed him outside to the waiting vehicle. Within moments they were well away from the scene; no one appeared to be following. Just to be sure Borobos ordered Inelefar to drive them around the city until she was absolutely convinced that they were safe, and the danger had passed.

"Turn at the next corner," she ordered Inelefar, then leaned back in her seat and remained quiet for a long time. When she finally spoke again there was a trace of optimism in her voice.

"Three days ago. Someone tried to assassinate Midlothian."

"A disgruntled citizen, I hope."

"A rebel. She very nearly succeeded. Unfortunately she was killed, but we now have many supporters like her, people who would gladly risk death to see Pulima Cos dead. I believe her government is in serious jeopardy. Her party has lost its popularity. It is just a matter of time before she is overthrown and replaced."

Poxiciti scowled. "She and her scurrilous companions may go, but there will always be others like them so long as we keep looking to those who promise to solve our problems. Stop here," he ordered. Before he climbed out he conveyed the briefest instructions. "You must leave this city and not ever return."

"Understood."

For the first time since Borobos could remember he reached across the seat and put his arms around her. "Please, Borobos, please be careful."

He departed in silence, and as the vehicle pulled away she watched him vanish into the shadow of the buildings. She did not hear Inelefar's voice until Poxiciti was out of her sight.

"Where to?"

"First I must convey important information to my contacts, then we go to city Anaxerxes."

As she leaned back Borobos sighed heavily. She hated to be parted from him and wished everything could somehow be different. If he knew only a small part of what she was planning to do he certainly would have tried to stop her. Nevertheless now she was on her way, and as the distance between them increased she knew quite possibly that she would never see him again.

Chapter 36

The journey to city Anaxerxes was equally long and uneventful. Instead of taking the air shuttle, Borobos chose the most onerous route, mainly because it was also the least likely to be watched. Parts of the main road were still under construction and there were numerous traffic snarls that tested even Inelefar's famous patience. But after two solid days of travel both were happy to have the city in their sight.

That afternoon Borobos hobbled into the administrative building. Inelefar's steady shoulder was giving her some assistance. Together, the two of them endured a brutish physical search for concealed weapons before finally being allowed into Pulima Cos's private suite of offices. As usual, Midlothian was there to greet them at the door.

"Sad to see you've recovered so quickly."

Ignoring her insulting remark Borobos pushed past her to find Pulima Cos's grotesque figure seated behind her desk, her one eye watching her as she limped forward. Pulima Cos smiled as she addressed Borobos with her usual sarcasm.

"How lucky for you to be able to walk again, Borobos. Let us hope that the next time something less fortunate doesn't befall you."

She made no attempt to conceal the anger that was within her, and likewise was equally rude and insulting. "I wish that for you every day."

Pulima Cos's smile decreased as she leaned forward across her desk. "You should thank me that my soldiers didn't recognize you at the sky port. Perhaps instead of saving your life they might have mistaken you for a rebel and spared me this meeting."

"There were people arrested? How many?"

"Only three were captured. Naturally these seditioners confessed their crimes and were punished."

"You mean executed."

"Of course. My only regret was that you were not among them."

"I am certain the ones you apprehended weren't anywhere near the sky port. Undoubtedly this was another convenient arrest to make yourself look good to the people. Those who you condemned were innocent."

"Yes. And they died. I assure you that more arrests are coming. And you're in the position to do nothing. There is only one reason why I still keep you alive, so I would give careful thought to your situation. For instance, where have been these past five days?"

"Sightseeing."

"Why not just kill her now?" Midlothian snarled. She glared at Inelefar, her hand caressing the segathar hide case which holstered her sidearm. "And what about you, pretty one?"

As a privileged scientist, Inelefar wasn't used to being addressed so discourteously, though he did manage to blurt out the same response as Borobos without it sounding too sarcastic.

"Lies, lies, lies!" Pulima Cos raged. "You think of untruths and speak only lies. I feel dirtied by your kind of lies. Now enough of this lying. No more lies. I want to hear only the truth." She terminated any further attempt to lie by indicating that Midlothian was ready to punish anyone who should try.

Ignoring Borobos's complaints of female brutality, Midlothian instead concentrated her efforts on Inelefar, who already was cowering beneath her clenched fists. "You will not even dare to think of lying to me. Admit the truth, or I will give you a beating to remember."

Feelings of despair crept in. Midlothian hovered over him, her ready fists bearing down.

"City Tsilix," he blurted out, speaking only because he had no tolerance for pain and did not wish to risk a beating.

"A very primitive city. A dot of scum on the ocean of civilization. Why were you there?"

"We were . . ." He glanced nervously at Borobos, then back to Midlothian who again was bringing up her fists. "We were recruiting new members."

"For what reason?" she asked him impatiently.

Inelefar was such a good liar. Borobos was surprised how well he lied, for the story she now heard him tell was vastly different from the truth. In any case, now that some civil communication had been reestablished she indicated to Pulima Cos the real reason for her visit.

"Word is spreading throughout the scientific community that you have a mystery animal in your zoo. Tell me, what are your plans for this creature?"

"For now it will remain alive. Only because it is a mild curiosity. I understand it is a very popular attraction with the people, a real profit-maker."

"I wish to see it today, conduct a rudimentary medical examination for my own scientific curiosity. Also, to study any existing records and biological tests. Is this possible?"

Pulima Cos straightened her stance of authority. "No."

Undeterred, Borobos went on, knowing that if her plan was to succeed then the only recourse was to bribe this greedy thing with lots of money. "I would pay handsomely for such an opportunity. Is 2000 konats enough?"

In light of this new offer Pulima Cos relented and said, "Then I permit it. For 3,000 konats, and it cannot be removed from the facility. Nor will you examine it without the presence of my guards." She indicated Midlothian would join them.

Agreeing to her list of conditions, Borobos left the office with Inelefar in tow. None of her movements betrayed what she was thinking, and so as they found their way outside the plan was made and her moment of triumph was one step closer.

By evening the zoo was closing to the public; people drifted outside. The building was now mostly deserted except for the workers who were busy feeding the animals. Greeting their party at the entrance, Boa Loam escorted them to the segathar pen. One of the guards was posted in the corridor while the second joined Midlothian and Borobos. Inelefar was in the adjoining laboratory preparing the examination table.

"And you say this was found with the creature?" Borobos closely examined the sharp tipped pole before handing it back over to Boa Loam. Midlothian's back was turned to them. How easy it would have been to run it through her.

"Why yes," Boa Loam answered. "Apparently to spear through animals. We found traces of blood on the tip. It may very well have been used to kill Epiphilinian citizens."

"Indeed. Then this is a very dangerous animal. How will it be retrieved from the segathar pen?"

"First it will have to be stunned," she explained. "And the segathars as well." Adjusting the stun level of her gun she handed it over to Borobos who studied it inquisitively. "At that setting the effects are nothing too traumatic. Temporary paralysis, followed by a state of disorientation, then a short duration of dizziness." She watched Borobos increase the stun level and cautioned her. "Be very careful. That setting will kill. Have you used one of these before?"

Borobos nodded. "Never." Without the slightest hesitation she swung around and pointed it directly at the guard. "Until now."

No one seemed to react when the guard crumpled and went down. Even Midlothian was surprised by the speed of which everything was happening. Yet before she could react the gun cracked again and she slumped to the floor. Borobos leaned over her dead form and disarmed her.

"Don't shoot!," Boa Loam pleaded, backing against the wall with both hands held shakily up in front of her.

Seizing her by the neck Borobos pushed her to the sealed double doors. "Open them," she ordered.

"Are you insane? The segathars haven't been put down yet. We'll be torn apart!"

She pressed the gun firmly to her head. "Do it now!"

During the commotion Inelefar had just returned from the laboratory with an armload of equipment. It made a resounding clatter as it crashed onto the floor, and as he looked over the sprawled bodies his eyes were wide with terror.

"What have you done, Borobos?"

"No time to explain. Here, take this." She handed him one of the stun guns. "There's another guard stationed at the end of the corridor. Take care of her." When he hesitated she pushed him backwards. "Go on!" She watched as he went away in silence, then turned to Boa Loam and said, "Now get these doors open."

Shortly there was a hum of noise as the first set of double doors slid open. Now only one more remained and Boa Loam wailed in protest as Borobos shoved her toward the next. They were almost there when she heard Inelefar's voice in the tunnel behind her.

"Stop." Turning slowly around Borobos saw that he was now pointing the gun directly at her. "Move away from there, right now—or die, Borobos."

"You! So it was you all along, Inelefar." Clenching her fists, every muscle in her body rippled with hatred and loathing. "You, who burnt down our building, caused all those deaths. Told Pulima Cos about all our plans, betrayed everyone, didn't you?"

"Shut up!" Inelefar snapped, quickly glancing back to see where the remaining guard was situated. "You. Go and get the guard." Boa Loam hurried out of sight.

"May you die a thousand deaths for your villainy," Borobos hissed in hatred. "Your bones ground up to dust, and scattered to the ends of the world. Why, Inelefar? Why did you do it?"

"You foolishly believe just as Poxiciti does, that our return to Epiphiline will force the polluters to change. He will kill us all! Why return to a dead world when we can have this one for the taking?"

"And wreck it just as we did ours?"

"We are what we are. If that happens here then we will find another world."

"No. I choose to return."

Inelefar regarded her with scorn. "Soon you'll be thankfully dead and forgotten. Your death will serve as a reminder to others what we do with criminals."

"If you wish to kill me—then do so now."

"You will not die that easily. First I must know where Poxiciti is hiding. Dead or alive, Pulima Cos will certainly reward me for bringing him to her."

"Your only reward will be to see your own death, traitor."

There was arrogance in his voice as he straightened his killing stance. "What are you talking about?" he sneered. "I am the one who has the gun."

"Wrong," Borobos smiled coldly. "To think I once trusted you. It is a good thing I stopped."

"I'm warning you. Move and die quickly."

Ignoring his threat she lowered her hands and reached for her belt. That was when Inelefar took aim and squeezed the trigger. Twice, but nothing happened. And the next thing he knew Borobos was standing over him as he died. Hearing the approaching footsteps she hid herself until they were close and surprised the both of them. They died too.

The alarm sounded as the second set of doors hissed open. Borobos swallowed as she stepped shakily into the segathar pen. She was taking an incredible risk. Nevertheless she had fully committed herself to this insane plan, and in doing so her fate now depended entirely on these blood-thirsty animals. Unpacking the lag gun which she had carefully hidden in one of the instrument containers, she now aimed it at the opposite wall and fired. A blue arc of light screamed toward its target. The ground shook violently beneath her as a tremendous explosion tore open the building to show a gaping, ugly hole. Now she set the gun down in front of her. And waited.

None of this had gone unnoticed. Ilon had watched the goings on from within the glass walls of his prison. Naturally his first thought was to kill this intruder, seeing it here now, standing this close. He took his first step forward.

"Go. Leave here. Escape." Again Borobos motioned towards the opening. "Outside. Go now."

Ilon looked straight at her, puzzled. Why was this Iranha trying to help them? His eyes lowered to the ground as he watched its foot push the weapon towards him. Why was it doing this? In the end he didn't care. All he knew was that the prison which had once kept him from the outside world was blown wide open.

Once Nagris realized that only this one unarmed Iranha stood between them and freedom she lunged forward, mouth agape, teeth shining, ready to strike death.

"Halt!"

The strength of Ilon's shouted order froze Nagris in her tracks. Her angry expression hardened, that even while she was smiling he could tell there was a darkness behind her teeth. Teeth that wanted to kill.

"Why stop now?" she demanded. "We can escape."

"I believe that is what this ugly thing wants."

"Then let us kill it and be gone," Krunod said.

Borobos was petrified with fear as the big segathars stalked around her. They were growling together, communicating what she believed was her death, but when the small creature answered them its meaning was abundantly clear.

"No," Ilon said firmly. "No killing. Let us be done and go home."

They parted enemies. Seizing the lag gun by the haft Ilon strode toward the opening, never looking back. However Nagris glared at Borobos as she passed by. Her fervent wish was to kill her—she still could—but obeyed Ilon only because there would be plenty of other Iranha to kill.

Borobos watched the last segathar drag its tail outside and vanish from sight. They were gone, but the fear of death was still with her. Her legs were wobbling so badly she collapsed under her own weight. Struggling to her feet she walked back through the double doors and stopped suddenly. Now seeing the corpses the full impact of what she had done started to sink in. She had killed everyone, had freed dangerous animals. She was a murderess, a criminal, who would be pursued, hunted down, punished.

Perhaps the segathars should have killed her, yet even as she heard the running footsteps, saw the armed guards coming closer, she knew that she would be dead very soon.

Chapter 37

Ilon was running, trying his best to keep up with them. The weight of this gun was slowing him down, and so he cast it aside and kept on going. All he could see was the tumult of broken branches and crushed vegetation where his overanxious companions had crashed through the undergrowth. He jumped over the trunk of a decaying tree, almost stumbling into them as he came to a fast halt at the outermost wall of the complex. Strange looking animals were crowding nearby, now mewling feverishly at the sight of them.

"The final barrier," Nagris said. "Use your weapon, quickly, and we shall all be free of this place at last."

"I threw it away. It was a burden that would only bring the Iranha to us that much faster." Instead he was looking up at the wall. "Can you jump that high?"

"Easy for me," she said. "What about you?"

"Come down here," he motioned.

Clasping both hands around her neck Ilon clung on tightly as she in turn closed her arms around him. Her big legs tensed. "Hold on."

They were the first ones over, with Sekak and Krunod quickly joining them on the other side. "That was easy," Sekak said.

"We're not out of the Iranha city yet."

Overhead a gusty breeze pushed rain clouds across the sky. It had just recently stormed and the running water collected in the muddy tracks where an Iranha machine had just recently driven through. Bright lights suddenly appeared from behind. The hunters instinctively stood motionless and silent. However, Ilon took advantage of their natural camouflage and stayed hidden behind them until the machine rumbled past. Once the danger was over they were quickly on the move again.

The edge of the city loomed closer than ever. Under the darkness of night three shadowy figures darted across a roadway, so suddenly and stealthily that they were gone in an instant. Up ahead, Ilon heard the muffled screams of the Iranha, saw the near invisible forms of the hunters standing beside the corpses. Here he could see that the gates of the city were wide open.

"Straight ahead to the field." Nagris's teeth cracked solidly together, so great was the emotion. "To freedom."

This much anticipated moment had come, and everyone hurried outside, happy to see the city growing ever more distant. However,

Ilon couldn't run any further, and collapsed into the grass, gasping for air before Nagris ordered the others to halt.

"You call that running? Why a newborn still fresh from its mother's womb could run faster than you. You are slowing us down. Now come on." She prodded him with her clawed foot. "We can't stay here."

"Can't go any farther," Ilon puffed. "Go on, leave me."

"Never. You are coming with us," she said forcefully. Leaning over, she picked him up in her arms.

Krunod was looking toward the city. "Will the Iranha come after us, Ilon?"

While no one was in pursuit, he knew they would be coming very soon. "Yes, certainly. I think we better leave."

To be able to jump again was a huge improvement over their slow-footed escape. It was near daybreak when the great forest slipped under the sky and very soon they were jumping beneath the trees. No one wanted to stop now, though it was not until midday when they finally reached the encampment.

The shock of seeing it deserted quickly replaced his eagerness to be home. All over there were signs that the Iranha had been here, evidenced by the scored tread marks and the deep craters where their weapons had blasted. But what had been the fate of his hunters? The absence of any recent tracks indicated that no one had come back, yet it was too soon to tell if any had escaped. A search of the burrow only worsened his fears. Finally it was Krunod who spoke aloud what the others were undoubtedly thinking in silence.

"Could they be dead?"

"No," Ilon said ill-temperedly.

"It is very possible that they are," Nagris grimly agreed only because the Iranha were accomplished killers. "But we are still alive."

"Better had I been here with them."

"Then you might be dead too," she disagreed. "We should be thinking about leaving this place."

Ilon had already made the outward decision to go, but inwardly his thoughts were in turmoil. Were the trods all destroyed, or had everyone managed to escape? Even more importantly, were his mother and sister still alive? Somehow he had to know for sure. This single concern usurped all other concerns, though he had to be pragmatic about his chances of finding them alive. Telling Nagris to wait for him he slipped back inside the burrow and found his riding harness.

"Here, put this on," he told her.

Under the shadow of the trees they slipped back onto the field and headed north-west, making a wide swing of the Iranha city before steering toward the desert. Digging in just after sunrise the next morning they slept through the heat of the day, then awoke and pressed on forward.

The barren landscape did not begin to change until they saw a dark line swelling on the horizon and knew the forest was ahead of them. Here they jumped through a grass filled plain and killed their first nentenen. No one had hunted in a long time, so perhaps this was the best one they had ever eaten. Sekak sank his teeth into the nentenen's thick shank and swallowed juicy mouthfuls of the sweet, bloody meat. Untying his bundle of wood, Ilon built a small fire and roasted his portion of meat before kicking sand over the coals and packing up the largest pieces.

Night soon became morning and the day passed quickly by. It was well after dark the next evening when they discovered a hunter's gnawed remains laying under the cold glow of the full moon's light. A gruesome trail of bodies led them back to the sand burrow, there making yet another grisly discovery.

"Just as I feared," Nagris growled. "All dead. Trod Skulgol is no more."

Seeing all of these skeletons laying about caused Sekak to wail in anguish. Most of his existence had been spent living in a cage. There he had known only the comforts of his prison cell. Now he was very quickly discovering that life outside was even grimmer than the one he had left behind.

"Where can we go where the Iranha have not already struck?" Krunod asked.

"Trod Karipace is a single day from here. Yet I fear the worst," Nagris admitted gloomily.

"Then do not forget today," Ilon told them. "Because there is only the darkness of tomorrow." He bent and picked up the first bone. "Now we bury these dead and sing their death song."

The hunters had great fear about the trek. To Ilon there was no mystery at all about what lay ahead. Either the same butchery had befallen trod Karipace, or they were still alive. Those were the only sure possibilities, and so at dawn when they reached the rim of trod Karipace's hunting territory they roared with happiness as seven hunters bounded forward to greet them.

No one had ever seen anyone like Ilon before. The onlookers debated loudly in his presence, and still they were not even sure what he was. Indeed he had captured their interest. They poked his soft flesh with their fingers, touched his dark fur, although they thought better of doing this when one of them received a rough slap on the snout.

The strangers were escorted back to the sand burrow and introduced to Karipace, an old female with few teeth and a bad arm that hung limply at her side.

"What is it that you seek, hunters?"

"Why the same as you." Ilon pushed his way past the others and faced the old hunter. "To see our world free of the Iranha."

Karipace was shocked more by his appearance than his speaking ability. "And what are you, creature?"

Before he could answer Nagris spoke in his place. "Our liberator. The one who is to tear down our enemy and bring us peace."

"So the stories are true after all," Karipace said. "I did not think to believe them, and yet here you are." She studied him momentarily. If she was pleased to see him then she hid it behind her voice of disappointment. "You do not look like the savior I expected."

"How I look is unimportant. Rather the future that I bring you and all Egris—is important." When Ilon told her of the future he spoke with an enthusiasm that intensified. Those who listened were forced backwards by the strength of his words. "We can attack them, defeat them, send them back home. We can win!"

Nonetheless Karipace did not share his excitement, or his future. "Had I known the future as I know it now, I would have altered nothing. There is only one sure course, and that is the one we are on. We are simple hunters who understand simple things. However this is not a simple thing. You ask us to risk our lives following you, attacking an enemy who we know cannot be defeated. It is better to stay away from them. We want to cause no more trouble, only to live our lives in peace."

"Peace," Ilon hissed. "Peace. That word is as alien to them as I am to you. There will never be peace, only killing, for that is what they have chosen for us."

Shaking her big head she said, "Then I am sorry. Perhaps you ask too much of us."

In part Ilon agreed with her arguments, but not her assumptions. "You have no choice. Understand that they are killers. The only life that exists for them is killing us. So do not think they will stop killing just because you wish to live apart from them. Wherever you hide they will hunt you down and kill you. I offer you the only choice. To choose anything else is to choose death."

"How will you do what no other Egris has been able to do?" Karipace asked skeptically.

She was certainly not easy to convince. Ilon laid out in detail what he had already accomplished and what he was still planning to do. He even explained exactly how the Iranha could be defeated. His listeners were polite, nodding appreciatively whenever he spoke of his past successes. He had earned their encouragement, but none of their support. In the end he was disappointed with their reluctance to fight. To them it was simply better to flee than fight. How could he make them understand that they were really running away from survival, and instead heading straight for extinction?

Most in the trod decided that night Ilon's plan was too dangerous. No one wanted to die unnecessarily, especially defending a cause that they had no possible chance of winning. Karipace's mind was set and her orders were firm. They were staying here.

Even Nagris, known to many of these hunters, could not influence their decision to remain. In spite of her great efforts she finally gave up. "It is just as you said. No one will fight them."

As Ilon climbed up onto Nagris's back and strapped himself in he could only shake his head. His dire warning had accomplished nothing. He had encountered such resistance before, though never this strong. Karipace was too stubborn, too unwilling to risk change, and that would bring about her end. Worse, he knew as he turned his back and headed for the field, trod Karipace would soon be no more.

They followed the track of the second moon until moonset, then dug into a dune and slept for the day. In his dreams Ilon dreamed of his mother and sister, was reunited with them once again. By the time he awoke the days of dread that had oppressed him were gone for good. He was now sure that they were still alive.

It was the following evening when the hunters reached a small hill that looked down into a shallow valley filled with clear water from some faraway mountain. Here they had to stop and make a decision.

"Where will we go now?" Krunod asked. "Back the way we came? To the empty forest?"

"No," Ilon answered. "Instead we head north, cross over the Un desert to the Olahn territory."

"The Olahn?" Nagris said with wide eyes. "That is a long journey. Many days and every one full of danger. Why do we trek there?"

"Trod Horhon must be there..."

"Might be there. Your gut feelings could get us all killed. Why should we risk traveling on the open desert in pursuit of a trod that might not even exist?"

"I can think of no other alternative. Can you?"

She couldn't. Every direction she turned was as uncertain as the next. Behind there was nothing for them. Ahead was something, so on they went.

Eventually the rock strewn hills spread apart; the grass started to thin out. High drifts of sand soon began to appear and after only a half day's travel they were already deep in the desert. With the worst yet to come, Krunod and Sekak already wanted to turn back. If Nagris felt the same way then she at least never said it aloud. Just before sunrise they came upon a natural spring where the water welled up through the ground. Animal tracks scarred the muddy banks. Dark forms, too wary to be eaten, were seen running away to safety.

"Drink your fill," Nagris ordered. "This may be the last we see for a long time."

An arid wind was blowing breezily, bringing up a light dust that Ilon brushed from his eyes. "We have gone far enough for today," he said. "Rest here, then we hunt tonight."

Fresh water. Fresh meat. It was a good idea and there were no dissenting voices. They choose a shady spot on the eastern slope of the dune and dug into its side to wait out the day's scorching heat.

At dusk the hunters were on the prowl again, their bodies melding into the evening shadows as they crept in absolute silence toward the watering hole. There they surprised a small herd of crested mullatods by the water's edge, killing one before sending the others off in a flurry of dust and panic. Unwrapping his dwindling supply of wood Ilon built up a fire. After he was through he put out the fire and repacked the burnt bits of wood for later use. He was used to this life on the move and learned to take advantage of every situation because the next day was never the same as the last.

"We stay the night, then tomorrow at dusk we leave," Nagris said firmly. "The path we are on is a long one. The Olahn is still days ahead of us."

"After tonight," Ilon agreed, "then we keep moving."

"Where will we find your trod?" she asked in earnest of his belief that they were still alive.

"I don't know yet." He acknowledged the truth and thought little of the consequences. The journey begun, the destination unknown, his only certainty that wherever they headed his trod would be there.

At hearing this, Krunod and Sekak, even Nagris, were sorely tempted to turn back. That would have been their first choice, but because there was nothing to return to they reluctantly decided to stay.

With the hunting now finished and the long evening still ahead of them the hunters had little to do. After eating their fill of meat they were moving about sluggishly and so they lulled near the water's edge. Few words were exchanged and this suited Ilon because he felt depressed. He knew the others were angry with him for leading them on this foolhardy expedition. Perhaps this future he was seeing was wrong. His whole life he had been fighting the Iranha, and to what end? What had he accomplished? He was filled with self-doubt and did not want to fight anymore. Upset as he was he realized this was too big a decision to make right now. What he needed was some time to be by himself to think, so he picked up his spear and headed up the side of the dune.

The night was peaceful and the sky was filled with a profusion of stars. The second moon was sinking below the horizon, but from atop the dune Ilon watched the gibbous moon's light die below in the still waters of the watering hole.

"Ilon."

Someone called out his name and he spun around suddenly to see a dark shape at the bottom of the dune. He watched as it started up the slope toward him. Too small to be one of the hunters, he decided. His spear was raised, but he dropped it the instant he recognized the hunter who now stood before him. Clad in animal skins, carrying a spear, her long black hair was flowing off her broad shoulders. Ilon was close to tears for the memory of her had never died.

"Aisahl?" Aisahl, who like a mother had comforted him and taught him everything he knew of the old ways and the life of the hunter.

"Ilon." She pushed her spear into the sand and stepped forward. "I am here. Now we must talk."

Chapter 38

Ilon was so dumbfounded by Aisahl's presence he was utterly speechless. To see her now, alive, was too much for him to bear. When he looked at her he saw only dark memories of the past. He remembered the Uta who murdered her, and how he had buried her in the cave and mourned her loss. She was dead. Dead. Unthinkingly he told himself this over and over as he peered at her and groped for an explanation.

"You should be dead."

"She is dead," Aisahl admitted, before adding, "And so are you."

She was speaking the old way, her one hand swinging downward so that it literally translated as *one-who-sleeps-in-the-ground*.

Now he was genuinely puzzled, and a little frightened. He struggled for the right thing to say, in a language he had not spoken for ages. But after all he was still Taal. Maybe he had forgotten it during his life here, yet as he searched through his thoughts the words and hand movements came together one by one.

"I don't understand. Who are you? What are you?"

Aisahl merely smiled. When she reached forward to touch him, Ilon stumbled backwards. "Don't touch me!"

Fumbling in the sand for his spear he seized it up and thrust it forward threateningly. "Stay back," he warned her. Tears streaked his face; he had conflicting emotions. Part of him wanted to believe that this was really Aisahl, while the other part of him believed it could just as easily be some devious kind of Iranha trickery.

Aisahl frowned at him. "I thought I taught you never to show your fear?"

"I fear the thing that dwells within you, for though you speak and look as she who I remember—you are not her."

"Part of me is Aisahl, her genetic material, the memories of her that you had. In many ways I am her." She dropped her spear at his feet. "I wish you no harm, Ilon. If it is my form that distresses you, then I will assume another."

Although it was a strange offer which he only briefly considered, he signified rejection. With his hand still firmly on the killing spear he stared at her in resolute silence, his eyes never leaving her. Aisahl, or whatever she was now, made no further attempt to touch him; his spear point guaranteed that. Yet since her existence could not be denied he was soon forced to believe that her mysterious appearance was beyond even the Iranha's capabilities. Indeed, whatever power had brought her across the gulf of space and time was beyond his understanding. So the moment she sat on the sand and started to talk he listened attentively to her every word.

"I did not want to be the one to tell you, but too many things have already happened and so I must. You remember our life together as I do, and you know that you are Taal, or, as the Uta who now fill our world now call us, Neanderthal. But you also must know that the lives we lived were so long ago in the past that our world is new and changed."

"As is this world," Ilon said.

"This is not our world," she agreed. "Look and see that your hunters are as different to you as night is to day. But here, as there, you have a ruthless enemy, a witless destroyer who wishes to wreck everything in it just as the Uta did, and continues to do. This is no coincidence and I will soon tell you why."

There was a brief pause before Aisahl continued; this time she was using the Egris vernacular, the syntax of her statements coming so simply and clearly to him that Ilon scarcely noticed when she changed over.

"You know of the Iranha machines, know that they crossed through the emptiness of space to bring their swarm here. But there was another machine, one that stalked between the stars hunting for worlds as you would hunt for food. It was a thinking machine, a living machine, which created other machines like itself and dispatched them throughout the galaxies. Far in the distant past, thousands of lifetimes ago, one of these machines visited our world and used our people to bring to life the Uta whose ancestors eventually destroyed us."

All at once her meaning was appallingly clear. "Like the Iranha! Is that what you are trying to tell me? That there are other worlds where this same thing has happened?"

"Many more. Thousands more. As many as you can see stars in the night sky."

Ilon gasped for air as his lungs suddenly emptied. So many? Now he knew for certain that there was nothing he could do. Nothing at all. Never in his whole life had he felt so completely and utterly helpless. The Iranha would eventually win, other worlds would collapse and die, and he would be long dead, his bones ground under the feet of his oppressors. His hand closed around the cold wood of his spear. This creature looked and talked like Aisahl, yet nevertheless he wanted to kill her.

"You caused all this?"

She tilted her head slightly. "The ones who sent me. They constructed the machine. Ages ago they built wondrous machines, left their own world and traveled to the stars beyond. It was a time of discovery and new ideas, a time of creating things never before imagined. Never once did they dare to think that what they created would turn against them." She stared at him, her eyes moist in the cool of the desert. "None of this was supposed to happen."

"It did happen," Ilon told her roughly. "You and your kind are criminals who deserve to die. All these deaths are your fault."

"Not entirely. But you are right; a large portion of the blame is ours. Those of us who remain regret what has happened and would change it if we could—we cannot."

He was not encouraged at all by her admission. Even what she had just said now made it seem all the more certain that the Iranha would keep on killing. And like his old home, this world and everyone in it was about to become extinct.

"Too many have already died, more will die, I will die, while all you offer us are empty words of consolation. It is not nearly enough!" Ilon shouted angrily.

Aisahl stood by impassively while he continued berating her. Blaming her would alter nothing. The past was immutable, was as dead as those hunters whose skins now decorated the Iranha cities. What had been done could not be undone, so she swung her arm and motioned for him to be quiet.

"You are lucky to be alive, Ilon. When I found you, your life was near its end. Had I not—"

"So it was you!"

Now he remembered, the bright light, the excruciating pain and terror. Thinking about it now made him shiver all over with cold. What had she done to him?

"You are not the same Ilon," Aisahl carefully explained. "That one died long ago. Fortunately I was able to preserve his genetic material. That is, you are an exact copy of him. Also, the memories that you have are his. His entire life's experiences and knowledge as well."

At hearing this Ilon fell back, unable to speak. Deep down he had always suspected he was not the same person. Aisahl's unsettling disclosure now confirmed that. He was two different people living two separate lives. Part of him belonged to someone else, but the part which was Egris belonged exclusively to him. Despite his present life he had no desire to break the bonds of the past. After all, deep in his heart, he was still Taal, and so long as he remained alive, Ilon's memory lived on through him.

"Not everyone was lost," Aisahl continued telling him. "Your kind was not wiped out completely. I found others."

"Others?" Tears filled his eyes suddenly. He could not stop himself from thinking her name. "Lende?"

"I cannot say. Not yet. First we must talk some more."

He had always believed himself to be the sole survivor. However his happiness diminished when Aisahl pointed out the dim and distant star which once was his home. For him that life ended long ago. Nothing that he wanted was there now. This was his home. So while she spoke in great detail about her plans for him, it was not until he started to tell her about his own plans that she made it perfectly clear he was to return.

"Go back? To a world that crawls with Uta?" He firmly shook his head no. "I think not. The Uta are there, the Iranha are here. What is the difference?"

"A lot of time has passed, many things have happened. You cannot imagine the changes."

"I can imagine the Uta have changed it for the worse. Again I must say no," he said forcefully, this time signifying strong refusal, *death-from-spear.*

"There is one important thing still yet to be told. These other Taal I spoke of . . ." Her voice trailed off so that the full impact of her next words would be felt. "They live now, among the Uta."

His eyes went wide. "Taal lives in our world again?"

"Hidden from the Uta, and yet right under their noses." Aisahl sighed. "I have tried to make things right. So you understand the reason why you must return. Believe me," she told him, "one day you will return."

"If that day comes then you must know I will not go willingly."

"Understood. But what must happen will happen. When your task here is accomplished."

"What have I accomplished?" Ilon said bitterly. "Each day we are closer to defeat. Upon my death the only thing I shall leave my followers is the knowledge that those who trusted me died for nothing."

"You are on the right track, Ilon. Had I not brought you here these Egris would certainly be doomed. They are stubborn to change, helpless against an enemy like the Iranha who changes all the time. But you have taught them new things, launched attacks which have brought you successes."

"And failures," he said. "They learn slowly—and die quickly. How can we defeat so powerful an enemy, how?"

"I see Egris, lots of them, fighting at your side, joined in battle against the Iranha."

"I can't do it anymore," he protested. "The Iranha are winning. Can even you not see this? If you have the power of life and death as you say then you can stop them, destroy them as they have destroyed us."

Instead Aisahl rose to her feet and arched her arms for speaking. The finality of her movements was as firm as her answer. "No. We will not aid you in killing. Above all other things is our recognition of all life forms—including the Iranha. That must be clear."

"And the Uta too," he growled. To Ilon it was perfectly clear. This cold creature of death would sooner see them wiped out than lift her hand against those whom she had inadvertently created. Had he been holding his spear at this very moment he surely would have driven it through her. Aisahl must have known what he was thinking because she took a step backwards and waited until his anger was spent.

"Then I curse the day you found me. As I have lived and died once already, to live and die again never seeing the end of my enemy is a burden too unimaginable to bear."

"You wish to defeat these Iranha, don't you?"

"With my whole being. I have no other purpose than to see them driven away in defeat—forever."

"Then it will happen," she said simply.

Ilon scowled. "And how will I ever bring that many fighters together?"

Aisahl's broad smile brightened her face. "What you said just now is happening."

He had no idea what she meant, so he proceeded to address what he thought was his most important concern. "The Iranha will never leave this world peacefully. Without your help how are we to overcome our enemy?"

"What you wanted the most—I have already given you. Remain here. In the morning you will see your future. Now I must go," Aisahl said abruptly. "May you be successful in all of your ventures."

"Wait!" Ilon cried out. "Don't go yet."

But Aisahl ignored his desperate plea to stay and was turning away, was looking up at the night sky, at the shimmering stars beyond. Suddenly there was bright burst of light followed by a searing wave of heat, and when Ilon rubbed his eyes open she was gone. The scorched marks in the sand were the only indication of where she had once stood. Picking up his spear he hurried back to camp to tell the others what had just happened.

"Unbelievable," Nagris gasped out after Ilon finished recounting his whole story. "And she told you to stay here?"

"Until the morning," Ilon nodded.

"What then?"

He simply shrugged.

Chapter 39

Some of the stars were beginning to fade in the sky. Glancing eastward, Ilon saw the sun coming up over the ridge of dunes. "Get some sleep. Tonight we go on."

In a short while everyone was digging into the same bank. Nagris was curled up inside her burrow, almost asleep when she suddenly slipped her head out of the hole as though something had disturbed her. A speckled gnar scurried past, a small, carnivore with its jaws clamped around some limp animal it had killed. Nothing else moved.

Moments later, after she was back inside with her eyes closed tight, she opened them again. Now she had felt something. Further investigation took her outside to the watering hole where she discovered mysterious ripples on the water's surface. Then she felt the faint trembler hit just as some of the sand broke loose and cascaded down the hillside. Looking into the bright sunshine Nagris saw a dark cloud building on the horizon. A dust cloud. Perhaps a wind storm was coming. That or something very big was coming this way.

Krunod was fast asleep when Nagris reached inside his burrow and grabbed him by the tail, dragging him outside. This rude awakening caused him to bellow at her. Silencing his noisy protest she ordered him to be attentive. "Listen . . . There. Did you feel that?" A head-shake confirmed that he had. "Wake the others. Hurry."

Soon the running hunters joined her on top of the dune. Nagris wasted little time showing them the huge dust cloud which stretched all the way across the northern horizon. There was a dull, steady rumbling sound as the ground shook beneath their feet.

"There and there," she pointed. "This one from the north, the other from the west. Two groups."

"What could be coming?" Krunod asked.

"Iranha!" There was immense fear in Ilon's voice as he spoke aloud their name. Surely the Iranha could not have tracked them to here, could not have found them out so soon, although apparently they had.

"Look again," Nagris said confidently. "You will see that they are not Iranha—but Egris. Lots of them."

It couldn't be. She had to be mistaken. Ilon refused to believe her, steadfast in his belief that the end was closing in. Yet as he watched this seemingly indistinct line coming closer, he was able to make out some of the leaders. Creatures with huge heads, long legs and tails, creatures that looked amazingly like hunters.

"More coming from the south," Sekak informed them.

Krunod now noticed a faint cloud on the eastern horizon and knew there were hunters coming from every direction.

From where he was standing they appeared to be all converging on this very spot, for as they drew nearer Ilon could see that they were indeed heading straight for here. Even though he saw them with his own eyes, he was completely mystified. What power had driven so many across the desert, to this one place, to where he was now? Then it struck him. What he wanted most was to bring all Egris together, and the creature who was Aisahl had given him just that!

The approaching stampede sounded like thunder, the ground was trembling, shaking, the roiling dust so thick that the sky behind was blacked out completely. Nagris led Krunod and Sekak to the bottom of the hill where the first Egris were gathering. Only Ilon stood alone, and as they crowded around the bole of the dune he found himself overlooking a sea of hunters. Hundreds and hundreds of faces, their jaws stretched open in the warm sunshine, rows of white teeth glinting. It was the most wonderful, incredible thing he had ever seen in his entire life.

By late-afternoon hunters were continuing to stream in and by the time the sun dropped below the horizon there were too many to be counted. In this whole wide world he could not have imagined so many Egris in one place.

"Ilon!" It was Horhon who raced up the slope to greet him. Seizing him by the waist she hauled him into the air and screamed excitedly. "You are here! Alive! You look well fed too. Say something."

He smiled as he smoothed his hand against her face, and felt her tremble with happiness. "Once we were separated by the Iranha, driven apart. No longer. Now we are joined together to fight them."

Horhon looked below at the hunters' swelling ranks, amazed by the sight of so many. "You did this?"

"I wanted this. What made you come here?"

"To find you," she grinned. "In my dreams you were alive in the desert."

"Why that is what brought us out here too," he said, surprised.

"Three days ago we left with trods Targasesk and Sandisand. As we traveled we met more and more hunters. Others told me that some of the trods have trekked for ten days. Then I could only wonder why so many were coming this way. Now I understand."

Ilon was thinking out loud to himself. "She must have done all this. Planned everything so that it would happen exactly this way."

"Who?"

"It no longer matters. What matters most is that we are all here together. Now we must act before these hunters break apart and leave for good."

Horhon knew exactly what needed to be done. "You must speak to them, and everyone will listen."

"I am afraid of that," Ilon confessed.

"You shouldn't be. It is exactly as I foresaw. I have dreamed and longed for this moment since your birth. These hunters will follow you." There was satisfaction in her voice. "But first you must convince them, make them want to fight."

He hesitated, yet this was his one chance, his only chance, he knew, for an opportunity such as this would never come again. "The Iranha have attacked them, chased them, killed many. They are afraid. To make them fight, they will need to see that we can do to the Iranha what they did to us. Your gun. Let me have it."

By the time he was ready to speak it was dark and the first moon was just beginning to appear. Yet even as he climbed to the top of the hill and peered over the sprawling mass of bodies, he had grave doubts about the outcome. So he lifted his gun and squeezed the firing mechanism, knowing the grim fate awaiting them all if he should fail.

The thunderous sound and bright light was an instant attention getter, and those who were in the outer circle now pressed forward to see what they could learn of this strange and terrifying noise stick.

"Hunters!" Ilon shouted. "The time has come for us to put aside our fears and mistrust. Today you must think of only one thing: the Iranha. There is not one among you here who has not suffered because of them. Had they remained on their world the peace you had always known would have continued unbroken, and you would still be living as you remembered, never knowing that these poisonous creatures ever existed. But the Iranha are here, to hunt us and kill us, to infest our world with their poisonous garbage and stinking cities, to destroy here what they have already destroyed there. What we need to do is fight them. So you ask how we fight this kind of creature, a creature who seems impossible to kill. Do not think them so powerful. They can be killed. Look at me, the weakest among you, and still I have killed Iranha."

His bold words elicited a rumble of disbelief, though it gradually subsided when many of his supporters in the crowd assured the onlookers that this was in fact true. Yet Ilon had to seize the moment while there was still time, as many of his converts were just barely convinced.

Just then another blue arc of light screamed overtop of the hunters' heads, and those who turned to see where it went saw the huge crater where it impacted, then felt the ground shake. Shocked gasps circulated throughout the crowd. Many of the onlookers were still recovering when a second explosion, then a third, rocked the screaming audience.

"This is a thing of mass destruction, a weapon of unimaginable killing power which we stole from the Iranha and now possess. Do not fear it. What was once theirs is now ours. We can kill as they kill, destroy as they destroy. But that is still not enough. What we need are hunters who will fight with us, and who will keep on fighting until these Iranha are defeated and destroyed. Some of you are thinking no. Do not think these Iranha will forget you. For those of you who walk away today, I promise they will kill you tomorrow. Your cowardice is defeat for every one of us."

He could not impress upon them enough the importance of that, and so he spoke about the impending battle, describing concepts and strategies which for most were difficult to grasp. But slowly and carefully he worked his audience, until everyone could see in their minds exactly what he wanted them to see. A long blank of silence followed after he was finished; everyone was thinking. Finally the crowd began to stir and the first shouts that he heard soon became a groundswell of support as thousands joined in. They were going to fight!

"You have done it!" Horhon cheered. "We will fight the Iranha and win, destroy their cities, drive them away from here for good. When do we go?"

"Immediately," Ilon said as he held out his riding harness.

She stepped backwards and flatly refused to take it from him. "No. There is someone else more suited for this honor, and he is waiting below." As she gave the signal the crowd parted and let this single hunter through. With some shouted directions from Horhon he found his way to top of the dune and halted before them.

Ilon smiled. "Krugjon."

"Yes, it is I," he grinned. "It pleases me to hear your voice again, Ilon."

"I see you are eating well. How goes the hunting?"

"Badly. I have sorely missed your eyes."

"And I have missed your teeth, great hunter. So you have found me and now we must never be separated again. Here." He gave him his riding harness and Krugjon slipped it on.

"I want to kill Iranha."

"Soon," Ilon said. "Very soon."

It was just after daybreak when the first in the procession started to move. There was a pale glow over the eastern horizon. Raising his hand Ilon gave the order to depart. Krugjon snapped his big tail and took off into the air as the great line surged and rippled behind him. That first step had started the journey back. Now they were heading for home, straight for the Iranha city.

For city Anaxerxes.

Chapter 40

"**I** bring a message from Nolum Gar, who is head jailer of the city correctional facility."

The low ranking dreg had carefully memorized her master's exact words, had repeated the message over and over in its entirety until it was perfect. But now as she stamped forward into Pulima Cos's domineering presence, she felt her throat constricting and hoped she would not forget a single word.

"Borobos, who is her prisoner, refuses to cooperate. Nolum Gar deeply regrets that she is unable to make this treasonous creature talk and sends her apologies. Regrettably the information that you wished for is not forthcoming."

Though Pulima Cos had leaned back in her wet chair the messenger could feel the intensity of her anger and started to tremble with fear. Should she continue and risk a possible beating, or wait until she was commanded to speak further?

"That is because Nolum Gar is too soft on her charge. Obviously she has no stomach for torture. Very well." Her aides surrounded her as she gestured, and each in turn bowed before her and hurried away. In the end only she and the dreg remained in her office. "You will instruct your slack master that I wish her to send the prisoner here to me. Immediately. Now leave me."

That was her final command. Bowing her head in lowly servitude the dreg about-faced and marched hurriedly through the doorway.

Now Pulima Cos was alone with her thoughts. Borobos's reluctance to speak was an irritating annoyance, albeit an inconvenience which she would surely and swiftly correct. Were Midlothian still alive she would have dealt appropriately with Borobos. Not like that weakling Nolum Gar, who grew squeamish at the very thought of inflicting pain. But it would be done. After all, everything she planned and worked for was contingent on Poxiciti's capture. So far, since her efforts to capture him had failed she was now more determined than ever to find him and rid herself of him. For as long as he was free he would continue to stir up the people against her, to cause all sorts of trouble as he had done in the past. She cursed him and his kind. Environmentalists were like trees that needed to be burnt down and plowed under. Only then would she be able to plant what she wanted. What she really wanted was to see the both of them dead, Poxiciti and Borobos together. That day, she was sure, was coming closer.

Later four heavily armed guards hauled Borobos into Pulima Cos's chamber. She was chained and manacled though she managed a dignified entrance, standing defiant and straight whenever the guards pushed her on. Aside from the ugly bruising on her face she was otherwise in good appearance and had held up reasonably well since her capture. However, as Borobos faced her old nemesis again she knew this was all suddenly about to change.

Pulima Cos acknowledged her presence then reinforced her own position as the dominant authority. "So—you still refuse to confess your crimes. Nevertheless I know that it was you who murdered Midlothian, leader of the city, and you also who deliberately released dangerous animals on our citizens. For these and all of your other crimes you certainly deserve to die. But before I issue your death warrant do you have anything to say?" Borobos stood solid and silent, her eyes burning into Pulima Cos like a blowtorch. "No matter, I will soon have what I want. Every co-conspirator will eventually be captured, tried, and executed. Your environmental movement is all but extinct."

"I sincerely doubt that," Borobos sneered. "Only someone as stupid and arrogant as you might believe that. For every one of us you imprison ten more will rail against you. The harder you try to stamp us out the stronger we become."

Hearing this Pulima Cos fought to control her emotions; her fists were clenched and she was shaking with blind rage. "You will tell me exactly what I want to know. You will tell me where Poxiciti is. Why because if you don't . . ." Pressing the control panel on her desk the door slid open and a tall, muscular female stepped through. She stopped directly in front of Borobos and awaited her orders.

"Meet Maranastis," Pulima Cos smiled wickedly. "She is an expert at encouraging information from difficult cases like yourself, Borobos. She has assured me that if you haven't talked by the time she is finished you will not be alive. Perhaps you would like to say something before she begins."

Borobos's eyes were cold with hatred as she turned her back to her, and waited.

The first blow wasn't too painful, nor was the second. Nolum Gar's guards had inflicted worse beatings, had beaten her unconscious and left her to wake up in her own blood. So what could this hired thug do to her which she had not already endured? After all she was well accustomed to pain and had spent some of her harshest years in Midlothian's jails. However as the beating wore on, Borobos began to realize this brutal creature was indeed going to kill her, regardless if she talked or not. Maybe, she half-hoped, her death would come with the next blow.

Pulima Cos nodded approvingly, was enjoying the sight of her opponent sprawled on the floor, battered and bloodied. Something splashed onto her purple gown. Blood. "Be careful," she complained. "You're getting too much blood on my furniture." Her primary concern was her expensive segathar rugs, and so before Maranastis struck again she quickly ordered her attendants to remove them at once.

The beating continued uninterrupted yet Borobos remained silent. She was in incredible pain when Pulima Cos finally intervened and ordered her assailant to cease.

"You see, Borobos? I can make her stop. I can end this for good. Just tell me where Poxiciti is. Tell me where he is and you will live."

All she heard from her was a gurgle of response; Borobos made a rasping noise as she breathed with great difficulty. Dried blood clotted her mouth, thickly caked her skin. Obviously Pulima Cos would get nothing from her in this state. Motioning to one her attendants who was standing nearby she issued orders.

"Bring her some water." She pointed at Borobos, then to the floor. "And clean up this mess."

The delay had given Borobos enough time to catch her breath. Her skin pulsated as it hissed hoarsely for air. After shaking the stinging blood from her eyes, she saw the attendant staring at her. "What do you want?" she demanded harshly.

A thin male wearing the black band of servitude around his neck stepped forward hesitantly. "Something to drink?" He held forward a flask of clear cool water which Borobos pushed back with her manacled hands.

"No."

"But you must be thirsty. Here. Drink some," he insisted. This time when he held up the flask to her he made a subtle hand motion which only Borobos saw, and understood.

In all likelihood her torturer would eventually make her talk. Too much was at stake to risk that, for with the information she possessed Pulima Cos could destroy them all. So she had to die. She would die so that everyone else would live. Unknowingly her body trembled with the enormity of her decision. Yet there was no other possibility, no way out, and reluctantly Borobos accepted this fate as her only alternative. She looked deep into his eyes.

"Yes, give me some water." Draining the flask she handed it back and watched as he hurried out of the room. It would not be long now.

"Shall I order Maranastis to continue?" Pulima Cos asked her. "Or would you prefer to tell me where Poxiciti is?"

With as much sarcasm as she could muster Borobos faced her enemy and said, "Who is that?"

Grunting angrily Pulima Cos stepped out of the way as the big female closed in with her fists, picking up exactly where she had left off. Borobos must have taken a dozen body blows before she began to stagger, and then collapsed.

Maranastis bent over her and touched her neck. "She is dead."

"So soon?" Pulima Cos scowled as she glanced at Borobos's lifeless corpse. "How unfortunate that the information she possessed died with her. Perhaps you killed her too hastily."

"Not I," she replied firmly. "Killed by poison."

Despite her shock Pulima Cos forced herself to push through the surprise and anger of this news. "Poisoned? How?"

"Self-administered. I suspect abarlaq. Easy to conceal, hard to detect. And only a medical examination will confirm its presence. The tiniest quantity can be deadly. It would've had to have been taken orally, probably within the last few moments prior to death. She must have been carrying it with her."

Of the four guards the one who was in charge stomped forward and vehemently disputed her unfounded accusation. "Impossible! I guarantee that she was thoroughly and properly searched. Twice. Make no mistake about that. She could not have obtained this or any other poisonous substance while in my custody."

"Then someone in this room gave it to her," Maranastis deduced.

That same thought must have been with Pulima Cos too, because one of her advisors leaned forward and whispered something that made her look suddenly at her coterie of servants.

"Where is he?" Pulima Cos demanded. It was soon obvious to those in her entourage that whoever she was searching for was no longer in the room. There was more whispering, some exchanges with her other advisors, then her guards were summoned and given their orders. "Have him found and brought to me at once. Alive."

Walking over to Borobos's dead bulk she kicked her as hard as she could, furious that she had been deprived of the opportunity to see her die decently. "Very clever. Had I suspected one of my own servants of collusion he would be dead just as surely as you. Will be dead," she corrected herself as she signaled the closest of her attendants. "See that this ugly thing is properly disposed of. May Poxiciti soon join her."

Chapter 41

"**I**s that the city you spoke of?"

Ilon stood perfectly still as he looked out across the shimmering, dust-filled plain. The daytime sun had reached its zenith in the sky. Overhead small clouds drifted by, while further away their moving shadows ran up the walls of the faraway city.

"It is. It crawls with Iranha. They are in there right now."

His newest acolyte trembled with excitement as she sniffed the air and sensed their invisible yet ominous presence. "I have never been this close to an Iranha city before. When do we attack them?"

"Tonight," Ilon replied. "At dusk. Although we cannot hope to conceal so many hunters, until we reach the city the cover of darkness will be to our advantage."

"And what then?"

"Kill Iranha," he said simply. "As many as you can."

While he talked his audience became more and more confident and could see exactly how this would happen. His strategy was simple. Once they were inside the city the hunters were free to attack and kill as they pleased—just so long as they continued until there were no Iranha left.

Ilon looked at their eager faces and knew they were ready for battle. Even if he was to die at this very moment they would carry on without him. His will had brought them all here, but their hatred of the Iranha would take them on to the city. Gangahar had told him that even now thousands of new arrivals were coming in off the field to join them to fight against their brutal oppressor. Thousands. They were an unstoppable killing power that soon every Iranha would come to fear. Once when that had seemed so impossible, when instead it was the Iranha who invoked fear and death, they were the scared ones. No more! Now this and everything else had suddenly changed to favor them. Indeed, all those years they endured and suffered well prepared them for what was certainly and inevitably coming. Even now he saw a glimmer of victory, and as he turned about and strode confidently back into the forest, those who trailed behind him felt for the first time since the beginning there was hope again.

Back in their war camp was a frenzy of activity and excitement. Lag guns were being distributed, and those who volunteered to carry them now listened attentively to their drill instructors. It was a satisfying sight, seeing this immense army and reveling in the impending battle which would rid them of the Iranha at last.

Already many of these hunters had broken apart from their own trods and were mingling together, talking with one another. What they talked about most was the Iranha. Everyone was telling their own story, recounting the unfortunate circumstances and those in their trod who had since died. They spent the better part of the day disseminating this information, and while it was sad to hear, each hunter swore an oath that they would personally avenge the dead.

In the meantime there were other diversions—one of these was Ilon. Many still had not yet seen the Egris who was not Egris, so whenever he happened to be nearby they suspended their talking to marvel at his strangeness. Later, when he approached some hunters who were locked in a heated argument a large group crowded behind him and listened on.

"What is wrong?" he asked the nearest, an argumentative female who he recognized from an earlier encounter.

"We have nothing to eat," she complained. "You bring us here without food, expect us to fight with empty stomachs. Maybe we should go hunting right now."

Ilon was amazed how this thick-skulled creature could think of nothing else but food. So much was at stake that to think of anything else other than the Iranha was almost an act of treason. Instead of plunging his spear into her as he should have done, he regarded her with contempt to show how little he cared for her or her feelings.

"I can see you are a hunter who prizes food far more than the lives of your companions." His eyes were ablaze with anger yet he spoke clearly so she would hear his every word. "Eat tomorrow, fat one. We came here to kill Iranha today. If you wish to fill your stomach then fill it with this." He reached downward and picked up a handful of Egris dung.

His listeners gave a whoop of laughter when they saw this. The hunter was so taken aback by his forcefulness and command that her jaw slackened and hung limply open; she was speechless. After he left, the laughter ebbed slowly away and the crowd dispersed. But a few of the watchers followed him to see where he would go next.

Meanwhile Horhon was waiting expectantly for Ilon's return. He had been gone since the morning, though Ilon had promised to meet her before nightfall. Even so, the day was getting on and dusk was that much closer.

Just before dark Horhon heard someone calling her name. Out of the corner of her eye she recognized the familiar figure coming closer, then fell back on her tail and expressed genuine surprise.

"Saskakel—is that you?"

The big hunter grinned. The world might have changed but he was still the same old Saskakel. "We parted so long ago, Horhon, yet it seems like yesterday."

There was a touch of formality in her voice. She had not forgotten the past, the harsh words, or why he had left the trod. "It pleases me to see that you are well. Did you find another trod that was more to your liking?"

All at once the smile left his face and he was grim and silent before he answered. "The Iranha killed many," he said bitterly. "I watched them die, saw the deadly creatures who skinned them."

"I am sorry for what they did," Horhon lamented. "So many have died."

"It was my mistake. You said many things in the past and I should have listened. When we first parted I believed the Iranha would eventually leave, that the killing would be over for good." He lowered his head. "I was blind to the truth."

"Perhaps," Horhon smiled. "Now enough said of the past." She reached out and grasped hold of his hands. "I am glad that we are together again, old friend."

"As am I." His hands were trembling when he looked directly into her eyes. "Old friend," he said. Friend.

Overhead the sky was darkening and beginning to lose some of its color; faint stars appeared overhead and flickered down. By the time the sun touched on the horizon the attackers were already in position on the field. Ilon sat in the grass holding his lag gun, was looking out across the plain at the Iranha city beyond. Gangahar came over and crouched low beside him. He too had a lag gun slung across his shoulder.

"All is ready. Is it time?"

"Soon."

So they waited in absolute silence, watching as the red sun sank lower and lower, until the field was barely illuminated. Rising slowly to his feet Ilon climbed up onto his mount, pulled the reins tight; Krugjon snorted nervously.

"Hunters!" Eighty thousand were riveted to his every word. Ilon raised his arm. "Ready!"

The air rumbled with the sound of their claws snapping into place. Tails straightened, legs tensed. As Ilon glanced westward the dying sun glinted in his face, and when he blinked his eyes open—it was gone. Now there was only the empty field between them and the Iranha city.

"Go!"

Chapter 42

The first of the attackers were away. The battle had begun.

Thousands of hunters poured onto the field, leaping, jumping, striding forward, an unstoppable wall of death that was steering straight towards the city. Dust clouds churned under the darkening sky. The sound, like thunder, boomed across the open plains. A large herd of skrill, clumps of green brush still dangling from their beaked jaws, galloped away in the opposite direction. Nearby, a flock of soros feeding on a corpse, arrowed back into the air.

Ilon, riding astride the thick shoulders of his companion, held tightly onto the reins as Krugjon's powerful hind legs flattened the grassy terrain and shot back into the air. Now he was sailing high above the ground, the wind was howling in his face, and he felt the thrill of exhilaration to be part of this fighting force.

At the same time Ilon was trying to concentrate on the battle strategy, trying hard to picture things clearly in his mind and envisioning how they might be. Would the Iranha be waiting, ready with their guns? In his mind's eye he was already inside of the city, was enjoying the killing and destroying, watching all of it crumble to the ground. He wanted it to be exactly this way, just as he imagined it now. However as the gravity pulled him heavily back into the saddle, even these happy thoughts were drowned out by the thunderous noise of the attackers.

Horhon and Gangahar were jumping alongside him, keeping pace, while the others who flanked them formed a straight line that stretched sightlessly into the dark. They were going forward, advancing on the city, and the invisible line which marked the turning point was now behind them. The plan was made and they were part of something that could not be changed. Even if Ilon wanted to stop, it was too late. To alter their course now, to change it in the slightest way was suicide. Surprise was their only advantage, for if they started back and regrouped, the Iranha would certainly be ready for them the next time, and they would never have this chance again. So why stop now? He had lived all his life for this day, this moment, to deliver his enemy this stunning blow from which they would never recover. He gripped the reins tighter in his hands as he hurtled closer and closer toward his destiny.

Chapter 43

Nequit, Pulima Cos's personal secretary, burst into her master's quarters and ran straight to her bed. This was the second time in her presence tonight and Pulima Cos had promised her instant death if she returned again. Nevertheless the importance of this news she bore was worth risking her life to bring.

Seeing Nequit coming through the doorway one of Pulima Cos's male companions shrieked aloud and pulled up the covers about him. The other, a servant of low rank who undoubtedly was sleeping his way to a promotion, dismounted her and assumed a sitting stance with his legs splayed open so that Nequit would see his private parts.

When Pulima Cos looked up and saw that her secretary was standing at her bedside, watching her, she was possessed by a cold killing rage. "You stupid, insensate, mindless, unthinking, half-witted . . ." she said coarsely, hurling as many insults as was possible before her next breath cut her off. "How did one so brainless ever come into my service? It is a wonder you are even capable of listening to my simplest instructions. I told you that I was not to be disturbed, and yet twice I am forced to bear with your unwanted attentions. I should have you killed, maybe I will. Explain this intrusion at once before I make up my mind."

The messenger gazed momentarily at her repellent naked body, then looked away. "Apologies for my bold entrance," she panted, for she had run quickly here to bring her this startling information and her skin was still gasping for air. "This news came in only moments ago. Apparently one of our transports flying into the city has just reported passing through an immense dust cloud. Their on-board tracking system has picked up a large animal herd on the move, coming this way."

"Coming here? To my city?" Pulima Cos looked at her disbelievingly. "What kind of animals? How many? Where are they now?"

Shaking her head no to each one of her interrogatives she replied, "Unknown. Regrettably the pilot was not that specific, although she did state that their number appeared large enough to pose a possible danger to our citizenry."

"Well then, dispatch my reserves outside immediately. Surely they could use some target practice."

Moments later Pulima Cos was returning to her bed when she suddenly felt the floor tremble slightly beneath her. The next time it happened the tremor was a little stronger. Decorative ornaments hanging on the walls began to rattle; the dull distant sound was like rolling thunder. Although it was too dark outside to see anything the metlaglass window was vibrating in its frame; still the rumbling grew louder.

After summoning her aides Pulima Cos hurriedly pulled on her robe and went to the doorway. The shrill sound of the city's emergency alarm was blaring in the corridor. The whole building was shaking now. People were running in a panic through the hallway, shouting. She forcibly stopped a dreg who was running past.

"You. What is happening out there?" she demanded.

"Something outside—attacking now!" the dreg screamed hoarsely. She tore herself away and raced for the stairwell.

When Pulima Cos returned to her chamber she was very much afraid. Nor did any of her aides improve her present state of mind, for the answers they supplied were vague and interpretive. While they babbled she was pacing the floor, thinking and worrying. If this was a battle, then who were they fighting?

****

"Do you see anything yet?" The hahlok commander hovered over her charge, trembling, eyes wide with fright. Perhaps it was foolish to have brought her soldiers outside the protective walls of the city. Standing here now it felt like an earthquake, and she fought just to keep her balance.

"Wait, I see something!" one of her dreg shouted over the deafening noise.

"There!" another shouted. "Moving on the field!"

While the soldiers had powerful guns and could kill or destroy moving targets indiscriminately, nothing had fully prepared them for what was now approaching. Under the bright glare of the floodlights the dark forms of the attackers were emerging out of the dust cloud, thundering swiftly forward.

The frightened commander let her thermal visor drop to the ground, so great was her shock. "Segathars! Shoot them! Shoot them!"

The sound of gunfire erupted across the defensive line. The soldiers started firing in panic, shooting aimlessly at anything that moved, though it was mostly the air that they struck.

Unfortunately for the hahlok commander, her last view was of an airborne segathar, its teeth-filled mouth smiling death as it came down on top of her.

"Retreat!" a soldier screamed. "Back to the city!"

It was a slaughter. The slow running Iranha were easily cut down and torn to pieces. The hunters kept on killing and stopped only because there was no one left to kill. Nor were they content to wait here for replacements—they wanted to kill more now.

As the first wave stormed the city's outer perimeter only the impenetrable, high wall kept them at bay; the front gates were closed and barred. Now only this barrier stood between them and the Iranha, between them and total destruction.

Jumping off of Krugjon's shoulders Ilon trained his gun on the great doors. The air hissed and crackled around him as the electrical charge struck. A large portion of the wall crumbled down and collapsed into its own dust.

"Inside!" he screamed. "On to victory!"

****

The hastily convened meeting had drawn together some of the city's most important leaders and functionaries, summoned here by Pulima Cos herself to discuss serious and grievous matters concerning the fate of their city. In attendance were five of her senior hahlok commanders. From the grim and set expression on each of their faces it seemed the fate of the city was already sealed. Those of the lowest station stood outside the crowded circle of confidants and advisors. From there they listened and tried to understand some of what was happening. Yet those who were fortunate enough to see the view screen closed their eyes to the grisly event now taking place outside. The scene that unfolded was a shocking one. Personnel monitors specially fitted on each soldier relayed the carnage back to a stunned and horrified audience.

"Segathars," Pulima Cos hissed in hatred. Turning to Malhasbus, her most experienced military advisor, she directed her harshest criticism yet. "Evidently you did not dispatch enough of our soldiers outside, commander. Your failure. I shall not forget that. Now—what can you do to harden our city's defenses against this beastly invader?"

First Malhasbus conferred with several of her top aides before responding. The tone of her voice, the shape of her stance, indicated a great reluctance to answer. "Honestly—nothing. We're totally unprepared for an invasion of this magnitude," she admitted nervously. "Who among us could have imagined such a thing?" Glancing warily at the view screen she pointed out what was already frighteningly obvious to everyone else in the room. "They're at the outer wall surrounding the city. Look—here and here." She indicated a dark cloud rising alongside two different branches of the wall. "Are they not digging?"

Barbis Lim, a high ranking military official, added further to this grim report by saying, "I seriously doubt the wall will keep them out for very long. However, the inner wall of the old city has been fortified and might hold them back temporarily."

"What do you mean temporarily?" Pulima Cos demanded. "Are we not safe here?"

The commander looked at her gravely. "No."

"We cannot hope to stop them all," Malhasbus continued. "Some of the buildings might keep them out long enough for us to shore up some of our key defenses. There is a high probability that the city generators will be one of their primary targets. I suggest we send in more troops to protect our most critical installations."

"They are stupid animals!"

"I sincerely hope you are right," she responded uneasily. "Because if they get inside the city, if they reach any of our occupied buildings— people will die. However, if their attack is guided by intelligence then I think this city and everyone in it will die destroyed." Those who were listening to the tense silence could hear the sound of their own hearts beating. "We still have time to act. Lives can still be saved. Shall I give the order to evacuate?"

Pulima Cos could barely restrain the blinding rage building within her. "Leave? Abandon our city? Never!" she screamed, hammering her fist against the wet metal of her desk. "I think you are grossly overestimating their chances of success, commander. I want every one of your soldiers equipped with a lag gun." Such was her order that even her lowest ranking officers took umbrage.

"That will demolish this city," Malhasbus protested. "I strongly suggest small arms. We need only to kill them—not obliterate them."

"Very well," Pulima Cos huffed. "Now carry out your orders. The next time we meet I want to see a city full of dead segathars, or I promise it will be your own hide that will decorate my floor."

Obeying her command the crowd quickly dispersed, everyone had their own duties to perform. When Pulima Cos was once more alone she summoned Nequit into her presence.

"Have my private shuttle prepared for immediate departure."

Despite her confidence that the soldiers would dispatch these filthy creatures, she was too important to let herself become their next meal. So she would leave. In the meantime, while her shuttle was being readied she demanded an update on the battle. A lowly dreg escorted her downstairs, taking her straight to Malhasbus. A temporary command post had been set up in the building's main lobby. From here the battle leaders directed their troops, shouting urgent orders to messengers who hurried away into the night. Others returned moments later with the latest information. Aides stepped forward, conferring briefly with their superiors before they settled back and waited to be called upon again.

When Pulima Cos arrived Malhasbus was seated, her hands drawn up about her face. The news was very bad.

"The segathars are inside the city," she told her gravely. "I do not know how they did it but several of our key positions have been overrun. Evidently they made us think they were coming under the wall. Instead, while we were sending our troops to meet them the bulk of their attacking force came through the main doors."

Pulima Cos's eyes widened. "How?"

"Unknown. There were no survivors." Speaking slowly, choosing her words carefully, Malhasbus revealed every detail of the ambush, everything she knew, though when she was through she had no solid answers, only uncertainties. "I believe we have seriously underestimated their intelligence. I can only hope now that their intention is to remain on the streets, otherwise the killing will escalate."

Her anger increased. Pulima Cos looked coldly at her and wanted her dead. She was furious with Malhasbus's efforts so far and did not disguise her contempt for her ineffectual and incompetent leadership.

"Then you had better be quick in your task to exterminate them and bring about order, commander. I expect nothing less. Now if that is all then I leave this matter in your charge."

Her dismissal could not have come at a worse time. Across the street a fiery explosion suddenly ripped through the building. The sheer force of the blast smashed into the front wall and sent a deadly hail of metallic shards flying into the startled crowd.

Struggling to her feet Pulima Cos looked over the bodies. She heard screams of pain all around her. Blood was dripping from her own fat face. "Where did that blast come from? Who fired it?" As if in answer to her question several dark forms leapt past—and then it was horrifyingly clear. "The segathars have weapons!" She could no longer control herself. Seizing Malhasbus by her scrawny neck she started to throttle her. "Our weapons!"

While the wounded were being attended to, a soldier came running, panic-stricken and too confused to speak. After they gave her some water and calmed her with words of encouragement, she managed to talk.

"We are losing the battle. Even now our city is on fire, people are dying." When her next words came her eyes were wide with terror. "The segathars have lag guns. It is just a matter of time before—"

Suddenly, overhead the lights flickered, then the room faded to darkness. There were loud gasps, shouts of alarm.

"They've cut the power." A communications officer rose from her desk and flung down her dead headset. "They've cut the power! We're all going to die!"

"This is a catastrophe," Malhasbus shouted over the confusion. While she was struggling to see in the darkness the emergency lights cut in and the room glowed an eerie green. She felt only despair, yet still maintained her stance of authority lest Pulima Cos know what she was thinking. "Did I not warn you that something like this might happen?"

"Shut-up!"

"No. Why die unnecessarily? It is obvious our city is doomed. Unless we evacuate without delay all is lost."

Before she could give the order a single gun shot rang out and Malhasbus slumped to the floor. Pulima Cos stood over her smoking corpse, her gun leveled at the stunned onlookers. "The next one of you who disobeys my commands will die just like her. Now get back to your stations."

There was no time to waste. She had to leave the city at once before disaster struck. "You and you," Pulima Cos ordered the two dregs. "Come with me."

With the elevator out of service it was a long, slow climb to the top of the building. Panting, her face dripping with sweat, Pulima Cos finally reached the end of the stairs. It was here she posted her armed guards at the door.

Outside the whole city was blacked out except where the streets below were lit by the light of the fires. Sparks were beginning to spread from one building to the next. Looking across the skyline she heard several more loud explosions, saw the red mushroom clouds rising upwards. Her city was burning.

As instructed, her shuttle was waiting on the rooftop so she climbed aboard and took her seat. "Pilot, take me to city Tykrerek at once."

This simple command was greeted by silence. As she started to angrily repeat her order the chair swung around and the pilot faced her. The pilot who was unmistakably Poxiciti. Pulima Cos was aghast.

"You! How did you get into my city?"

"You've become rather unpopular, Pulima Cos. It seems a lot of people want you dead." He lifted his gun and trained it on her. "I, especially. But that would be too easy, killing you here. Instead we will go downstairs together and join those who you were ready to abandon."

"Idiot!" she roared with rage. "Can't you see we're under attack?"

Poxiciti paused, listened. "Yes. Wonderful, isn't it?"

"Have you lost your mind? If we don't escape from here we'll both be killed, torn to pieces, eaten."

"Then it is my dying wish to see you killed first."

"What is it you really want? Money, power? I can give you all that and more. Anything you desire."

Poxiciti laughed hysterically. "Your city is falling. That is what I desire, to see you pulled down with it. May I be cursed for all eternity for the day I set foot on this world, for allowing you and your profiteers to come here to plunder and slaughter at will. Enough. It is ended now. Since you know these segathars bring death here to Anaxerxes I see no reason to think that they will stop when there are other cities to conquer."

"Why not stop them?" she pleaded. "Do our people deserve this kind of death?"

"Stop them, from taking back what is rightfully theirs? I have no intention of doing that. It is over, Pulima Cos. Your reign, your city, your world. Those of us who survive will return to Epiphiline to be where we belong. But you—you go downstairs to face the death you deserve." He waved his gun. "Move."

"No," Pulima Cos cried out in anguish. "Not like that."

She had no other choice. With Poxiciti behind her, his ready gun jammed in her back, she stumbled along the pathway to the door, all the while thinking of possible ways to escape. When she pressed the switch and the door slid open that was the moment she made her move. Seeing the two armed soldiers suddenly appear in the doorway startled Poxiciti, but was all the time Pulima Cos needed to lunge inside past the guards.

"Shoot him!" she screamed. "Shoot him!"

Before the first dreg could get her weapon up Poxiciti took aim and fired. She emitted a muffled scream as she took the full blast in her chest, then stumbled backwards and disappeared down the stairs. But by the time the second guard recovered enough to return fire he was gone.

"Go after him," Pulima Cos ordered. "Search the rooftop. When you find him—kill him instantly."

While she stood waiting in the doorway, looking outside and wondering why it was taking so long, the dreg finally returned.

"Nothing. He is gone."

She was outraged. She would order her soldiers to search for him, find him and bring him back. She would leave no stone unturned, would scour this city until he was found. Her thoughts were on what next to do when the guard swung around in her direction and cried out a warning.

"Fire!"

By the time they reached the shuttle thick smoke and flames were pouring out the hatchway. She stood by helplessly and watched it burn. There was no doubt in her mind whatsoever who had done this. Pulima Cos stared at the burning wreckage and cursed his name over and over.

Trapped here in her own city, with thousands of rampaging segathars on the loose, fires burning out of control, and only one sure fate now awaiting her.

She was going to die.

Chapter 44

The battle was going poorly for the Iranha.

Fires were cropping up everywhere—and no one was stopping to put them out. Ripped apart bodies offered grave evidence of the city's imminent collapse. There was no longer a skirmish line to separate the opposing forces anymore. Instead, those Iranha soldiers who still remained alive were scattered throughout the streets and buildings, effectively cut off from anyone who knew what was happening. As soon as they walked out into the open their attackers would leap from out of the darkness and sink their teeth into the nearest before leaping away. The Iranha were unused to waging this kind of guerrilla warfare within their own city. They were better adapted to fighting in the open against a civilized enemy. Unlike the Iranha, the Egris knew nothing about organized warfare. They were tenacious predators who knew everything about stalking and killing prey. This was their realm, where their front line simply charged in, attacking and killing as many as they could before the soldiers' concentrated gunfire cut them down. Regrettably, some of them were killed, but the swarms behind them kept coming and coming until every last Iranha in their way was dead.

From the beginning it was the Egris who were the better equipped army. The sorilox rifles which the Iranha soldiers used were no match against the much bigger lag guns. Few Egris possessed them, though the volume of damage they produced was incredible. Whole city blocks were ripped apart; buildings were engulfed in flames, while smoking rubble rained down onto the streets. Then it was no surprise that the Iranha reacted with horror and shock when they learned it was their own weapons being used against them and their city.

The destruction was glorious. The sheer magnitude of the damage far exceeded even Ilon's expectations. He was running well ahead of the others; Krugjon was leaping high as he steered him down a deserted street. They reached a spot on the road where many corpses were strewn about. The battle here must have been fierce, for there were as many Egris as Iranha piled together, silent and unmoving. So many dead. A hunter lay sprawled out in front of them, her jaws closed tightly around an Iranha soldier's midriff. Ilon saw her glazed over eyes and knew she was dead. He suddenly felt a great revulsion and fought to control the flood of emotions as he pulled on the reins and jumped away.

It had been a long night of killing and Krugjon was eager to keep on killing more. Though he was blind he was an adept killer nonetheless. Blood stained his teeth where earlier he had bitten into his enemy—and still he was not yet finished, so great and powerful was his hatred. Even now as he was leaping forward he heard something off to the side and veered straight toward it despite Ilon's orders to turn back.

The sharp crack of an Iranha gun echoed in his ears and the next thing Ilon knew, he was being thrown sideways, falling out of control. The force of hitting the ground must have knocked him unconscious because the first thing he remembered was blinking his eyes open to see the full moon directly above him. Struggling back onto his feet he felt a sharp pain spear through his arm. Krugjon lay motionless on the road; Ilon hobbled forward to reach him, fearing the worst.

"Krugjon, can you hear me?"

"I can," he answered weakly, but it was a short while before he was able to speak again. "My leg. I cannot move it." And then came the grim words, "I fear it is broken."

This was not good news. To a hunter like Krugjon who relied on his jumping skills a broken leg meant he was as good as dead. Most Egris just simply chose to be killed on the spot rather than face a life of immobility. He knew exactly what Krugjon would want him to do.

"You understand," Krugjon told him. "Now you must kill me, Ilon. Do it quickly."

Tears welled up in his eyes. "No. I cannot. Once long ago I let that happen to someone else. You are my friend, and I will not kill you here in the city of the Iranha."

"The Iranha will die with me!" he roared.

Deep down he knew Krugjon was right. It was what he would have wanted for himself. Still, even if it was death that Krugjon wanted, what happened next would never have been his choice. Coming out of a building, the sound of the heavy feet, the outline, was unmistakable. Alone, weaponless, trapped, Ilon pushed hard against Krugjon as the Iranha soldiers stalked closer.

One of the soldiers stopped abruptly when she spotted them. The sight of Ilon must have surprised her because her gun arm slackened, but it did not remain there for very long. Lifting her weapon she took aim.

For Ilon the end could not have been any closer when two hunters landed behind him so suddenly that he scarcely noticed them until the ear-splitting sound of a lag gun erupted in his head. When the smoke cleared there was nothing left of his attackers, just a mound of smoldering ash where they had once stood. Gangahar pulled on Ilon's arm and tried to shake free the great fear that possessed him.

"Are there other Iranha?"

"I . . . I don't know. These ones came out of that building over there."

With his lips peeled back, Gangahar fired off round after destroying round. Targasesk soon joined him, both their guns blazing as each new explosion ripped into the metal structure and sent flames and debris shooting out in every direction. Within moments the entire building collapsed into a ruin of rubble.

"They must be dead now," Targasesk said with immense satisfaction. She kept her weapon ready, hoping there would still be more to kill.

"What of Krugjon?" Gangahar asked gravely. "Can he move?"

Ilon turned to face him, his voice crackling with emotion. "No. His leg is broken."

"Then he wishes to die?"

"That is not my wish," Ilon said forcefully, positioning himself so that he was now standing between them. "If you kill him then I will kill you too. Is that clear?"

"You are making a bad choice. To not kill him when he chooses to die."

"I know. But you must let me do this for him. There is still one thing that can be done. So until tomorrow comes will you obey me?"

Despite what Gangahar believed was best for Krugjon he obeyed only because the battle was not yet finished. Beating the Iranha was of greater importance, and so he allowed Ilon to make the decision and simply agreed.

Gunfire echoed sporadically up and down the street. Targasesk listened intently. "Their armed forces are withdrawing. Their city is on fire. We have won."

"Only this one battle," Ilon said. "We must keep up the offensive. Do not give them the chance to regroup. Now it is quiet. But that could mean they are preparing to launch an attack of their own. Can we be so impetuous to quit now when total victory is just around the corner?"

"You are right, of course."

"Take your hunters up that street. Death is everywhere, so be careful to look," Ilon warned them. "There might be other Iranha hiding in those buildings too."

After issuing quick orders four other gun toting Egris soon joined them. "You will stay here with Krugjon?" Gangahar asked him. Ilon's solemn nod affirmed what he had already surmised. "We will soon return."

To a large extent the battle had already been fought and won. Now only a few pockets of resistance remained, though this was the deadliest part of the hunt so the hunters proceeded with utmost caution. Those who accompanied Gangahar and Targasesk now concentrated their guns on either side of the street where the Iranha might have entrenched themselves. Their teeth clenched, guns blazing, they continued with the onslaught. Together their combined firepower leveled much of the adjacent streetscape; crumbling buildings exploded into flames. Even long after their weapons were silenced the walls were still collapsing. Nevertheless the fighting continued. Those Iranha who managed to escape outside were gunned down; anyone they saw was chased after and killed on the spot.

From where he stood Ilon could see the destruction unfolding, the flattened buildings, the dead bodies. He wanted very much to join his companions now. Of course he couldn't leave Krugjon here by himself, so he knelt back down beside him and continued with his work.

Krugjon grimaced intensely while Ilon felt with his hands where the two broken bones had separated. "What is it that you are doing?"

"Hold very still," he ordered. "Can you do that?"

"I will try," Krugjon promised, although he felt a little trepidation of what was coming.

What Ilon did next was so painful that Krugjon screamed in agony as he first pulled then twisted his broken leg. After repeating this excruciating procedure again he felt himself slipping into unconsciousness.

Later, after Krugjon awoke he gradually became aware that the throbbing pain in his leg did not hurt so much now. He was curious so he started to pull himself up only to feel Ilon's hand pushing him back down.

"What is this you have done?" Krugjon asked him, feeling the two straight lengths of metal lashed to his leg.

"It should hold your leg steady for now, until the bones mend together," he explained. "Understand, that for this to happen you must not move too much."

His mouth widening, Krugjon said, "Then I will be able to jump again?"

"Yes," Ilon told him confidently. "I believe you will."

It was at that exact moment when he caught sight of two figures scurrying away. One of them in particular attracted his attention. Had he not recognized the flowing purple gown it might have been just another ordinary Iranha running for its miserable life. Searching through the rubble he found what he was looking for, then started off in quick pursuit.

Pulima Cos was running as fast as she could, though her gross weight limited her speed to almost a plodding pace. After running as far as she could, it was too much, she suddenly ground to a halt and spat out a mouthful of foam. Huge drops of perspiration dribbled off her fleshy face. She bent over, wheezing and gasping for air. When she regained some of her breath, only then did she hear the fading footsteps and look up.

"Wait! Wait! Come back! I order you to come back here!"

Still unable to move, she stared helplessly at the fleeing soldier. She was being abandoned. Furious, she wanted to kill her. Drawing her sidearm she fired in the soldier's direction—missed. Possessed by rage she hurled her gun at the wall as hard as she could. It made a sharp crack as it struck and dropped in pieces. As the haze of anger began to clear from her head she realized her stupidity. Suddenly horribly afraid, Pulima Cos was alone on the streets of her city. Without a gun.

What she had not noticed was that now there were two shadows on the wall, hers, and someone else's. Something else. Spinning around Pulima Cos recoiled and screeched in absolute terror.

Roaring in rage Ilon drove the metal shaft's jagged point deep into her. Blood spurted when he pulled it free and struck again. The more times he stabbed down, the more difficult it was to restrain himself. All the bad memories flowed through his arm. It was this same creature who had imprisoned him, who had brutalized and tormented him. For all the destroyers, for all those who came to take what was not theirs, for all the Uta and the Iranha, and the others on worlds unknown to him, this was his bloody vengeance for all of them.

Pulima Cos crumpled, her fat bulk sprawled in her own pool of blood. Not dead yet—but soon. Her breaths hissing out of her skin were short and shallow, she was very close to death, and when her chest collapsed she breathed her last breath.

And died.

For the first time since he could remember Ilon felt a tremendous sense of relief. And yet, unknown to him, the Iranha who had killed so many would kill no more. Perhaps it was finally over. Perhaps. With one eye still on his dead quarry he watched as several hunters approached, the high wall of flames shooting up behind them.

"Their city is destroyed!" A tall, battle scarred female roared with happiness. "We have done it!" She introduced herself as Inlaptep, one of trod Targasesk's hunters who had served Ilon during many of their previous raids on the city.

"Tell me," he asked her, "What news of the battle? Are the Iranha all dead?"

"Some escaped. No matter," she assured him, "we will track the rest of them down and kill them too."

"I search for Horhon of trod Horhon? You have seen her?"

Her headshake indicated no, though another of her eight companions arched his neck and spoke. "I have."

Smiling, Ilon said, "Good. Take me to her now. We are not finished with these Iranha yet."

Chapter 45

A fresh replacement of guards was just coming on to take the morning watch. Since learning of the attack on city Anaxerxes, their own city was on the highest possible alert and security was tighter than ever. Armed guards patrolled the city perimeter. Although information was scant, every citizen felt on edge. There were all sorts of wild rumors going around. Every citizen was talking about last night, though no one actually knew what had really happened.

Though it was almost daylight the sky was under the cover of thickening clouds. A dull rumble of thunder told the watchers there would be rain before the morning. Traffic in and out of the city was restricted. The big inter-city transports hauling supplies were impounded and searched. The guards were under strict orders to look for anything suspicious, so when one of them spotted a dim beam of light on the highway she scrutinized it closely as it approached.

As the vehicle pulled to a stop in front of the main gates the guard immediately walked over to speak with the driver. "State your business here?" she said brusquely.

"Tell me, who is in charge of this despicable city."

She was taken aback by this low male's insulting tone and touched her gun threateningly as she leaned forward. "She is Oneteesel. The same Oneteesel who would have you scourged for speaking so crudely of her city—so be careful."

"I might have guessed," he snorted derisively. "Pulima Cos has surrounded herself with cronies and racketeers, so why not her? You will take me to her immediately."

The guard's voice was insolent. "You dare speak that way? And who are you to command me?"

The driver stared at her with widening eyes, then spoke ebulliently, saying, "I am Poxiciti."

Automatically her gun went up and she called the alarm. Within moments the vehicle was completely surrounded and Poxiciti was subdued and forcibly dragged outside. He did not resist, however everyone who was present bickered and quarreled over who would be the one to take him to Oneteesel, since his captor might profit from the outstanding reward.

Oneteesel had already been summoned from her sleeping chamber and now was waiting expectantly while Poxiciti was brought before her. He was manacled and chained about the wrists and feet, could barely walk for all the weight of his restraints.

"So we meet face to face at last, Poxiciti. Certainly this is an unexpected surprise, having you here now as my prisoner. I am told that the price on your head would fill a small room." Reaching across her desk she pinched his bare shoulder. "No reward will be greater than handing you over to Pulima Cos myself."

"I can see that you and her eat from the same garbage pile," he said insultingly. "Do not count your money yet. I am here in your city, but not as your prisoner. Rather I came here of my own free will to warn you—"

"You?" Oneteesel's rude roar of laughter cut him off. "You warn me?" After another round of laughter she leaned back in her wet chair and hoped this interpellation would be a brief one. "About what?"

"By now Pulima Cos is hopefully dead. Since her city is only a short distance away from city Soligcetis I can only assume it will be the next logical target."

"Of what? Attack?" She snorted derisively. "I heard reports of segathars running wild on the streets of her city. I can assure you that if they should try coming here to my city Tykrerek then we are ready to put these animals down."

"You know nothing. If you did you would be very afraid. The enemy you think you can stop—you cannot."

Oneteesel looked confusedly to her hahlok commander who was standing nearby. "Do you understand any of his nonsense? What is he babbling about?"

Sogonogona shrugged feebly. What information she possessed she personally believed was ludicrous and did not want to appear foolish in front of her superior, so she declined to answer.

"I find these bonds uncomfortable." Poxiciti rattled his shackles. "Remove them, unless of course you want to imprison me and never know what horrendous fate awaits your own city."

As a longtime money-maker Oneteesel never allowed her personal feelings to interfere with business transactions—especially when the seller possessed something she desired. Nevertheless she was irritated, though bent her arm to his request. "Now—tell me."

"The segathars that you skinned and profited from have launched a well-organized attack against city Anaxerxes. It is now in their possession. What you do not know is that they have lag guns, and undoubtedly what remains of the city will soon be leveled to a dust pile."

"Segathars with lag guns, the city destroyed? Impossible! You lie."

Poxiciti considered her the stupidest adversary he had encountered yet. "You idiot. For what reason do I need to lie?" he argued, coarsely. "Or perhaps a segathar attack here might make it abundantly clear that they intend to wipe us out." He looked over at Sogonogona and saw that something was deeply troubling her. "Tell her commander, you must know something, don't you?"

Again she responded by shrugging her shoulders, only this time accompanying her movements was a low voice that every listener had to strain to hear.

"It is true," she admitted. "Witnesses reported seeing armed segathars in the city. Of course segathars are stupid animals so naturally I believed the reports had to be wrong."

"And you did not think this important enough to bring to my attention?" Oneteesel angrily rebuked her in front of everyone. "I want no excuses, only an immediate explanation."

"It is too late," Poxiciti broke in. "What is done is done. City Anaxerxes is no more. Pulima Cos and her evil empire are finished. She misled you, corrupted you, and now she is dead, as will soon be all her supporters. So you must decide between your loyalty to her—which will certainly and inevitably lead you to your own death—or you can retain the privilege of your rank and join me. But you will do exactly as I say, and when I order it."

"Never!"

"Think again about what I offer you. The salvation of this city—or the death of it. Now choose."

"It is I who gives the orders in this city."

"No more. You forget I am still a member of the Vulana, the rightful governing authority which was taken by force, overthrown by violence. As its only surviving and democratically elected member I hereby assume command of you and your armed forces."

"Then join your traitorous companions now," Oneteesel hissed. She was in a murderous rage, reached for her gun and held it up to his face. Before she could squeeze the trigger a second gun cracked and she slumped to the floor and died. Her death had come about very suddenly and the shocked spectators reacted by seizing her still armed assassin at the front of the line.

"Stop!" Poxiciti shouted. "Enough. There will be no more bloodshed. The killing is ended. This one is the last." He looked over his audience and saw that Sogonogona, still holding her gun, was his only opposition. "And how about you, commander? Will you join your master in death, or obey me?"

Sogonogona lowered her weapon slowly. "I obey."

"Then inform every citizen to commence with this city's evacuation. Inform the other cities as well that we leave immediately."

"Leave? Where will we go?"

"Home to Epiphiline," Poxiciti said with pleasurable finality. "Back to where we belong."

Chapter 46

"It is done. It is over at last," Horhon said triumphantly. The hot sun was beading down on her face as she squinted to see what remained of city Soligcetis.

"This is only the second," Gangahar said beside her. "Why stop when there are still more cities to conquer?"

"The Iranha now know that we Egris can kill and destroy too. Let them think about these two cities. Let them decide if they want to stay here and risk losing another."

While he was thinking about that she discarded her lag gun and started to untie the small bundle which was bound about her waist.

"What is that you have?" he asked her inquisitively.

"Megog. What remains of her physical body. She saw this day long ago, and wanted to be here. It was her dying wish that I bring her to the battle, to be among the dead, those who gave their lives to see this end." Unsealing the container she let Megog's ashes spill out. A breeze blew and settled the dust across a wide swath of ground. Now, with her task completed, Horhon could leave this place knowing she had fulfilled her promise. It was time to go.

Like all other occasions the celebration was a short one since food was always a hunter's primary concern. And while many of the hunters talked of new friendships and inseparable bonds which would last forever, after the dead were buried the trods soon departed for home. Few might meet one day, but the vast majority would never see each other again.

Horhon had known this all along, for just as sure as the brightness of day became night, the light of this moment would soon diminish to a dim spark. Because the Egris had no accurate means of recording their history everything they accomplished here today would eventually be lost forever. To some degree that was happening already. Once the battle ended the Iranha were no longer in their future, but in fact were now a part of their past. What Horhon needed to do was to somehow keep the memory of this moment alive.

In just five days after city Anaxerxes and city Soligcetis were leveled the hunters found city Tykrerek empty, and so it too became a smoking pile of ruin. Nothing remained of it but the charred outline where their fires had burned, and the twisted metal and rubble which had once been buildings. By the time the hunters reached the outlying cities they found them abandoned too and knew then that the Iranha were gone for good.

"We have found another Iranha city." Saskakel was just returning from the desert, was covered with dust and sweat, though appeared eager to speak his message. "Shall we tear it down just like the others?"

"No. Leave it," Horhon said firmly. "Perhaps I was mistaken to go along with this cleansing. In our haste to rid us of the Iranha completely I see that what we have also done is to erase the very memory that we seek to keep. Destroy nothing else, for anyone who might come upon these relics may glimpse the past and remember us for the bloody battle which we fought and won. May this never happen again."

Saskakel bowed his head reverently to show that her instructions would be obeyed. "As you wish."

The first days passed uneasily and everyone expected the Iranha to return, although as more and more days slipped by the great fear that possessed them soon began to ebb. No one could remember so long a time when the Iranha had not been talked about. And yet each new day passed like all of the others, monotonous and empty, though everyone fervently hoped their lives would remain exactly that way.

In the spring the goud returned to the tree-top plains and the hunters ate well every day. Krugjon was improving, so much so that when his bindings were finally cut he was able to stand up and walk for the first time. Before he was finished he was promising everyone that he would be jumping and would soon be joining them on the hunt. Sanbat bore the trod's first child, and that must have encouraged the other females because three more were soon coming.

It was almost too good, this placid life all of them were living. Horhon was suspicious, sure that something was about to change. For many days now she had felt this way, unable to shake the feeling that something was going to happen. She did not know what exactly, only that she would be powerless to keep it from happening.

Then early one morning, she jumped in off of the field. The others were still out hunting but would be back soon. For some unknown reason she had felt the urge to return home, though now as Krugjon greeted her at the entrance his unsettling news was her answer.

"The creature from far away that Ilon told us of. It came back this morning. It is with him right now. Inside."

She hurried in through the tunnel. It was so strange to see the two of them standing side by side together, for it was like looking at another Ilon. Had he not waved to her she might never have guessed which one was which, though once her eyes left him she focused all of her attention on the intruder. Its unwanted presence here could only mean the peace and order of their lives was about to change. Undoubtedly now this was going to be revealed.

"The time has come for Ilon to leave," Aisahl told her.

"No," Horhon moaned. Slumping backwards on her tail she crossed both hands and blocked out its face in an attempt to forestall hearing it speak.

"You know that he must go."

"I know only that we will be parted, and it is not a good thing for a mother to be separated from one of her own."

"He is here because I brought him here. Brought him to you, Horhon. You know this. You have always known this. Now he wants to return to his own world."

"Only because he cannot stop you," Horhon hissed. She caught herself wondering if this creature could be killed. A single bite and Ilon would be going nowhere.

"I shall, of course, take him back," the creature who was Aisahl admitted. "But it was he who made the decision to come with me. If he still wishes to remain here with you then let him say so now."

"Is this true? You want to go with it?"

Only partly true. Actually he had no choice, and despised this creature for making her think he wanted to leave—he did not. He now gritted his teeth and the words caught in his throat. "I will return," Ilon tried to assure her.

"Will you? That is hard to believe. With the Iranha gone and we Egris now free, what is here to keep you from going back to your own kind and not ever returning?"

"Only you. You will always be my mother. That is a bond that can never be broken."

"Don't go back there," Horhon pleaded with him. "I know you cannot leave me."

"I can. I must. My future lies elsewhere."

"Why now? Why return to those Uta creatures when you can stay here with us?"

"It is too difficult to explain why, although I think you already know."

She did not answer him directly; the long bout of silence that followed was acknowledgment enough. His mind was made up and Horhon knew it was futile to convince him to change what he most wanted.

"And what do you want me to tell the others?"

"Tell them . . ." Ilon's back was turned, tears streaked his face, and the only thing he could think of to say was, "Tell them goodbye."

"Understood. Then you will leave here. Will you ever come back?"

"One day, I promise. Now—I must go."

"And you, strange one, will you bring him back to me alive?"

The creature who was Aisahl smiled. "That is the way I found him."

While they walked outside, Ilon held onto his mother's hand to comfort her. Deep within himself he was struggling, fighting to change his mind. Not that he really ever wanted to leave her. But despite how he felt about staying he knew from the very beginning that one day he would return to his past. That day was here now, and so he was going.

They reached a spot on the dune and separated. Krugjon, Horhon, stood by looking on. Tears ran down Ilon's face as one last time he lifted his hand and bade them both farewell. At that very instant a brilliant flash of light enveloped him. Horhon instinctively forced her eyes shut. After the light faded only the depressions in the sand showed where they had once stood.

"What happened? Tell me what happened," Krugjon asked, his words rushing out faster than he was able to speak. "Is he gone?"

"What he came here to do is finished," Horhon answered him. "You know what he has done. The Iranha are gone." She then spoke to him with great unhappiness. "Ilon is gone."

"I believe he will come back soon."

Horhon glanced skyward and sensed he was up there somewhere, moving out beyond their world, toward one of those fading points of light. That was where he belonged now. Perhaps his world and hers would never come together again. As she turned and took her first step home a tear ran down her face. A future without him now seemed more certain than ever. And life would be as it had always been—the life of the hunt. Still, even more certain than that, Horhon knew she would never forget. She had already dreamed too many dreams to ever forget.

"I am hungry, Krugjon."

He smiled.